PANACEA EXODUS

BOOK 2 OF THE PANACEA TRILOGY

L. Ana Ellis

FIRE-FORGED BOOKS
Alexandria, VA

Sign up to be updated on future book releases at
fireforgedbooks.com

Copyright © 2022 by L. Ana Ellis

First edition December 2022

ISBN 979-8-9851474-5-2 (paperback)
ISBN 979-8-9851474-6-9 (hardcover)
ISBN 979-8-9851474-7-6 (large print)
ISBN 979-8-9851474-4-5 (ebook)

Cover design by Jeff Brown Graphics
Editing by Tayler Bailey McLendon of Bailey and Bloom Ink
Sensitivity read by Michelle Mosely-Pace
Book Layout © 2016 BookDesignTemplates.com

Published by Fire-Forged Books (an independent publisher of speculative fiction)
Contact us: info@fireforgedbooks.com
Visit Fire-Forged Books at fireforgedbooks.com

Content notice on publisher's website: https://fireforgedbooks.com/content#Exodus

Dedication
To Nicky, Midnight, Yarpy, and Pax
for providing me company through the pandemic;
And to my beta readers, Brian, Kate, Karen, Grace,
Brooke, and Melissa, who provided me with the support
and encouragement that kept me going.

**Technology cannot keep us from death,
but it can keep us from life**

-Area 52 saying

Amaya—works with legacy computer systems, Nyala's sister, is struggling with guilt over things that have happened in the past

Amoco—neuroscientist and programmer, Director of Research for Panacea Corp

Bren—stayed in Area 52 to take care of June's pets

Cooper—still bitter three years after being dismissed from his position at a university, upset because he didn't know that he was Grace's father

Dan—sheriff's deputy in Area 52, was kidnapped by the expedition team

Elliat—reporter, blogger

Georgia—designs digital items, especially historical reconstructions and clothing

Grace—Mariela and Cooper's daughter, deceased

Hank—martial arts instructor who grew up in a res-home

June—Mariela's mother, wife of Oscar Stafford, used to work at Panacea Corp, lived in Area 52 for sixteen years

Liam—CEO of Panacea Corp, was thrown out of a helicopter over the Gulf of Mexico

LP—highly advanced digital being who is modeled on Liam, has been deleted

Mariela—acting CEO for Panacea Corp

Nyala—Amaya's sister, organizes protests against Panacea Corp

Opali—young girl, advanced digital being, Sofi's daughter, has been deleted

Oscar—Mariela's father, former head of Panacea Corp

Petra—founder of Area 52, over one hundred years old (according to her birth certificate, that is)

Sofi—Mariela's sister, Opali's mom, lives in the Panacea metaverse

T-Rock—survivalist, former Zazora player, was bitten by a rattlesnake, has never met a nature metaphor that he didn't like

Viola—the new Director of Research for Panacea Corp, used to date Cooper

14 Years Ago
Nighttime in Area 52

Mariela lifted Grace and held her close. The young girl put her arms around Mariela's neck and rested her head on her mother's shoulder. The man who had carried Grace for most of the last six hours hovered nearby, waiting among the pine trees edging the driveway. The house at the top of the gravel driveway beckoned, as if inviting them in—the porch light welcomed with a soft yellow glow; the balcony running along the front of the house suggested lazy afternoons of wildlife watching and nights of moon gazing; the twinkling lights wrapped around the banister of the steps to the balcony hinted at playfulness; and the thick stands of pine trees surrounding the house said this was a place where a child could explore and have adventures.

Grace shifted in her arms. "I'm cold, Mommy. Are we almost there?" The poor girl was drenched and exhausted. They were all exhausted.

"Yes, we're here." She needed to get Grace out of the rain, but her arms refused to let her daughter go. Maybe they could stay here just a few more minutes. The steady drizzle ran through Mariela's hair and mixed with her salty tears. At least Grace wouldn't know she was crying.

Just a few more minutes, and then they would go.

A light flickered on in the house. Mariela's heart warmed to see the woman in the window standing at what must be the kitchen sink, washing some plate or maybe a pot. Her heart pounded against the walls of her chest, threatening to break her rib cage. She had to get this over with, even if that meant handling things differently from how she had originally planned. She set Grace down. It was now or never.

She knelt beside Grace and helped her put on a child-sized backpack stuffed with a change of clothes and her favorite stuffed animals. Mariela placed her hands on Grace's elbows and looked at her. The resemblance to her father—the dark honey eyes and thick brown hair—was striking.

She should have told Cooper. She should have told him everything— about how Grace was his daughter, about how she wasn't dead. Mariela should have asked for his help, but she had buried herself so deep in lies she didn't know how to climb out. Now there was nothing to do but continue to tell them.

"Do you see that woman up there?" Mariela pointed to the house where the woman was still standing at the sink. Grace nodded. "Do you remember who she is?" Mariela asked.

Grace bit her lower lip and shook her head.

Mariela took a deep breath. She just needed to keep it together for a bit longer. "She's your grandmother," Mariela said. "I need to say goodbye to this man here," she nodded in the direction of the man hovering at the edge of the woods, "so I want you to knock on the door and when your grandma opens it, say, 'Abuelita, it's me, Grace.' Did you get that?"

Grace nodded. She was so serious, so young.

"Okay, go along now. I bet your grandma will make us some hot cocido quemado that we can drink by the fire." Mariela smiled and stroked Grace's cheek. "Go get warm and get into some dry clothes, and I'll be there in a few minutes."

Grace turned and headed toward the staircase. She didn't look back, thankfully. Mariela inched off of the gravel and onto the thick carpet of pine needles, never once turning away from Grace. The stairs were big for the young girl; Grace had to put in a little extra effort with each one. She was about halfway up the steps when Mariela got to the trees. Mariela grabbed the man's elbow and pulled him back with her, farther into the darkness of the trees, but still close enough to see the house. Grace's knock on the door was faint, but seconds later the door opened. The woman looked confused at first, but then smiled a big smile and kneeled down to hug Grace.

That was all Mariela needed to see. "Come on, let's go," she said to the man. Without waiting for him, she turned and walked as fast as she could into the dark.

The man caught up to her. "Are you sure that's what you want to do?" he asked in a low voice. "Are you really going to leave her there, without even talking to your mother at the very least?"

"Yes."

"That's cold."

"Don't judge me…what's your name again?"

"Bren."

"Bren, I appreciate you helping me. You saw me struggling and you offered to help out, which is more than most people would have done and I appreciate it. But don't judge me."

Not that she cared what the man thought, or if he was judging her. The rain slipped down her face obscuring her vision, and she stumbled over the spongy pinecones and scattered branches. There was a hiking path up ahead. Once they reached it, they would be able to move faster and get away from here. She couldn't face her mother. Not with what she had just done.

CHAPTER 1

Nine Days Until the Umbrella Falls

April 2115, Dawn on Tuesday

Cooper hated everyone in the hovbus with him, even the ones he liked. The sixteen hours the seven of them had been stuck in the bus together were without a doubt the worst hours of Cooper's life. Cooper even hated the sunrise that punctuated the jagged lines of the far off mountains and he despised the clouds that burned with color as they hovered over the hostile desert. Sure, some people would consider them beautiful, but to Cooper the sunrise was just another reminder of how long he had been stuck in the small, enclosed space of the hovbus.

The bus sped along the highway heading toward the Outside, beyond the Outer Ring of the city of Glorietta Pass, bringing them closer to when he would have to explain to Mariela that her eighteen-year-old daughter—*their* daughter—had been accidentally shot and had died a death that left them heartbroken and with no other option but to bury her in a shallow grave in the desert. He hated the desert.

"Grace didn't deserve to die," Georgia said, just as she had said multiple times before. "I should have been the lookout instead of her."

The people around Cooper then had the exact same conversation they had been having for the last who-knows-how-many hours. Hank told Georgia not to beat herself up; Georgia told Hank he was minimizing her feelings; T-Rock told Georgia there was no way she could have known what would happen and that it was his fault. On and on it went, *ad nauseam*. Then Deputy Dan said he was responsible for Grace's death, which was actually true, but had also been said many times before. Cooper was sure he was going to hate them all for the rest of his life.

They should have reported in to Mariela with an update about the trip. She was the one, after all, who had planned the expedition to the isolated Area 52—an area concealed from the world by an umbrella of advanced technology. But while the maintenance on the backup servers had gone as planned, no one wanted to tell her that her daughter had died. Or that they were holding Dan, the deputy from Area 52 who had accidentally shot Grace, hostage until they could figure out what to do with him.

With nothing to do but stare at the other passengers for hours, Cooper felt like their faces were burned into his memory banks. There was the petite and silver-haired Georgia, a designer of digital items who was un-failingly kind yet also firm, especially with Hank, an over-grown manchild who appeared to have never had any gainful employment other than as a martial arts instructor. Although on the scrawny side, he might have been considered handsome by some. Unlike T-Rock, a block of pure muscle who was known for his survival skills both as a Zazora player and in the solid world, who ironically had managed to get bitten by a rattlesnake.

The quietest ones were June and Amaya, who both seemed to have retreated within themselves. Maybe they were, like him, inwardly judg-ing everyone else in the hovbus and thinking about how they would rather have toothpicks shoved under their fingernails than continue to sit in an incredibly tiny space with people who they had come to hate.

And there wasn't anyone Cooper hated more than Dan, the Area 52 deputy. Dan thought the entire world outside of Area 52 was awash in radiation, no matter how many times they told him that the levels of ra-diation were perfectly normal and there was no Nuclear Armageddon of 2035. Dan returned to it stubbornly, as though their explanation might be different the next time he fretted about the radiation.

Cooper closed his eyes and tried to tune out the conversation around him. He sighed. In another hour they would be home and he would be free of this never-ending torture.

Cooper needed an off-switch for his brain. A switch that would let him sleep and stop thinking. With the job to perform maintenance on Server AA completed, Cooper's brief period of employment was coming to an end. It had been nice to have a job again after so long without one. Not that he had looked lately.

Since he had returned home a year ago from fighting in the Arctic War, he had been…adrift. Unmoored. Signing up to fight in the Arctic War was probably the best decision he could have made after losing his teaching position at the Academia Veritas Virtual three years ago. At least he felt like he had something to offer when he was in the Arctic.

Unable to find sleep, Cooper watched the large, concrete block pod warehouses surrounded by chain-link fences pass by in a blur. No other cars passed them. Nothing but warehouse after warehouse. Each almost indistinguishable from the next. Concrete block after concrete block. Lulled into a half-sleep, he startled awake when a stump-like, buck-naked man ran out of one of the warehouses.

"Hovbus stop!" Cooper swayed forward as the hovbus immediately decelerated.

Amaya looked over her shoulder at the man running towards them. "Isn't that Elliat Exis? The journalist?"

The naked man charged through the unguarded gate in the warehouse's chain-link fence and ran full force into the hovbus. His face smashed into the window and he pounded on the slowing vehicle while running along beside it.

"Help!" Elliat cried out, his voice straining and his eyes wide with fear. "Please help!"

The vehicle came to a full stop.

"What in the world?" June asked. "Why is a man pounding on our window in the buff?"

"I don't know," Amaya said, "but I'm going to find out."

Deputy Dan's eyes widened as he stared at Elliat pounding on the window. "What is wrong with you all? Is that how exposure to radiation makes people act?"

"Dan, how many times do we have to tell you?" Amaya snapped at him. "There was no Nuclear Armageddon of 2035, your village Elders told you that so you wouldn't want to leave the protected zone of Area 52. There is *no* radiation other than the usual amounts."

"Then why does everyone from here seem so deranged?" Dan asked.

Dan had a point. Things had been tense during the time they had been cooped up in the vehicle, first because of a sandstorm, and then during the drive home. Dan watched them that whole time with the look of someone who was scared stiff because he didn't understand who they were or what they were going to do with him.

"I met Elliat during a protest I went to with my sister Nyala about a week ago." Amaya's natural hair bobbed from the motion of yanking on her shoes. "I'll go talk to him. Cooper, can I have your digital skin clothing?"

"You want me to go home in this?" He looked down at the plaid shirt and denim jeans that Grace had picked out for him in Area 52. He had planned to change back into his digital skin before they got home.

"I can't talk to him if he's not dressed," she said. "It's not like a lot of people are going to see you before you get home." She stood up, leaning over slightly so she wouldn't hit her head on the roof of the hovbus. Elliat's renewed pounding on the glass made Georgia jump.

"Oh alright." Cooper pulled his digi-skin clothing out of his backpack. He tossed the clothing to Amaya. She opened the door to the bus and stepped out. He exited the hovbus after her.

Elliat came running around to meet them. "Thank the Oracle," he panted. "You have to help me."

"Here, put this on." She threw him the clothes.

"You want me to wear this?" He took the clothes but let them dangle from his fingers with disdain.

"You don't want clothes?" she asked him.

"Clothing is an artifact of societal expectations that developed when we needed clothing to deal with the weather. I find it to be unnecessary on moderate days such as this one. But fine, if it makes you comfortable, I'll put them on."

"I appreciate you accommodating my societal expectations," Amaya said drily.

He pulled the shirt over his head and put the pants on. They adjusted to fit him.

He put his hands on his hips. "Happy now?"

"Yes."

"You have to help me." He paced back and forth while wringing his hands. "Everything's gone off the rails inside."

"What do you mean?" Cooper asked.

"It's better if you see for yourself," he said. "Come take a look."

Whatever made Elliat flee the building sparked Cooper's curiosity. "Okay," Cooper said. "Let's go then." He turned toward the hovbus. "Is anyone else coming?"

June, Hank, Georgia, and Dan exited the bus behind them.

"Hey guys, I'm going to stay here," T-Rock said from inside the hovbus. "Even with the antivenom for the rattlesnake bite, moving around hurts like a million bees stinging me at once."

"What are you all wearing?" Elliat looked at them almost as skeptically as Dan did. "Is that *plaid?* Why is everyone wearing plaid, except for that guy," he pointed to Dan in his Area 52 law enforcement uniform, "who looks like he's dressed for retro-cop Halloween. And her..." He pointed at June but stopped short when he looked at her. "June STAFFORD?" His voice broke on her last name. "June Stafford? I thought…" He paused, apparently for the first time at a loss for what to say.

"Do I know you?" June asked.

"June, don't worry about him," Cooper said. "He's a blogger/wanna-be-journalist who thinks he knows a lot more than he actually does."

Elliat huffed. "I had some very reliable sources who said that her husband may have killed her when she disappeared sixteen years ago."

Cooper took Elliat's arm and turned him toward the warehouse. "I'm sure they were *very* reliable. Elliat, what was it you wanted to show us?"

June didn't move. "I'll stay with T-Rock," June said. She headed back to the hovbus. Maybe it was the lack of digi-color on her skin, but she seemed older and more tired than Cooper remembered. He shook his head—*don't be dense, Cooper*—they all looked older and more tired than they had sixteen years ago.

Elliat slipped through a hole in the chain-link fence and then held one side open for Cooper to climb through. Elliat moved stiffly but with a hurried pace toward the single door in the looming concrete block warehouse. The others followed along behind them.

"Where are we?" Georgia asked. She turned in a circle taking in the landscape around her.

Cooper couldn't answer her; he had no clue where they were either. The only thing he could say for sure was that they were in the Outside of the Outer Ring of the city. If he had to guess, they were about thirty minutes from Oscar Stafford's estate, but that was as much as he had figured out.

"I've been here before." Behind him, Amaya hunched over to step through the fence. "It was around a week ago, and it was the day that he," she nodded at Elliat, "moved into his pod." Her brow furrowed, one eyebrow higher than the other. "Elliat, what's going on? Did you exit your pod?"

"Yes, but not the normal way," he said.

It was the first time Cooper had ever heard of a not-normal way of exiting a pod. "What other way is there?" he asked.

"You'll see," Elliat replied. "Follow me."

At the entrance to the warehouse, the heavy steel door stood open.

"Why is the door open?" Amaya asked. "Where are the guards?"

Hank swung the heavy door back and forth. It glided smoothly. "It should be locked."

"Right," Elliat motioned for them to go through. "Follow me inside, but don't leave the waiting room just yet."

A pungent smell burned Cooper's nostrils. Every door leading from the plain white, unadorned waiting room was open, their magnetic locks apparently not working. A handful of uncomfortable chairs that looked like no one ever sat in them lined the walls of the room.

"Where's the manager?" Hank asked Elliat. "When Georgia exited her pod after thirty-two years of pod living"—he placed a hand on Georgia's shoulder—"the pod manager told me that for security reasons no human was ever allowed into the inner storage chamber unless they were entering or exiting a pod or conducting necessary maintenance. But look at this—even a raccoon could wander in without a single person or door to stop it."

Georgia walked around the edges of the room examining the bare walls. To Cooper it looked like she had moved to get away from Hank. The tension between Georgia and Hank—Georgia mad at Hank for his apparent carelessness and Hank mad at Georgia for being mad at him— had been part of what made the last seventeen hours so intolerable. This nightmare trip couldn't be over soon enough.

"This warehouse doesn't have a manager." Elliat sniffed. "It's completely automated."

"No manager?" Georgia asked, her eyebrows raised. "I didn't know there were warehouses without managers."

Elliat shrugged. "I don't make much money blogging, so it was what I could afford."

"Do you make *any* money blogging?" Hank asked. Hank's tone of voice made it clear he thought Elliat was second-rate hack. Cooper was inclined to agree with him.

Elliat ignored him. "All the warehouses this far outside of town are pretty cheap. Corporate used to send someone out if there was a problem, but now even the repairs and pod insertions are automated." He turned to Amaya. "Where's your sister? Not that I'm missing her. She's a pill."

"I don't know." Amaya looked away. "I've been trying to reach Nyala for hours now and I can't. Ever since Panacea went offline I can't reach her."

"The outage probably messed with her chip," Elliat said, seemingly unconcerned about Nyala's lack of contact. "It surely messed things up here."

Cooper didn't believe Elliat's glib assurances that there was nothing to worry about with Nyala. It had been twenty-one hours since all the digitally stored information in the world had disappeared for around twelve hours and then mysteriously reappeared. Nyala should have been able to be in touch by now.

Elliat turned to address them. "Before we enter into the storage area, I need you all to prepare yourselves—it's not going to be easy to see. Or smell."

Finally, they were going to see what the fuss was about.

"Are you ready?" Elliat asked in what could only be described as a *very serious* voice that seemed to be setting up a dramatic reveal.

"What is this place?" Deputy Dan asked, spoiling Elliat's reveal. Usually no one answered when Dan asked questions, but this time Amaya responded.

"Some people like to spend all their time in the metaverse…" Amaya said

"What's the metaverse?" Dan interrupted.

"It's virtual reality—the digital stuff that tons of people have made…on their computers, and it all connects together. People who live in the virtual world need to have their bodies taken care of, so their bodies are in pod environments in large buildings like these called warehouses, but they spend all their time in the virtual world."

"They spend *all* their time in virtual reality?" Dan asked. "Don't they lose their ability to interact in the physical world?"

"They do," Georgia said. "Some even forget the solid world exists and that it can affect them. But most of them never plan on leaving the virtual environment, so it's not a concern for them. I used to live in a warehouse like this, until I left my pod and learned how to walk again."

~~~~~

Dan hung back near the warehouse entrance where it would be faster to escape. They kept telling him there was no Nuclear Armageddon of 2035, but these people didn't behave normally. No one was paying attention to him; he should just make a break for it now and take his chances in the desert.

"Are you ready?" The guy who had run out to greet them—not
~~~~~

wearing a stitch of clothing—asked with his hand hovering near the door handle.

The woman named Amaya answered the guy, "Okay Elliat, let's see what's got you all worked up." She didn't seem to like Elliat much, but then she didn't seem to like Dan either. Maybe she didn't like anyone.

Elliat took a deep breath and opened the door onto the largest room Dan had ever seen. Elliat appeared to expect them to follow him. It was probably a bad idea, but Dan couldn't help himself—he followed the man into the gloomy chamber. The emergency lighting was clearly inadequate and a safety risk, with pockets of harsh light mixed with dark spots where Dan couldn't see the floor.

The immense room stretched long, with some unusual metal structures that he couldn't figure out.

"Why is it so dark?" Amaya asked.

"The regular lighting stopped working," Elliat said. "Your eyes will get used to it."

He wished he had his gun back. Ahead of him, Amaya turned down one of the aisles. The gangly man named Hank followed Georgia, an effortlessly elegant woman, in the other direction. The wild-haired man called Cooper was behind him.

Did he really know all their names? Yes, because he had spent seventeen hours with them in a small hovering vehicle. He knew more about them than he ever wanted to know. Now, they were looking at something inside this large building where people lived in 'pods.' Sure, they had tried to tell him that there was no radiation, but then what did they really know? They said his leaders lied to him, but what if their leaders were lying to them?

Dan turned down an aisle. The large metal structures loomed on both sides of him. He walked slowly, making sure to keep an eye on his six. His foot caught on something on the floor. It tipped him off balance and sent him hurtling onto the concrete floor. He rubbed his kneecap where it had slammed into the floor. Too late, his eyes adjusted and the item he had tripped over became visible. It was a body. A dead body. The body of a thin, nothing-but-bones, woman with long hair and no clothing.

He scrambled backwards on the floor. "What *is* this place?"

On the other aisle, Amaya was singing a song—haunting and spiritual, sad and forlorn, it seemed to be asking forgiveness. Hank and Georgia joined in, and their voices sent the song echoing throughout the building.

Dan picked himself up off the floor and brushed the layer of dust off his pants. *What was he going to do with the body?* Where he was from, he would have been responsible for it. But he didn't have jurisdiction here. *What had killed her? Would anyone investigate what happened? Would someone bury her or would they just leave her there?*

A hand grabbed his ankle. He startled and almost fell onto one of the pods.

"Kill me," the woman said in a raspy, foreign-sounding voice that he could hardly hear.

He looked around him, checking for threats. It didn't feel safe. This place—there was something wrong with it. Amaya's *Kyrie* haunted him, he could barely see the woman begging for his help, and he didn't understand where they were or why she was lying on the floor wanting to die. His eyes blurred. He couldn't breathe.

The woman's hand slipped off his leg but still clung to his pant leg. "Kill me," she said again, the raspy whisper barely making it out of her mouth. He kicked his leg to loosen her grip on his pants. Freed from her grasping hand, he fled the building.

~~~~~

Cooper looked up the aisle Dan had just sprinted out of. *What had spooked Dan so much to make him run outside like a scared sheep?* There was a woman lying on the ground near where Dan had been standing. Cooper ran up and kneeled beside her. She grabbed Cooper's arm with a weak grip.

"What happened to you?" he asked her.

"I was hungry." Her body tensed and she took a few fast, shallow breaths. Her mouth formed words with difficulty, just like Georgia's had when she left her pod after many years. "I needed"—she paused—"to get food." She closed her eyes. Her teeth clenched and her breathing was labored.

Elliat hovered behind him. "All the warehouse services, including the food drips and waste removal, stopped after the Black Screen."

"The Black Screen?" Cooper asked.

"When the metaverse went out. It was like staring at a black screen for twelve hours. When the virtual environment came back on, none of the life support worked."
~~~~~

The woman tightened her grasp on his arm. "I was hungry." The woman was close to emaciated. Elliat had implied this warehouse was one of the cheaper ones; they probably kept their residents on an even more restricted diet than usual.

"And something happened?" Cooper asked the woman.

"Tried to climb…down ladder. Too weak." Her grip on his arm loosened for a second.

"And you fell?"

"Yes."

There was an access ladder to the vertically stacked pods not far away. The pods were stacked probably fifteen high, with the top ones near the soaring ceiling. It was impossible to tell how high she might have fallen from. Based on how she was lying, with her back twisted and her legs not moving, it looked like her back was broken.

"I'm in…a lot…of pain," the woman said. Her voice was getting weaker.

"How long have you been lying here?"

"Don't know. I jumped at…four?"

She had been lying there for thirteen hours. Cooper shuddered. It was an agonizingly long time to be lying injured on the concrete floor. Based on his experiences back when he was working search and rescue, she probably didn't have long to live. Her breathing had the wheeze of a death rattle and her skin was cold and clammy. He didn't have anything to warm her with, so he took off his plaid flannel shirt and placed it over her. He sat beside her on the cold concrete floor, held her hand in his, and waited.

In the distance, there were sounds of the others moving around and at times talking quietly, but now that it was quiet he also heard other voices. There were faint cries of "help" and the occasional "over here." At least one person was sobbing and another repeated "I'm so hungry" over and over. Someone else complained she had soiled herself. There was the sound of someone in one of the high-up pods vomiting, and the vomit hitting the ground a fraction of a second later. The smell of vomit mingled with the stench of excrement and urine. Elliat was right—it was an assault on the senses.

With his eyes adjusted to the light, he could see maybe half the pods had open covers and people sitting up in them. Others changed their covers from opaque to clear as he was watching and their occupants' voices joined the others calling for help.

Elliat moved on to join Hank and Georgia about a third of the way down the long row. *Where was Amaya?* Cooper hadn't seen or heard from her in a while.

Elliat looked into one of the pods with an open cover. "I think this one's detoxing," he said.

Hank joined him. "Sir, are you okay?" Hank asked. There was a pause with no sound. "How can he be detoxing? Doesn't the warehouse control the substances that go into his body?"

Georgia joined Hank and Elliat. "Some warehouses are more lax in what they allow than others," Georgia said. "Some of the cheaper warehouses, especially the ones people can actually afford to live in on the basic advertising income, allow pretty much anything in any amount as long as the person pays in advance. Those warehouses don't care if the person becomes addicted or not."

"Is there anything we can do for him?" Hank asked.

"Do you have any detox injections?" Elliat asked.

"No. Doesn't the warehouse have any?"

"Probably, but where?"

"Cooper," Hank yelled back down the aisle to where Cooper sat with the woman, "is there anything we can do for him?"

"Not without detox injections," Cooper yelled back. He had never felt quite so helpless, not even in all his days of doing search and rescue.

Hank said something to the fellow who was detoxing and moved on. He was too far away for Cooper to hear him but it sounded like an apology. Hank pushed a large button near one of the ladders.

"The rotating mechanism's not working," Hank said. "There's no way to get the higher up pods down to the ground level."

"Nothing's working," Elliat said. "Haven't you been listening to what I've been telling you?"

"How did you get out?" Hank asked Elliat.

"I climbed. I've only been here a week so I can still climb down the ladder."

"Can you rotate the pods manually?" Georgia asked.

"I don't see any way to do that," Hank said. "I can climb up and start carrying people down."

The rattling breathing of the woman reeked of impeding death. Cooper tightened his grip on her hand. It wouldn't be long now.

Hank climbed up the ladder closest to him. When he got up to the pod above the bottom one, he leaned over and spoke to the woman in it. With what appeared to be careful delicacy, he pulled her onto his shoulders in a fireman's carry. "She's super lightweight!" he called out, placing one arm around the woman and looping the other arm around the ladder so he could slide down as he descended the ladder.

It was a relief when he placed the woman on the ground. She wasn't able to support herself, so Hank gently propped her against the bottom pod; not long after she slid to the side and laid on the concrete. Cooper could feel the cold air of the concrete working its way through his jeans. If he felt cold, the unclothed woman had to be freezing.

Hank was already ascending the ladder to get the next person. Elliat and Georgia had gone further down the aisle checking on people who were in bottom pods. It was slow going, but Hank was managing to get people down the ladder in about five minutes per person. Cooper did some calculations—the typical warehouse could house 12,000 people. Even if this one was only half full, and assuming Hank could carry twelve per hour, it would still take him around 1,000 hours to get them all out. They would be dead by then.

Was there any point in helping them out of their pods? If they couldn't walk, how would they be better off? A burst of sunlight shot in through the door as Amaya strode in from the outside. So that's where she'd been.

"I've checked some of the other warehouses nearby and they are in the same situation," she said. "I also saw Dan in the hovbus, and he is freaked out."

"I'm surprised Dan didn't take the chance to run off," Cooper said.

"I'm not," Amaya said. "Where would he go? It's not like he has any clue how to get home and he doesn't know anyone here."

"Good point."

"What's he doing?" Amaya nodded toward Hank, who was carrying his fifth person down.

"He's removing people from their pods."

"There's no way we can help them all."

"He seems determined to try."

"It's a fool's mission. And without food it won't do them much good." She looked at the woman. "Is she okay?"

"No, she's close to death."

"I'm so sorry." Amaya sat down by the woman and placed a hand on her shoulder.

Elliat and Georgia worked their way toward Cooper and Amaya, stopping to talk to some of the people in the lowest pods.

"Elliat," Amaya asked, "does anyone know about this?"

"I contacted the authorities after about ten hours when I figured out that the automated systems probably weren't coming back online. It's been eleven hours since then. They informed me they were 'dealing with lots of issues' and will get to the warehouses when they can.

"I've told the people not to leave their pods, but it's not like they are listening to me. Like this lady," he pointed to the woman that Cooper was sitting next to, "they panic but they don't have the strength to get out. As far as I know she's the only one who survived."

"We should check for others," Georgia said.

"And do what?" Elliat asked. "Good luck finding any medical supplies."

"At least we can keep them company," Cooper said.

The death rattle had been going on for half an hour now. It wouldn't be much longer before the woman passed. Her grip on Cooper's hand loosened and she no longer seemed to be aware of the people around her. No other survivors had been found outside of their pods. None, that is, except for the ones Hank had carried down the ladder as he continued in his futile attempt to help them.

"I can't see," a woman Hank had helped said. "My eyes are blurry."

"Mine too," said another man.

"That's normal," Georgia said. "It'll take your eyes a while to start seeing normally again."

"Hank, give it up," Amaya yelled down the aisle. "It's a hopeless endeavor."

"I don't take orders from you," he yelled back.

"That's true," Amaya said under her breath. "You never have, even when you were supposed to." Then louder, more to Cooper and Georgia than to Hank, she said, "Even if we can keep these people alive for a while, they'll quickly run out of food and we will as well if we stay here. Even if Hank keeps helping them out of their pods, it will still take months for him to get all of them down. And that's not even including the thousands of people living in the three other warehouses up the road have the exact same problem."

"I know." Cooper didn't like it, but they couldn't help these people. He would talk to Mariela when he got back and see if she could send help. Her employer, Panacea Corp, was one of the world's largest corporations. Mariela would have access to resources they didn't have. At the very least they could send food. These weren't Panacea Corp's warehouses, so it wasn't Mariela's responsibility, but she would make sure they got help. Mariela had a lot of faults, but she was always willing to help out.

"Didn't you used to do search and rescue?" Hank yelled at him. "Why aren't you doing more to rescue these people?"

"One part of doing rescues," Cooper yelled back, "is knowing when any attempt to help will make things worse."

The woman's rattling breathing went quiet and her hand went limp. Cooper felt for her pulse.

"She's gone," he said. He closed her eyes. He reached for his shirt, and then stopped with his hand hovering in the air. It seemed wrong to take his shirt off of her. He went back and forth on whether to take the shirt, finally deciding the right thing to do was to leave it.

"Are you all okay with leaving?" Amaya asked.

"Yes." Cooper and Georgia spoke at the same time.

Elliat grabbed Amaya's sleeve. "Take me with you."

"Sorry," Amaya shook her arm to remove Elliat's hand. "There're too many people here for us to help them all. It wouldn't be fair to the others if we took you." She turned to where Hank was starting to climb up another ladder. "Come on Hank, let's go."

Hank stopped a couple rungs up the ladder. "I can't leave them."

Amaya turned toward the door. "Okay, let us know when you're done in a couple months and we'll send a car for you."

"Okay," Hank yelled back.

Was he really fine with being left behind? "Hank," Cooper said, "we'll get Mariela to send someone to check on them. But come on, let's go. There's not much you can do for them now and we're all exhausted."

Hank didn't respond right away. "On my way," he finally said as he headed down the ladder.

"Don't leave us," a soft voice cried out.

"We'll send someone for you," Cooper spoke loudly to the room because he was unsure where the voice was coming from.

"How long until someone comes for us?" another voice called out.

"I'm sure it will be soon," Cooper said. The truth was, he didn't know. From what Elliat had said, it might be a while before any help got out there. More and more voices spoke up with increasing urgency as they turned to leave.

"Get me down from here," someone called out in a small voice. "Don't leave me."

The voice came from high up in the pod lifts. Nearby a gentleman had his pod open.

"We'll die if you leave us," the man said.

"You're not going to die," Cooper replied. If only he could be certain of that he would feel better.

"I'm *not* staying here." The man reached for the ladder, grabbing it with one hand and pulling himself to a standing position. His legs trembled underneath him and his grasp on the ladder was tenuous.

"Don't." Hank started to climb up the ladder. "Sit down and I'll get you."

"I'm coming with you," the man said. He lifted one trembling leg out of the pod and placed it on the ladder. His entire body quivered.

"Please, sit down," Amaya said.

With visible effort, the man pulled himself onto the ladder. For a second it looked like he might make it, but his legs trembled and buckled. He tumbled headfirst over the side of his pod, plummeting until he slammed into the concrete floor.

Cooper's heart pounded.

Elliat ran to the man. "Stay in your pods, I tell you, stay in your pods." His voice broke with frustration.

Georgia headed toward the man.

"He's dead," Elliat said.

Georgia stopped walking toward him. Amaya took her arm.

"Let's go," Amaya said. "There's nothing more we can do to help them."

Hank wiped his eyes and followed them. Cooper stopped to look back at the rows and rows of stacked pods. These people would get the help they needed, right?

"Cooper, are you coming?" Amaya called from the door.

"Yeah, I'm coming." He followed the others out through the lobby to the exit door. The transition from the cool, dark interior of the warehouse to the light of the rising sun blinded him. He shaded his eyes with his hand and made his way back to the hovbus.

Elliat ran after them. "Take me also!" It was clear he wasn't giving up. "You're not leaving me."

"Call a transport," Amaya said.

"I've called. They're all booked. For the entire week. I made a reservation for next week but I can't handle staying here that long and I'll probably die without food and water."

Amaya spun around to face him. "Elliat, you're *not* coming with us." She was angrier than Cooper had ever seen her. "You think June Stafford wants to share a ride with you? After all the things you said about her over the years? How you said that she had committed suicide? Or blamed her husband for killing her? Or said that her family had mismanaged Panacea Corp? We'll send some help, but you're staying here."

So *that* was why she was adamant that Elliat couldn't come with them. Cooper should have thought of it. The Stafford family had been kind to him over the years, and June was like a second mother to him. Why hadn't it occurred to him it would be tough for June if they offered Elliat a ride?

Elliat stopped talking, apparently unsure of how to react to Amaya's anger.

"I didn't think…" he said. His shoulders slumped. He rubbed his face and stopped following them.

With Elliat no longer bothering them, they got into the hovbus. T-Rock had his eyes closed, his face pinched from the pain. June was napping, and Dan was staring blankly at nothing. He looked like he had just realized he didn't have anywhere else to go and they were the best friends he had.

June woke up as they got settled. "How did it go?" she asked.

Cooper didn't want to talk about what they had seen. He shook his head. "Not good." He pushed some icons on his monitor and the hovbus glided forward. Elliat chased after them, yelling nonstop.

Cooper rolled his eyes. "Doesn't he ever give up?"

"Who?" June asked.

"Elliat Exis."

"The blogger? I read some of his stuff while you all were inside. He has some interesting theories."

"Well don't worry, we're not taking him with us."

Elliat was surprisingly fast considering he didn't look like he was in good shape, but as the hovbus picked up speed Elliat fell behind. He developed a limp and then finally stopped, put his hands on his knees, and panted.

"Hovbus stop," June said. The bus slowed. "I don't like this. Let him come with us. We have one extra seat; we might as well allow someone to use it."

Cooper shrugged. If June was okay with it, who was he to object. When the hovbus came to a complete stop, he opened the door and motioned for Elliat to join them. Elliat smiled, ran toward them as fast as his limp would allow, and hopped inside.

"Thank you, thank you, thank you!" He said while trying to catch his breath. He turned to June, "I promise I will only write flattering things about you in the future."

Nine Days Until the Umbrella Falls

Tuesday Morning, cont.

Mariela peered around the curtain on her office window. The horde of protesters outside the Panacea Corp headquarters was dwindling, but the chanting still pulsed through the air, rising up to her office on the top floor of the Panacea Corp headquarters building. Listening to the veiled threats in the chants only made waiting for a message from the team all the more excruciating.

She was probably going to wear holes in the carpet from pacing.

Finally—an alert pinged her chip with a message from the team. It was only a brief message—Amaya said to meet at Mariela's father's estate in half an hour. Not long after the first, a second message from Amaya followed. But instead of having more details, all it said was, "Bring a cryogenic tag." A cryogenic tag? She wasn't even sure what it was or where she would find it. She would have to ask Amoco Cadiz, a neuroscientist who worked for Panacea Corp doing chip research.

She sent a message back to Amaya. "What do you need it for?"

"A prisoner." Amaya's brief response alarmed Mariela.

"Is everyone okay?" she replied immediately.

"Will share more details later," was all the response she got.

Mariela sent out another message to Amoco. "Amoco, I need you in my office right away. Bring a cryogenic tag, whatever that is."

Amoco probably would have preferred she send a messenger pigeon instead. Mariela sometimes indulged his quirks, but she wasn't in the mood to run up to the pigeon rookery on the roof today.

She rubbed the back of her neck. It still burned from where two thuggish Panacea Corp bodyguards had injected a substance next to her embedded chip, a substance that let them illegally monitor the activity on her chip. If the bodyguards, or as she liked to call them, brutes, were monitoring her chip activity right now, hopefully they didn't know enough to realize that asking for a cryogenic tag was highly unusual.

Her reflection in the window showed the side of her lip was swollen.

She pushed away the memory of the brutes slamming her head into the window of the helicopter and splitting her lip. Even with the healing spray her doctor had given her it was probably going to scar. With any luck, the scar would make her look tough and like someone not to be messed with.

Amoco must have been in the building already because he showed up within minutes. He sported his usual vest with a pocket watch, cane, and tophat. The cane was completely decorative—even though he used prosthetics on the lower half of his legs, he had no need for the cane. She wouldn't be surprised if he twirled the cane on occasion just for fun.

Amoco spread his arms wide in greeting and kissed her on the cheek. "My dearest Mariela, let me first say how glad I am to see you and how concerned I was to hear your trip to Bolivia had been cut short. I was also taken aback that your bodyguard chose not to return with you."

It was a long story she couldn't afford to tell Amoco right now. Not with the brutes monitoring her chip.

Mariela leaned on her desk, half standing and half sitting on it. "Did you bring the tag?" she asked.

Amoco nodded and held up a palm-sized silver box with etchings on each side.

"What is it?" Mariela asked.

"Decades ago, when we first attempted to revive people who had been cryogenically frozen after their deaths, we collaborated with the government to develop a security protocol. In the event we successfully brought someone back to life, they granted us ten security tags that could be used wherever identity checks were needed. The only stipulation was, in addition to the ID number, the tags had an additional label of 'medical experiment.'"

Upon closer examination, one of the etchings on the silver box read 'for medical use only.' "Have we ever used any of the cryogenic tags before?" Mariela asked.

"We have never successfully revived a cryogen, so there's never been a need. Once someone is declared dead, it turns out they are in fact quite dead and, despite our best efforts, refuse to be brought back to life." Amoco placed the box on the desk. "Can I assume it was not requested for use on a cryogen? Did the travelers bring someone from Area 52 back with them?"

"I guess so. I'm not getting much information." Mariela sighed.

When she realized they were bringing someone back with them she had briefly hoped it was her mother or daughter, but they wouldn't be prisoners and neither of them would need tags as they had profiles already. Her daughter Grace's profile had been inactive and marked as deceased years ago, but at Mariela's request Amoco had reactivated it before the team left for Area 52.

She felt completely in the dark. "All I know is I need to take the tags to my father's estate where I'm going to meet them."

"Were there any encounters with your mother or daughter?" Amoco asked.

"I don't know!" It got under her skin that the team hadn't provided more information. She was the one who had planned the expedition, after all. She deserved to know what had happened. "My mother's chip is online, and a tracking identifier found Grace's chip but then the chip went offline." The panicky feeling returned. "Why don't they tell me anything?"

"I understand your concern." Amoco picked the box up and tucked it into his vest pocket. "I will accompany you to your father's estate. You will need my assistance to install and activate the tag. Not that I would miss hearing what happened."

Mariela dreaded hearing what happened. Between the lack of communication, the prisoner, and the ping from Grace's chip before it went offline… Her stomach caught in her throat—something bad had happened. The only thing she could do right now was to head out to the estate with Amoco and get some answers.

~~~~~

Cooper stared out the window of the hovbus at the narrow road passing through the grounds of Oscar Stafford's estate. They arrived not thirty minutes after leaving the pod warehouse. The only stop had been to drop Elliat at the Levanto monorail. As the hovbus wound its way up the long winding driveway to the estate, Cooper's breath became shallow and his hands started to shake.

Insisting that he be the one to tell Mariela about Grace's death had seemed like a good idea a day ago, but now it seemed like a ridiculously bad idea. The eleven hours they had spent sitting in the hovbus waiting for the storm to blow over seemed like a distant memory, and his request to be the one to tell Mariela seemed like an even more distant memory.
~~~~~

Cooper had been angry she hadn't told him Grace was his daughter, and at the time he had some idea he would confront her, but now he realized he was about to tell a mother that her daughter had died.

The feelings of anger and grief were so strongly mixed in him he wasn't sure he could sort them out and be able to talk in any sort of coherent way. The growing dread that settled into his stomach almost made him want to stay in the hovbus with the people he had begun to loathe during the hours he had been confined with them.

June held a napkin tightly gripped in her hand, rubbing it between her fingers and passing it from one hand to the other until it shredded into small pieces. Cooper had almost forgotten it was her home as well. Caught up in his own problems, he forgot she had her own stress to deal with. It must be difficult seeing her husband Oscar for the first time in sixteen years.

The hovbus glided to a stop in front of the main estate house. Mariela ran out of the house, down the steps, and across the open area to where the bus was parked. She called over her shoulder to Oscar as she ran ahead to greet them. June punched a button and the door of the bus opened with a hiss.

Georgia took a deep breath and looked at Amaya. "Are you ready?" She took her pack out from under her seat and held a hand out to Amaya.

Amaya nodded, her mouth pressed tight and her eyes wet with tears. She grabbed her pack and exited the vehicle holding hands with Georgia. Neither of them looked at Mariela. They set their packs down and, standing next to each other looking like twin statues, they slumped and looked at the ground. Mariela ran up and pulled them into a close embrace. They hugged her back.

Cooper tried to collect his thoughts as everyone else exited the bus. Only June remained with him.

"You don't know what to say either?" he asked her.

"How do you say hello to the husband you haven't seen in sixteen years?" June asked. "How do you say you're sorry for leaving to the daughter you left behind?"

Cooper put his arm around her. "Well, I consider you to be the good news. So which first—the good news or the bad?"

"Normally, I advocate for bad news first, but in this case, I think I should go ahead." She wiped her eyes. "Are you going to be okay?"

"June, I don't know how to talk to her. How do I tell her that her daughter is dead when all I want to tell her is how angry I am with her?"

"You'll figure it out," she said before giving him a long hug back. "We'll figure it out. Cooper, there's no easy way to do it, and any way you say it, it's still going to hurt and sound wrong. Just say whatever comes to mind and it will be good enough."

~~~~~

"What's wrong?" Mariela asked. Amaya and Georgia either couldn't or wouldn't answer her. "What's wrong?" she demanded again.

T-Rock and Hank exited the vehicle along with another man she didn't recognize. He had to be the prisoner.

"Where's Cooper?" she asked.

"He's fine." Amaya answered through her tears. "Give him a minute."

What did he need a minute for?

Her father and Amoco joined them. She grabbed her father's hand. "Something's wrong but I don't know what." She had an idea what it was, but she still hoped she was wrong. She had to be.

A grey-haired woman with a sad air about her exited the vehicle. *Mom!* She ran forward and grabbed ahold of her mother. As a grown woman in her mid-forties, Mariela thought she didn't need a mother anymore, but once June hugged her, she didn't know how she had survived without her. Mariela had worried about the team running into her family members in Area 52, but now that she had seen her mother, she had no doubt it was the right thing. She was elated. Secrets be damned. What good were secrets anyway if they didn't get revealed eventually?

But that also meant they knew about Grace. Was that why Cooper didn't come out? Was he angry with her for lying to him, for telling him Grace was dead instead of the truth—that she had taken Grace to Area 52 after her chip failed?

"Mom, where's Grace?" The thought she had been trying to avoid pushed its way in. "Something happened to her, didn't it?"

"Ask Cooper," her mother said. She was crying also. Even the prisoner appeared to be crying.

"Let's go," T-Rock said to the new guy, giving him a push toward the house.

"Cooper?"
~~~~~

He was stepping out of the vehicle now, looking almost gaunt although he hadn't lost any weight. His eyes were dark and angry. He held himself gingerly, like he was in pain.

Mariela's words caught in her throat. "Cooper, what's wrong? What happened to our daughter?"

~~~~~

Why did he say he would be the one to do this? How did he imagine it would go? Cooper tried to speak but couldn't. The tears in Mariela's eyes glistened. She already anticipated the worst. And her question had confirmed Grace was his daughter. He let that sink in. Grace had been his daughter. And he had lost her.

He was angry with Mariela about so many things, but for a moment he didn't see the woman who deceived him. Instead he saw she was in pain. He wanted to go to her, to comfort and to be comforted, to acknowledge the connection they shared to Grace. But the anger froze him. Anger that he only knew his daughter a week before losing her. Anger that Mariela would keep such a big secret from him. A thousand emotions pushed on the inside of his skin, trying to get out, like he might burst open and the tangled knot of emotions he had stuffed inside would explode.

"We left…" He couldn't finish. He sniffed and wiped his nose with back of his hand. "We buried her at the base of the mountain."

What a peculiar torture this was. The only person he wanted to be comforted by was also the person he couldn't let himself get close to. He wanted to go to her, but he also wanted to walk away and never talk to her again. He wanted to tell Mariela how Grace had grown up to be a self-assured, intelligent young woman with a quirky personality. But his feet stuck to the ground like they were in concrete.

Amaya and Georgia stepped in to comfort Mariela. June hurried to her husband and held his hands in hers while saying something to him. There wasn't any point in sticking around. He could go to his cottage and let the others sort out the seething mass of human emotions he left behind. He would find emotional relief in solitude.
~~~~~

CHAPTER 3

Eight Days Until the Umbrella Falls
Wednesday

The moment Mariela saw Cooper come out of the hovbus that morning she had known. She had hoped it wasn't true, hoped that Grace was still alive, that her chip had gone offline because she had decided to stay in Area 52. But Mariela had known. She just had to be honest with herself.

Back at her favorite park bench, the leaves swirled around her like they had when she had first talked to Amoco about planning the trip to Area 52. Back then, she had been so optimistic—she was going to get in touch with Grace and become part of Grace's life again. There was no guarantee the team going on the expedition would find Server AA, or be able to do the maintenance on it, but the trip should have been safe. No one should have died.

Now they had a deputy from Area 52 who Amoco had tagged this morning as a cryogen but who was very much alive and would have to be dealt with, Cooper was understandably mad at her because she hadn't told him Grace was his daughter, and she was having to send her staff to deal with the crisis at the cheap warehouses outside of town. It wasn't her fault their owners had done minimal maintenance and the warehouse's systems couldn't handle the outage. No matter what they did to get the warehouses back online, no matter how soon they got it done, Panacea Corp would still get sued. The only silver lining was that her mother was here.

Mariela sighed. It had been a long day. Before she left the estate, Georgia had told everyone she was planning to return to her pod. Amaya had hugged Georgia and promised she would use her terminal to stay in contact, Mariela's mother had suggested to Georgia that they both get together with Mariela's sister Sofi, T-Rock had hugged Georgia and told her he would visit, and that guy they called Deputy Dan surprised everyone by also hugging Georgia. Mariela had been told that he hadn't intended to kill Grace, but she was having a hard time forgiving him.

Hank had also hugged Georgia, and told her he would see her later that week in their martial arts class.

"I might not be there for a while," Georgia had said. From what Mariela could tell, she blamed him for Grace's death even though it had been Dan who pulled the trigger.

Hank had opened his mouth to speak and then shut it again, apparently unable to find the words to tell Georgia he loved her. Or at least that's what it seemed like he had wanted to say. Mariela almost felt sorry for him.

"Hello Mariela."

Mariela startled. Two beefy men towered over her.

Oh hell no.

The brutes. The ones who had injected a substance next to her chip that allowed them to monitor everything she did. They could also kill her remotely if she didn't do whatever they asked. She crossed her arms and leaned back against the park bench. "What do you want?"

"Lots of interesting stuff going on in your life Mariela," the man she knew only as Brute One said. "Luckily for you, I don't have the time to watch what's going on in your life, and I don't care how you spend your day or how many secrets you have. I don't care because the kill switch is all the leverage I need to get everything I want."

Brute One had always been the more difficult one. Brute Two was friendlier and less dangerous, but unfortunately Brute One appeared to be in charge. Brute One was also easy to identify by his broken nose.

Mariela's heart pounded, but she wasn't going to let the brutes know that. "Like I said, what do you want?"

"We got something good in the works," Brute One said. "For now, I just wanted to remind you about the kill switch."

"Like I could forget. The thing burns like hell."

"Good. That way you won't forget about us. We'll be coming to you soon with what we want. Be prepared, because you may have to do some things you don't like."

With their message delivered, the two brutes left her alone. She wanted Amoco to disable the kill switch as soon as possible, but the brutes had threatened to set it off if she ever tried to disable it. She rubbed her temples. She needed to figure out a way to let Amoco know about the kill switch without the brutes knowing.

~~~~~
~~~~~

Amaya hadn't planned on coming back to the Stafford estate. Ever. After Amoco and Mariela deleted the LP100 model digital ghosts without letting her know, she also hadn't planned on talking to either of them ever again. But she didn't know anyone else who could disable her chip, so she was back at Mariela's family's estate one day after they had gotten home, sitting at the conference table in the library watching Amoco as he prepared his tools.

The house's library, with two walls completely covered in bookshelves filled with print books, was probably the most beautiful room on the planet and the only upside of being back at the estate. Amaya took a couple of the leather-bound books off of the shelves, felt their rough pages, and breathed in the hundred-year-old smell.

Her sister Nyala had finally contacted her late the evening before and said she was on the train back from Bolivia. Nyala wanted to support Amaya even though she was still on the train, so she joined them over a monitor. Her face, with the landscape of Mexico passing by in the background, filled one of the windows in the library. In the adjoining windows, Amoco had the Zazora game playing while he got ready. Mariela sat at her desk drumming a pencil on the table. She seemed distracted and it wasn't clear why she was there because she didn't talk to anyone.

"Amaya, are you sure this is what you want to do?" Nyala asked.

"How can you ask me that?" Amaya asked. "I've lived without a chip, or more accurately without knowing I had a chip, since I was fifteen."

The situation that had led Amaya to take meds so she would forget she had a chip was complicated. In the two decades since, she at times had wished she had a chip, so it was no wonder Nyala was grilling her on whether this was what Amaya really wanted to do.

"I just want to make sure," Nyala said. "This needs to be the right decision for you. Not because you think it's something you have to do."

"I'm sure." People with chips had excluded her, belittled her, and looked down on her. Even when the exclusion was unintentional, like forgetting she couldn't attend their graduation party without a monitor or projection suit, it still stung. Now that she could be a member of that group, the idea of spending time doing things only chipped people could do only made her feel lonelier. In the end, the decision to permanently disable her chip was easy. She sat down at the table where Amoco was getting his tools ready. "Let's do this," she said.

Amoco stood behind her. "Lean your head forward."

Amaya did what he requested.

He put his hands on the sides of her head and palpated the back of her neck where it met her head. He then rummaged around in his bag, mumbling to himself as he did so.

Deputy Dan strolled into the room, his eyes open wide as he took in the library, the windows turned into screens, and the medical equipment on the table. "Is this the kidnappers' hang out?" he asked.

No one replied. Amoco set a device that looked like half a metal cuff on the table and looked up. "How are you adjusting to your medical experiment tag?" he asked Dan.

"It burns." Deputy Dan rubbed his arm where the tracking and identification chip had been inserted.

Amaya should probably stop calling him Deputy Dan, as he wasn't a sheriff's deputy here. But she had gotten used to it and it felt right for him, even if he was now wearing some pre-programmed digi-skin clothing rather than his uniform.

"Thank you for sharing that detail," Amoco said. "It is important to have this information if we ever successfully revive a cryogen. Please be assured you are providing invaluable assistance."

"Would have preferred not to. Am I free to go where I want now?"

"Of course. But please be sure to contain your wanderings within the grounds of the estate."

Dan nodded towards the windows that had the game on them. "What's that?"

"It's the Zazora game." Amoco had a large screen on one window showing one team and three smaller screens on another window—one displayed the hazard bidding numbers, another showed the other team, and the third was a shot of some of the fans in the arena.

"How many people are there?"

"I have not been informed of the attendance, but a typical game has about 100,000 people in the stadium."

The main camera switched to a wide angle shot of the arena.

"That's more people than we have where I live." Dan pointed to a group of spectators near the top of the screen whose seats defied the laws of physics. "How do those people not fall down?"

"It's in the metaverse."

"The meta what?"

"It's not real." Amoco must have tired of answering Dan's questions, because he switched off the Zazora screens and continued getting his gear ready. Dan stared at the window where the screen had been. He then wandered around the library looking at the books and artifacts decorating the shelves as he went.

"Amaya, are you ready?" Amoco asked. "It may sting."

"Go for it."

Amoco put one device on her head and then held another to the back of her neck in the area where her chip was located.

"Disabling chip…now."

A sharp pang stabbed into the back of her head and then intensified. *Holy crap that stung.* The pain ended as abruptly as it had begun. Amaya panted while she waited for the muscles that had tensed in her body to relax.

A smile crept onto her face. The chip had tempted her to use it, telling her that it would be different, better this time, or that a few minutes in Panacea wouldn't hurt. The only way she could get away from it was by turning it off and making sure it stayed off—permanently. She was glad her chip was gone. She had rejected what others found to be so valuable, and she didn't regret it for a second.

She also felt like maybe for once she had lived up to the ideals that Nyala had set. Nyala had a functional chip, but she was never tempted to use it. She felt no need to make a statement about chips, because she had already been making a statement for the last couple decades.

Amaya rubbed the back of her head. "Mariela," she asked, "what happened to Liam? It seems odd that the CEO of the world's largest corporation hasn't been seen or heard from since the Black Screen."

"He stayed behind in Bolivia."

"And then what happened?"

"I don't know. I haven't heard from him."

"And he left you in charge of Panacea Corp?"

"Not exactly. I don't think he expected to disappear. I'm just in charge until he returns."

"Did you kill him?" Nyala asked.

Nyala was probably joking, but who knows, maybe she actually thought Mariela was capable of killing Liam.

"Why would you think that?" Mariela said. "Of course I didn't kill him!"

Something about Mariela's voice sounded wrong—it was too high, too defensive. Surely Nyala's suspicions were just the wanderings of a paranoid mind. It was inconceivable Mariela could be a killer. On the other hand, Mariela did leave her own child in Area 52, told everyone her daughter was dead, and lied to Amaya about her plans to delete the LP100 models, so maybe it *was* conceivable she was a killer.

And had Mariela known that Opali, her sister Sofi's digital daughter, would be deleted when the LP100s were deleted? While that would be considered a property crime rather than murder under the law, the pain Sofi felt when Opali was deleted was the same as if her daughter had been solid flesh.

Amaya pushed the thought away. Mariela had been her friend for over a decade. She couldn't be a killer. But she was hiding something.

~~~~~

Mariela didn't like lying to Nyala and Amaya. But what could she say to them? Except for Amoco, it seemed like everyone on the team—Nyala, Amaya, Hank, Georgia, Cooper, even that guy they brought with them— was mad at or mistrusted her for some reason or another, and she couldn't defend herself because of the brutes monitoring her chip. Or in some cases, like with Amaya, she couldn't defend herself because there was nothing to say. Mariela had made the decision to delete the advanced LP100 model ghosts, and she had done it against Amaya's wishes. There wasn't any way she could make it better with Amaya. Not now, at least. Maybe not ever.

Julio knocked on the door of the library. "Mariela?" he said.

"Come in, Julio," Mariela said, looking up from her desk.

Julio walked a couple feet into the library. "There's someone here to see you. I tried to send her away but she was quite persistent." He looked back toward the doorway as a stunning redhead walked through. Mariela sighed. The woman was one of the last people she wanted to see.

Julio looked apologetic. "She says she's the Director of Chip Research for Panacea Corp."

Amoco huffed. "That is impossible. *I* am the Director of Chip Research."

Mariela stood up and put her hands on her hips. "No introductions needed." She gave the redhead her most disdaining look. "Viola and I have known each other for some time now. What isn't clear to me is why
~~~~~

she thinks she's the Director of Chip Research."

Viola pulled herself tall with her shoulders back in her sky-high heels and power pencil skirt. A slight scent of lavender accompanied her as she walked across the room. "Liam hired me before he left on the trip to Bolivia. Since Liam hasn't been around to let you know, I thought I would stop by and let you know myself." She paused in front of the table and assessed Amoco. "You must be Amoco." She looked down her nose at him. "I'm so sorry to be the bearer of bad news, but Liam was going to reassign you as soon as he got back."

"That is patently preposterous." Amoco sat down with a thud.

"Viola," Mariela walked out from behind the desk and approached the vixen while maintaining a cautious distance, "I don't know why Liam would have hired you, especially without telling me, but until he gets back I'm in charge, so you can consider yourself out of a job until he shows up."

"Okay." Viola looked as cool and collected as ever as she nonchalantly dropped her bag on the couch and sat down with the constrained athleticism of a tiger poised to pounce. "But you might want to consider that there was a reason Liam didn't tell you. I doubt that he will be happy with you changing course while he is missing." She crossed her legs and draped one elegant arm on the back of the couch. "He might even see it as a sign you took advantage of him being gone."

If only Viola knew how much Mariela planned to take advantage of Liam's 'disappearance.' She wasn't responsible for his death—that had been his bodyguards, AKA the brutes, who had threatened her with death if she told anyone that they had thrown him out of the helicopter—but she wasn't sad to see Liam gone. And she wasn't going to keep following his misguided agenda.

Mariela sat down in the armchair farthest from Viola. "Viola, I'll contact you if I need your services. In the meantime, I suggest you start looking for work elsewhere."

"Careful Mariela, or people might start a rumor that you caused Liam to go missing." Viola leaned forward and lifted her bag with one finger. "I can see I'm not wanted here so I'd best be going." The redhead flipped her hair over her shoulder, rose fluidly from the couch, and strolled toward the door. Then she stopped and turned. She tucked her chin in and rubbed her forehead. "Is…Cooper around?" Viola no longer sounded like a power player, but vulnerable instead. It almost made Mariela feel sorry for her. Almost, but not quite. If Cooper didn't want to see her, Viola only had herself to blame.

"Be realistic, Viola," Mariela said. "Are you seriously be thinking you and Cooper could have any sort of relationship after what you did to him?"

Viola lifted her head and sniffed as she turned back to the door, and without responding, she left.

A slam of the front door moments later conveyed that Viola had left the residence.

"I want everyone here to understand," Mariela said, "we will *not* tell Cooper about Viola." It was a good thing Cooper hadn't been there. "He has enough to deal with right now without having to know that his manipulative and vituperative ex-girlfriend may have taken Amoco's job."

"Was she the one that outed him as unchipped?" Amaya asked.

"Yes, she's the one."

"They were dating?" Amaya asked. "That's a pretty low thing to do to someone you are supposed to care about. No wonder it makes him so mad."

"What happened?" Nyala asked.

"They were romantically involved," Mariela said, "until three years ago when she tried to chip-jack him. When she realized she couldn't chip-jack him because he didn't have a chip, she outed him to the Academia Veritas Virtual as being unchipped. He was fired. And now he's spent most of the last year puttering around my father's house."

"He did fight in the Arctic War," Amoco said. "Let us not forget he served his country for two years."

"Oh right," Mariela rolled her eyes, "while serving his country he also hid away from everyone he knew and engaged in a form of self-sacrificial punishment by volunteering for some of the most dangerous assignments. Let's not forget that." She was still angry with Cooper for volunteering to fight in that stupid war. He could have died.

"What's chip-jacking?" Dan asked. Mariela had almost forgotten he was in the room. He was lurking silently in the corner, blending in with the bookshelves.

"Chip-jacking involves using a device to download info from someone's chip without them knowing it," Amaya said. "It's a breach of privacy."

"This happened to Cooper?"

"*Almost* happened. You can't chip-jack someone who doesn't have a chip. But then Viola figured out that he had been pretending to be chipped; she outed him, and people got mad."

"He was dismissed from his position," Amoco said.

"Right, he got fired. Which is why we aren't going to let him know that Viola is around."

"Mariela," Amaya looked around at the others in the room, "we won't tell Cooper. But maybe you should."

~~~~~

While Amoco chatted with Amaya after Dan had left and Nyala had signed off, Mariela came up with a strategy to ask Amoco for help with deactivating the kill switch. There wasn't any room for error—if the brutes figured out she was trying to deactivate it, they would use it to kill her. And while it was probably unrealistic for them to monitor her chip activity all the time, she couldn't know when they were monitoring it. She had to assume anything she said might be overheard, and anything she saw might be seen.

She planned to take advantage of a blind spot—without specialized equipment, it was exceptionally difficult to spy on a person's movements through their chip. Mariela's plan was to write what she needed from Amoco without looking at the paper as she was doing so. That way there would be no visual data for the brutes to review.

On one piece of paper she wrote, *Don't react and keep your responses vague.*

It's a matter of life-or-death, she wrote on another.

By the time Amoco turned to leave, she had three pieces of paper to share with him. Mariela called out to Amoco before he headed out the door with Amaya. "Amoco, could you stay behind for a moment? I'd like to discuss some things with you."

He sat down at the desk across from her. "How may I help you?" he asked.

Being careful to make sure the paper did not show up in her field of vision, she pushed the first piece of paper over to him.

"I want you to know that if I have anything to say about it," she said, "Viola will not take over your position." She pushed the second piece of paper over. "Do you understand me?"

"Most certainly," Amoco replied.
~~~~~

She pushed the last slip of paper over to him: *Liam's guards placed a 'kill switch' on my chip. It can kill me and monitors everything I do. Need you to deactivate it. Do it without telling me. If bodyguards find out, they'll kill me.*

"I'll be sure to advocate for you with Liam." She paused, hoping Amoco would understand what she wanted. "Am I understood?"

"Yes. And in return let me assure you, you have my loyalty."

She sighed. He had understood. She heard crinkling as Amoco wadded up the paper. He would figure out some way to save her. He would have to. She couldn't live in constant fear that the brutes would kill her. There had to be some way to fix it.

~~~~~

Six hours of walking and Cooper still hadn't reached the downtown area of Glorietta Pass. He did have blisters and a sunburn to show for his efforts, though. His original plan was to go all the way to Panacea Plaza and then maybe walk home again, but at this point he had maximized any cathartic effect from walking. The prickly bag of emotions that had propelled him to start walking hadn't left him, but further walking didn't seem like it would help any more. Apparently, he couldn't sweat out his anger and frustrations, or his sense of betrayal and loss.

The most direct path to Panacea Plaza from the Stafford Estate had taken him down the ironically named International Mall—a trail, mostly deserted in the heat of the day, that happened to travel through the campus of the Academia Veritas Virtual headquarters. To one side of the trail, green lawns seeded with thick grass stretched to brick buildings with faculty offices. On the other side, a lake with a fountain separated the trail from the administrative offices. That side was where he had been fired three years ago. He turned his back on it and looked at the side with the faculty offices.

This side was where he had spent some of the happiest years of his life. Sure, he had been in constant fear someone would figure out he was faking being chipped, or that they would realize he didn't have the credentials they assumed he had, but he had found teaching to be fulfilling and worth any fear he had about being discovered. Now, three years after being dismissed in what had been the most humiliating episode of his life, he was drawn back to the building.
~~~~~

He headed up the grassy slope to the closest brick building. On the fourth floor, in the corner office facing towards Panacea Corp headquarters, was his old office. The office he had been rewarded with after his classes had seen the highest enrollment of the school for three years straight. Not a single student was in sight, but that wasn't unusual. Most of them never set foot on campus or in a classroom. They took their classes virtually and were lucky to see even one prerecorded lecture, much less a live, in-person lecture.

He stopped with his hand on the door to the building. Was he really thinking of going in? Of taking a chance on running into his former colleagues, most of them so-called friends who hadn't bothered to contact him after he got fired? There was only one person he actually wanted to see, an old mentor who had reached out to him a number of times and even had expressed interest in buying one of his iron artwork pieces.

Shame had kept him from returning her calls at the time, but something had changed in him. He wanted to talk to her now. Maybe she was even still interested in his artwork. He could use the money to buy the headstone he wanted for Grace's grave. Not that Oscar Stafford wouldn't have willingly given the money, but he wanted to buy it with his own, earned money.

He pulled open the door and entered the light-filled lobby. The cool, air-conditioned air rushed out of the building and tickled the hairs on his arms. On the far side of the empty lobby was the school's only lecture room. He strolled past the unused couches and pushed open the swinging door to the large auditorium with tiered rows of seats that used to fill with students during his lectures. The lights came on as soon as he entered.

He wandered down the steps to the front of the room. The room had a new, musty smell, but also a familiar smell Cooper had never been able to place. Now it just smelled to him like learning. From the flat area in front of the seats he took the steps up to the stage. It had the same podium he remembered with viewing screens at the back of the stage. In the back of the room, behind the students, were more screens plus the camera that sent his image to the virtual students.

During his time at the Academia, he had been a professor of digital antiquities, lecturing on stuff like the internet, the development of pod warehousing, and the early days of the metaverse. But in looking at the podium covered in dust, lonely and forgotten, he realized that it was an antiquity. He ran his hand along the top, leaving dusty streak marks behind. The auditorium had been constructed for faculty that wanted to record live lectures, but it turned out no one other than Cooper wanted to record live lectures. It was all part of a world that no longer existed.

If only he had been open about not having a chip, he could have lectured so much more honestly about life as an unchipped person. Not that he would have been hired if he had been honest. It was a virtual learning institute after all. Unchipped people, by default, didn't attend and didn't teach there. Well, there was no point in dwelling on it now. He wiped his hands on his pants and left the stage.

At the swinging doors back to the lobby he turned around. Maybe someday he would be back there. Maybe he wasn't as unwelcome as he had worried about. His tentative plan to see Helema, his mentor, became concrete. And while he was there, he might just see what she thought about him returning someday. If Helema didn't support him, then nobody would. It would be nice to feel like he had a purpose, like he was contributing to the world again.

Thankfully he had the elevator all to himself on the way to the fourth floor. He turned left off of the elevator. The hallway ran in a big loop around the edge of the building. Faculty offices with windows were on the outside. On the inside were the bathrooms, storage closets, and windowless offices for student workers. Most of those had been empty while Cooper was there. In fact, most of the faculty offices were too, with both groups preferring to work from home for the most part. Even the faculty members that worked from home, however, kept offices that they would use on occasion.

Cooper walked past his old corner office. It was still empty. Had it been empty for the entire three years since he had been fired, or had someone come and gone? Farther down the corridor, Helema's office was also empty. He turned the corner and continued the loop around the building. More offices were empty. Where was everyone?

He followed the hallway around the building, checking each office name plaque for Helema's name. He was at the fourth corner office, the one that contained the dean's suite, when he finally saw it: Helema Prax, Dean of Technological Advancement Studies. Cooper smiled. Good for her—she had been promoted. He pushed open the door. The suite's deep walnut walls and academic vibe was exactly the same as when he had worked there.

The expressionless woman at the assistant's desk inspected him, her lip raised in the beginning of a snarl. "Cooper O'Connor. *So* nice to see you."

Her heavily sarcastic voice was unchanged from when he had worked there. She had disapproved of him before she found out he was un-chipped, then her opinion of him had plummeted so low she had basically stopped acknowledging his presence. Cooper looked on the bright side— it was a step up she even said his name or bothered to be sarcastic with him. An open door to the side of the reception room led to the corner office where, out of sight, Helema was talking with someone.

"I'd like to talk to Helema," he said.

"*Dr.* Prax's busy."

She obviously didn't approve of him using Helema's first name.

"I'll wait."

"She may not see you. She's very busy."

"I'll take my chances." Now that he was there, he was sticking it out no matter how many assistants were rude to him.

He sat down on a couch in the waiting room. Snippets of the conversation in the corner office reached him.

"Tell her she should have known she couldn't hire someone to do her final project for her."

A minute or so of silence.

"I don't *care* if she was using the principle of comparative advantage and that her time is better spent creating content—it's not an economics project."

More silence.

"She can take a zero on the assignment or be expelled from the class. If she doesn't like that tell her she can talk to me."

The conversation appeared to end not long after. A few minutes ticked by. Cooper finally gave up waiting for the assistant to let Helema know he was there.

He stood up. "Should I go on in?"

"Hang on," the annoyed assistant said. She finished rearranging some school spirit items on her desk, and then walked to the office door. "Dr. Prax, Cooper O'Connor is here to see you without an appointment."

Cooper held his breath.

"Cooper? Of course, show him in." Helema sounded pleased to see him.

Cooper exhaled. He had been more worried than he had realized.

He stood from the barely used couch and realized he was covered in dust and dried sweat. He probably should have cleaned up a bit, but Helema wasn't one to judge.

"Cooper, so good to see you!" She hurried over to him, then stopped short and gave him a once over. "What, are you homeless now? I thought Oscar Stafford had taken you in."

Maybe he looked worse than he had realized.

"Sorry, I just walked from the Stafford estate."

"Goodness—all that way? You *must* be in a dire state." She leaned forward and gave him an air hug. "I'd give you a bigger hug but I'm not sure I want to get that close."

He laughed. He had known her long enough to hear the affection in her voice and to not be offended by her blunt honesty. "Do you have a minute?" he asked.

"Sure, for you, anytime." She looked over at the assistant. "Why didn't you tell me he was here sooner?"

"You're very busy," the assistant said. "It's not like he works here anymore."

Helema said something that sounded like "pshaw" and turned to walk into her office. "I'm going to fire her someday."

"Yeah, you say that every day," the assistant called after her.

Helema wore the flowy clothes of someone who valued comfort but also didn't want to look unprofessional. Her gray hair was covered up with digi-spray, but she didn't bother trying to hide her wrinkles. In her job it probably added to her authority to look older.

Cooper followed Helema into an office that was at least twice the size of his former office. Unlike the other offices that had to make do with regular windows, the dean's office had floor-to-ceiling windows on two walls and a sitting area in the corner. Off to the side, an immense wooden desk surrounded by bookcases had two chairs facing it.

The view through the windows was similar to the one that he for so many years had stared at from the office on the other corner. The concrete, mostly windowless Panacea Corp headquarters, taller than most of the other buildings, was the prominent feature among the skyscrapers of the Inner Ring of the city. In the near distance, just beyond the grassy lawns of the Academia, were the older, shorter, pre-disaster-proofing-era buildings of the Middle Ring.

Helema gave him some water with ice before sitting down on one of the couches. She encouraged Cooper to sit on the other. Cooper drank thirstily. They chatted for a while about mundane things—how the weather was hot, the traffic was bad, the students ungrateful. Typical things. After five or so minutes, Helema looked serious, "When you didn't return my many calls, I never thought I would see you again."

"I wasn't in a place to speak to anyone…but it made me feel better knowing I wasn't totally forgotten."

"Love you or hate you—I don't think anyone here has forgotten you."

Cooper shifted in his seat. "Speaking of people who hate me—there's something I wanted to ask you about, and I want an honest opinion." He hesitated for a moment. "Is there any possibility for me to return? I miss teaching."

Helema paused before responding. "Well, I'm the dean of the department now, and I would be for it, so that should go a long way. As long as there's no one in administration or higher up the chain who opposes, I don't see why not." She leaned forward and rested her elbows on her knees. "I got the impression that teaching virtually without a chip may have been somewhat physically challenging—do you think you're up for it again?"

He didn't hesitate. "Yes."

"You know some students won't respect you because you don't have a chip, or will try to test you to see if you can handle it?"

"Yes. I've had lots of experience with being treated poorly since I left here." It was sad how true the statement was. "I've become accustomed to ignoring it."

Helema looked at the table, her eyes unfocusing before focusing on him again. "Let me look into this and I'll get back to you. Give me about a week or so."

"Great." Cooper was grinning like a fool, but he couldn't help it. "I look forward to hearing from you." He didn't want to get his hopes up, but it would be great to start feeling useful again. Like he had some value to the world.

"I'm happy to do this. You were one of the best professors we've had. Since you've left, things haven't gone well here. We've lost students to the Chicago Academy and had to cut some faculty."

That explained the empty offices. But if the school was hurting for funds… "Is funding a problem? I don't want to put you in an awkward position."

"Don't be silly. You always paid for yourself. Students liked that you actually lectured. You brought enough students into the school to cover your salary and then some. Not to mention there was a substantial group of students who were upset when we fired you, and left to the Chicago Academy afterwards. I think the people who wanted you gone were more than upset when they realized that part of their salary came indirectly from your efforts, and that we had to let them go because we couldn't pay them."

It was a complete revisioning of the narrative he had been telling himself over the last three years. In his head no one had supported him, no one had cared when he was gone. He had been thrown away like used tissues. Well, he *had* been thrown away like used tissues, but it turned out there were people who had cared about that tissue. "Why didn't you tell me this sooner?"

"Why didn't you return my calls?"

Oh, right. "Sorry."

"Dr. Prax," the assistant knocked on the door. "Your next appointment is in five minutes."

Helema nodded at the assistant. "Thank you." She turned back to him. "Cooper, before you go, I just wanted to say I'm sorry about what happened. I thought the decision was wrong. I said she shouldn't be allowed back. I was overruled, but I want you to know I was against it from the beginning."

"Against what?"

"You don't know? Viola Adams has returned as a researcher in a joint project with Panacea Corp."

Cooper stood up so abruptly he knocked his water over. "She's done *what*?"

CHAPTER 4

Seven Days Until the Umbrella Falls

Thursday

A contact request from Viola woke Mariela up. *Ugh.* Not how she wanted to start her morning. She glanced at the clock. After the last two days, Mariela had hoped to begin her day later than five am. Looks like it wasn't going to be. She sat up in bed, stretched, ignored an unusually high number of pending news alerts, and accepted Viola's call with no video.

Viola was wearing workout clothes and had a light sheen of sweat, but somehow was also perfectly coiffed and glowing as usual.

Mariela didn't bother trying to sound pleasant. "Viola, what is it?"

"Mariela, I don't know why you hate me. We were friends once."

"I don't remember ever being friends with you." The few dinners they had as a group when Viola was dating Cooper didn't make them friends. Because let's face it, Mariela was never going to be friends with anyone who dated Cooper. Mariela may not be able to commit to him, but that didn't mean she was going to like anyone else who did. But she *had* introduced Viola to Cooper, so maybe they had been friends at one point. It was difficult to remember, though. All she could see now was bitch.

Viola sniffed. "Well, *I* believed we were friends once. I'm heartbroken to hear you don't feel the same way."

"I…" Mariela stumbled in her search for words. Viola's comment left her tongue-tied and trying to determine if she had been rude. She probably had been. "I—"

"So," Viola interrupted her, "what did Cooper say when you told him I was in town?"

"I didn't tell Cooper. I thought if you wanted him to know you were in town, you would tell him yourself."

"You're very short-tempered this morning when I'm the one who should be short with you for not letting Cooper know I was here."

Mariela shook her head. "Not my responsibility."

Viola's voice when she responded sounded small and uncertain,

"Does Cooper ever talk about me?"

"No," Mariela answered. It was a brutal but honest answer.

"But maybe he thinks about me sometimes?" Viola asked.

"I'm not able to read his mind, so I couldn't answer that question." He probably did think about her, considering she had ruined his career. Viola's insecurities around Cooper were as unjustified as they were annoying, considering Viola had injured Cooper more than the other way around. Mariela yawned again. "Maybe if you wanted him not to hate you, you shouldn't have tried to chip-jack him. And, just a thought, maybe you shouldn't have revealed that he was unchipped to his employer."

"Mariela, I know I shouldn't have done it. I don't know what I was thinking. I think I was just jealous at the time because I could tell he was pulling away from me. I really want to apologize to him. I know it's a huge favor to ask, but would you be willing to put me in contact with him?"

"No."

"Oh. Okay. I guess I didn't expect differently. I was just hoping maybe we were still friends."

"I guess not." Mariela thought they had already established that they weren't friends. She rubbed her eyes. "Was this why you woke me up at five am? To talk about Cooper?"

"Oh, sorry, I thought for sure you would be awake by now. Don't you have a lot of work to do?"

Yes, she had a lot of work to do. Thanks, Viola, for reminding her. Was chatting about Cooper the only reason Viola had called her at this ungodly hour? "So, that's it?"

"No, I still haven't told you the main reason I called."

"Okay. Go ahead."

"It looks like we're going to be working together after all." Viola smiled slyly. "I suggest you check the news reports." And with a quick goodbye, Viola disconnected.

Seconds later Mariela got one more message from Viola. It was short, simply saying, "Looks like you didn't kill him. I always believed you were innocent."

Mariela told her most recent news alert to show on the wall.

Business Today

"All the business news you need to know"

April 11, 2115

Liam Price, Chair of Panacea Corporation, Reappears
Around 2 a.m. Panacea Time this morning, Liam Price, Chairman of Panacea Corporation, was found by oil rig workers as they were heading to the mainland of Mexico. According to the workers, Liam was unconscious, sunburned, and floating on a parachute. The parachute was a small, custom-made one that when stored would be almost imperceptibly hidden in his jacket. He has been taken to a local hospital where he is being treated for strained muscles, sun exposure, and dehydration. He is expected to make a full recovery.

Panacea Corp has not commented. According to the influential business blogger Elliat Exis, Panacea Corp board members loyal to former Chairman Oscar Stafford may have caused the recent outage, also called the Black Screen, of the Panacea Metaverse as a distraction from their attempts to depose the new chairman. Elliat Exis said he looked forward to hearing Mr. Price's account of what happened.

Elliat Exis also mentioned that he recently personally confirmed that June Stafford was still alive. Stafford disappeared approximately 16 years ago during the Chip Crisis of 2099, and as recently as March of this year Elliat Exis had hypothesized that she may have killed herself. Exis stated that Stafford did not appear to show any signs of the mental illness that had plagued her before her disappearance. Exis did not have any information on where she had been for the last 16 years.

Seriously, Elliat? Mariela had never met him, and hoped to never meet him after all the untrue things he had written about her family over the years, but the team had just saved him from his non-functioning pod warehouse, the least he could do was show her family a little positivity.

What would Liam say once he was better? Would he remember that the brutes threw him out of the helicopter? Would he think Mariela was behind it? Would he even be capable of imagining that his own avatar had ordered the hit?

~~~~~

It took walking up ten flights of stairs for Amaya to reach Nyala's apartment. It wasn't a surprise the elevator was broken; something was always broken in her sister's apartment building. Usually it was the food dispensers, but the elevators were a close second. Amaya took a second to catch her breath and let the burning in her legs subside. After a minute of deep breaths, she trudged down the dark hallway to Nyala's door. She knocked on the door as she opened it.

"Good morn—" She stopped mid-greeting. At the table, looking like he was deep in conversation with Nyala, was the blogger Elliat Exis. "Why are *you* here?"

"I find your sister to be the most bluntly opinionated person I have ever met." He said it like it was a compliment.

"Thank you." Nyala nodded at him. She obviously took it as a compliment.

"You're welcome." He nodded back at her.

Elliat and her sister were friends? When did these two get so chummy? "What is going on here?"

"It turns out," Nyala said, "that we share a certain…distrust…of one large corporation in particular."

Elliat and Nyala had bonded over their dislike of Panacea Corp—what was the world coming to?

"I'm not a fan of Panacea Corp either," Amaya's words caught in her throat, "but Nyala, he," she nodded at Elliat, "spreads rumors and lies about people we care about who work there." She remained standing just inside the door. She could have sat down at the table with them, but that might encourage Elliat to stay.

Elliat made an odd huffing noise. "I never report something unless I believe it to be true."

"You believe a lot of stuff," Amaya said. "And Nyala, I never expected you to be defending Elliat." It was like an alien had abducted her sister.

"I can help him see that some of the stuff he writes isn't true," Nyala said with a half-smile. "He can also be helpful to us."

"Or you might find out that everything I write is true," Elliat turned
~~~~~

and spoke directly to Amaya. "It's important to stay open-minded. For example, right now I'm researching a piece about how a group of people connected to Panacea Corp may have deleted all the groundbreaking LP100 advanced model digital ghosts, including one—an avatar for the CEO—that was quite effectively serving as a vice president of Panacea Corp…and that had taken away the job of your friend." His smug impression said that he felt confident he would find evidence to support his ideas.

This time Amaya huffed. "You didn't seem to think the CEO's avatar was so effective a week ago—you wrote that he 'frenetically jumped from one inane project to another.'"

"Well, I've reevaluated."

Amaya crossed her arms. "I can tell you now that I didn't have anything to do with his disappearance." It was stretching the truth, but it felt close enough to the truth for Elliat.

"Let's just say that the appearance of you, June Stafford, a former lover of Mariela Stafford, and a motley group of some other folk—one with a rattlesnake bite as well as a bewildered fellow wearing an outfit from who-knows-where—right at the time the ghosts were deleted was highly suspicious."

"Elliat," Nyala stood up, the expression on her face showing that she had finally had enough of him, "I've enjoyed our talk, but I think you need to leave now."

"But why?" Elliat looked confused. "I thought we were on the same page about exposing wrongdoing by Panacea Corp."

"It's one thing to look in to the corporation, but when you accuse my sister of illegalities, that's where I draw the line."

Elliat gave a knowing nod. "Family is important." He stood up and held his hands clasped in front of him. "Of course it would be awkward for me to expose your sister's misdeeds."

"There *were no* misdeeds." Amaya barely caught herself before adding 'on my part.' Elliat would have surely caught the implication that there were misdeeds by other people. What Amoco and Mariela did was wrong, but there wasn't anything to be gained by having Elliat expose what happened to the world.

Amaya moved to the side so as not to impede Elliat's exit in any way.

Elliat stopped with his hand on the doorknob. "Of course not. We'll just pretend that's the truth when we're talking here." He waved his hand in a circle to indicate the room.

"It *is* the truth!" Amaya exclaimed.

"Sure, sure." Elliat nodded. "I'll see you next week?" he snapped his fingers and pointed at Nyala.

"You'll bring the wine?" Nyala asked.

"You bet!" Elliat said.

"Okay, I'll see you then," Nyala responded with a smile.

Elliat opened the door. "And I promise to wear clothes again, because I know this one," he pointed a finger at Amaya this time and made a clicking noise, "gets upset when I don't." He walked out the door, letting it slam behind him.

Amaya huffed. If only Elliat not wearing clothes was the most upsetting thing she had to worry about right now. How could Nyala agree to meet with him? "Why did you say you would see him again?"

Nyala's dog Fido emerged from the back bedroom and nuzzled Amaya's hand. She scratched his head. Obviously he wasn't any bigger fan of Elliat than Amaya was.

Nyala smiled. "It's better for keeping an eye on him. That way I'll know what he finds and maybe I can even influence what he writes about it. Plus, I kind of like him."

"Seriously? No one likes Elliat. He's a conspiracy theorist and a hack journalist."

"That's kind of mean. Why are you being so defensive? *Did* you delete the ghosts? I won't tell Elliat, I just want to know what I'm dealing with here and how much I'll have to work to cover it up."

"No, of course I didn't." Amaya walked to the glass balcony door and looked out. The view of downtown from Nyala's apartment never ceased to impress her. The old-fashioned apartment building may not have had weatherproofing and was only one disaster away from falling down, but it was roomy and had a stunning view.

"But you know who did delete the ghosts?" Nyala asked.

Amaya rolled her eyes. She hadn't even gotten her tea yet and Nyala was already interrogating her. "No one on the expedition deleted the ghosts." Once again, it seemed close enough to the truth, as neither Amoco nor Mariela had gone on the expedition. Normally she would have told her sister everything, but Nyala's recent friendship with Elliat made her reluctant. "Can I get some tea?" she asked, sounding more annoyed than she had intended to.

"Sure." Nyala stood up, took a teacup out of one of the kitchen cabinets, and held it under the hot water dispenser. "So it was someone *not* on the expedition, and you know who it was."

When was Nyala going to let it go? Amaya was saved from having to come up with an answer by a knock on the door.

"Are you expecting anyone?" she asked Nyala.

"No. Sometimes Trevor stops by but he usually just barges in without knocking. Can you open it?"

"What if it's a serial killer?"

"Why would it be a serial killer??"

"I don't know. But shouldn't you check the camera first to make sure it isn't?"

"Alright." Nyala set the teacup down and tapped the mini-screen next to the sink. She laughed. "Oh, you're gonna love this."

"Who is it?"

"It's not a serial killer. Go ahead and open the door."

The door squeaked as Amaya opened it. Everything about Nyala's apartment building always seemed like it was about to fall apart. On the other side stood Hank, looking dejected with his head down and shoulders slumped.

"What are *you* doing here?" she asked as she held the door open for him.

Hank looked back over his shoulder as he walked in. "Did I just pass Elliat Exis? Are you talking to him?"

"Not if I can help it," Amaya said.

That must have been enough for Hank because he sat down at the table in the chair that Elliat had just gotten out of.

"Oh, I guess we're sitting now?" Amaya joined him at the table. First Elliat and then Hank. It was an odd day.

"I was just making some tea," Nyala said. "Did you want some?"

"Sure."

Nyala took out another teacup. "So why are you here?" she asked. "Did you get in a fight with the other kids on the playground?"

Amaya smiled. Nyala could do patronizing better than anyone.

"I need someone to talk to," Hank blurted out. "Georgia's ignoring me, T-Rock hates me, Cooper blames me for Grace's death—"

"We all blame you for Grace's death," Amaya said.

"Yeah, well so does Mariela, June, and probably Dan, though that's kind of ironic considering he's the one who actually shot her. The only friends I have left are the guys from back in the res-home, and I can't exactly talk to them about this."

Nyala set a teacup in front of Hank along with a selection of teas in a box. "So what do you need to talk about?" She walked back to the kitchen and started filling the other teacups.

"Everything." He looked up at the ceiling and took a deep breath. "I blame myself for Grace's death. And for Georgia not talking to me. It's really lonely without her around. And I couldn't help those people at the warehouse." Tears crept into his eyes; he wiped them away quickly.

The pause that followed wasn't awkward, at least not for Amaya. For her it was a reconsidering. Reconsidering whether she had been wrong about Hank—too quick to dismiss him, to see him as shallow and immature, always willing to pick a fight, not having much to offer to anyone other than Georgia. All those things were still true, but for the first time Amaya saw there was something more to him.

"Okay," Amaya said. "Talk. Tell us what's on your mind."

Hank looked at the table, apparently lost in thought. "First," he said, "you may not want to check your news alerts, because that blogger just posted about you."

Nyala carried the two teacups to the table. She put one in front of Amaya and kept the other for herself. "Go on. What did he say?"

"He's saying he thinks Amaya is responsible for deleting the ghosts."

"That ass!" Nyala said.

"But it's not all bad. He's saying really nice stuff about Nyala. He's calling her 'the savior of the unchipped' because of her promos she does educating about the barriers faced by the unchipped. He even posted a mockup of her in a flowing robe riding a white horse."

"Great," Amaya said, "just what I need. You know that now she's going to be insufferable?"

Nyala laughed. "I can't help it if Elliat recognizes my true genius while you've been exposed as the petty criminal that you are. In fact, you're not even a petty criminal, deleting that many advanced ghosts would make you a felon multiple times over."

"I know Amaya didn't delete the LP100 ghosts," Hank said. "She would never do that."

"Thank you, Hank," Amaya said. Maybe he wasn't so bad after all.

"Plus, I heard Mariela and Amoco talking about it beforehand."

Amaya spit out some of her tea. "And you didn't think to say anything to me?" Amaya put Hank back in the category of people she didn't like.

"I didn't understand what it was. It was only afterwards that I put all the pieces together."

Nyala raised her eyebrows. "So, it was Mariela and Amoco."

Now that Hank had spilled the beans it was a relief. Her words came out in a rush, like they were finally breaking free after being held in for so long. "Mariela asked Amoco to add some code to the program and didn't tell me about it. It was a complete betrayal."

Hank slouched in his chair. "And then Georgia betrayed me."

Amaya's mouth dropped open. Did he really just say that about Georgia? "Being mad at you for acting like an idiot is not a betrayal."

"But why does she still have to be mad at me? Couldn't she just yell at me some and move on?"

"It's not that easy. She's really mad at you right now. You need to give her some time to get over it."

"I don't have time." Hank sounded like petulant child.

"Why not?"

"If I give her time, she'll get used to being in her pod, and I don't think she'll be willing to go through all the pain and nausea again that she went through when she left the first time."

"It's a chance you'll have to take," Amaya said. "You can't make her stay out of her pod, and if you try, it will only make things worse. Let her do what she needs to do and when she's ready, she'll contact you. In the meantime, find something to distract yourself with."

"Nothing distracts me anymore." He looked around the room. "I'm bored by all of it."

"Why don't you start a business helping people who want to leave their pods readjust to the solid world? You were really good at helping Georgia with her readjustment."

"I know. But that was because it was Georgia, and I cared about her."

"Maybe you could care about other people."

Hank sat up straight.

"Those people in that pod warehouse, they were starving and scared. I cared about them. Maybe I could help them out."

"Great idea." Nyala patted him on the shoulder. "Now go do it."

"I will. Thanks to both of you—you've been really helpful."

Nyala raised her eyebrows like she wasn't quite sure but didn't want to say anything. "Glad to help."

"Hey, do you think I could talk to you all again some time? I don't really have many friends I can confide in."

This was too much. Hank had never been friendly with her, in fact he had been outright rude to her, and now he wanted to use her and Nyala as confidants? She crossed her arms. "I suggest you talk to those guys you know from the res-home."

"Don't be mean, Amaya," Nyala said. She placed a hand on Hank's shoulder. "Of course you can talk to us."

"Thank you! It won't be a lot, I mean, it may be, but it won't."

Hank hopped out of his chair and not seconds later had given them both side hugs and was out the door.

Nyala looked at Amaya. "This is a really weird day."

"That's for sure. Why did you tell him he could talk to us? He's been a jerk to me."

"He reminds me of the kids I meet when I go to inspect the res-homes. I guess I have a soft spot for him because I know how difficult it must have been for him growing up."

"You've developed a lot of soft spots for people lately."

"We're going to war, Amaya. You can never have too many friends in a war."

"Who are we going to war with?"

"Panacea Corp."

"Okay, why?"

"They're too powerful."

It was true, Panacea Corp was too powerful, but Amaya didn't want to go to war with them. She wasn't even sure what that meant or what they were fighting about or hoped to gain from it. But she had made a pledge to herself that she would be more supportive of Nyala's causes. And Mariela and Amoco, both senior employees of Panacea Corp, had screwed her.

"Okay, let's go to war. What do we do?"

"I don't know. I'm still figuring that out."

For a moment neither said anything.

"Nyala, what happened to you on the trip with Mariela? I know you didn't choose to stay behind and let Mariela go home without you."

"I was drugged. By Liam's bodyguards. They took Mariela and left me unconscious on the train. I woke up hours later and I eventually made my way back home."

"What happened to Liam? How did he end up in the middle of the ocean?"

"I don't know. I bet Mariela could tell us but for some reason she's not talking. I don't think she threw him out of the helicopter, but it's Mariela, so you never know. What happened on your expedition to do maintenance on the server farm?"

"So much happened. It was awful but it was also wonderful. Or at least it was wonderful until it was awful. Hank and T-Rock got arrested and—get this—hog-tied by that deputy, we went to a rodeo and a hoedown, Mariela's daughter was wonderful but then…we lost her." She had cried so many tears over Grace's death. Sometimes it felt like she had no tears left, but the tears still rushed down her cheeks. "We made Deputy Dan come with us because he shot Grace and we didn't know what else to do with him."

"It broke my heart when I heard about Grace. I never knew her as an adult, but she was such a spirited and bubbly kid." Nyala took a sip of her tea. "I knew it wasn't safe for you to go on the trip."

"Nothing happened to me."

"You were in danger." Nyala idly stirred the tea. "You went to a rodeo? Where *were* you? I've seen that deputy guy and he is *not* from around here."

"I'm not supposed to tell you because I signed a non-disclosure statement."

"But this is war, and normal rules don't apply in war."

"This is war," Amaya repeated, more to herself than Nyala. "Okay, but you can't tell anyone else. This place is wonderful and will get ruined if people find it."

"How about this—I promise not to tell anyone else unless I have your permission to do so."

"Okay, I hope I don't regret this." She took a breath. "We were in Area 52."

"Really? What is it? Military installation? Site of an alien spaceship crash landing? Where they faked the moon landings? Wait, was the rodeo an alien rodeo and was the hoedown held on the stage where they faked the moon landings?"

"It's a retro colony. A bunch of semi-luddites. They believe 2005 was the year of technological supremacy because, according to them, that's when humans had the best balance with technology. I don't think their communication technology could even be called smartphones. They're more like moderately intelligent phones. And no one has implanted chips.

"A group of Elders stops any attempts at technological advances. And they've lied to the kids and told them the rest of the world is contaminated with radiation, so they can't ever leave because, according to the stories they've been told, they'll die if they do. The only people who remember the truth are the adults who founded the place eighty years ago, and most of them have passed away. That's why Dan—the deputy— is so freaked out. He thinks he's being poisoned with radiation."

"Area 52 really exists?" Nyala leaned forward. "What was it like? I'd really like to see this place."

"It was amazing and I wish I could take you there, but the only living Elder didn't like us, and then we kidnapped Dan, so I'm not sure what would happen if we went back."

"Wow, you guys were some serious outlaws on this trip."

"Sort of. We tried not to be, but it didn't work out liked we hoped.

Now that Amaya had given up on sticking to her non-disclosure agreement, she couldn't wait to tell Nyala everything. Her words tumbled over themselves as she started filling Nyala in. There was so much to tell.

CHAPTER 5

Seven Days Until the Umbrella Falls

Thursday, cont.

You've survived worse, Cooper. Much worse. You can handle a simple dinner. Sure, he had faced enemy fire when he had rescued stranded ships during the Arctic War, but that wasn't making it any easier to get to dinner at the estate. Reminding himself he had survived a search and rescue mission during the Snow Storm of 2080 that had lasted for over forty-eight hours in sub-zero temps wasn't increasing his confidence that he could handle facing all 5'5" of Mariela.

The only way Cooper was going to make it the rest of the short distance from his cottage to the estate house was to remind himself of how good Oscar and June Stafford had always been to him. *Why had Oscar and June even invited him to dinner?* Surely they must know how awkward it was for him to be around Mariela right now.

He headed up the brick path that led to the back entrance of the house. The house glittered from the lights in the large entry hallway and the dining room. Was it his imagination that the dining room table, with its candles, flowers, and fine china, was set for five?

He didn't have to wait long for an answer as Amoco rushed out of the back door and down the short flight of steps leading up to the house.

Amoco panted with the exertion of running. "Cooper, I am so glad I caught up with you."

"Hey, Amoco, what's up?"

"Has Mariela informed you of what Liam's bodyguards did to her chip?"

Cooper was always the last one to hear about anything. "No, what did they do to her chip?"

"They placed a substance on it that allows them to track her, monitor her chip activity, and terminate her life should they decide to do so."

Cooper's heart skipped a beat. "Is that like what…someone…tried to do to me?" He didn't want to say Viola's name out loud, lest it summon her.

"More concerning than that. Viola was using chip-jacking technology that allowed her to access information stored on a chip. The substance used on Mariela adds the ability to kill the person, so I would say it is a step worse."

That was an understatement. "Is there anything that can be done?"

"Any attempt to deactivate the kill switch will alert the people who installed it, and before it can be deactivated, they will certainly kill her. There is no safe way to deactivate it quickly enough. There may be another way," Amoco continued, "but the problem is, Liam has been found—"

"What?"

"—and he is surely going to replace me…" he paused like he was going to say one thing, but then changed his mind. "So I cannot expect to have the resources of Panacea Corp to work on it for much longer."

"Is there something I can do? Why did you come to me?"

"I need you to take Mariela to Area 52. I cannot suggest it to her, or at least not as a step towards deactivating the kill switch, because that may tip off the people who installed it. But if we can get her there, and inside the Faraday cage provided by the Area 52 umbrella, then I can probably deactivate it without putting her at risk."

"Probably?"

"There's always risk, especially with endeavors such as these with no precedents."

"Can't you try to deactivate in kill switch in your family crypt? Isn't it also a Faraday cage?"

"That is a reasonable solution, but as I am unsure how long it will take me to devise a solution, I believe Mariela will be more comfortable in Area 52 where she move about freely rather than cooped up in my family crypt."

"So what do you want me to do?"

"I have already put the process in motion by suggesting she go to Area 52 with her mother so June can inform the people they know there what happened to Grace. I also suggested she hold a gravesite memorial service for Grace. And they might want to consider doing something with that hunky sheriff's deputy you all abducted while you were there as well."

Hunky? Interesting choice of words, especially considering Dan was a murderer. "We can't take him back. Dan shot Grace."

"Understood. But there is not much point in keeping him here, is there? It's not like he is going to stand trial or go to jail."

"No." Fewer than ten people outside of Area 52 knew the true nature of the isolated area. Most thought it was a military installation or a secret government site, and had no clue it was where a bunch of people eighty years ago had gone to get away from technology. They lived in the past, staying away from any technology from after 2005. They also cut themselves off from the rest of the world.

June had asked for information on Area 52 not to be revealed, so Deputy Dan was never going to stand trial. Cooper could see Amoco's point that it at least should be discussed, although it seemed wrong to let Dan go. But really, what were their long-term plans for him? Were they going to hold him indefinitely? Who would keep an eye on him? It wasn't a responsibility Cooper wanted.

Through the windows of the dining room, Mariela, in a glowing digi-skin dress with no back, entered the dining room with her parents. The gauzy dress made her look almost ethereal, angelic even. He tried not to notice the flow of the dress around her legs, the fabric briefly clinging to them each time she moved.

"We had better get inside," Cooper said. "We don't want Mariela to see us talking and ask what we were talking about."

"Agreed. Before we adjourn, I have one more matter to discuss. We will need to schedule a time so I can show you how to inject the neutralizing fluid to deactivate the substance."

"What? I thought you were going to do that?"

"Me? I have no plans to go to Area 52. I dislike perspiring and I find physical exertion to be undesirable. I will prepare the substance, and you will inject it."

"I would rather not. June knows doctors in Area 52, I'm sure they can help. Or June could do it. She's good with stuff like that."

"I believe I am not overstepping when I say everyone thinks you are the best person to do it."

"Why would I want to go back there? Last time I was there someone ended up dead."

"Mariela needs you to do this."

"Hey, you guys." Mariela stuck her head out the door to the backyard just as the dusky rose color of her dress changed to a dusky violet. "Why don't you come inside? Dinner is starting soon."

Cooper gave Amoco a pointed look conveying that the conversation wasn't over and then headed on inside.

When they arrived in the dining room, Mariela had taken the seat at the far end of the table. June and Oscar had chosen to sit along the side facing the window. Amoco took the side seat facing in, leaving Cooper the end of the table across from Mariela.

The conversation during dinner was light, not really touching on any topic for too long. Or any of the topics that Cooper felt like actually needed to be discussed. They would be having dessert soon, and if Mariela didn't bring up the trip to Area 52, he would have to. It didn't seem fair he had to do this. He wanted some space from Mariela, from everyone, and so far he could barely get an hour to himself. Why was it so hard for people to leave him alone?

"Do you have any interesting stories from your trip?" Mariela said to Cooper.

He looked at June. *What was there to tell?*

A deep voice from behind Cooper said, "There was the time I arrested Hank and T-Rock for trespassing." Cooper looked over his shoulder. The 'hunky' Deputy Dan leaned against the doorway to the entry hall. *What had Amoco been talking about?* Dan wasn't all that good looking. Too tall. Looks that were too commonplace.

Cooper pushed back from the table, his chair scraping across the floor as he stood up. "Dan, you weren't invited here."

Mariela stood at the same time, her dress turning to a deep crimson. She kept her eyes fixed on the table and didn't look at Dan. Mariela, who kept every emotion stuffed deep inside her, appeared to be on the verge of tears. Her voice quivered when she spoke. "You need to leave!"

Cooper didn't like Dan any better than Mariela did, but after spending seventeen hours stuck in a small bus with him, he was a little more used to the guy's presence. "Come on, Dan, let's find someplace for you to hang out where you won't be bothering people." He took Dan's elbow and half led/half pushed him out of the room. "How about you spend the rest of the night in your room?"

Dan snatched his arm away. "You all will have to figure out what to do with me at some point."

Cooper again took ahold of Dan's arm and, using more pressure than before, turned him to the door. "I know, but not tonight."

Cooper led him to the guard's station in front of the house, where the guards agreed to confine Dan to his room for the night. Dan put up just enough resistance to make it clear he wasn't happy about it.

Mariela was slumped on a bench in the entry hall with her elbows on her knees and her head in her hands when Cooper got back to the main house.

"Where did everyone else go?" Cooper asked.

Mariela sat up. "My dad was tired so he went to rest and my mom went with him. Amoco decided to head out, but not before giving me a long speech that we need to figure out what to do with Dan. I told him if he was so worried about Dan, he could conduct medical experiments on him."

She wiped a tear from her eye and laughed. "He said okay. And then he left." She wiped another tear from her eye, doing it quickly, like she was hoping Cooper wouldn't notice that the tear had been there. "It's just, why does Dan have to stay here? Here, where the people who cared most about Grace have to see him every day."

"We could take him somewhere else, but your mom wanted to keep an eye on him."

"I just don't understand it."

"I don't either. I think your mom feels some responsibility for him because he's from Area 52, and she got attached to the people there."

Mariela's tears flowed faster. It was rare for Mariela to cry in front of him. Or anyone. Her tears did something funny to his heart. *Why did he let himself get involved in this stuff?* He put his arm around her; she leaned into him and buried her face in his chest. She smelled like vanilla.

She picked her head up from Cooper's chest, sniffed, and said with more composure, "I want you to take me to see where Grace died." She sat up straight, wiped her eyes, and stopped crying. "Amoco had this idea—he said we should have a memorial service to properly honor her."

Blast Amoco for putting him in this position. He didn't want to spend a long day traveling with Mariela to Area 52. He didn't want to be stuck in a claustrophobic hovbus for hours on end. He didn't want to remember what happened to Grace. He had so many reasons to not do it, but if it was the only chance they had to deactivate the kill switch, then he had to.

"Okay."

"Okay you'll take me?" Mariela wiped another tear from her eye.

"I'll take you."

"Thank you, thank you!" She smiled but her cheeks still glistened with tears. She unhygienically wiped the back of her hand across her nose. "I really have to stop crying."

"You know I won't judge you if you cry," Cooper said. He absent-mindedly stroked her hair until he realized he was doing it and made himself stop.

"I can't allow myself to be emotional." She wiped the tears off her cheeks. "Emotional women aren't respected. If we cry people think we're weak."

"Well, I already don't respect you, so no need to try to make a good impression on me." With his arm still around her, he shifted so he could look her in the eyes. She smiled at his teasing, her eyes puffy from crying.

"You look like a puffin," he said. "A very unrespectable puffin."

Mariela laughed out loud. She wiped her face with her hand again and sniffed.

"Do you think it will be safe for us to go to where Grace died?"

"I think so. There shouldn't be anyone there."

"I can't handle losing any more people."

"You won't." He hoped he wasn't making a promise he couldn't keep.

"Do you ever think of doing search and rescue again?"

Why was Mariela asking him about that now? "Not really. Do you think I should?"

"Absolutely not. People only seem to get lost when the weather's really bad, and it's too dangerous for you to be out in weather like that."

Cooper wasn't surprised that Mariela didn't want him to do it. She had been afraid of the weather, and of losing people close to her, ever since her biological parents had died in the Snow Storm of 2080.

"Well, no need to worry. I've aged out."

"What do you mean you've aged out?"

"The upper age limit is thirty-five. I turned thirty-six last year."

"Oh. I'm glad you've aged out. Because you would do it again if you could, wouldn't you?"

"Probably. At least I felt useful back then. But I'd rather be back teaching at the Academia Veritas."

There was a silence that lasted a couple seconds. It felt comfortable to be with Mariela, but he couldn't let down his guard and assume that he wouldn't get hurt by her. She sometimes let him get close, but she never let him stay close.

"Why didn't you tell me Grace was my child?" he asked.

"I couldn't. I don't know why. I think I was afraid you would be angry with me, and I couldn't deal with that."

"Of course I would have been angry with you. But you still should have told me."

"I know." She sniffed.

The gauzy fabric of her dress transformed to a cool and calm shade of light powder blue. Was it paranoid of him to think that she was overriding the pre-programmed color sequence to choose his favorite colors?

He pushed his thoughts about the dress aside. "You should have given me a say in whether she stayed here or went to Area 52 after her chip failed."

"I know."

"You lying about Grace—saying that she was dead—was probably the worst thing anyone has ever done to me. You stole fourteen, no— eighteen years we could have had together."

She looked at him but didn't speak. He could tell she regretted it, at least on some level. But it was always difficult to tell with Mariela whether she really understood, especially now she had her emotions under control again.

"I wish I had handled it differently," she said quietly.

He removed his arm from around her shoulders. "I don't want to take you to Area 52." Sometimes brutal honesty was the best policy. "I care about you but when I spend time around you, I just feel manipulated."

"I know."

Getting too close to Mariela, or even enjoying her company, was always risky. If he let himself feel something for her, she would push him away sooner or later. Usually, it was sooner rather than later. "I'll do it because of Grace, because I want to go back and honor her memory."

"Thank you, Cooper." She ran her hand through her hair. "I'm sorry. I'm kind of messed up when it comes to you. I can't truly love anyone else and yet I don't know how to be together with you."

"Lying to me about Grace was the death knell in any chance we ever had of being friends again."

"Cooper, I know I've pushed you away, but please don't be angry with me. I can't stand it."

Bile rose into his throat. Mariela had been his oldest childhood friend, but she had lied to him, kept secrets from him, and made decisions that affected him and people he cared about without giving them any say. How could she claim that she cared about him? *Is that what friends do?*

He stood up and backed away from her. "I have to get back to my workshop." He turned on his heels and fled.

Six Days Until the Umbrella Falls

Friday

For Mariela, it was just another day at the office—another day, another meeting with the boss who might accuse her of murder because his disloyal bodyguards had thrown him out of a helicopter that she also happened to be riding in. Even though the hit had been ordered by his digital avatar, there was a good chance she would get blamed for it.

It was Liam's first day back in the office and Mariela didn't want to talk to him but it would look worse if she didn't. The walk from her office to Liam's executive suite dragged. Her heavy feet barely lifted off the ground. When she raised her hand to knock on the open door it felt weighted with concrete anchors. How would she explain why she didn't go to the police? Honesty was out of the question—the last thing she wanted was for Liam to learn about the kill switch.

"Come in," Liam said after she knocked. The only signs that he had been thrown out of a helicopter were that he stayed seated and a cane leaned against his desk. "Have a seat. I'll only be a minute."

He may have had the power to make her anxious, but she didn't have to let him know that. Liam's perverse personality displayed power through showing that he could control other people's emotions, so she sat up straight in her chair, folded her hands in her lap, and sat perfectly still.

Liam's intimidation tactics included never using the conference table or the couch in his office; instead, he always sat behind his desk, raised his chair as high as it would go, and replaced the guest chairs with shorter straight-backed chairs. His guests, always half a head lower, were stuck fidgeting in the uncomfortable chairs. Today Liam added to the effect by having her wait as he finished up some other task.

"I'm glad you're safe," she said. It was a true statement on some level. "I was scared when your bodyguards threw you out of the helicopter." Also a true statement.

Liam pushed what he was working on to the side. He took out a stress ball with a happy face on it, leaned back in his over-stuffed leather chair, and threw the ball from hand to hand.

"Of course." He rolled his eyes. "You're obviously overjoyed to see me."

The stress ball went from right to left and back again.

"Listen," Mariela said. Maybe honesty was the best approach. "You and I don't get along. I'm not going to say I enjoy spending time around you or even like you. But that doesn't mean I wanted you dead, or enjoyed your apparent death in any way."

In one motion, Liam caught the stress ball, leaned forward, and rested his arms on the desk. "I heard you reversed my decision on Viola and Amoco, putting Amoco back in charge of research and telling Viola she wasn't employed with us."

"You never shared the change in personnel with me. I was implementing company policy as I was aware of it. Did you want me to start taking people's word for it that you were planning on hiring them?"

Liam leaned back in his chair. "Well, Viola's back in now and Amoco's out."

"You're firing him?"

The stress ball went back and forth, its happy face grinning at Mariela with evil deviousness.

"I don't trust him," Liam said. "He might as well be a lap dog for your family."

"Is that wise given that we are down an employee now that LP is gone?"

Liam grunted.

Mariela mentally kicked herself for bringing up LP—that was a can of worms she didn't want to deal with. She sat perfectly still, hoping that Liam would forget the mention of his now-missing avatar.

Liam stood up and leaned on his desk, his rigid arms holding him up. A slight wobble was the only sign he had been badly injured. "Mariela, if I ever find out you had something to do with me getting thrown out of that helicopter, or with LP disappearing, I will personally throw you out of a helicopter some place where they will never find you. Until then, you are suspended."

Mariela huffed. Just as well. She didn't want to be there anyway.

~~~~~
~~~~~

Mariela's favorite park bench wasn't helping her focus like it normally did. She did her best thinking here, but lately it seemed like no matter how much time she spent sitting on the cold plastic bench her mind was just as cluttered as ever. Maybe she should ask Amoco to join her next time. It would be nice to have some company considering that everyone else seemed to be mad at her.

Eight hours had passed since Liam had suspended her that morning, and she was still trying to wrap her head around it. Ever since entering the workforce, she had worked for Panacea Corp. Who was she if she didn't work for them? Eight hours of contemplation hadn't gotten her any closer to the answer.

She was doing what she usually did when something was bothering her—sitting at the park watching the leaves swirl around—until a leopard-print four-inch-high heel crushed the leaf closest to her. Mariela followed the leg from the offending shoe to the gorgeous redhead that was wearing it. Great. It was Viola. Dressed to the nines as usual. How did people keep finding Mariela at her special bench? She needed to find someplace new before any more enemies managed to catch up with her.

"Hello, Mariela." Viola sat down without waiting to be invited.

"Hello, Viola." Mariela sighed. As usual, Viola looked impeccable. The fabric of Viola's tailored dress didn't have the texture and sheen of digital skin. Sure, Mariela's digi-skin dress was great. It never got dirty and in seconds Mariela could change it into whatever she wanted. But there was something about real fabric…and the way it still looked soft even with the rough texture woven into it.

Something about Viola made Mariela feel small, and it wasn't just that in her impossibly high heels Viola was almost a foot taller than Mariela. No, it was like Mariela was in the presence of someone more strategic, and more ruthless, than Mariela was or ever could be—someone simultaneously both menacing and mesmerizing.

Viola cleared her throat. "I'm sure you've known me long enough to know that I do my research. It's important to me to know the people I am working with on all levels. So you can imagine my surprise when, as I was doing some, shall we call it 'experimental' research, I discovered your chip has been compromised."

Darn Viola and her advanced technology. She was going to get Mariela killed.

"I don't think we should be talking about this," Mariela said. "You could be putting both of us in danger." Of course Viola and her unique chip-jacking skills had to show up just at the same time that Mariela's life, in addition to her privacy, was threatened by the brutes' control over her chip.

She moved to stand up. Viola stopped her with a hand on her arm.

"I don't think you need to worry," Viola said. "Neither of us is in danger. This morning, after you met with him, Liam asked me to review the video capture from the helicopter. I saw a situation where Liam's interests and mine were closely aligned and I took advantage of it. I told Liam I had reviewed everything and you didn't have anything to do with his bodyguards throwing him out of the heli. So Liam took care of his bodyguards not long ago."

Mariela shivered. Was Viola saying what Mariela thought she was saying? She leaned back against the bench. It was a lot to process.

"I know you don't have a high opinion of me," Viola continued, "but I'm not a violent person and it doesn't suit my temperament to be involved in that kind of stuff. It was the least I could do, and I'm sure you would have done the same for me."

It was such a relief to not have to worry about one of the brutes having an itchy trigger finger and killing her. Viola had removed the concrete anchor weighing on Mariela.

Before Mariela could put her thoughts into words, Viola continued speaking. "I saw something else on the video I didn't tell Liam about, because my interests did not align with his in that area."

"Which was?"

"Your chip was compromised. Trust me, I will not share this with Liam." Viola toyed with a dainty chain around her wrist. "There's one more thing, Mariela."

"Yes?"

"First let me say that I really respect you as an equal, and I hate to do anything that might hurt one of my fellow sisters. Especially as women in positions of power, we are always fighting an uphill battle and we have to support each other."

"Yes, of course." Where was Viola going with this?

"There's something I would like in return for helping you. Something I need you to help me with."

"Okay, what is it?"

"It's Cooper. I've tried to deny my feelings for him, I've tried to tell myself I burned that bridge and that it was pretty clear he was also setting the bridge on fire from his end, but I just can't forget him."

"Well, that's ironic—the one man you really want to be with is one who doesn't have a chip so you can never know his secrets." Mariela was enjoying this. "Sounds like being all-knowing isn't everything it's cracked up to be."

"I'm sure, Mariela, you could analyze my feelings for Cooper to death, but I just think he is truly an outstanding person. I like him because he is special, not because he doesn't have a chip."

"Can I ask you something? About Cooper?"

"Sure."

"Why did you try to use the chip jacker on him? Didn't you worry he wouldn't trust you after you violated his privacy?"

Viola scoffed. "Listen, I'm not so naïve as to believe everything a partner says to me. I've been lied to before, on more than one occasion. He was being hesitant about continuing the relationship once I left to go back east. I sensed he was pulling away from me and I wanted to know why. And guess what—I was right. He did have a secret and he *was* lying to me. And to everyone else. And I found that out. If I had just trusted him and not checked for myself, he would have gone on lying to me."

"Okay, I get it. You had a good reason for treating him poorly." Mariela hoped her sarcasm wasn't lost on Viola. "So what do you want from me?"

"You know you can't commit to him, so please do me a favor and don't stand in the way of his happiness with someone else. I'm asking you to convince Cooper that there is no hope that he can ever be with you—"

"Done." It seemed pretty clear Cooper had given up on her, so that part of what Viola wanted was easy, though Mariela regretted admitting it as soon as she said it.

Viola shifted on the bench. "Okay, I was expecting more resistance there…but then there's the second part."

"Which is?"

"I truly regret what I did. I've come to realize that his deception—the way he acted like he had a chip when he didn't—it wasn't the sort of deception I had encountered in the past. It wasn't about me. It was something he got into and then didn't know how to get back out of. I understand him now."

"Okay. I'm still not sure what you want from me."

"I need you to convince Cooper to have a conversation with me. Just one. So he can see I've changed."

"I'm not going to try to convince him of anything. I don't even want to tell him you're here. Or working for Panacea Corp. He was just starting to do better and then Grace…someone close to him…died and now he's having a hard time of it. It won't help him to know you're here or to have conversations with you."

"I understand. All I'm asking is one small favor in return for helping you. I kept the information from Liam about the kill switch. I made sure Liam not only knew you weren't involved in tossing him from the helicopter, but I also told him you didn't have anything to do with the LP100 model ghosts being erased, which I think we both know was a *big* lie." Viola swept her bangs out of her scheming face. "If Liam finds out I lied, I'll lose my job. I would have protected you regardless, but I think this isn't a huge favor to ask in return."

Viola's guilt trip was successful. But if Mariela was going to help Viola, she would get something in return. "I have one request in return."

"What is it?"

"That you make sure Liam doesn't fire Amoco. You can put him to work on whatever, but it would kill him to not have his job."

"Alright. And if I do that, you'll help me?"

"I don't like it, but I'll tell Cooper you're around and would like to have one conversation with him. After that it's out of my hands."

"Wonderful!" Viola looked quite pleased as she clasped her hands in front of her chest. "Thank you! And Mariela, don't worry—I have the access codes to your kill switch, so I can deactivate it as soon as you help me out."

What?

Viola had the codes?

Mariela's body felt like it was sinking into a deep hole, one she would never get out of. The access codes to the kill switch hadn't died with the bodyguards—of course Viola had gotten ahold of them. For one short minute Mariela had felt free, but now she was owned again. And this person, this picture-perfect woman who was one of the top chip researchers in the world, was cunning enough that the two brutes would seem docile in comparison. Mariela shivered despite the warm weather. Viola would be difficult to outplay.

~~~~~

After a beautiful spring day, the night turned stormy. It was a short walk from her father's house to the cottage where Cooper lived, but the rain came down in sheets, lashing the trees until it finally drenched her.

Convincing Cooper to meet with her hadn't been easy. Even though he had agreed to take her to see where Grace had died, Cooper still wasn't talking to her outside of quick logistic questions for the trip such as setting the date or arranging supplies.

Mariela wasn't sure how he would react to finding out about Viola. It's not like Mariela was likely to have much influence over Cooper, yet Viola was unlikely to let it go until Mariela at least tried to convince him. As if Mariela could control what Cooper did.

Would Viola really deactivate the kill switch once Cooper met with her? Viola wouldn't want to give up that kind of power.

When she got to Cooper's porch, he had the door open. Through the screen door she saw him in the soft golden light of the living room, flipping through his laptop browser on the couch with both his dogs pressed up close against him. Lightning flashed and the wind picked up, chilling her. She set her dress to vibrate and it shook off most of the water and evaporated the rest. It warmed her slightly but didn't completely take away the chill from the wind. She took the open door as an invitation to go on inside, but knocked lightly on her way in to let Cooper know she was there.

"Cooper, how are you?" Cooper looked over his shoulder at her.

"You mean besides my daughter—that I didn't know I had—being dead?" He put down his screen. "I'm great. Just great."

"*Our* daughter." Correcting him would set him off, but she couldn't help herself. It was nice to finally have it out in the open, to finally talk about *their* daughter, even if it made Cooper angry with her. If only she had had the courage to do it while Grace was still alive.

The dogs, Spot and Lucy, jumped down from the couch and ran to greet her. Mariela crouched down and let them lick her face. After a few seconds of dog slobber, she headed over to the couch and sat by Cooper. Lucy immediately jumped up between them and put her head on Mariela's lap.

Almost as immediately, Cooper got up and moved away from her to sit in the armchair. Fine. If he didn't want to sit next to her that was understandable. Mariela scratched Lucy behind the ears. On the other
~~~~~

side, Spot curled up next to her, his soft fur warming her.

"Spot, Lucy, come here." Cooper patted his thigh as he called to the dogs. Without hesitation the mongrels abandoned Mariela and jumped onto Cooper's lap.

Mariela crossed her arms. "That was uncalled for." Cooper didn't have to be so petty. Surely the dogs could still enjoy her company even if Cooper didn't. And it's not like he looked comfortable with the two dogs crammed into the armchair with him.

Cooper scratched behind Spot's ears. "They're my dogs."

The message was clear. Cooper wasn't going to share with her. Large raindrops splattered against the window. Chilled again, she took advantage of her administrative access to light a fire in the fireplace.

"Come on, pups," Cooper said to the dogs as he stood up and deliberately moved between Mariela and the fire. The chill in the air came back. The dogs settled around his feet. "I don't want you to get too comfortable. You're welcome here for only as long as it takes you to tell me whatever it is that you need to tell me."

"Then let's get to it," she said.

"Let's."

Was he really going to leave her on the verge of shivering just because he was mad at her? That was a stupid question. She already knew the answer. But she wasn't going to give in without a fight. She used her chip to turn on the heater. Hopefully by the time Cooper noticed the heater was running more than normal the place would be warmer and they'd be done.

"Fine." Mariela stood up.

"Fine." Cooper crossed his arms.

She wasn't even sure what they were talking about anymore. "I'll get on with it."

"I suggest you do that."

"Viola is back."

If Cooper was surprised by the news, he didn't show it.

"So the manipulative bitch is back," he said. "How does that concern me?"

"She wants to talk with you."

"I don't care what she wants."

"She has control of my kill switch."

For the first time, Mariela thought she saw some sort of reaction from

Cooper. It was just a brief flinch and then he quickly returned to a neutral expression.

"She won't use it," he said.

"What?"

"She won't use the kill switch."

"Do you really want to take a chance on that?" It sounded like he was saying he wouldn't talk to Viola.

"It doesn't really concern me either way," Cooper said.

"Wait—are you saying you don't care if she kills me?"

"Listen, she's unethical, prying, scheming, and lots of other negative things, but she's not a killer. And you're her mentor. She wants what you have. She wants to be you. Sometimes I think it was the only reason she dated me. She would never kill you. You're a Picasso to her."

"She thinks I have a nose on the side of my face?"

"And asymmetric eyes." Cooper smiled. "But however bizarre looking you may be, Viola looks up to you."

Mariela laughed. For a moment she saw the old Cooper. The Cooper that liked to joke around with her and say stupid things. A ping on her chip caught her attention. It was a message from Viola. She used her chip to view the message. It said, "Cooper's right that I admire you, but he's wrong that I won't kill you. I have a vision of where I want to be, and I can get there more easily if you're out of the way. So stop flirting."

No surprise—Viola *had* been spying on Mariela through her chip, but it was still jarring to know. She wasn't just reviewing what Mariela had said after the fact—she was watching at that very moment.

"Mariela, are you okay?" Cooper asked.

She must have checked out while she was reading Viola's message. "Yeah, I'm fine. Except Viola sent me a message that she would kill me."

"She won't. It's a bluff." Cooper softened his voice. "But if it makes you feel better, I'll go talk to her."

"It would make me feel better. Thank you. I know this isn't easy on you."

"It's not." Cooper moved back to the armchair, letting the warmth of the fire reach her. He leaned back in the chair, draped his arms over the sides, and closed his eyes. "It's hot."

Oops. She quickly used her chip to turn the heater back to its original setting.

Cooper sat up. "Did you turn the heat up?"

She opened her eyes wide and adopted her most innocent expression. "I don't know what you're talking about. The heat is exactly where it was when I got here."

"Mariela, you need to leave. I'll talk to Viola tomorrow."

She wanted to stay talking with him, to learn about what Grace was like as an eighteen-year-old, but she understood if Cooper wasn't willing to talk to her about Grace. She had gotten what she came here for, and it was the best she could hope for. She said goodbye and headed back out into the rain.

CHAPTER 7

Five Days Until the Umbrella Falls

Saturday, mid-day

Amaya rested her arms on the red metal table tucked under a cheery yellow awning in the plaza. The scents from multiple food vendors combined into an enticing mix. The towering, weatherproof buildings surrounded the cobblestone square on all four sides, with the Panacea Corp headquarters building across the square spanning the length of the entire block.

Nyala had come up with the random idea that it would be fun to plan activities for the afternoon but make them a surprise for Amaya. *We need to have some fun after everything that's happened*, Nyala had said. And so far, it had been fun. They had spent the last hour sitting in Panacea Plaza, eating lunch and talking about all the things that needed to be said between them.

It was a pleasant spring day, perfect for hanging out with her sister. The air was warm, and a cool breeze kept it from being hot. The brick plaza was perfect for people-watching. A father hurried by, pulling his two small kids after him. At a table nearby, a young couple was feeding each other grapes.

"So, Nyala, what do you have planned for us next?"

Nyala looked at the time on her Everything, "we had better get going. It should be starting soon."

"What should be starting soon?"

"The Panacea Corp press conference. We need to stake out our spots for the protest."

"The protest?" Less than a week ago, Amaya had committed to being more supportive of Nyala's protests, but now that Nyala was asking her to participate, her motivation slipped away. More accurately, it ran away. "That's your idea of a fun afternoon?"

A drone buzzed up to their table at top speed, hovered at eye level, and apparently decided nothing interesting was going on. It went on its way as quickly as it had arrived.

"Don't worry," Nyala said. "I know protests aren't your thing. That's why you're going to be doing an interview with a reporter who wants more information about why we are protesting."

"Why *are* we protesting?"

"We're protesting Panacea Corp's research on chip implantation in adults. It's highly dangerous and unethical, and takes advantage of vulnerable people. Their new neuroscientist, that Viola woman that Cooper used to date, will be talking about it today. It's too bad Liam showed back up because Mariela never would have allowed Viola to do this kind of research."

It wasn't her idea of a fun afternoon, but Amaya resigned herself to speaking with the reporter. "I guess I can talk about why it's so dangerous. Still not my idea of fun. Is the reporter friendly to the cause?"

"I'm not sure yet. You'll have to tell me."

Oh well, it would be better to have her words misconstrued than to have to hold a sign and shout along with the other protestors, "Be a hero, stay net-zero!" over and over again. What did that mean anyway? As a rallying cry, it sounded good, but it didn't really make any sense.

"Since we don't know if the reporter is on our side or not, I'll ask for the right of review before anything I say is published just in case. Anything else on the agenda?"

"Why yes, there is. After we are done here, I was thinking you could use a martial arts lesson."

"Wait a second—is the reporter who's interviewing me Elliat and the person who is going to teach me martial arts Hank?"

Nyala shrugged. "Maybe. Do you care?"

"You realize that both of them have been repeatedly rude to people you care about?"

"It's just that I feel sorry for them. Plus, you are going to use the interview with Elliat to learn what he has figured out so far. It'll be like a reverse interview. Or an undercover interview, where you're spying for us. And I would feel *so* much better if you learned martial arts. It seems like things are getting less safe—with what happened to me on the train, and Mariela having the kill switch forced on her, and Grace getting shot. Hopefully you'll never need it, but it would make me feel better if you knew how to defend yourself."

"I can't believe you planned what was supposed to be a fun day for us with two people I dislike."

"Oh, come on, you know it's going to be fun."

It probably would be. Nyala had a knack for making things interesting, to say the least.

"So where's Elliat?" Amaya scanned the plaza for him. "I might as well get started having 'fun.'" There were lots of drones flying around, and some protestors were starting to gather near the broad steps up to the main Panacea Corp headquarters building, but no Elliat. Among the protesters were some people she knew already and a throng of new people, all holding signs supporting a variety of causes.

The size of the gathered group impressed her. "Looks like your protests are drawing in bigger crowds," she said.

"Ever since Panacea went down people have been really riled up. A lot of them are protesting the Black Screen outage and the loss of their LP100 model digital ghosts rather than the chip research, but if it helps get attention for the cause, then I'm all for it." Nyala scanned the area. "Let's see if we can find Elliat. I don't want you to be late for your interview."

Steps stretched the entire length along the plaza side of the Panacea building, which itself took up an entire city block. Protestors had completely overrun the steps and gathered around the entrance in such numbers that it would be difficult to get in or out of the building. To the side of the entrance, a group of guards formed a circle around a podium, creating a small oasis around it.

Amaya followed Nyala as she headed toward the growing group of protestors at the end of the steps near the Levanto cart downramp. In the corner of the plaza a steady stream of carts pulled up to the downramp and opened to reveal groups of people arriving. People flowed from the carts, some joining the group at the bottom of the downramp, while others joined the group gathered near the podium.

A cheerful and oversolicitous woman approached them with signs and stuck buttons to their chests. "Here you go! Don't forget to chant!"

Amaya wanted to kill her.

A group of drones, some surveillance, some media, hovered over the protesters.

"Oh," Nyala pointed across the plaza, "look who showed up for the protest!" In the direction she pointed, Hank was strolling towards them. "I didn't know if he would make it."

"Yay, he made it." *Why* did Nyala insist on being friends with Hank?

"I know he can be a jerk but that's how he survived growing up in the res-home. He's been helping out with the warehouses that had the malfunctions. Plus, I think it's nice he wants to join the protest," Nyala tried to reason.

"It's probably because he doesn't think the unchipped are worthy of getting chips."

"At least try to keep an open mind about him."

"Okay, okay. I do feel *a little* sorry for him because Georgia is so mad she's not talking to him," Amaya admitted.

"See, now was that so hard?"

Nyala could be so annoying sometimes.

Elliat, wearing a Hawaiian shirt and sandals, took a seat at a table not far away and waved Amaya over to join him.

"Hey, I see Elliat over there," she said to Nyala. "I'm going for my interview." With feet that dragged, she headed to the table where Elliat sat.

Amaya gave Elliat all the talking points. About how chip implantation had only been shown to be safe in kids younger than six months old and there hadn't been any research done to make sure the people getting the experimental chips wouldn't suffer brain damage; about how the research subjects were required to waive their right to sue the company; about how there was no guarantee an adult brain would even understand how to interact with a chip; and about how the research was targeted at vulnerable people and how it was better to give people without chips more options for employment rather than do high-risk research on them. Talking with Elliat made her nervous, but she did a good job of presenting the information.

She almost forgot to tell him that she wanted the right of review before he published anything. "Elliat—"

Angry words erupted behind her.

"You!"

Amaya whirled around. Liam Price was staring at Nyala with surprised, intensely angry eyes. He was pointing at her, his arm looking like it might jump off of his tense body. "*You* were on the train! With Mariela."

He appeared to have just exited the Panacea Corp building side exit with Viola. With the help of his guards, he was making his way through the still gathering protestors to the podium when he had noticed Nyala. Viola had a blank, confused look on her face.

Nyala stepped toward Liam with her head held high. "You drugged me and left me unconscious on a train in Bolivia." Nyala's face was redder than Amaya had ever seen it.

Hank also stepped forward. Was he trying to protect Nyala from Liam or Liam from Nyala? Liam closed the distance between him and Nyala. Amaya saw his cane for the first time. It wouldn't look good for Nyala if the confrontation became physical.

Nyala stepped around Hank. "You kidnapped Mariela!" The crowd gasped.

Liam held his ground. "She threw me out of a helicopter in the middle the Gulf of Mexico."

The crowd had gone completely silent and still, as if worried Liam would notice them and stop talking.

Liam stood tall. "I think she paid me back fully and then some."

Nyala lunged and grabbed his shirt, sending him staggering. His cane slipped out of his hand and the off-balance Liam wobbled as he tried to right himself.

Amaya's chair clattered to the ground and her feet hit the paving bricks and she sprang into a sprint towards Nyala.

Nyala was either going to hurt Liam or get hurt. A pack of bodyguards swarmed around them. One held onto Hank, another steadied Liam, and two more grabbed a struggling Nyala by both arms and pulled her away.

"Wait!" Liam's thundering voice stopped all motion. Amaya froze. Liam waved away the cane that his bodyguard held out for him and limped over to where the two bodyguards held Nyala. "I know you're involved somehow; I know you share some of the blame for LP and the other ghosts being deleted, and when I figure out how to prove it, you will spend the rest of your insignificant life in a squalid jail. And while I could charge you with assaulting me, I'm going to let you go, because I want you to run off and remind your friend Mariela that I'm on to her." He sneered. "She should count her days as a free woman, because they are almost up."

Liam turned back to the enthralled crowd and raised his voice. "Listen up—you see how I am today? How I have lost the strength I used to have, and my leg is injured?" He raised a hand and pointed at Nyala. "It is *this* woman's fault!" The crowd murmured. "Do you want to know who caused the outage?" He pointed at Nyala again. "It was *this* woman!" The crowd roared. "Do you want to know who deleted your ghosts? Deleted your personal property so thoroughly it could never be recovered, and left you without the companionship of your ghosts, or their income?" He stabbed his finger in Nyala's direction. "It was *this* woman!!"

His voice rang in Amaya's ears.

He looked at Nyala and growled, "Go tell Mariela that I'm coming for her." Liam held out a hand to the guard holding his cane. Cane in hand, he spoke to his guards: "Let her go." The guards let Nyala go so abruptly that she landed hard on the ground.

Hank shook off the guard holding him and grabbed Nyala's elbow to help her up. "We need to get out of here." Hank looked over his shoulder at the crowd that was just starting to process what Liam had said. "Come on!" He glanced back at Amaya. "Run!"

Hank bolted toward the Levanto ramp. Amaya sprinted at top speed after him, with Nyala right behind her. Amaya glanced back. Groups of people from the crowd were chasing after them. The enthusiastic woman who had given them the signs put her shoulder down and ran full speed into one of the chasers.

They were on the edge of the crowd, but what would happen once they got out of the plaza? Would they be trapped in the narrow streets?

"There's a cart arriving!" Hank angled toward the cart upramp. The cart door opened and a family got out. Hank flew around the startled family with Nyala and Amaya not far behind. Seconds after, he slammed the door shut just as a group of angry people hit the side of the cart.

Using the voice activation feature was impossible with all the noise outside. Amaya jabbed the control panel. She needed to enter a destination somewhere, anywhere but here. How was she supposed to focus with all the pounding on the side of the cart? After a couple attempts, she entered her apartment complex and the cart started moving.

"The weather for the next fifteen minutes is seventy-five degrees Fahrenheit. Expect clear skies," the auto-weather on the cart said.

"Off," Amaya snapped. Her breath came in ragged gasps and her chest pounded from the run and anxiety. She clutched her chest. Maybe if she held on tight it wouldn't explode.

"What happened to Elliat?" Nyala asked. "Did you finish your interview with him?"

Amaya took a couple deep breaths before responding. "We were almost done with our interview when I heard the confrontation. I ran over and I didn't see him after that."

"Did you get any useful information from him?"

"No, we got interrupted before I had a chance to ask any questions."

"Speaking of Elliat," Hank said, "he just posted something you are going to want to see." Hank pulled up a video on the cart's monitor. "It's the entire confrontation between Nyala and Liam."

At the beginning, Elliat's exo-cam was focused on Amaya. After Liam called out, the camera angle widened to include Liam and Nyala. The recording showed almost everything just as Amaya remembered it— her chair falling over, Liam's accusations, the mad dash for the Levanto cart. Almost everything, but… "Parts of it are missing," she said. "He cut out the parts where you said Liam drugged you and kidnapped Mariela."

"I'm sure somebody else will upload the whole thing."

"Yeah, but Elliat has millions of followers. Maybe billions. Lots of people are going to watch his video."

"You would not believe this news alert that Elliat just posted," Hank said. "Here let me put it on the screen."

In breaking news, Liam Price accused known dissident Nyala Gidada of causing last week's outage of Panacea and deleting the advanced LP100 model ghosts. Nyala's sister, Abrihet Amaya Gidada, another known dissident, agreed to be interviewed by me today about their uprising. She said they intend to do whatever it takes, including civil disobedience like today, in order to stop Panacea Corp from providing the unchipped access through embedded chips to the Panacea metaverse.

This is a surprising position for Gidada to take, as giving the unchipped access to chips would go a long way toward addressing inequality between the chipped and the unchipped.

"I thought you were going to ask him for right of review?" Nyala seemed a little pissed.

"I was…but I got distracted when Liam yelled at you. I never asked him."

"The rest of the post gets weird." Hank used the back of his fingers to scroll some more of the text onto the screen.

Liam's golden hair shown in the sun as he asserted his deft leadership skills and put the unruly protester in her place. Despite being senselessly assaulted by her, he magnanimously agreed not to press charges. He also urged the crowd to be calm, and to allow the justice system to do its work rather than to engage in vigilante retribution.

"I am so going to kill him." Nyala waved the text off of the screen.

"Nyala, this isn't a huge surprise. It's exactly the sort of thing Elliat has always written."

"I thought we had an understanding." Nyala's Everything lit up with a contact request. "Well wouldn't you know—look who had the balls to contact me." She held up her arm for them to see Elliat's picture blinking on her Everything. "I'll let it message."

"Why don't you answer it? See what he has to say for himself?" What could Elliat have to say to her sister after what he had written?

"Okay. If you want." Nyala shrugged her shoulders as she hit the button on the Everything that let the others hear. "Elliat," she said, "what's a traitorous weasel like you doing contacting a nice girl like me?"

"Nyala, I'm sorry, but I had your best interests in mind!"

"You did?" Nyala raised an eyebrow.

"Yes, I saw an opportunity and I took it. First, I had to publish something because my boss knew I was there so he knew I would have video."

"Did your boss know that Liam's golden hair was shining in the sun?"

"I wrote that for a reason—so that Liam would trust me. I'm sure you know the best way to get dirt on someone is to let them think you can be trusted."

"It's also a good way to get your friends beaten up." Nyala's voice was more plaintive than normal. "Elliat, you could have said something to calm down all the people who now think I'm responsible for deleting their ghost companion, family member, employee, or whatever. Not to mention they think I'm responsible for the outage where people died!"

"Well, yes, that is unfortunate. But you know how people don't remember stuff. Within a week it'll be totally forgotten."

"In a week I'll be dead."

"I'll fix this Nyala. Trust me, I will. I'll write about an even bigger scandal. I just need to figure out what."

"Elliat, you can't fix this."

"But—"

"You can consider our collaboration ended." Nyala swiped the call off with a dismissive wave of her hand.

Amaya absent-mindedly looked at the buildings as the cart passed them. It felt like something significant had changed in her life. Liam, with the one extremely public and inaccurate accusation of her sister, had changed everything for all of them. They were going to be targets of abuse and harassment, and no public place would be safe for them.

Not even her apartment would be safe. By now any number of people could have accessed her address and might be waiting for her. She changed the cart's destination to the Levanto downramp at the edge of town. The only place they would be safe right now was the Stafford estate. She ordered a car to meet them at the downramp and then went back to looking at the buildings passing by the windows in a blur.

"I'm going with you tomorrow," Nyala said.

"Where?" Amaya asked.

"When you go to Area 52 to pay your respects to Grace. I loved her too, I want to see this place, and I think it would be best if I got out of town for a bit."

~~~~~

Cooper set his ironwork on the worktable in the gazebo and stepped back to get a better look at it. It was a complicated piece with overlapping tendrils that had no pattern. He wanted to get it just right—if he did it right, the viewer should look for patterns in the piece but even after staring at it for hours, not find any. It represented the chaos of the world and his feelings about the meeting with Viola.

Sure, Viola had control of Mariela's kill switch, but like Cooper had told Mariela, Viola wouldn't use it. He considered skipping the meeting, but as much as he thought Viola was bluffing, it wouldn't do to not go and then later find out he was wrong.

After a brief meeting that Amoco had requested, he would drag himself out to meet with the traitorous queen of vermin. On the other hand, maybe Amoco would say he had found a method to disable the kill switch, and Cooper wouldn't have to meet with her. Why did Viola want to meet with him anyway?

He sat down at the worktable and inspected the artwork. "You're going to be beautiful," he said to the piece.
~~~~~

"I hope I am not interrupting."

Cooper startled. Amoco was right beside him, having hovered up silently in his mobile chair.

"Amoco! When you're in your chair you need to cough or something so I know you're here. I thought my artwork had started talking to me."

"My apologies." Amoco reached out to run his hand along the piece. "Your hobby is quite impressive. I was not aware you had such talent, such mastery over the metal. I see how you bend it to your will and in doing so create masterpieces that are haunting yet equally fascinating."

Haunting. That was probably the best word anyone had ever used to describe his artwork. Maybe Amoco would buy one. Cooper could use the money. It wasn't like he had any other source of income right now. Oscar, thank the Oragle, let him live in the cottage and eat in the main house for free because Cooper's iron artwork didn't bring in much money. Especially as Cooper didn't like to let the pieces go. It felt like sending a child off to live with a family of unknown character. In an ideal world where he didn't need money, he would never sell any of them.

Amoco leaned in closer. "What are you working on? The intricacy and detail are stunning."

"It's a piece I was thinking of giving to Oscar, but then I realized it's a stupid idea. But I still want to finish it. I hate leaving a piece unfinished." It had been a misguided idea from the start. Mixed in with the tendrils representing chaos, the twisted metal represented the danger Oscar was in when he had the chip burn, and the reddish hue of the metal evoked the blood that had been spilled. The overall effect was striking—haunting, as Amoco had said—but it wasn't exactly what most people liked to hang on their living room walls. He pushed it away and turned to Amoco. "So have you made any progress figuring out how to deactivate the kill switch on Mariela's chip?"

"I have made some progress, but am limited by my inability to test the solution. If it does work as planned, an additional complication is that it may also disable her chip."

"It's a chance she'll have to take. I don't think Viola would ever hurt her, but Mariela can't live with that uncertainty. Plus, what if someone gets control of the kill switch from Viola?"

"I am sure Mariela would agree with you without reservation. I agree as well, it is a chance we must take. Have you set a date for the trip?"

"Mariela has said she wants to go as soon as possible. So as soon as the treatment is ready, we can be ready to go."

"I am in the process of fine-tuning it. It may be as much as a week still. It would be expedited if I could convince Viola to let me biopsy the kill switch site."

"I'll let you talk to Viola about that."

"Of course. I also intend to create a diagnostic tool you can use to verify the kill switch is deactivated. Mariela should not exit Area 52 unless you have confirmed the kill switch is inactive. The Faraday cage surrounding Area 52 will protect her while she is there by blocking any signals from outside the umbrella, but she will be exposed once she leaves."

"We'll make sure it has been deactivated before she leaves. I'm going to need some support, so I'm going to ask some of the people who went to Area 52 before to go along with me. People who would be interested in attending the memorial service as well."

"Who did you have in mind?"

"T-Rock, if he's feeling sufficiently recovered from the rattlesnake bite. Amaya. Georgia if she's willing to wait to go back into her pod."

"And Hank?"

"I think not."

Hank was the last person Cooper wanted to spend time with. Other than Dan, that is.

"June should go with you. She is your connection to the community there. They will trust her if Mariela ends up needing to stay there."

"True."

"And Dan? He should be returned to his home."

Was Amoco really suggesting they take Dan back to Area 52 after everything they did to get him here? "Dan is staying here."

"You can't keep him here forever," Amoco argued.

"It was what the team decided. And we can't really take him back now."

"You can take him back as you will already be there. If Area 52 wants to keep their citizens in the dark about the rest of the world, it will be up to the Elder to convince him not to talk about what he saw. I suggest the team revisit the decision now that you have had some time to think about it."

"I'll mention it to the team to see what they think. For all we know, Dan might not want to go home. How will he explain having disappeared for a couple weeks?" Cooper asked.

"The National Enquirer was made for situations such as these. He can review a couple back issues to come up with whatever outlandish story he fancies."

"I'll see what the team has to say about it. What time is it?" The interrogation with Viola was at three.

"It is half past two. It quite baffles me how you survive. You could at least get an Everything like the other unchipped."

"I survive by not having appointments or any sort of commitments." Having no schedule made his life much easier even if it did make him feel unneeded. "Amoco, it's been good to see you, but I'd better be off to meet the woman who betrayed me."

"Mariela?"

"No." How could Amoco not know he meant the *other* woman who betrayed him? "Viola."

"Viola, of course! I apologize for my denseness. You have so many women who have betrayed you, it is cumbersome to keep track of."

"Right." He didn't need Amoco reminding him of his unfortunate relationships with women.

Amoco touched the small piece of metal in the center of the artwork. "Is that Oscar's chip, may I ask?"

"Correct."

"Are you intending to give it Oscar?"

"I was going to, but giving him something with the chip in it that almost killed him is kind of morbid. Plus, I'm fond of it, and I think someone else may find it grotesque."

"Indeed. If you are open to considering a change of course—would you be willing to present it to Viola instead?"

"Why?"

"People think that when a chip goes through chip burn it does not function anymore. But usually there is some function left. If you can get Viola to keep this in her house or office, she does not even have to hang it up, but if it is there, I can use it to listen in on her conversations. Even if she places it in the back of a closet, we may not hear much but it will be more information than we have now about what she is up to."

Making the decision to spy on Viola was easy. Making the decision to give her his artwork was much more difficult.

He held the intricate piece in front of him. "Don't worry, you'll be okay," he said. "She'll treat you well. She only treats humans like crap." He turned to Amoco. "I'll do it."

CHAPTER 8

Five Days Until the Umbrella Falls

Saturday, afternoon

"Come in, Cooper." Viola rose from the oversized desk in her lavishly appointed office and headed over to greet him. Her furniture had clean, flowing lines but the walls appeared to be gilded and the curtains were made of thick golden brocade. Viola ran a hand over her already smooth hair—the only hairs allowed to deviate from her prim ponytail were two perfectly coiled tendrils on either side of her face.

It was the first time he had seen Viola since…since she had ruined his life. Three years and he was still bitter about it. And now, when he had started to see some hope in the future again, she showed up.

"It's so good to see you." She leaned in to kiss his cheek. It was difficult not to turn away, but antagonizing her might make things worse for Mariela. He was going to be polite, but there were limits to what he could handle.

He shoved the ironwork piece at her. "This is for you." His voice sounded flat and awkward, but he didn't care. Viola took hold of the artwork but Cooper didn't let it go. *You'll be okay,* he said internally to the artwork. *She won't appreciate you, but don't worry, I'll get you back some day.*

Viola tilted her head and looked up at him with oversized eyes. "You brought me a gift?" Her voice sounded a little rough. Was she actually choked up about this? "Thank you, Cooper!"

"Here." With one last sigh of regret, he handed it over to her. Viola held it up at arm's length to look at it. He tensed. Oscar's chip was well hidden—he had covered up the chip with some additional ironwork, but if she looked closely, it was possible she might spot it.

"Thanks." It didn't sound convincing when she said it. Like she was happy to get a gift but unsure what she thought of it. "I'll find someplace good for it." She set the artwork down on her conference table. With only six chairs, it wasn't as large as Mariela's had been, but it was big enough to give her authority. She motioned for Cooper to sit across from her.

"Please, have a seat."

He ignored her and wandered over to look out the wall of windows. "What do you want, Viola? I'm not going to pretend I want to be here." He rubbed the fabric of the thick curtains between his fingers. Definitely not digi-skin. He let the curtain go and turned to look at the room. "I'm only here because Mariela thinks you might kill her."

"That's silly. You and I both know I won't kill her. You were right when you said that I was bluffing. I'm not a killer and I'm offended Mariela even thinks there's a possibility I could be. But you and I are both predictable, and I knew you would do anything to protect Mariela. Even if it seemed unnecessary, you wouldn't take a chance that she could get hurt."

Except for one wall, the walls didn't look like they were digi-skin either. He walked to the table, running his fingers along the wall. If he had any doubt that the rough texture wasn't digi-skin, Viola's grimace confirmed it. Whatever the wallpaper was made of, it wouldn't clean itself like digi-skin.

"Okay, so you figured me out. Why am I here?"

"Because you can't say no to Mariela?"

Cooper rolled his eyes. "I mean, why did you want to speak with me?" He took a seat at the table.

"I owe you an apology. I never meant for what happened to happen. I just…I know I seem confident, but…I have a hard time trusting in relationships. I've been burned before. So I thought I had to know if you were being truthful with me or not."

"So you thought the best way to find out if you could trust me was to violate my trust by trying to chip-jack me?"

"I'm sorry, Cooper. I really am. When I told the Academia that you didn't have a chip, I didn't know it would result in you getting fired."

It was a bitter memory. Despite all the good will he had built up with the Academia over the years, despite having the most highly attended classes and being the most frequently requested speaker, the higher-ups at Academia Veritas hadn't waited ten minutes to fire him after Viola told them he didn't have a chip. Not because he deceived people about having a chip, but because he let them assume he was a credentialed academic and they finally figured out he wasn't. But they had hired him without asking about his credentials, so was that really his fault?

"Why did you feel the need to tell them anything?" he asked her.

"Considering you had just tried to chip-jack me, it's not like you could pretend to have the moral high ground."

"I was mad that you hadn't been honest with me about not having a chip. I thought we were close, and then I find out there is this really big deal you've been keeping from me and I realized I had been deluding myself thinking that we were close."

"So you punished me."

"I didn't think of it like that—not at first. But over time… You're not the only one who suffered—I've been through a difficult time these last couple years as well. I know it was self-inflicted—I'm not saying it wasn't my fault, but I lost the best relationship I've ever had. I had to come to terms with my own stupidity."

"Took you a long time to realize that."

Viola had the audacity to tell him about how she had suffered? To make matters worse, she put her hands on top of his.

"I truly regret what I did to you. I was angry and didn't fully think through the consequences for you at the time. I want to make that up to you. I owe you; I just need the chance to show you that how I acted isn't how I really am."

Maybe he could use her guilt to his advantage. "I'll make you a deal—I'll get back together with you if you disable the kill switch. But only after it's disabled completely and irrevocably." Viola would probably see through his bluff, but offering to get back together with Viola seemed easier than taking Mariela on a trip to Area 52.

"Ha, no, I can't do that. I'm not feeding your savior complex. But I won't stop trying to win you back legitimately."

"You're going to be waiting a long time."

"You know Cooper, I'm surprised by how little you show up in the feed from Mariela's chip. It seems like you two don't talk to each other much anymore."

He moved his hands from under hers. "I'm not sorry you didn't take me up on my offer. I don't even know why I said it considering I don't think you would kill Mariela anyway."

"I wouldn't. But I would consider making life difficult for her. I'm sure I could pull that off with the power I have over her chip."

"I thought you had agreed to deactivate the kill switch once I met with you."

"You know that's not going to happen. Relinquishing that sort of power requires getting something in return."

His teeth grinded together. It was just like when they were together—Viola always put her needs above everyone else's. "I'm not sure I expected any different from you."

Only one option was left—whatever Amoco was planning to do to deactivate the kill switch.

"Cooper, there's one more thing I find interesting. Elliat Exis posted some information saying June Stafford had returned. It said she was traveling in a hovbus with a group of other people, including a man who claimed to know nothing about pod warehouses. Would you know anything about that? It seems curious that she could have just disappeared for sixteen years and then suddenly reappears."

"Sorry, can't help you." It was time for him to hit the road before Viola asked any more questions that he didn't want to answer. He stood up.

"Cooper, sorry, there's one more thing."

Cooper rubbed his forehead. He couldn't wait to get out of there, but the smallness in Viola's voice stopped him. She sounded worried.

"What?"

"Who came up with the kill switch? I mean, I didn't do it. Amoco's the only other neuroscientist who is capable of developing this kind of technology, and he says he didn't do it. I believe him, and even if I didn't, I don't think he could come up with something *this* good. He's a bit of a hack, if you ask me. I know you probably just think I'm saying that out of professional jealousy, but he's been working on chip implantation in adults for decades and hasn't made any progress, so there's no reason to think he would have any luck with using a chip as a weapon. Because that's what this is. A weapon."

"It's not a very efficient one."

"No, it's a highly targeted one. It's more about having control over someone rather than killing them. The threat of killing them is just a way to gain control—you see how effective that was with you?"

He nodded. "Right, I didn't even believe you would use it and it still worked."

"If deployed in just the right way, the kill switch could be a very effective weapon. You were in the military—how would you use it?"

"Let me think about that."

"You're not going to tell me anything, are you?"

"Absolutely not." He wasn't going to share his ideas with Viola under any circumstance. She had a number of contracts with military organizations—her chip-jacking tech had been created for the military to scan data on people's chips—and he didn't trust her. No, he would think about how it could be used, but he wouldn't share it with Viola.

~~~~~

According to June's sources, Elliat Exis had been showing up at all of her old haunts. Apparently reappearing after disappearing sixteen years ago was newsworthy. If they didn't hurry, he would probably pop out of the shrubbery and accost her with questions. She looked back at the wide-eyed man in his late twenties who was lagging behind her. "Hurry up, Dan." She brought Deputy Dan to get him out of the house. Plus, it would do him good to get some answers as well.

If he didn't hurry up though, she might regret bringing him. Four days ago, when they had given Elliat a ride in the hovbus, he had asked her questions non-stop. Even though she said 'no comment' to even the most innocent questions, it got tiring after a while. She didn't want to go through that again today.

"What is this place?" Dan stared, his mouth open, at the large building at the top of the steps. He would never have seen anything quite so imposing while growing up in Area 52. The large building loomed tall in front of them, its steepled roof embellished with a stained-glass rose window. At the apex a marble statue of a woman with wings and a flowing dress leaned out from the roof as though she might take flight. In the square behind them, thousands of truth-seekers milled around.

"It's the Oragle." June started up the broad marble steps to the arched entrance door. "People come here when they are seeking answers."

"Are you seeking answers?" Dan eyes remained fixed on the building while they walked up the long flight of stairs to the entry.

June waited for him on the landing. "I have questions about many things. Like whether to return to Area 52. I loved the way of life and I have many people I care about there, but my family's here."

Dan nodded. "I want to go back. Miss my family. And my home." Dan avoided making eye contact. "Will I ever be able to go back?"

June paused with her hand on the large metal ring that served as a door handle. "I don't know. It's not just up to me. If you do go back, there are other people who would have to agree to it as well."
~~~~~

"Why don't you take me back? I'm not afraid of my fate. The Elder can hold a hearing and if she decides it was an unjustified or negligent shooting, I'll face the consequences."

"You could end up going to jail."

"I trust the Elder's wisdom. I have always followed Petra's orders; if she sends me to jail then so be it."

"Maybe you shouldn't be quite so good at following orders."

June pulled open the heavy wooden door and entered the large rectangular central room with soaring clerestory windows. After the vestibule, a large soup pool took up almost all the floor space except for the columned aisles going around the pool. The dappled light of the south-facing stained-glass windows reflected off the metallic grey of the fairly empty main soup pool. Only a few of the private loge boxes lining both sides of the long hall above the lower colonnade appeared to be occupied.

Dan looked over his shoulder. "What *is* this place? Why am I here?"

"I think you could use some answers as well. About what happened with Grace."

"You're the only one who sees how what happened with Grace bothers me. The others just think I'm a monster."

"That's because they don't know you."

To the right of the entrance, a worn marble staircase rose grandly up to the second floor.

"Our loge is up this way." June motioned up the staircase. "Dan, if we were back in Area 52 right now, would you try to arrest us?"

"Not sure. If that contract says you can be there like you all told me, then it's not lawful for me to try to stop you. So I don't think so."

"But what if Petra told you to? You've always done what she asked in the past."

"I thought what she asked was lawful." He shook his head. "Never thought she would mislead me." From the second floor, they took a smaller staircase with deep carpeting and creaking steps. Dan paused on the landing. "Why would she do that?"

"Sometimes people bend the rules to protect things and people they care about. Petra probably thought she was doing what she had to do to protect the people there." June starting walking up the stairs again.

"Doesn't make it right."

"No, it doesn't." On the third floor June turned down a dark carpeted hallway. In the dim light the number 324 was barely visible.

"This is our loge." June's eyes adjusted from the dark hallway as they entered the light-filled small room with a balcony overlooking the main room. Dan stood without moving, staring at the small pool set into the concrete floor with a gently pulsing metallic liquid filling it to the brim.

Dan scoffed. "A hot tub? How do you get answers from that?"

"Get in and I'll tell you about it." June popped off her shoes and after grabbing the clear balcony railing for support, she lowered herself into the pool. It always gave her vertigo if she looked over the edge of the balcony to the main soup pool below, so she kept her eyes fixed on their pool.

"In my clothes?" Dan avoided eye contact. June didn't mind immersing herself *au naturel*, but she had chosen to wear clothes to avoid making Dan uncomfortable.

"The liquid won't stick to your clothing, so you can leave your clothes on if you want." She lifted her hand up to show how the liquid beaded up and dropped back into the pool.

Dan took off his shoes and squatted on the walkway that ringed the pool. He drew his hand through the thick substance, leaving ripples that radiated out.

"Is it mercury?"

"No. It's not anything you would recognize because it was created after Area 52—where you live—sealed itself off from the rest of the world." She leaned back and felt the slight vibration of the soup liquid heat her neck muscles.

Dan got over his hesitation and slid into the pool. He sat awkwardly on the pool bench, his straight back not touching the side of the pool.

"Will this do something to me?"

"That depends." June sat up. Explaining the soup, and the soup halls, was complicated. "So you know how in Area 52—where you live—you have the internet?"

"You can just call it Area 52. I know what you're talking about now."

"Okay, thanks. Right now, we are in a soup hall. This liquid," June picked up some of the liquid and let it run through her fingers, "is the soup. The soup is like the internet. It doesn't work the same way, obviously, but it does the same thing. It stores information, lots of it, and gives people access to that information."

"By bathing in it?"

"Not a requirement. Soup pools can transmit the information to embedded or external chips—no physical contact is required. The larger the soup pool, the farther it can broadcast the signal. And soup pools can communicate with each other; so once again, no contact is required."

"How close do they have to be?"

"It depends on the size of the soup pool. That pool in the central hall is a large pool—it can transmit for miles. The pool we are sitting in now might be a good size to cover a large household."

"What happens if some of the liquid gets out? Like if I splash it out of the pool? Is the information stored in it lost?"

"That's kind of the genius thing about soup pools. Every drop is instantaneously synced with all the others, so if one drop, or an entire pool, is lost, it doesn't really matter."

"So we're swimming in the internet?"

"Right."

"Why?"

"I come here to consult the Oragle."

"What's the Oragle?"

"It's our collective source of wisdom. Sometimes we consult the Oragle to see what other people have done and to learn from other's mistakes or successes. Other times we consult the Oragle for advice. I find it helps me feel more centered. It's more effective with a chip, but some people say it works even without one. You should try it out. Maybe it will help you."

"What do I do?"

"You submerge yourself up to your neck in the soup or float on your back and think about the question you would like insight into. Like I'll be thinking, 'How can I reconcile my desire to return to Area 52 with my desire to be close to my family?' Then you relax and let the answers come to you."

Dan closed his eyes and leaned back until he was floating. "What should I ask it about?"

"Something that you need insight into. Or that you need help making up your mind about."

"How about 'Should I run away from these disturbed people?'"

"That will work."

"Now what?"

"You just sit quietly and see if an answer comes to you."

With Dan settled, June relaxed. The soup hall was unusually quiet. The only sound was the trickling of the soup waterfall into the main pool. June consulted information on setting priorities, decision-making, even whether family should come before the self, until she ran out of obvious searches. She looked for other people with similar experiences, but this was one of the few occasions where there weren't any other people like her.

Five minutes passed, and not having made any progress in finding an answer to her first question, June switched to the other question, perhaps more pressing, that she wanted to consult the Oragle about. *What should we do with Dan?* she asked the soup internally so that Dan wouldn't know. The answer came to her almost immediately, and seemed obvious once she had it. At least she knew now what she would recommend to the group.

"Miss June," Dan said quietly, floating on his back with his eyes still closed. "Are you sure there's not any radiation here?"

"Positive." Not any more than the usual, at least. "And please, just call me June. Any progress on your question?"

"Yes."

"What did you decide?"

"I want to go home, but I'm not going to run. Whatever you decide I should do, whatever my punishment is, I'll take it. I won't complain."

CHAPTER 9

Five Days Until the Umbrella Falls

Saturday, late afternoon

"I just swept for bugs not long ago." Amoco showed Cooper into his home office. "I wanted to make sure no one was spying on us while we were spying on Viola. But to be extra safe, when everyone else gets here, we'll go meet in my Faraday Cage."

Amoco sat down at a desk that was almost completely hidden underneath the pile of items on top of it. The office, in a corner room of Amoco's house that was old enough that it had wooden shutters to protect it from the weather, overflowed with stuff—papers, books, collectibles, vintage computer equipment—all piled high on shelves, desks, cabinets, and most of the floor.

It was the most impressive collection of nostalgia Cooper had ever seen—better than any museum, but with the items thrown around wherever a free spot could be found rather than on display. Old maps and paintings with overly-detailed frames propped themselves on the bookshelves. On a shelf he saw a compass, a protractor, and slide rule. Some feathery, plumed thing was stashed in a corner. "You have an amazing house."

Cooper sat down in the only unused chair in the room. The old rolling chair with wooden legs and a worn leather seat squeaked and jolted to the side, leaving Cooper leaning backwards and unbalanced. He sat perfectly still, unsure if any move would topple the chair over.

"Be careful with that chair," Amoco said. "It is a little lopsided."

That warning would have been more useful *before* Cooper sat down. Amoco stood up and pushed his chair towards Cooper. "Here, have mine, it's safer."

"No, no need." Cooper changed the subject before Amoco insisted they switch chairs. "Is the chip working?"

"It is!" Amoco sat down and rubbed his hands together like an evil mastermind plotting his next plan for world domination. "Shall we commence our espionage? She was talking to her assistant when I heard you at the door." He pushed a button on a device sitting on a small cleared area on his desk. A woman, presumably the assistant, was speaking.

"…I'll make sure I have those numbers for you by the end of today," the woman said.

Amoco turned to Cooper. "It is quite unfathomable to me why Viola gets an assistant. I was in the employ of Panacea Corp for ten years and I have never had an assistant." He sniffed. "Viola's tenure is a mere week and yet she is provided with an assistant."

"I feel sorry for the assistant," Cooper said in a low voice. "Not only is it Saturday but it's late on Saturday."

A rustling noise was the only sound picked up by the chip for a few moments.

"Would you like to go over your schedule for next week now?" the assistant asked.

"She needs someone to keep her schedule?" Amoco's offended tone made it clear what he thought. "I believe we are beginning to grasp the larger picture of why she needs an assistant."

"Shhh. I can't hear what they're saying." How was Cooper supposed to hear anything if Amoco kept talking all the time?

"Of course. Commencing silence." Amoco leaned in closer to the device, his head cocked to the side.

"Not right now." Viola's confident voice was easily recognizable.

"That's her!" Amoco whispered in a way that was more like an excited hiss than a whisper.

"I know!" Cooper said, also whispering for some unknown reason. It wasn't like Viola could hear what they were saying.

"We can go over it later today," Viola continued. "I need to give Amoco a call right now."

Amoco bolted out of his chair before Cooper had even processed what Viola had said.

"What did she say? She's contacting me?" In a matter of only seconds, Amoco smoothed his hair, ran his hands over his vest to flatten out any wrinkles, and then adjusted the watch fob hanging from it. "How do I look?"

Cooper raised one eyebrow in amusement. "Amoco, don't tell me you're concerned about how you look for Viola?"

"No, of course not." Amoco sat down, crossed his legs, and leaned one arm on the back of the chair in way that appeared designed to convey maximum relaxation. "I would never worry about such trifling matters as that."

"Then you don't care that you have a piece of hair sticking up?"

"What? No…" He ran a hand over his hair again, then looked at Cooper. "Just one moment, are you deceiving me to evaluate my reaction?"

"Yes." Cooper smiled.

"I respect her," Amoco said. "She is the only other neuroscientist at my level. I value her as an intellectual equal. Or almost equal. Plus, you know Viola is not my type."

"Of course. It seems to me you have your eye on that 'hunky' sheriff's deputy."

"If I did, would you blame me? However, I have a saying, 'Do not waste your time on something you cannot have.' And since I expect you will soon be returning him to his home, he is firmly in the category of something I cannot have."

"I don't know what's going to happen with Dan. It depends in part on what June recommends after she consults the Oragle, but it also depends on the rest of the group. We're going to talk about it when the others get here."

"You know my thoughts on what you should do. Now if you will excuse me, I need to answer Viola's contact request before she decides to go talk to her assistant about her schedule."

"Of course. I'll give you some privacy." He planned to sit in the hall so Viola didn't know he was there. He preferred it that way.

"No need to go far," Amoco said. "I will put the call on speaker so that you may listen as well."

Cooper pointed to the device they were using to spy on Viola as he headed out of the room. "Don't forget to turn that off."

In the hall outside Amoco's office, Cooper settled on a bench.

"Amoco," Viola said, "I need a favor from you."

The husky sound of her voice took Cooper back to times he preferred not to remember.

"How can I be of assistance?" Amoco asked with a quiver in his voice. Cooper had never seen Amoco so nervous.

"I'm worried. We don't know who created the kill switch. We don't know who else might have a copy of the codes. Someone else could have them and use them to control Mariela."

Huh. That sounded like the pot calling the kettle black, but Viola didn't seem to notice her hypocrisy.

"We don't know if anyone has more of the fluid. They could inject Liam, or you, or me. We need more information on the potential for the kill switch to be deployed as a weapon."

"Your argument is persuasive." It wasn't hard to imagine Amoco stroking his goatee. "Perhaps I could persuade Mariela to allow me to biopsy the area where they injected the substance so that you can study its properties?"

"That would be perfect."

"I don't think Mariela will be easily convinced."

"I need you to convince her. If you can get the biopsy, you can use the information to come up with a way to deactivate it and I'll research it to make sure it can't be used as a weapon. I know I've tried to use the kill switch to my advantage"—so she *did* recognize her hypocrisy—"but I never would have used it and I think we need to make sure no one else does as well."

"You have quite convinced me and I must confess, I was thinking the same thing," Amoco said. "She cannot be safe until we understand the mechanisms through which it works and we can stop similar applications in the future."

Cooper let out his breath and relaxed his shoulders. He hadn't realized how tense the call had made him—he was hunched over, his arms wrapped tight around his waist, and he felt light-headed. He took a couple deep breaths and slowed his heart beat.

"Might I provide one more suggestion?" What was Amoco going to suggest to Viola? Cooper slid down the bench closer to the door.

"Of course," Viola said.

"Until we can resolve this problem, Mariela would be best protected by being placed in a Faraday cage where no electronic signals can reach her. That will keep anyone from activating the kill switch or eavesdropping on her chip. I have a number of such facilities; I would like to place her in one expeditiously. Liam has conveniently suspended her so she won't be missed at work."

"I have no concerns about that. Where are you going to place her?"

"If I may be quite direct, as you hold the codes to activate the kill switch, I think it would be best if I not tell you where she will be placed.

While I have the utmost respect for your work, I have yet to come to a conclusion about your character."

"Your lack of trust disappoints me. I would never hurt Mariela. Just make sure I get the biopsy information I want, then I don't care what you do."

Good job, Amoco! He had managed to get Viola to agree to letting Mariela go into a Faraday cage and to not being told her location. And now Amoco could safely biopsy the kill switch site. Viola might even think it was her idea. It might be a mistake to trust Viola with anything, but it felt like they were making progress.

~~~~~

The air of the crypt felt cool and refreshing on Amaya's skin. The Faraday cage in Amoco's family crypt was deep underground and so well insulated that no electronic signals could enter or leave it. It was Nyala and June's first time in the crypt, and they watched the floating sparks with the same amazement Amaya had felt the first time she saw them.

Amoco, Cooper, Hank, and Georgia rounded out the group planning the trip. Cooper had confided in her that he didn't want Hank involved, but June had invited him because Hank wanted to participate in the memorial for Grace. Hopefully he wouldn't get anyone killed this time. They all settled into a circle of chairs and with the soft shushing of the closing door, they were cut off from the rest of the world.

The logistics for the trip were detailed but straightforward enough. Cooper reminded them how to get in and out of Area 52. They would have the memorial service for Grace and then pass through the portal into Area 52 so they could deactivate the kill switch without putting Mariela in danger.

"If we are unsuccessful in deactivating the kill switch," Amoco said, "I am going to recommend to Mariela that she stay in Area 52 until I am able to devise another option."

"If we stay in Area 52, how will we know if you've come up with another option?"

"I used the information that you gathered last time you accessed Server AA to develop a communication device," Amoco said. "The entire area is a Faraday cage, so no communications can travel in or out over airwaves, but because Server AA—Panacea Corp's backup server farm—is on a wired underground connection we can use it to talk. It will
~~~~~

require going to the server room right after you get to SkyWater and connecting the handset to the main server. Amaya, are you okay with doing this?"

"Of course." SkyWater was the largest village in Area 52 and the closest to the portal. It would be easy to get to the Server AA access point in a cemetery outside of the village. From there it would be a simple task to get to the server room and install the communication device.

"I can make something that will look like the communication devices we saw last time," Georgia said.

"We should decide now who will be staying with Mariela if she needs to stay in Area 52. I'm thinking Mariela, June, Amaya, and Nyala," Cooper said.

"Georgia and I can stay also," Hank said. "They could use our support."

Cooper looked at Hank. "We can't send that many people into Area 52 again. It would draw too much attention. June needs to go to take care of her house, Amaya needs to set up the communication device and they'll need someone to read the weather, which Amaya can do also. Mariela obviously needs to go, and Nyala should go because I'm pretty sure Amaya would want her to."

"That's right," Amaya said.

"But—" Hank was interrupted by Cooper.

"You're not going into Area 52."

Hank closed his mouth. The matter was decided.

If they were going to stay in Area 52, they would need gear similar to what they had taken on their last trip. Somewhere in an out-of-the-way room at the estate, there were packs with the supplies from the last trip. Stuff like a syntho-fire for cooking, pup tents, weather equipment, and first aid kits. "When we get back to the estate," Amaya said, "I can go through the packs from last time and put together four travel bags just in case we need to stay in Area 52."

"I'll give you the portable device I used to program the digi-skin" Georgia volunteered.

"That leaves the last task of the meeting," Cooper said. "We need to discuss Dan and whether he will be going back to Area 52 with us. June, as the person who knows him the best and who lost the most, what do you think?"

"I've spent a lot of time thinking about this," June said, "and I've asked the Oragle about it, and I think we should take Dan back. He doesn't belong here, and we can't keep him here forever. Is he just going to wander around the estate until he dies? If people disagree, I'm open to other options, but I know the one thing I don't want, and that's any involvement from law enforcement here. I don't want the secret of Area 52 to become known."

"Thanks, June," Cooper said. "What do the others think? Amaya?"

"I think Dan should be returned to Area 52 because that's what June wants," Amaya said. Back when Amaya was in charge of the expedition, she had made it June's decision. She hadn't changed her mind. It should still be June's decision.

"I say we keep him here," Hank said, "or preferably shoot him."

No one was surprised by Hank's answer. No one bothered to respond either.

Georgia said she agreed with June that he should go back. Was Georgia agreeing because that's how she was, or to spite Hank? Even though it had been four days, the rift between them didn't seem to be getting any better. Georgia still didn't seem to be talking to Hank.

Cooper fidgeted. "It doesn't seem right to take Dan back, but it's impossible to try him without revealing the secret of Area 52, so there's really nothing we can do with him. We can't send him out to live on his own because he couldn't get a job or rent a place to stay or do anything that involves needing an ID, because the cryogen tag…"

"Revived cryogen tag," Amoco corrected him.

"The revived cryogen tag would draw too much attention. Also, I don't think Oscar wants Dan wandering around his place for the rest of his life," Cooper explained.

Hank rolled his eyes. "But you think Oscar's okay with you wandering around his place for the rest of your life?"

June bristled at Hank's remark. "Oscar has been very clear that Cooper is welcome to stay as long as he would like," June said.

"Thank you. June, will you be staying in Area 52 or returning here?" Cooper asked.

"I don't know," June said. "I still have to figure that out."

"So the only strong objection I'm hearing is from Hank."

"I don't care," Hank said even though it seemed like he did care. "Do whatever you all want."

"So then we're decided that Dan will go back?" Cooper asked.

"It's decided," June said.

"That's taken care of everything then. This meeting is over." Cooper immediately stood up and walked out of the room without waiting for any of the rest of them.

Amaya hurried to catch up to Cooper, with Nyala not far behind her.

"Cooper, are you heading back to the Stafford estate?" Amaya asked.

"I was planning to. Why do you ask?"

"Can Nyala and I travel with you? We're staying there because there are large and rather angry crowds camped outside of both our buildings."

Nyala caught up to them. "When I try to get people to protest," Nyala said, "I have to drag people out, but Liam makes some statement about me being responsible for deleting the ghosts, and suddenly everyone's a protester."

"All our social accounts have been completely overwhelmed with messages dripping in vitriol" Amaya said. "Really hateful stuff."

"I don't want those people at my protests anyway," Nyala said. "They just lob hateful and violent threats based on unfounded allegations. *My* protests are much more civilized."

"Clearly, we don't want those people at our protests. For many reasons."

"Our protests?" Nyala raised an eyebrow at Amaya.

"I go to them too."

"Sure, okay, they can be 'our' protests."

Cooper rolled his eyes. "It's fine if you want to ride back to the estate with me."

~~~~~

Hank fell into step beside Georgia on the walk back to the house. Georgia may not want to talk to him, but he had to at least try. He cleared his throat. "Georgia, you look like you are doing well." Why did he sound so awkward? He could have asked her how she was doing without sounding so formal. "Was it difficult leaving your pod again?"

Georgia didn't look at him or slow down. "I didn't go back."

She didn't go back? *How could she have not told him that she didn't go back to her pod?* Where was she staying for the last four days? He wasn't used to her not sharing important information with him. It was like she was a thousand miles away—he could talk to her but he couldn't connect with her.
~~~~~

"Why didn't you tell me?" he asked. She could have stayed with him, like she did before.

"Hank…" Now she sounded sad. "After Grace died, I felt like you were partly to blame, and I needed some time away from you. I still do. And I'm not sure that's going to change."

His heart stopped. "Don't say that unless you really mean it."

"Do you remember when we were in the Levanto cart a couple weeks ago, and I told you that sometimes…?"

She trailed off but she didn't need to finish her sentence for him to know what she was going to say. He remembered that evening with vivid clarity. She had been mad at him for confronting Cooper, even though Cooper had been acting like an ass. She had made one point very clear: "You told me to pick my battles," he said.

She stopped walking and made eye contact with him. "Right. And you didn't do that."

The look in her eyes—was it betrayal? Had he let her down that badly? "I didn't really understand…that other people could get hurt."

She started walking again. "I really appreciate everything you did for me. Your friendship was invaluable, and you changed my life. But right now…I don't see us ever being like that again."

She ducked her head and sped up. He stopped walking and let her go. He couldn't force her to be his friend. It was just…it was just really painful to lose the best friend he had ever had.

~~~~~

Mariela jumped up from her chair as soon as the group entered the library. "Where have you all been?" Cooper, Amaya, Nyala, Amoco—she hadn't expected such a contingent all at once. They must have had a meeting, but that didn't excuse them from not contacting her earlier. "It's been hours since I've heard from any of you—"

"How often do you normally hear from us?" Nyala asked.

"—and after I saw all the people outside your apartment—both of your apartments—I tried to contact you and the message didn't show up as delivered, so then I tried contacting everyone else and none of my messages were delivered—oh, I see that they have been now—but I'm just worried about you all. Did you see Elliat wrote another awful article?"

She had said too much. If Viola was listening to what she was saying,
~~~~~

she would know that none of them had been in contact for hours and might be able to guess that they were plotting something. If Mariela could guess it, so could Viola. She needed to shut up before she said something that would get them in trouble.

Amoco motioned for her to sit and set a large leather bag he was carrying on the table. "Mariela, I believe a chat is in order."

A chat sounded like bad news. With Amoco one could never tell, it could either be about his pigeons or it could be that her chip was going to kill her. "Okay." She waited quietly for him to say something.

He paused. Mariela sat down and started counting the seconds. His longest pause ever had been over a minute. The pauses usually meant he was going to say something difficult or dramatic. So it wasn't going to be about his pigeons. She was going to die.

"Come on, tell me!" She didn't mean to bark quite so loudly at him. Her desperation was starting to show. She was so bored—without her job she had nothing to do, and other than a few details, the others didn't involve her in planning the trip to Area 52 because they didn't want Viola to find out, and most of the people she cared about weren't talking to her. She had moved the furniture around in the library that morning, but that only kept her entertained for so long. With nothing left to distract her, she was free to worry all day. She dug her fingernails into her palms. Amoco couldn't be rushed. So she counted.

After fifteen more seconds he finally spoke. "I spoke with Viola today, and we agreed that you should be placed in one of my Faraday cages until we can find a way to neutralize the kill switch."

"Can't she just use the codes to deactivate it?"

"Well, see, there is an issue. We don't know where the kill switch came from. So we don't know who else might have a copy of the codes. We think it safest if you are disconnected until we can make sure that no one else can access your chip."

"Okay, I'll go into your Faraday cage after Grace's memorial service tomorrow." That would be easy enough to do as they were planning on taking a trip into Area 52 anyway. Mariela was pretty sure that was Amoco's plan as well, but he hadn't said so to keep Viola in the dark. As much as his crypt was an interesting place to visit, she didn't intend to spend any significant amount of time there.

"There is another matter. I would like to biopsy the area around your chip to get a better understanding of the kill switch substance. That way

I think I can be more effective in creating something to permanently deactivate it."

"Okay. Is it safe?"

"Well, there is a catch, as you might say. Viola would also like access to the biopsy. She is concerned this technology was developed to be used as a weapon, and she would like to study it so she can create a way to address it if that should ever happen."

"Viola wants access to the biopsy? After she tried to manipulate me by threatening to kill me?"

"If I may counsel you on this matter," Amoco said, "this course of action seems wise to me. She is going to work with me on neutralizing the kill switch before she begins her research on whether it was designed to be a weapon. As people say, 'two minds are better than one,' and she is a talented neuroscientist."

How had she ended up in this position, where she had to trust Viola? "Alright, on one condition. Viola must stop monitoring my chip. Immediately. I want her sworn word." If Viola gave her word, chances were she meant what she said.

"One moment," Amoco said. "Let me contact her. Please feel free to talk amongst yourselves in the meantime." Amoco stepped over by the large picture windows looking out onto the lawn.

Mariela turned to the others. "So when are we leaving for the memorial service?"

"As soon as possible," Cooper answered. "We are going to do the memorial service at sunrise, so we'll leave about six hours before that."

Mariela was used to being the one to make decisions. She didn't like having decisions made for her and then being told what to do. But in about eleven hours they would be inside Area 52, and she would be able to be herself again. She dropped heavily back into her armchair. Amoco sat down in the chair next to her.

"Viola has agreed to stop monitoring your chip. She has also agreed to let you wear this." He held up a flowered headband chip blocker. She hated the thing, even though she once started a new fashion craze when she had worn it in public at Amoco's insistence.

"Why didn't you give this to me before?" She adjusted the band with the buckle in the back of her neck over her chip.

"There was the possibility disconnecting your chip from the soup might automatically trigger the kill switch."

"What?" That seemed like something she should have been informed of before putting the headband on.

"I determined it was a very low probability event. I knew if I mentioned to you the possibility, it would cause an undue amount of stress given the low probability."

Mariela found herself unable to respond. Should she yell at him for not warning her or thank him for not telling her?

Amoco picked up his leather medical bag and put it on the table. "Are you ready to proceed with the biopsy?"

"Let's get it over with."

Mariela looked away from the needle that he pulled out of his bag. He put a sterile towel on the table and then set the needle and an antiseptic wipe on it. He added two cell culture dishes to the towel and opened their lids.

"Take off your headband and lean forward. Cooper, can you hold her hair out of the way? I am going to biopsy a couple sites because I want to understand how far the substance has spread."

Amoco was quick and efficient. He palpated the site, swabbed the skin, prepared the needle, and took the first biopsy before she even knew he was going to do it. The biopsy stung, but considering that the site continued to itch and frequently burned, having needles stuck in the nape of her neck seemed trivial. Amoco pulled out needle after needle from his bag until he had covered the area all around her chip. He placed a large curative bandage on the biopsy sites and Mariela slipped the flowered headband back on. She adjusted the buckle and breathed more deeply once it was in place.

"Amoco, will you be able to figure out a method to neutralize the kill switch before we go?" Mariela asked.

"I hope so. I am going to work all night on it and Viola has agreed to do so as well. But if I cannot get it done, I suggest you stay in Area 52 after Grace's memorial service tomorrow, unless you want to stay in my crypt until it is done."

"Not at all. Your crypt is cold, boring, and creepy."

"I am sorry to hear you think that because you will be staying in it tonight. It would be misguided to take a chance on your headband slipping off in the middle of the night and someone activating the kill switch, so I expect that you will return to my place with me."

"Nooo, no, that's not a good idea."

"I must insist. However, you will not be there long as you are leaving at midnight for Grace's memorial service. A benefit of having you close by is that should I need additional biopsy samples I can get them from you." He placed covers on two dishes where the samples were suspended in blue gel. "Might one of your father's guards take one of these dishes to Viola at the lab? She is going to run one set of samples through her equipment while I will of course run my samples through my equipment."

"Of course. Whatever you want." Mariela sighed, unable to keep the disappointment from her voice. Was this what her life was to be now? Not able to make any decisions for herself?

"If I am able to devise a disabling solution before you leave for Area 52, would you like me to attempt to disable it before you leave my crypt? Or would you prefer to wait until you get to Area 52?"

"I'll wait. If disabling the kill switch doesn't work then I'd like to just stay in Area 52."

Amoco nodded his head. "Of course."

"Mariela," Amaya stood up, "there's one more thing we can tell you now that your chip is blocked. Dan will be going with us. We're returning him to Area 52."

"What?" She sat up straight, considered, and then slumped back in her chair. "You know what, I don't care. I'm sure you had a good reason for deciding to reverse your decision." Mariela felt agitated and restless. She got up and moved to her desk chair. "Sure, it would have been easier if you had never brought him here if you weren't planning on making him stay, but I really don't want to have him around." She threw up her hands. "So fine. Whatever. I'm just glad no one will be able to set off the kill switch. As long as I'm not in danger of dying at any second, I really don't care what we do."

Mariela twirled her pen while they called Dan into the room and told him that he was going with them. She didn't like running into him in the hallways, so if the others had decided to take him back, she would grit her teeth and sit in the same vehicle with him for the six hours it would take to get to Area 52. But once they were there, he could go his own way.

"Dan," Amoco said, "considering you will be leaving us tomorrow, do you mind coming back to my place and letting me run some tests on you while we are waiting for Mariela's biopsy results? It would be fascinating, from a scientific standpoint, to learn how living in Area 52 has affected your physiology."

"Sure. Don't see why not as long as it doesn't hurt."

"Completely non-invasive and pain free. I swear."

"Alright."

Amoco turned to Cooper. "I will expect you a half hour before midnight, when I will provide you with whatever I have prepared. You can pick up Mariela and Dan at that time."

Cooper shrugged. "Okay, see you then."

"I will take my leave," Amoco said, nodding to the others in the room. "Mariela, Dan, may I suggest we depart?"

CHAPTER 10

Four Days Until the Umbrella Falls

Saturday, almost midnight

It was almost midnight and Cooper was tired. It was the time of night he should be going to be bed, not picking up people who he didn't want to spend time with. He sprinted up the five or six steps to Amoco's door and knocked loudly to make sure Amoco heard him the first time. He was in a foul mood and didn't feel like waiting around. After what seemed like an interminable amount of time, Amoco finally answered the door in his bathrobe. Shouldn't Amoco have been expecting him?

"Please, Cooper, come on in." Amoco held the door to his front hall open wide. "Please take off your shoes."

Cooper slipped his shoes off and followed Amoco into the kitchen. It was a country kitchen featuring exposed beams with metal light fixtures hanging from them. Amoco sat down at a table with three devices on it. He picked up the one that looked like half of a cuff. "You'll put this on the back of her neck," he held it next to his neck to show where it was supposed to go, "and then you'll push this button to deploy the device to deactivate the solution. It will sting but—"

Amoco stopped mid-sentence as a shirtless Dan walked over to the fridge in his socks and boxers. Dan yawned, rubbed one eye, opened the fridge, got out the milk, took a swig, and put it back. "Hi Cooper," he said and walked back out.

Cooper leaned close to Amoco and whispered, "He looks very comfortable here."

Amoco blushed. "I like for my guests to be comfortable. I endeavored to ensure that his needs were taken care of."

Cooper used his best angry whisper voice: "What happened to 'not wanting what you can't have?'"

"Well, as it happens, I was thinking too big. It turns out that as long as I adjusted my thinking so that what I wanted only took twenty minutes, I could have what I wanted."

"Is twenty minutes how long it took for the biopsy results to process?"

"Yes, and it was a blissful twenty minutes. Then I got right down to work and did not stop. Well, there was one five-minute break. But other than that, I took not one single break from work."

Cooper rolled his eyes. "Speaking of your work, let's get back to it."

Amoco held up an unremarkable looking device. "It will take about five minutes for the neutralizing nanodes to do their work, and then you'll use this," he nodded at the other device, "to make sure her chip still works and that the substance has been neutralized."

"Is that it?"

Amoco nodded. "Once you have the results of the deactivation, I would much appreciate being informed of its success or lack thereof."

"We'll keep you updated. If there's not anything else, I'd better tell Dan to put his shirt and pants on so we can go get Mariela."

"I'm ready." A fully-clothed Dan stood in the doorway to the kitchen.

"Let's go then." Cooper walked out the front door without waiting to see if Dan followed him.

Dan caught up with him after Cooper was down the front steps and heading around the corner of the house to the backyard.

"I've never done that before."

"What?" Why was Dan telling him this? "I really don't want to know about it." Cooper picked up his walking pace. They had barely started down the path to the crypt and Dan already was more chatty than Cooper had the energy for.

"Yeah, of course. Just wasn't expecting that to happen."

"Listen, Dan. You shot Grace. I've learned to tolerate you, but I really don't want to be your friend, and I don't want to hear about your personal life. And the sooner we can get you back to Area 52 and out of my hair, the happier I will be."

"Right." Dan nodded. "Understood."

They walked in silence through Amoco's backyard to the crypt entrance. There was nothing about today that Cooper liked. He didn't like that uncontrollable circumstances were forcing him to spend time around Mariela, he didn't want to spend hours in a hovbus with Dan, he didn't want to have a memorial service even though he had loved Grace. He was just still so angry that she was taken from him after only getting to spend a few days with her. A memorial service wasn't going to make that better.

On top of all that, he suspected Amaya was responsible for deleting the ghosts, probably with the collusion of Mariela and Amoco, and he didn't like that not a single one of them had been honest with him about it. He had trusted all of them at some point in his life, but right now he didn't trust any of them.

He had agreed to go on the first expedition thinking it was to do routine maintenance on a server farm, but then found out he was being used for an agenda he didn't support. He never had any complaints with the advanced LP100 model ghosts, and that made being used to help delete them all the more infuriating. After he returned from taking Mariela to Area 52, he was going to cut ties with the lot of them.

As they walked to the crypt, Cooper got madder and madder. By the time they were at the entrance to Amoco's crypt that doubled as a Faraday cage, Cooper was stabbing at the keypad to open it. He pushed the door lightly and it creaked on its hinges as it swung slowly inwards. The sparks floated down but their playfulness clashed with his mood. They seemed to mock him and draw attention to how cranky he was. He and Dan walked down the short walkway and found Mariela lying on a thin cot in the main chamber with a pillow under her head and a sheet over her legs.

"Oh, thank goodness," Mariela said as she hopped to her feet and started scooping up her bedding. "That was the worst night of my life."

"Don't forget your headband." He pointed to the flowered device laying cast away on the floor.

"Oh, right." She picked it up and adjusted it on her head. She looked like she was five years old wearing it. "What's Dan doing here?" She didn't sound any happier about it than Cooper felt.

"Amoco was doing some 'tests' on him."

"Why?"

"He wanted to see how living in Area 52 has affected him."

"I'm healthy," Dan said. "So he says."

"I'm sure that was the assessment," Cooper rolled his eyes. The guy was obviously healthy. If Amoco's tests didn't yield anything more than that, then they were a complete waste of time. "We'd better go. If we don't head out now, we'll be late meeting the others."

"You would not believe how happy I am to see you," Mariela said as she scurried up the walkway, barely avoiding tripping over her bedding.

So Mariela was going to be chatty. Hopefully Dan would talk to her because Cooper didn't feel like talking.

"That place is so creepy!" Mariela waddled from the bulkiness of the bedding. Cooper thought about offering to help her and then decided not to. Mariela was an empowered woman; she could ask for help if she wanted it.

"I felt completely safe in there," she continued talking to him and ignoring Dan, "because there's no way anyone is going to find it, considering it's behind a hidden entrance and two locked doors, but even though I felt without a doubt safe, I was also completely terrified."

Apparently, it was going to be a long explanation, but Mariela seemed perfectly content to keep on talking even though no one was responding.

"I was afraid to turn out the light because it was complete darkness and I was worried I would never find the light switch again. I don't think I slept even five minutes. And what was even worse…"

How long was this monologue going to last?

"…is that I had nothing to entertain myself. I hadn't thought to save anything to my chip's solid storage. Did you know that without Panacea access there is nothing to do? I mean *nothing*. I kept thinking of stuff to do and then realizing I couldn't do it without Panacea." She dropped the pillow and quickly doubled back to pick it up. "Is that the equipment you are going to use to fix me?" She nodded at the devices that Cooper was carrying.

"Yep."

"Oh, great. I'm really looking forward to getting rid of this flowered headband thing."

Amoco was waiting for them on the steps to his house. Back in his typical waistcoat and vest, he greeted them as they approached the front of the house. "Dan, one minute of your time, if I may." They both looked shyly at the ground. Dan scrapped the dirt with his toe. Amoco fiddled with his watch fob. "It has been a pleasure," Amoco said, glancing up with a sly smile.

"Pleasure's all mine."

Amoco pulled Dan into a kiss that was equal parts scorching and tender. Mariela looked like she couldn't be more surprised if the way her mouth dropped open was any indication. "When did that happen?" she asked.

"Sometime last night," Cooper replied.

"Wasn't Amoco supposed to be working on deactivating the kill switch??" Mariela dropped her pillow again.

"He's a good multi-tasker." Cooper didn't feel like explaining any further. "Come on, Dan, let's go! Mariela, give Amoco his bedding back. We have to get on the road."

~~~~~

Three hours on the road, another three to go until sunrise and the memorial service. Even with eight people in it, the darkened hovbus was almost completely silent with no sound other than the hum of the vehicle's movement and Mariela snoring ever so slightly. Amaya had been trying to sleep but she struggled to get comfortable, so she shifted in her seat and stared out the window. The blackness outside had a loneliness to it that seeped into Amaya's soul.

It was a larger hovbus than the one they had used before, and the seats were different. The decision to take the larger bus had been made when they thought there would be ten people traveling, but then Oscar got sick and T-Rock, still suffering from the snakebite, decided to stay back. Instead of smaller seats in a ring around a center space, these were larger, fully reclining chairs with pivoting seats in rows along the windows and with an aisle between them. It was a huge improvement over last time when they were stuck staring at each other. It was peaceful to turn away from the others and gaze out the window at a nothingness that was only interrupted by soft lights from the occasional intrepid household that had chosen to live far from any town.

Dan leaned towards Amaya, his elbow resting on the arm of his chair, and spoke in a low voice. "Does the Elder, I mean Petra, know the truth? That there was no Nuclear Armageddon of 2035, no radiation poisoning from the fallout, nothing at all?"

"Yes, she knows."

"Why did she lie to us?"

"The decision to hide the truth was made when the colony was created. All the adults, the ones you call the Elders, agreed to it. They were afraid if the younger generation knew it was safe to leave, they would travel outside Area 52 and be seduced by the technological progress of the rest of the world. But now the only person still living who knows the truth is Petra."

"No one else knows the truth?"

"I don't think so. We don't know all that much about your group so we may have some incorrect information. But based on what we know,
~~~~~

Petra is the only one. And you."

"And the people out here don't know about us?"

"There are lots of rumors. People know there is something different about the area where you live, but they don't know what causes the anomalies. Most people think it's a secret military installation."

Nyala pressed a button on her seat, and it slid across the aisle to a spot close to both Amaya and Dan. Amaya didn't even know the seats could move like that.

"Who is Petra?" Nyala asked, also keeping her voice low. Mariela, at least, still appeared to be sleeping because the snoring continued. "I've heard her name mentioned by you all a couple times."

Cooper must have been awake, because he slid his chair over by them. Nyala adjusted hers to make room for him.

"She's this absolutely terrifying woman," he said. "She's smart, takes no grief from anyone, and apologizes for nothing."

"I'll second that," Dan added.

"She also hates us," Cooper leaned in closer to them, ignoring Dan. "When we were there, she wanted to arrest us."

"Right," Dan smiled. "She was going to have me do that."

"I remember, you were her willing lackey," Cooper said, quietly angry.

"Guess I was." Dan stopped smiling, but instead of looking angry with Cooper, he just looked sad.

"I'm curious," Nyala said, "after all you've seen, are you still her lackey?" Nyala had a way of asking difficult questions as casually as if she was asking him about the weather.

"I don't know." Dan's eyes unfocused, his thoughts apparently elsewhere. "I don't think so." He ran his fingers through his hair. "I don't know."

"When I look at him," June said from behind Amaya, "I see someone who has been humbled, who is no longer convinced he has all the answers." Now they all adjusted their chairs as June joined them. June made eye contact with Dan. "You're no longer that guy who assumes he always hits his mark."

Dan squirmed uncomfortably and looked away, the tears in his eyes clearly visible. Amaya sighed. A week ago, she wanted to kill him, and now somehow, he had made her feel sorry for him.

There was a moment of silence, and then Mariela, wearing a dress

Grace had liked when she was four because it was made out of lollipops, stretched and yawned. "It was so nice to get some sleep." She rubbed her eyes and looked at them. "What are you all doing?"

"Just talking," Amaya said.

"Did I miss breakfast?"

"You're three hours too early. Go back to sleep and we'll wake you when we get close."

"Okay," a still groggy Mariela laid back in her seat and closed her eyes. Not long after the gentle snoring started again.

"You guys have to hear this." Now Hank moved his seat to join them. "Good news for you Nyala, not such good news for Amaya, June, and T-Rock." Hank waited for people to adjust their seats so they could see him. "That blogger Elliat Exis has a new post. Look at this." Hank put the blog post on the hovbus's main screen.

Business Today

"All the business news you need to know"

April 14, 2115

By Elliat Exis ~ Now a regular contributor!

Group had chips offline before the Black Screen
In what may seem like a shocking twist to those of you who have been following my reporting on the role of Mariela Stafford and Nyala Gidada in last week's Black Screen, I have discovered that it is unlikely that either were the culprit of the outage as the evidence is currently pointing in a different direction. It appears that a group of people, including June Stafford, Abrihet Amaya Gidada, and the former Zazora player Ted "T-Rock" Richardson, were all offline in the days prior to the outage.

That unusual event, combined with the unexpected reappearance of June Stafford after her surprise disappearance 16 years ago, is highly suspicious. In addition, Amaya Gidada is believed to have permanently disabled her chip following the Black Screen. Could it be she is trying to hide something?

Four Days Until the Umbrella Falls

Sunday, dawn

The dusty and dry dirt surrounding the headstone scratched Cooper's hands as he patted it down. Putting up the headstone in the desert sand hadn't been easy, but with some specialized equipment and a lot of effort they got it upright. He pushed himself up off the ground and stood back to look at it.

Grace Barua Stafford O'Connor
A shining star who will always guide us
February 15, 2097 – April 8, 2115

The desert glowed with the radiance of the not-quite-risen sun. It seemed like a fitting reflection of Grace's radiance. "Okay, June, I think it's ready." Cooper used his jeans to brush the dirt off his hands.

June used her chip to turn on the hologram. Grace's image, made from light, emerged from the stone and expanded to a life-size projection in front of it. In the image, she was smiling like she had just said something funny. It was incredible to think that she had been his daughter. Saying goodbye was like having a piece of his heart torn out.

Mariela, Amaya, Nyala, Hank, and Georgia joined Cooper and June and the group formed a circle around the hologram and headstone. Dan, his hands stuffed in his pockets and his head down, stood off by the hovbus.

June looked around at the group. "Thank you all for gathering for this memorial service today." June handed them all some firedust. "We are here to prepare our hearts and minds to say goodbye to Grace." June wiped a tear from her cheek. "Cooper, would you like to say something first?"

Cooper had written what he wanted to say last night, but now that he was about to say it, it seemed inadequate. He didn't have any better words though, and probably never would no matter how long he worked on the eulogy. Despite his misgivings, he forged ahead with the words on his paper. "Grace, I wish I could have known you better. During the short time we had together, you were always positive no matter how bitter I was, and you challenged me in ways no one else could. It breaks my heart that we didn't have more time together."

His words seemed so inadequate, but at least they were heartfelt. Cooper tossed a handful of firedust on the ground before the headstone. The flickering flames burnt dark orange with traces of yellow.

"Mariela, do you have something to say?" June asked.

Mariela was stoic. "I gave birth to Grace, but I wasn't a mother to her." A single sob escaped. "Grace, I tried to give you the best life possible, but I'm sorry that meant I didn't get to be with you. I'm sorry if it was the wrong choice." Mariela tossed her firedust onto the ground.

Cooper's heart felt like it had turned to stone when he heard Mariela's words. If Mariela hadn't sent Grace away, Grace wouldn't have died; if Mariela hadn't written that letter encouraging Grace to visit her, Grace wouldn't have died. It was stupid to blame Dan when the real perpetrator was the woman wearing the lollipop dress and the flowered headband.

Not that there wasn't plenty of blame to go around—Amaya had told Grace to keep a lookout, Cooper had said she could come with them. No wonder they were letting Dan go; with so much blame to share, there was hardly any left to point at Dan.

In turn, each person shared a memory of Grace and threw their handful of firedust onto the ground. Georgia spoke of Grace's spirit and kindness, Amaya spoke about her intelligence and generosity, and Hank shared an anecdote of Grace playing with her dog. Cooper had to admit it was more touching than he had expected from Hank.

Going last, June spoke about Grace growing up, about all the good times they had, but also about the times when Grace was rebellious, or had been hurt by some careless insult from a friend. Through all June's comments was the theme of the many, many days they had spent in laughter and close companionship.

The ache in Cooper's heart grew louder.

"All knowing Oragle, provider of knowledge and insight," June said, "we commit to you the memory of Grace Barua Stafford O'Connor, beloved daughter, granddaughter, and friend. May her memory live on in your archives forever."

One by one, each person tossed their remaining firedust on the ground and repeated, "May her memory live on forever." With each new handful of firedust the flames rose higher and higher, engulfing the holo with purples and dark reds joining the orange and yellows. The sweat rolled down Cooper's back as the gentle warmth of the firedust spread. The fire grew brighter, larger, more intense, and then whipped into a tight column and disappeared into the ground, taking the holo of Grace with it.

The service was over, and Cooper didn't feel any better. Wasn't the point of a memorial service to help with grieving? Why had they gone to all this trouble when he still felt so heavy, so hopeless? When the holo was up, it was like Grace was with them again. But when the holo disappeared, it left a hole in its place, an emptiness. Gentle hands rubbed his back. Someone put an arm around him. Someone else hugged him. It didn't matter who because it didn't make a difference. The more that people tried to support him, the more he felt alone in the world.

~~~~~

Mariela picked up her pack from where she had left it leaning on the hovbus, and then went to stand nearby where the opening to the portal was. The ache in her heart had turned into a burning during the memorial service. An exhaustion had seeped into every fiber in her body. She just wanted to go home. The sooner the kill switch was disabled, the sooner they could get out of there.

She could feel the invisible field coming off the tesseract that pushed back anyone who tried to get close. It was reassuring in a way—there was no way she was going to accidentally walk through it. If she were going through, it would have to be on purpose.

One by one, the group members finished up what they were doing, picked up their gear, and came over to stand by Mariela. Even Dan stood awkwardly with them. Cooper, after retrieving the equipment that Amoco gave him, joined them last. He looked at the ground, avoiding eye contact with everyone.

With the headband on and unable to use her chip to change her clothes, Mariela used Georgia's digi-skin programmer to change into a practical outfit that fit her mood and the occasion—black pants and a plain, lightweight black sweater.

"Is everyone ready?" Amaya asked. They all nodded. "Okay, here goes. Remember don't touch the edges." She knelt down and pushed the blue rock that Bren had painted to show the keystone for the portal. An
~~~~~

arched opening the size of a doorway filled with jagged rays of light that settled into the edges with a blue sizzling electricity. The doorway opened onto a rock wall with what looked like a steep exit to the left. Just as it had last time, the smell of sulphur filled the air.

The portal was exactly how Mariela remembered it from her trip to Area 52 fourteen years ago. It was like a window that looked into another world. There was a small space to stand on the other side, and to go any further, you had to clamber up the steep sides of a hill. Once up about ten feet or so, the terrain opened up and gently rose in all directions from the opening.

"How does it work?" Nyala asked.

"You see that line of rocks there?" Amaya pointed to a row of rocks that were carefully laid in a long line extending both north and south until it disappeared over the next hill. "It shows where the tesseract is, thanks to Bren.

"Who's Bren?" Nyala asked

"Bren was the navigator on our expedition to Area 52. He stayed behind so he could take care of June's pets while she visited her husband."

"Got it. What's a tesseract?"

"I was getting to that. The tesseract is a bend in space—if you cross it, you will end up on the other side of Area 52. For you, it will feel like no time has passed but three days will have gone by. And you will be on the other side of the mountain range that we can't see but is right there." She pointed in the general direction of where she knew the mountains to be. "If you pass through the tesseract again to get back to this side, you'll lose another three days."

"Got it, don't cross the line," Nyala said. "This portal, it allows us a way to get into where the mountains are? And not get sent through space or end up three days in the future?"

"Correct. It's an opening in the tesseract. There's an entire community and a mountain range hiding right in front of us right now, and once we cross through the portal, we will be able to see it."

"And the point of the tesseract was to keep it isolated? So that they could avoid new technology?"

"Yes. They decided technology from the year 2005 was the best it was ever going to get, so they use only technology from that time period. But they knew that if they didn't isolate themselves it would be impossible to not be tempted to use the newer technology, especially for the kids. So they hid themselves in here, and to keep the world from finding them they put up the tesseract. Then to keep the kids from trying to visit the outside world, they told them that the rest of the world was suffering from radiation poisoning."

"I'm still not convinced there isn't radiation poisoning," Dan interjected.

"Tell it to the Oragle, Dan," Cooper said dismissively.

"What does that mean?" Dan asked.

The portal blinked multiple times and then disappeared.

"If I may continue," Amaya refocused the discussion, "it was eighty years ago when the community was formed here. It's also a Faraday cage that keeps digital signals from entering or leaving. For the same reasons as the tesseract—to stop people out here from finding out about Area 52, and to keep the people in there from finding out about us."

"That's why you need to go in there?" Nyala asked. "Because once Mariela is in there, the signals that could activate the kill switch won't be able to reach her?"

"Exactly."

"And all this tech existed eighty years ago when this place was created? It seems pretty advanced."

"Petra, the woman we were talking about earlier in the hovbus, is brilliant. Her inventions had the capacity to be some of the most life-changing ever. And she decided to use them here." Amaya swept her hand along the line of rocks showing the tesseract.

"We should probably stop talking and get on inside," Mariela said. "I'm aching to get this kill switch disabled."

"I'll get the portal." Amaya pushed the blue stone again.

The portal opened but this time, instead of showing the side of a hill, there was also a somewhat grizzled yet fit black man holding what looked like a cat carrier.

"Bren!" Amaya called out.

Bren smiled. "Fancy meeting you all here. Thanks for opening the portal for me—finding the stone is always a bitch."

"What are you doing here?"

"Taking Midnight here to see his mom." Bren held up the cat carrier slightly and stepped through the portal.

"That was nice of you!" June said. "But you didn't need to."

"Well Midnight and I thought we would head on home. Midnight misses her family and I miss my wife." Bren turned to June. "And don't worry, one of your neighbors has happily taken in Squeegee."

"Was Midnight giving you a hard time?"

"He was crying and looking for you." Bren's eyes narrowed as he looked at the group. "What are you all doing here? Because I sure would appreciate a ride home if you're heading in that direction."

Mariela hugged Bren. "There's so much to tell you. Let's go inside the portal for a minute so we can talk."

"Sure. No problem." Cat carrier still in hand, he passed back through the portal and clambered up onto the flatter ground above the opening. The rest of them followed him through the portal and to the left up a short, steep incline to a plateau.

"What is Deputy Dan doing here?" Bren asked. "People up in the SkyWater have been mighty worried about him. Sending out lots of search parties and stuff."

Dan shoved his hands in his pockets. "Told you they would worry about me."

"Bren, there's a lot to explain…" Mariela paused, uncertain how to tell Bren about Grace's death. "I can't tell you it all now, but Grace is dead."

His face fell. She could tell the news hurt.

The blue sizzle of the portal blinked, and Mariela reached for her headband. She would be so happy to be rid of the stupid flowered thing.

"Wait," Cooper stopped her. "Before you take off your headband, let me make sure no outside signals can reach us here."

Mariela paused with her hand already pulling off the headband. Reluctantly, she put the headband back on and lowered her hand. She sat cross-legged on a flat patch of desert between two creosote bushes, placed her bag in front of her, and waited patiently, or more accurately, somewhat impatiently, as Cooper laid his large canvas bag flat on the ground and put the various devices in a row on top of it.

Cooper spent a couple minutes arranging the items Amoco had given him, and Mariela was starting to wonder if he was ever going to do anything with them. She brushed some dirt off her black pants. She didn't need to—the digi-skin would clean itself, but there wasn't much else to do while Cooper got ready.

"You can stop fidgeting," he told her. "You're making me nervous."

"Okay." She stilled her body, but being patient was challenging.

He put the device he had been fiddling with down and said, "Okay, looks like you are safe to take your headband off."

Without hesitating Mariela swept the headband off and threw it on the ground.

Cooper picked it up and handed it back to her. "You may want to keep it in case this doesn't work. You might need it later."

"What if it doesn't work?" Would she be stuck living in Area 52 for forever?

"I'm sure it will work," Cooper said. "Amoco knows what he is doing."

"Didn't seem quite so sure when I talked to him," Dan said.

"Dan, what are you still doing here?" Cooper snapped.

"I'm waiting to see how this turns out."

"I suggest you start walking." Cooper looked at Hank. "Give him his bag so he can go."

"Here's your clothes." Hank removed the bag over his shoulder by the strap and slung it to Dan.

Dan caught the bag and put it under his arm. "Where's my rifle?"

"For obvious reasons, we kept that," Cooper said. "And we kept your handcuffs, as it didn't seem wise to give you those back either."

Dan looked like he might say something, but then changed his mind.

"You have your stuff," Cooper said. "Now hit the road. And don't come back."

With an uncomfortable look at the group, Dan turned and walked up the overgrown road. Mariela was glad to see him go. Hopefully that was the last time she would have to look at her daughter's killer.

Cooper turned back to her. "Okay, Mariela, are you ready?"

"Wait. The brutes told me that if I try to deactivate the kill switch it will kill me. What if that happens? Maybe we shouldn't do this."

"Amoco thinks that was just a bluff."

"He thinks? Why can't he be sure?" It wasn't the reassurance she was hoping for.

"He said that if the failsafe was going to be triggered by disconnecting from the soup, it would have been when you put on the headband."

"Oh. Right. Of course."

"But there is one thing Amoco wanted me to tell you." Cooper looked uncomfortable, like he didn't want to share what Amoco said. "If this doesn't work, you can never connect to the soup again. Because reconnecting could possibly trigger the failsafe."

"Let's get this over with. Whatever happens, happens." There wasn't much else to do at this point but to push forward. She drove any thoughts of being terrified out of her mind.

"Lean forward so that I can get to the back of your neck."

She leaned forward and rested her head and arms on her bag. Cooper moved her hair off her neck.

Georgia knelt on the ground by her and held her hand. Mariela squeezed it. Hopefully Georgia would know how much Mariela appreciated having her there, as it wasn't something she could put into words just now.

Cooper ran his fingers along the back of her neck, searching for the right spot. His fingers touched a tender spot—the spot where the substance injected by the brutes still burned sometimes, and where she knew her chip to be. Cooper's fingers kneaded her neck, palpating to discover the extent of the area. He kept one hand on her neck, and the other picked up the marker. She heard the click of the cap opening and the velvety feel of the marker tip circling the area. Cooper set the marker down and grabbed the device that looked like a metal cuff. He placed the cuff on the back of Mariela's neck. The coolness of it chilled her as it curved to match the curve of her neck. It was lighter than it looked.

Cooper held the cuff in place on her neck. "Are you ready?"

"Do it before I change my mind." She pushed aside any thought that it might kill her.

"Amoco says it might sting."

"It can't be worse than what I have now."

"Here we go."

Needles covering every millimeter of the cuff stabbed into the back of her neck. A liquid, cool, not hot like the kill switch, slipped under her skin. She jerked from the pain, her hands forming into claws. The headband fell back into the dirt. Seconds later, the pain subsided and Mariela let her head relax onto her arms. She needed a moment to recover.

Cooper set the device on the ground. "He was only able to prepare one dose," Cooper explained, "so let's hope this works. Amoco said to give it five minutes to work." He picked up the last device.

A couple minutes passed where no one said anything.

"Are you ready to check if it worked?" Cooper asked.

"Go ahead." At least she wasn't dead—if it was going to kill her it probably would have done so by now. She sat up.

Georgia squeezed her hand. Her mom knelt behind her and touched her back. Amaya looked nervous as she chewed on her nails. Bren watched as though he were watching a reality show, but he looked like he might have a bead or two of sweat on his brow as well.

Cooper fiddled with the device and it lit up. "This device simulates the soup. It's broadcasting a test signal."

"I can hear it."

"That's good. That means your chip hasn't been disabled. But now we need to check if the kill switch has been deactivated." He adjusted the device and then held it close to the back of her head. He stared at it for a long time, too long. He adjusted the device again.

"What does it say?"

"It looks…" Cooper stopped talking.

Mariela steeled herself for bad news. "Go on, tell me," she snapped at him.

"I'm sorry, Mariela. It looks like the kill switch is still active."

How could that be? Amoco had always been able to come up with a solution to every problem.

"Well," Cooper picked the bag up and started putting devices back in it, "I guess it is time for Plan B."

"What's Plan B?"

"I don't know. It's up to Amoco to figure out." Cooper finished putting the devices in the bag.

"I'm going to head back to let Amoco know that we weren't able to disable the kill switch. Amaya, you'll access the server room outside of SkyWater and set up the communication device so we can communicate?"

Amaya nodded.

"Mariela, put your headband back on. I'm going to open the portal."

"Cooper…" Mariela rubbed the back of her neck. The kill switch still burned, but now it was mixed with a freezing cold. If only the two would cancel each other out.

"What's up?"

"I don't think I can choose between living without a chip or living in constant fear of being killed by my chip."

"That's not going to happen. Amoco will figure out a way."

"Okay, but if he doesn't, if I have to disable my chip, will you help me?"

Cooper nodded. "Put your headband on."

Mariela wiped the dirt off her headband, slipped it onto her head, and adjusted it so the buckle was over her chip and the flower was in front.

"Hank, Georgia, Bren, you're with me." Cooper knelt down to press the blue rock that opened the portal. There was the shimmer, the expanding streaks of light, and then the door-sized opening appeared, showing the flat desert on the other side. Cooper jumped into the hollow just inside the portal opening. "Come on, let's go before the portal closes."

"Hank, let's go." Georgia hugged Mariela. "Mariela, take care. Amoco will take care of this, you'll see. And we'll see you back at the estate before you know it." Georgia didn't jump into the hollow like Cooper, but instead walked down the less steep side.

Hank sighed in a pouty sort of way and then followed Georgia into the hollow by jumping over the steep side.

He reached up toward Bren. "Hand me the cat carrier."

Bren passed the cat carrier on to him. The cat let out one long, complaining, howl.

"Come on, Midnight," Hank said to the cat. "Let's get you out of here."

Bren clambered down and followed the rest of them through. Not long after, the portal closed. Mariela threw her headband on the ground and sobbed. She didn't want anyone to see her like this. It was unprofessional and weak. But she couldn't help it. She put her head down on her arms and let the tears flow.

<div align="center">~~~~~</div>

Cooper wasn't looking forward to six hours in the hovbus. It was nice to see Bren again, and Georgia was always pleasant, but Hank's presence grated on his nerves. He tossed his bag over his shoulder. Might as well get on with it. The sooner they got on the road the sooner it would all be over. He glanced over his shoulder at the portal. It had closed behind him almost as soon as he stepped through.

"AHA!"

Cooper startled at the unexpected sound. Hank dropped the cat carrier. The carrier clattered to the ground, bouncing on one corner and then another. The cage bent and the door popped open; a black ball of fur streaked out and ran off in a panic.

"Midnight!" Georgia called out as the cat streaked past her.

Cooper turned to see Elliat emerging from behind the hovbus.

"I *knew* you were up to something!" Elliat declared.

The panicked cat headed straight to the tesseract, and there was nothing to stop it except the repulsion field. It seemed too panicked to notice the field even as it its fur stood on end. And with a crackling spark of electricity, the cat disappeared.

Cooper took a second to process what had just happened. "If that isn't just..."

Georgia stared after the cat, and then, with no warning to anyone else, bolted after it. The electric crackling of the tesseract made her short platinum hair stand on end and seemed to push her away. She leaned into it and struggled to move forward. A second later she disappeared.

"Georgia!" Hank called out. He bounced anxiously, looking almost as panicked as the cat. This time, Cooper knew exactly what was about to happen. Hank took off at full speed towards the tesseract. It seemed to push him back like it had Georgia, but he powered through it faster, and a second later, hair standing on end, he was also gone.

With the time distortion of the tesseract, even if they found the cat and returned right away, it would be six days before they got back. Cooper made a mental note to send a hovbus for them in six days. And there was one more thing he could do. He picked up the carrier and fit the door back into its slot. Like a disc thrower, he turned in a circle a few times to get some speed on the carrier and let it loose through the tesseract. Hopefully it wouldn't hit anyone on the other side and they could use it when they found the cat. The carrier's speed slowed as it hit the field, but it didn't stop completely, and not much later it too disappeared.

"What was *that*?"

Crap. Cooper had forgotten about Elliat. He spun around. "None of your business."

"I should say it is."

"Elliat, you can't report on this."

"On the contrary, this is going to be top-of-the-blog news!"

"Elliat, it's important people don't know about this."

"My job is to make sure people know about this. It's stuff like this I live for." Elliat took off running in the other direction. He disappeared around the hovbus and seconds later an engine started. Dust rose up from a small, off-road vehicle as Elliat pulled away at full speed. Bren, who always enjoyed a good drama, looked shocked but entertained.

"Well, Bren, I guess it's just you and me. Looks like we'll both get a lot of space in the hovbus."

"It's not my fault the cat escaped. I wasn't holding the carrier when it happened."

"I'm sure June will understand. Especially if Hank and Georgia get him back, which I'm sure they will."

"Wow. Man, I feel really bad about that. That was something how that blogger Elliat jumped out from nowhere. How did he find us?" Bren headed towards the hovbus. "That guy is a pest."

For a guy who appeared clueless most of the time, Elliat pursued the story with dogged determination. He shouldn't have been able to find them but somehow he figured it out.

"The good news is," Cooper said, "seeing the tesseract made him forget about the portal and whatever he was planning to confront us about. If people find out about the tesseract, it's not that big a deal, they'll just lose a lot of time if they go through it. If people find out about the portal to Area 52, that's a big deal."

Bren nodded. "That cat did us a favor."

"Come on. Let's get out of here before Elliat remembers the portal and comes back to interrogate us."

CHAPTER 12

Four Days Until the Umbrella Falls

Sunday, afternoon

Amaya was exhausted. The trip up the mountain was uneventful, and the weather beautiful, but it was six hours of walking uphill with just a few stops and bags heavy with their equipment. Mariela and Nyala, both in excellent shape, had taken the lead. They didn't appear to be talking much, in fact it looked like they might be competing to see who could go the fastest. Amaya wasn't getting involved in whatever was going on between them. She would much rather keep June company. They passed the time complaining about how their feet hurt, their legs were tired, or their backs were sore. Occasionally, they talked about the memorial service or reminisced about Grace.

After six long hours, they arrived at the entrance to the servers that Panacea Corp kept in Area 52. Hidden inside a cold mausoleum in the town cemetery was a door with an entry keypad. Amoco's device broke the code on the keypad in seconds, and the door swung open to show an elevator door. It was just like Amaya remembered it, cobwebs and all. When the elevator door opened, they all piled in and Amaya hit the down button. She brushed a cobweb out of her hair.

Nyala touched the oxidated metal of the elevator wall. "How long has this been here?"

"Panacea Corp agreed to give the land to the Area 52 settlers about eighty years ago," Mariela said, "so sometime around then. The settlers used the land to create a colony that only uses tech from 2005 and earlier."

"What did Panacea Corp get out of it?"

"Panacea Corp was allowed to place a backup server farm here. That's where we're headed right now."

"Why did Panacea Corp want to have servers here? Isn't it kind of out of the way?"

"The server farm, called Server AA, is located deep beneath the mountain, it's far from the other servers, and it works differently from the other Panacea Corp servers, so if something happens to the soup, it's possible these servers won't be affected."

The elevator, creaking and moaning, continued descending. Based on Amaya's previous experiences, it would take around three minutes to reach the bottom.

"Did something go wrong?" Nyala asked.

"First of all, so few people were told about the server farm that Panacea Corp pretty much forgot about it. Even people who had heard of Server AA didn't know where it was. Second, the people in Area 52 were supposed to allow Panacea Corp unrestricted access to the servers."

"I can say for sure that did *not* happen," Amaya said. "They did everything they could to keep us from accessing the servers."

"Right," Mariela said. "Technically they are in default because they didn't allow us access, which means Panacea Corp could take back the land if they wanted to. Except nobody but us knows they are in default."

"Liam doesn't know? Even though he's CEO now?"

"I only found out about this myself a couple of months ago, and I already didn't trust Liam at that point, so I didn't tell him."

Nyala raised her eyebrows. "Wow. Hopefully that won't come back to haunt you."

The elevator clicked to a stop and the doors opened. Amaya ignored the vast server room that opened up in front of them. Those servers belonged to Area 52 and compared to the next room, it was small. She went to a door to the right and placed Amoco's device on the side of the keypad. Seconds later the door opened onto a server room of almost unimaginable proportions. Amaya only needed the main server closest to the door, however. In the week since she had last been there, a thin layer of cobwebs and dust had built up on the servers. She wiped it off with her hand.

"I'm going to look around a bit," June said.

Amaya pulled the cube that Amoco gave her out of her bag, but something stopped her from putting it on the server. "Mariela," Amaya said, "it's not going to delete anything this time, is it?"

Mariela had the gall to roll her eyes. She could at least admit it was reasonable for Amaya to not trust her. Mariela shook her head.

Amaya activated the screen and placed the cube on the server. The program started running automatically.

"So, Mariela," Nyala asked, "did you delete the ghosts?"

Amaya paused what she was doing. Would Mariela admit to having deleted the ghosts? Mariela had taken a huge risk—they were considered private property and it was unquestionably illegal to delete them. Not to mention they were worth a small fortune.

"I guess there's no point in pretending I didn't do it," Mariela admitted as casually as if it were some minor thing, like copying the design of an outfit.

The anger Amaya had felt at the time washed over her as strong as when it had first happened.

"Not that I was there," Mariela continued, "Amoco wrote the program and Amaya uploaded it when she was doing the maintenance on the servers."

Something in Amaya exploded. She pounded her fist on the shelf holding the server. "Don't you dare lump me in with you and Amoco." It was long past time that she confronted Mariela about what happened. She had put it off while Viola was monitoring Mariela's chip, but now she could finally tell Mariela exactly what she thought about what they had done. "I said I didn't want to do it, and then Amoco put a program that couldn't be aborted into the maintenance program without telling me. You used me."

"I'm sorry, Amaya," Mariela said. "It had to be done. LP was too powerful."

Unbelievable. That was just like Mariela. She always felt justified in the actions she took—the consequences to others be damned.

"So you deleted Opali?" Nyala's voice cracked. "You deleted the daughter of your own sister?"

Mariela scoffed. "She was a *ghost*. Not a human. Not real."

Amaya spun around to face Mariela. "She was real to Sofi." Mariela's sister had cried non-stop ever since she lost the ghost that for ten years she had considered to be her daughter.

"It hurt me too, to lose Opali." Tears streamed down Mariela's face. "I hated to do it, but it was war, and she was a civilian casualty."

"Was it worth it?" Nyala asked. "Look at you—you have to hide in here because you could be killed any second. Was it worth it?"

"Yes, I paid a price too. I've lost my freedom, and I still might lose my life. But that just shows how important it was to get rid of LP. He ordered the brutes to kill Liam by throwing him out the helicopter, and with the kill switch, he would have been able to control me. Just think how much worse it would be if LP were still around right now."

"Enough!" June stepped up to the two women. Amaya startled at her appearance. "You both have good points. So stop arguing!"

"What about my point," Amaya risked more of June's anger, but she still had stuff that needed to be said, "that Mariela should have told me what she was doing since I ended up being mostly responsible, even though I didn't want to do it and I didn't know it was happening until too late?"

"If I had told you, you wouldn't have done it," Mariela said under her breath.

"All of you, stop it!" June said. "Amaya, you need to get the communication device ready, so focus on what you're doing. The rest of you, don't distract her."

~~~~~

Mariela punched the button on the elevator. Her mother made her feel like a little kid again when she told them to stop arguing. Nyala and Amaya had a right to be angry with her, but if she had a chance to go back and do it all over again, she would make the exact same decisions. Surely her mother of all people should understand that sometimes difficult decisions have to be made. When her mother left her family to live in Area 52, hadn't she made a difficult decision that ended up hurting some people?

The silence in the elevator got louder the longer they were in it. How much longer would it take to get to the top? The seconds dragged on. And dragged on. Eventually the door opened. The inside of the mausoleum was barely illuminated by light seeping in around the entrance door. Amaya stalked out and threw open the door to the outside. The sunlight rushing into the mausoleum blinded Mariela. Amaya stopped short and Mariela almost ran into her.

Dan was standing there with three other deputies, his rifle slightly raised. "Hands in the air!"

They all raised their hands. "Dan, you know we're not armed," Amaya said.

"I don't know anything. You could have a gun or knife on you that I don't know about." He turned to the deputies. "Frisk them. Take all their devices."

"Dan," June said, "what is this?"
~~~~~

"You're under arrest."

"For what?"

"Breaking and entering." He motioned with his chin toward the mausoleum. "Now be quiet. Next person who talks will learn what it feels like to be hit in the head with my rifle."

Mariela had a lot of things she would have liked to say to Dan, but there was no point. She kept her mouth shut. The others must have also figured that there was nothing to be gained by getting hit in the head with a rifle because they all stayed silent.

"Put cuffs on them," Dan said to the other deputies. "You're going to be held without bail until a later date."

As long as he didn't throw her out of Area 52, Mariela didn't really care if they were in the jail or at her mother's house. Sure, her mother's house would have been a lot more comfortable, but at least she wouldn't have to worry about the kill switch being activated at either location.

~~~~~

Amaya jumped at the sound of the holding cell door clanging shut behind her. Their cell, with a concrete floor and cinderblock walls, was across from an empty cell. It smelled musty with a side of sweat and a hint of urine. There was a small toilet in the corner with a privacy panel that wouldn't provide much privacy and hard concrete benches on two of the walls that were wide enough to lie down on, but nothing else. There wasn't even enough space for all of them to lie down at the same time unless two of them laid on the floor. Amaya sighed. At least she would have an interesting story to tell her kids someday. She sat down on the cold bench that was farthest from the toilet and dropped her head into her hands.

June was still trying to convince Dan to let them out, but her efforts seemed about as likely to be successful as cutting their way out through the thick door.

"I'm sorry, Miss June," Dan said. It was the only time Dan had shown any contrition since he picked them up. He had taken all their belongings, including their communication device, and for clothing he gave them slippers and jail uniforms in a dingy gray that said Property of SkyWater Jail. He never acknowledged knowing them when the other deputies were around. He had become an accomplice in keeping the residents of Area 52 from finding out that there was a thriving world outside the
~~~~~

umbrella.

June lingered at the cell door, looking out at Dan.

"Dan, why did you pick us up?" June asked him.

"Petra told me to."

"You're back to doing whatever Petra tells you?"

"She's the Elder. And it's my job."

"But we didn't break any laws. You know we have a contract that says we can access the servers."

"Never seen this contract."

"Well, it's not like I can show it to you while I'm in here."

"Show it to the judge when you see him."

"You know we'll never get to see a judge. Petra would never take a chance on having Area 52's secrets come out in a courtroom."

"Don't know about that."

"Tell Petra I want to see her."

"Yes, Miss June. She is planning on visiting you when she has time."

"Right. Because she is so busy."

"Lots going on around here. It's been keeping her pretty busy."

"Dan, can you do one thing for us?" Mariela asked.

"What's that?"

"We really need our communication device."

"You mean your phone?"

Mariela crossed her arms over her chest. "Yes. Of course I mean the phone."

"I can't do that."

"It's really important. It's how we will know when it's safe to leave."

"Sorry, can't give it to you. Prisoners can't have cell phones. I'll monitor it and advise you if I hear anything."

Mariela rolled her eyes and turned her back on Dan.

It seemed like they were stuck taking his word for it.

~~~~~

Amoco held the door to his house open for Cooper to enter. "I must say I was hoping to hear from you sooner. I have been eager to hear how the procedure to disable the chip progressed. In addition, I have been most anxious to discuss Elliat's recent blog post with you."

Amoco led Cooper into a room that was almost as full of curiosities as the office that they had been in last time. Instead of a desk though, it
~~~~~

had two leather couches. Amoco stood with his hand resting on the back of one of the couches while Cooper walked around looking at some of the items. It was too much for Cooper to take it all in, but he did see a model velociraptor skull. *It was a model, right?*

"Sorry it took me so long to get here," Cooper said. "I dropped Bren off at his place in the Outer Ring of the city first, then I went to the estate to drop off the hovbus where I filled Oscar and T-Rock in on everything that happened, and then I had to wait for a ride from Oscar's driver. It's been a long journey to get here." Cooper flopped down on Amoco's green leather couch. He was exhausted. "What about Elliat's latest post?"

Amoco tucked one hand into a pocket of his smoking jacket, placed the other behind his back, and lowered himself deliberately into a chair. "Have you had the pleasure of reading Elliat's latest post? I sent you multiple messages regarding to it."

"Sorry, I haven't checked my messages or the news. I find it's better not to know."

"It never ceases to surprise me how you manage to get by in this world. You are probably the one person on the planet who can go for more than half a day without checking their messages."

"It's a skill I've worked hard to cultivate. So, what is Elliat's post about? He intercepted us as we were leaving Area 52, so I can't imagine it's anything good."

"Let me read it to you." Amoco's eyes unfocused as he pulled up the post using his chip. "*Breaking news!*" Amoco focused on Cooper again. "This was published early this morning, around 7:30 am." A short pause and Amoco started reading again.

> This reporter promised to continue following the story of the deleted ghosts, and now this reporter's persistence has paid off. In addition, this reporter...

"I find it most annoying how he repeatedly refers to himself as 'this reporter,' don't you? But to continue..."

> ...this reporter has determined that many of Mariela Stafford's friends, or shall we say accomplices, had their chips offline in the days directly before the Black Screen and the loss of the advanced LP100 model digital ghosts. What has

not yet been reported is that the chips of these partners in crime all came back online at the same time in the same geolocation.

To learn more about what might be at this location, this reporter traveled to that location. After about six hours of travel through the desert, this reporter arrived at the location to find a large hovbus parked there, a recently placed gravestone for one Grace Barua Stafford O'Connor, and not a single person in sight. Some voices could be heard in the distance, but they were muffled and the owners of those voices were nowhere in sight.

This reporter then accessed the records on Grace Barua Stafford O'Connor and found a Grace Barua Stafford passed away 14 years ago and was buried in the family burial plot which is located on the Stafford estate. Now stick with me here—on her birth certificate, her father was indicated as an anonymous sperm donor, but one of the last names on Stafford's grave is that of Cooper O'Connor, Mariela Stafford's longtime associate. Suspicious, no?

To this reporter's utmost surprise, as I was accessing the information on Stafford O'Connor, four people appeared out of nowhere, one carrying a cat carrier of all things. Even more shocking, the cat escaped the carrier and while running away, DISAPPEARED INTO THIN AIR! Loyal readers of this blog, you know this reporter does not use all caps lightly, so let this indicate how astonishing this event was. The cat was then followed by two of the four people— Hank Silva and Georgia Bristow. Similar to the cat, they also disappeared.

The two-remaining folk, including Cooper O'Connor and a gentleman who I did not recognize, then yelled at this reporter saying that what this reporter had just witnessed could not be published. Of course, you see how that has turned out. The video capture of what happened is also available on the blog.

What a tangled web has been woven here! While the answers as to what happened and who did what still remain

elusive, this reporter will continue to untangle the web, and
will update all my loyal readers…

"He should have said 'this reporter's loyal readers' just to be con-
sistent," Amoco interjected.

…when I have more information.

"Again, he should have said, purely for consistency's sake, '…when
this reporter has…,' but that's neither here nor there. I would show you
the capture, but I am sure you know already what is in it."

"I'll watch it later just so I know what people are seeing," Cooper
sighed. Elliat was getting too close to the truth, but he felt so tired, even
watching a capture sounded like too much effort.

"To give you a brief update," Amoco said, "the other news reports
say a multitude of alien enthusiasts, thrill seekers, and conspiracy nuts—
many of my good friends included—have set off to the coordinates mentioned by Elliat. Also, can I assume that Hank and Georgia have gone
through the tesseract and that is why they did not return with you? And
that disabling Mariela's chip did not work, and that is why she, June,
Amaya, and Nyala also did not return with you?"

"Correct. It was just Bren and me in the hovbus on the way back.
Even the cat didn't make it. On the hovbus, that is. Hopefully it's still
alive." Cooper closed his eyes. The two hours of fitful sleep that he managed to get in the hovbus wasn't enough.

"Very well then," Amoco said. "There is also a problem with Viola.
After she helped me develop the ineffective treatment for the kill
switch—I blame myself, not her, for the lack of effectiveness—Viola
continued to examine the kill switch substance. I believe, based on what
I have overheard of her conversations through the bug we left in her office, she has used the results of her tests on the substance to develop her
own fluid to use to control the chips of the cryogens. She is planning on
using them to strike some targets in the Arctic, and she appears to believe
that doing so will allow them to make progress in the war while saving
lives."

"Huh. Amoco, don't you think I should talk to her to find out more
about this? If it saves life and shortens the war, I can't really complain
about her using it. But first I should probably learn more about it."

"Agreed. I have been working on reviving cryogens for decades now and I think I can conclusively state at this point they will never be revived. If she can use them for another purpose, then maybe some good can come from them."

"Okay then. I'd better get on that and I'll leave you to work on solving Mariela's chip problems."

"Very well. If you have no further need of me then, I will return to my labor on the kill switch."

CHAPTER 13

Three Days Until the Umbrella Falls

Monday

It took twelve hours before they heard Petra's voice approaching the holding cell. No access to Panacea meant that Amaya was more bored than she had ever been in her life. She actually looked forward to seeing Petra. It would be a nice break from the awkward silence of the last twelve hours. Even though they were stuck in the holding cell together, the four of them hardly talked. Maybe because any conversation felt awkward.

Amaya actually felt a hint of excitement when the aged and diminutive Petra came through the secure door into the holding cell area. Although slightly hunched, she still had an almost stately air about her. Maybe haughty was a better description.

Nyala sat up from lying on one the concrete benches and looked Petra over. "She's over one hundred years old?" Nyala asked in a low voice. "She doesn't look a day over ninety." If Petra heard Nyala's comment, she ignored it.

"June." Petra's voice crackled in the way the voices of the elderly often do. It was the voice of someone used to being in charge and whose voice conveyed the heavy weight of disapproval. "If it wasn't enough that you continue to be a thorn in my side, I see you have brought three new thorns with you. To what do I owe this displeasure?"

June stood on the other side of the bars from Petra. "Petra, we don't want any problems. We'll stay out of your way if you stay out of ours."

"And do you call kidnapping my most talented deputy staying out of my way?"

"You mean your most *loyal* deputy? The lap dog who never questions if what you are asking him to do is legal or not?"

Mariela stood up and grabbed the bars with clenched fists. "He killed Grace."

Petra turned her gaze to Mariela and looked her up and down. "He told me. He also told me that it happened in the conduct of his official duties."

June winced. "He was impulsive and reckless in discharging his weapon. How is it you don't have any self-doubt about what you have done? Don't you ever feel any tinge of guilt?"

"I have nothing to feel guilty for."

Mariela lunged and reached through the bars, her fingers grasping onto the front of Petra's shirt. "You killed Grace. You sent Dan after them and you killed her."

Petra and Mariela stared, unblinking, with their faces not six inches from the other. Nyala touched Mariela's clenched hand, gently drawing it back inside the bars.

"I think it goes without saying I didn't kill her," Petra said, not breaking eye contact with Mariela.

"Come on, Mariela." Nyala took her elbow and led Mariela back to the bench. "Let June talk to her."

"I have to agree with my daughter," June said. "If you hadn't sent Dan after us and given him the idea you would forgive whatever he did, Grace would still be alive today."

"June, I'm sure you remember how I warned you if you didn't leave the area, I would throw you and your friends in jail. I'm here to officially let you know that until you agree to be escorted to the portal by my deputies, you will have to remain in jail."

"No!" Amaya hadn't meant to call out, but the idea of spending another day in the jail was too much. It was cold and smelled like feet. She wanted a warm bed and a hot drink. Maybe even a fireplace. Instead, she had a frigid bench in a dank holding cell.

"You're bluffing," June said. "You wouldn't want your deputies to learn more about where we're from."

"That's not a concern. I've told the deputies that you, June, a person who they believe is a resident of this area, found a way to open the portal to the outside. While out there, you met these other ladies who have been affected by radiation poisoning. While you were outside the portal, you were also exposed to high levels of radiation. As a result of the radiation poisoning, you all have developed wild ideas, including that there was never a Nuclear Armageddon of 2035 and that you are perfectly healthy.

"Once you have gone back through, I have instructed Dan on how to permanently close the portal. My deputies know to stay at least ten feet away from you at all times in order to not be exposed to the radiation that your bodies emit. If the madness from the radiation causes you to approach them or you try to run, they are to shoot because it would be a health threat for you to run free or get too close to them. Dan is the only deputy who is allowed in here, and he will visit you once per day to see if you are ready to return to the portal. He will also bring you food. He is allowed to stay no longer than one minute for each visit because any more would expose him to too much radiation."

"You've really thought this out," June said.

"I want to make sure there is not a repeat of what happened before," Petra said in her imperial, disobey-and-suffer-the-consequences voice. "June Stafford, you are no longer welcome on this side of the portal."

"Well then, consider us conscientious objectors to your dictatorial rule over this supposedly democratic society," June said. "We can stay in this jail as long as it takes."

"So be it. Deputy Dan will be in to see you in twenty-four hours. Maybe by then you will have reconsidered."

"But we haven't eaten yet today," Nyala said.

"I'm sorry, but you've already had your one visit for today. And the deputy has been exposed to more radiation than is safe for today." Petra walked in a measured pace towards the door.

Nyala leapt up from the bench. "But there isn't any radiation!"

Petra, hand on the button to call the guards, turned back. "So sad to see what the radiation has done to your brain. It's like you actually believe you've never been exposed to unsafe levels of radiation." Shaking her head, Petra turned back to the heavy security door and pressed the button. Not two seconds later, Dan opened the door and Petra slowly exited.

June's hands grasped the cell bars with white knuckles until the door slammed shut. She angrily pushed away from the bars and sat next to Mariela. Her shoulders slumped and tears streamed in rivulets down her face. Mariela embraced her and leaned her head so that it was touching her mother's. June wiped her nose with the sleeve of her uniform. "I knew Petra didn't particularly care for Grace—she didn't like that Grace had a mind of her own—but I never thought Petra could be so heartless. At least Dan cried when Grace died."

No one said anything. Amaya tried to think of something to say, but really, there wasn't anything to say other than what June had already said.

"How long will we stay here?" Mariela asked.

"Until we hear from Dan that Amoco has found a way to disable your chip," June said.

"Our plan depends on Dan?" Mariela asked.

Amaya didn't blame Mariela for sounding skeptical. She felt the same way.

"Yes," June said. "I still think he will come through for us. He owes it to Grace."

"You're putting a lot of faith in him."

"I know. I wouldn't blame you all if you thought the radiation poisoning had gotten to me."

"What if Petra is right and we are all suffering from radiation poisoning that has so addled our brains we don't know it?" Amaya asked. It was a ridiculous idea but she couldn't help but at least consider it.

"Then I say bring on the radiation poisoning." Nyala never met a challenge she didn't like.

"Wait, shouldn't we have superpowers?" Amaya asked.

Nyala laid down on the bench where she had been sleeping when Petra arrived. "Yes," she said, "my superpower is sleeping on extremely uncomfortable benches despite how hungry I am. So stop bugging me and let me sleep."

"Fine." Amaya sat down next to June and Mariela on the other bench. The coldness of the concrete bit into her back. "My superpower is ignoring you."

Mariela and June ignored them both.

~~~~~

After getting him through security at Panacea headquarters, Amoco had quickly scampered off to deal with some "pressing" matter, leaving Cooper alone to talk to Viola. Cooper knocked on the door to Viola's office and waited impatiently during the couple seconds it took her to open the door.

"Cooper!" Viola smiled. "This is unexpected. Come in. I was sorry to hear the news. Amoco told me that the solution we came up with for the kill switch didn't work."

The digi-wall by the sitting area was black—most likely Viola had been watching something on it that she didn't want to be seen. She closed the door behind him and motioned toward the couch facing the black
~~~~~

wall.

"Unfortunately, it didn't." He sat on the arm of the couch. No need to get too comfortable.

"Personally, I think Amoco was too conservative. He was afraid of setting it off when we tried to deactivate it." Viola slid, catlike, into a spot on the couch. "Amoco's approaches are always too conservative, in my opinion. That's why he failed at solving chip implantation in adults. He was never willing to take chances."

Cooper wasn't interested in debating Amoco's willingness to take risks with Viola, but he couldn't keep himself from defending Amoco. "If taking chances means leaving someone potentially brain-damaged after failed chip implantation, then I think Amoco's caution is a good thing."

"But consider, for example, someone with a working chip who has a traumatic brain injury. If the chip is still functioning, we can use it to compensate for the injury, but if the chip is damaged or non-existent, then the road to recovery can be very long indeed. Can't you see how much good it would do if the chip could be replaced? If everyone had the option of having a chip? What a difference it could make in so many lives!"

Cooper hated that everyone with a chip seemed to think not having a chip was such an awful thing. Like life wouldn't be worth living if their chips stopped working. "Remember who you're talking to," he said to Viola.

"I never forget you don't have a chip. But look how you managed to get by—first, you relied on your incredible memory and the advanced tech that the Staffords willingly shared with you. That took a lot of intelligence and access to tech that other people don't have. It also involved a certain level of dishonesty. Then you chose to disconnect from the world. I mean, look at you—you don't even wear an Everything!"

"It makes my skin itch."

"Other people without chips don't have any of those options—they have to go out and scrape by however they can. And frequently it is nothing more than scraping by."

"Your concern for others surprises me."

"You've always underestimated me. Did you come to get your artwork back?"

"It was a gift." He did want it back but they still needed it to spy on

Viola.

"I just thought maybe you had gotten what you wanted out of it? Or do you still want to eavesdrop on my conversations?"

"You knew?" How long had she known they were spying on her? The whole time? If the artwork's cover was blown then he was definitely taking it back.

"I'm not easily fooled." She seemed to think about this for a second, and then added, "Or at least not anymore." Undoubtedly, she still resented that he was able to fool her into thinking he was chipped when they first met.

"Everything you said, you were okay with us overhearing?"

"Of course. I knew it would intrigue you." She looked at the black wall. "I want to show you something." The wall changed to show a warehouse-like room a with high ceiling and bright, industrial lighting. In the middle of the floor there were about ten people with pasty skin and no clothes holding guns facing in the general direction of a mannequin. On the left side of the screen, towards the corner, there was a balcony, with people standing on it who appeared to be observing those in the center of the room.

"Who are those people?" He pointed to the pasty-skinned people standing completely still in the center of the room.

"They're cryogens. People who, when they died, decided to have their bodies cryogenically frozen in the hopes they could be cured and revived at a later date."

"I know what a cryogen is." It bothered him that Viola felt the need to explain it to him.

"We've done a pretty good job curing what ails them," Viola continued, "but it's generally accepted we will never be able to revive them. And even if we could, who would pay for it? And chips that were implanted prior to 2050 are all outdated and won't run well with the amount of information we have in Panacea currently. If we bring them back to life they would become a welfare class—effectively the same as those without chips but with even greater limitations because they will have no skills for coping in the world today and no established income streams."

Cooper resented that Viola considered people without chips to be a part of the welfare class, but then he couldn't really disagree with her. He was living off of Oscar's welfare, and a lot of other unchipped barely got by on the pay-for-view advertising supplement.

And he had to admit, it was impressive she had gotten the cyrogens to stand up and hold rifles. "You can't revive them but you can get them to stand up?"

"Exactly! It was the tech from Mariela's kill switch that did it. Once I saw how it was constructed, it was a short jump to figuring out how I could use it to control cryogens as long as they had a chip. Did you know we have over 214,000 cryogens with chips in storage?"

"That's not something I'd be likely to know."

"Of course not. But it's enough to make a small army."

Nothing seemed to be happening on the screen. The three people on the balcony appeared to be talking among themselves but that was it. "What are we looking at?" Cooper asked.

"Training. I've asked them to hold off until we we're ready." She stood up and moved closer to the screen. "Okay, go ahead and proceed."

The people on the balcony, who had looked bored, now looked fully engaged in whatever was happening there. Was that bulletproof glass surrounding the balcony? Whatever the cryogens were doing with the guns looked like it wasn't quite under control yet. A man standing on the balcony made a motion with his hand. All the cryogens simultaneously raised their guns and pointed them at the mannequin.

"The mannequin has been tagged by the controllers as the enemy." She pointed to the people on the balcony when she mentioned the controllers.

The cryogens, again in a coordinated maneuver, pulled the triggers on their guns. One fell over backwards while another shot straight through the one in front of it. He was aiming at the target, but directly in between the target and the shooter was another cryogen that ended up taking the bullet in the back. Viola winced and turned away as the blood spurted out of the open wound in the cryogen's chest. Still looking slightly ill, she said, "Eventually it will lose enough fluids that it falls to the ground." The remaining cryogens lowered their guns.

"Fluids?"

"We fill them with a special cocktail to keep them running. They don't have any blood."

"Then why is it red?"

"Coloring the fluid made it easier to see when it was leaking. And some of the staff found anything other than red to be creepy because it looked like they were bleeding blue or green."

The red spots on the floor that Cooper hadn't looked closely at before now were clearly fluid from the cyrogens. This must have happened quite a few times. "Losing a lot of cryogens, are you?"

"Too many." On the screen, a pair of techs came out and dragged the fallen cryogen out a door off to the side. "We've stopped even trying to clean up in between attempts." Viola startled him by grabbing his arm. "You can see why we need you. I need you to help us come up with a system of efficiently distinguishing friend from foe, of helping them not kill each other, and other logistics. The movement part I think we've mastered—we're still making some tweaks to it but it's close to ready." Another cryogen walked with a wide stance onto the floor to take the place of the one that was shot. It wasn't natural enough to pass for a still-living human, but it was impressive how Viola's people were able to control its walking.

"Were you doing this instead of working on the solution for Mariela's kill switch?"

"I only started working on it after Amoco and I had already come up with a plan for the kill switch and Amoco was pulling it all together and didn't need my help. As you can tell, I've been working on this pretty intensively for the last three days—I haven't even been home to shower or change my clothes, but I would never put this above Mariela's well-being."

Now that she mentioned it, her clothes did look unusually rumpled. If she wore digi-skin, she could have avoided wrinkles and the slight smell they seemed to have. Whether she was being truthful about putting Mariela's well-being first was less clear.

The new cryogen was in place. The controller ran back towards the observation room.

"What are you going to use them for?" Cooper asked.

"There are some high-value targets in the Arctic, but anything we use to get close to the target, either human or machine, has a heat signature the enemy can detect and use to destroy it. The cryogens are unique in that they have almost no heat signature. We have drones that will be far enough away to be useful in controlling the cryogens but not so close as to be shot down. We'll use the drones to aim the cryogens towards the target and to determine human or machine targets for them to shoot at. Other than that, the details are pretty much up in the air. That's what I need your help with."

Viola jumped as another training exercise resulted in a repeat of the previous demonstration. She turned to the screen and yelled, "Can you all *stop* that until you figure out a better way for it to work?" She turned back to Cooper and sat down on the couch. "Cooper, you know this will save lives. If we don't send these cryogens in, we will be sending still-living humans. And we will never revive the cryogens." She flicked off the screen. "What do you say, will you help me out?"

"Why should I work with you? I don't exactly trust you."

"Because this isn't the same as before—we were in a romantic relationship and I was insecure and felt like you were hiding something from me. This time it will be purely professional. And you're the sort of person who can't say no to an important and interesting cause even if you're reluctant to do it."

Viola knew him better than he cared to admit—she was right that he was reluctant to work with her, but he would do it anyway. "We start with the ones that are the oldest."

"I agree. They are the hardest to control because their chips are the least advanced. If we can get those working then we should have an easy time with the others."

"Then I'm in." He grabbed his artwork off the wall. "And I'm taking my artwork back."

CHAPTER 14

Two Days Until the Umbrella Falls

Tuesday

Mariela was achy, cold, and hungry, and her butt hurt from sitting on the concrete bench. How long had they been sitting there with nothing to do? "No access to Panacea," Mariela said, "no messages, no blogs, no people, no nonsense. I never knew it could be this lonely."

"You get used to it after a while," her mother said, "and then it has the opposite effect. You feel less lonely and you stop missing Panacea." Mariela rested her head on her mother's shoulder. Nyala and Amaya were both attempting to sleep on the floor but appeared to failing.

"Is there anything you miss about your former life?" Mariela asked.

"I miss the people very much."

"Did you ever want to visit?"

"Of course I did. But I couldn't really do that, could I? I had Grace. I thought about taking Grace back and forth, but Petra wouldn't have allowed it. I also wanted Grace to have a semi-normal life."

Her mom had a point. When Mariela left Grace with her mother, she had made it almost impossible for her mother to leave. But there were so many times when Mariela could have used having her mother nearby. When she needed someone to talk to. To give her advice. To comfort her.

The buzzing of the door alarm announced the arrival of a visitor to the holding cell area. It was unusual, as Dan has already brought them their one meal that day. There also hadn't been anyone in the holding cell opposite during the entire two days they had been there. Or was it three? Dan had brought them food once, so maybe it was two days. The lack of sunlight in the holding cells was messing with Mariela's brain, and she was losing track of time.

A bit of sunlight streamed into the holding area as the door opened. So it was daytime. Dan held the heavy door for Petra. Petra looked almost cheery in a flowered shirt and multiple gold bangle bracelets. She stopped in front of the door to the cell and turned to Dan, "You can leave."

Dan nodded and headed out the door.

The sour expression on her face made it clear Petra wasn't feeling cheery, despite her bright clothing. "Why haven't you all left yet?"

"We like it here."

"Please do not make light of this. We need these holding cells, and the longer you stay here the more you interrupt the business of law enforcement."

"You could let us go."

"Don't anger me or I will make your incarceration permanent. Why haven't you had Dan escort you back to where you came from?"

"I can't go back," Mariela blurted out. Considering that two, or three, days had passed and Amoco hadn't contacted them, at least according to Dan, she might as well start getting used to the idea that she could be here a long time.

"Has the portal malfunctioned?" Petra asked. "Are you physically incapacitated in some way? Have you committed a crime for which you wish to avoid incarceration? What in heaven's name could be so serious that it keeps you from returning?"

"Someone placed a substance around my chip that they can use to spy on me or, they said, kill me if I don't do what they want. I think they're dead now, but I don't know who has access to the codes or where the substance came from. I can't leave until someone figures out a way to deactivate it."

For a brief moment Petra looked disconcerted. Maybe that woman wasn't all ice-cold steel after all. But then she recovered her composure. "If you hadn't gone placing electronics on your brain where they don't belong, you wouldn't have to worry about this sort of thing."

Mariela huffed and rolled her eyes. "Thanks, that's helpful."

"What did the substance look like?"

"Mercury. And it looked like it was boiling."

"Did it sting when it was injected?"

"It stung like hell. I thought I was going to die."

"These people, the ones who had the substance, do you know where they got it from?"

"No, that's part of the problem. We don't know where it came from, who has the access codes to it, or if they have more of the substance."

"I know where it came from, but not how they got a hold of it. Or who might have access to it now."

"You do?" Petra had Mariela's attention. Even if Petra didn't have all the details about the kill switch, Mariela would take whatever she could get. "You have information?"

"Didn't I just say that?"

Didn't Petra understand what a rhetorical question was? "Where did it come from?"

"I created it back in the mid 2030s."

"And no one knew about it for…eighty-five years?" Nyala asked. "Why haven't we heard of it before now?"

"Yes, it was eighty-five years ago." Petra looked like it was trying her patience to talk to people she considered to be so slow. "Let me walk you through what happened. Around 2030, five years before this colony was founded, the first chips were implanted in humans as a result of my research for Panacea Corp. In the following years, it appeared the chips were going to be successful. But despite my success as a young researcher, I became concerned about the implications of my work. We were running headfirst into adopting more and more complicated technology that we didn't really understand or have the ability to control.

"When the government asked me to create a way for chips to be monitored so they could use it for espionage, I was reluctant, but complied. Around that time, I found the people who had the idea for this colony, but they were having difficulty making it happen. I was curious about what they were doing but couldn't see myself signing on for such isolation. I liked creating new technology too much to give it up for tech that was decades old. Even so-called smartphones weren't going to be allowed, and I had a hard time imagining life without one." Petra snorted at the memory.

"What's a smartphone?" Nyala asked.

"Shush! Let me finish, and then you can ask questions. The final straw was when they asked me for technology they could use with certain groups of people—foreign leaders and the like—using the threat of death as a way of manipulating them and the monitoring function as a way of tracking compliance. I created what they asked for, it was just like this kill switch that you are describing. But I couldn't shake the feeling I had created something evil. Before I gave the formula to anyone, I destroyed it. I made sure every single backup, every single snippet of the formula, was obliterated. And I committed myself to building what you see here."

She lifted her arms.

"But nothing is ever completely erased," June said.

"Unfortunately, that appears to be true. Someone must have found the formula and reconstructed it."

"But this is good news," Mariela said. "If you created the formula then you must know how to deactivate it. Or you can figure it out, if you're so brilliant."

"Nothing about you makes me want to help you with your predicament. You abandoned your child here and you're disrespectful to your elders. My only motivation is to get you out of here. But no matter my willingness to help, you're still out of luck because what you call a kill switch can't be deactivated. Once the substance has been injected, it attaches to your DNA and gets into your bone marrow. The only thing you can do is disable or block your chip because whoever has the codes needs the chip to communicate with the substance. So instead I suggest you find a way to permanently block your chip."

"Is there nothing else that can be done?"

"How do you feel about DNA editing and bone marrow transplants? Have those procedures gotten any less risky over the years?"

Mariela felt so tired. "Still risky." Up until this point, she had been hopeful things would work out, but now that she was finally getting some answers, she was losing hope that she could both keep her chip working and be safe.

"You can always disable your chip. There are bigger concerns, even more serious than your self-centered worries that could be easily solved by deactivating your chip."

She ignored Petra's jab about her chip. Obviously, Petra didn't understand how important a working chip was. "And those concerns are?"

"Whoever found this code could use it on others. It's part of the reason I destroyed it. No person or government should have that kind of power."

"I think we all agree on that," Mariela said.

"Do you think the people who injected you were the ones to find the formula?"

"I don't think they had the intelligence." The brutes were obviously pawns in the game, not the mastermind.

"Can you ask them where they got it from?"

Mariela rolled her eyes. "They're dead."

"Do you know who they were working with?"

"The digital ghost—avatar is probably the term you are familiar with—for the CEO of Panacea Corp gave the substance to the goons who injected me."

"Can you ask him?"

"Deleted."

It was Petra's turn to roll her eyes. "If you wouldn't keep deleting or killing everyone who might have some answers, this would be easier."

"I didn't say I did any of those things."

"I'm sure your hands were dirty in some way."

"Can you help us with this or not?"

"I will not. It won't affect the people living here, as June is the only one with a chip, and she is expected to be leaving with the rest of you." Petra looked at June as if she could stare her out of Area 52, and then returned to her usual haughty look. "My concern is only the people under my umbrella; I washed my hands of the rest of you long ago."

CHAPTER 15

One Day Until the Umbrella Falls

Wednesday

The cat was nowhere to be seen when Georgia arrived on the other side of the tesseract. She checked the date. It was Wednesday. It was hard to believe that in what felt like seconds, she had lost three days.

Seconds later, his hair sticking straight out, Hank emerged from the tesseract. It was the happiest she had been to see Hank since Grace died. There were a lot of things she was worried about—she worried she wouldn't be able to find the cat, and if she did, she wasn't sure she would be able to get it back through the tesseract without being clawed to the point of needing stitches. Leaving the cat in the unforgiving desert wasn't an option. Facing a difficult task, she was glad to have Hank's company.

"That was wild," Hank said. "Three days gone in a second!" He smoothed down his hair, or tried to. It was still full of static, and it popped back up as soon as his hand passed over it. Hank laughed. "You should have left your hair long—imagine how ridiculous it would look sticking a foot out from your head."

Georgia had to admit it would have been amusing. "I wonder what the cat looks like." They both laughed at the idea of the long-haired cat with his fur sticking straight out.

The cat carrier appeared mid-air where the tesseract was and went flying past them. It clattered to the ground near some bushes.

"Well, that was helpful," Hank said as he went over to pick it up.

"I don't suppose they could have sent some tuna as well?" Georgia said.

Georgia wiped away of bead of sweat before it could roll into her eye. It was boiling hot, and she didn't look forward to spending any more time in the heat than necessary. "One thing that was nice about living in Panacea—I didn't have to deal with heat like this. I never missed having sweat rolling down my back."

"That's because you never felt anything at all."

Hank had a point. Temperature, in particular, was difficult to replicate in Panacea, so most people didn't bother trying.

Georgia walked around the area, looking for signs of the cat. The desert had a surprising number of hiding places. Large creosote bushes that a cat could easily fit under, small rolling hills that would hide a running cat, and large cat-sized holes in the ground that Georgia did not want to go sticking her hand into. She sighed. They were never going to find the cat.

"Found her!" Hank called out from beside one of the bushes. Georgia joined him and saw the cat, hunkered down under one of the low-lying bushes. It looked ready to make a break for it at any moment.

"Can you get the carrier and I'll see if I can get close?" she asked.

"Sure."

"Move slowly."

Moving at a snail's pace, Georgia sat down and, with the utmost patience, scooted ever closer to the cat. Hank grabbed the carrier and knelt nearby. Georgia moved one inch closer; the cat moved deeper under the bush.

"Let me try," Hank said. Georgia sat back and let Hank have some space.

He talked to the cat in a low voice and moved steadily towards it. "Midnight." His voice was smooth and lyrical. "How've you been? A lot has happened since I last saw you. I bet a lot has happened in your life as well."

The furry thing actually moved toward Hank and shoved its head into his hand. Hank scratched the kitty under the ears. It was like Hank and the cat were best friends. He picked it up, scratched him under the chin, and then slipped him into the carrier.

"My cat never would have gone into the carrier that easily," Georgia said. "You're like the cat whisperer."

"Cats like me." He scratched the cat on the head and then closed the carrier door. "We had a bunch of orphan kittens once at the res-home that I grew up in. I bottle-fed them until they could live on their own. When they got bigger, they would all sleep on me at the same time. Sometimes I couldn't move when I woke up in the morning." He stood and picked up the carrier. "Shall we head back? Waste another three days passing through the tesseract?"

"Can you put Midnight in the shade for a bit? I have a lot of angry clients who are wondering why they haven't heard from me in three days. I think there's enough of a signal here I can send them some message about how I've been sick and they probably won't hear from me for another three days."

"Sure, but what shade?"

"How about the tree over there?" She pointed to a tree that couldn't be more than seven feet tall. Its small crown provided a couple feet of spotty shade.

"Okay, I'll put the cat under that 'tree.' But it's really hot out here so let's not stick around too long."

"I'll be quick."

The three of them wedged themselves into the partial shade of the tree. Georgia contacted her clients as quickly as she could. She also requested that T-Rock join her at Above the Zócolo, one of her favorite cafés in the Panacea metaverse. It was odd to feel so far from home but also to be able to access all the places where she normally spent time in the metaverse. The mixture of familiarity and unfamiliarity was disconcerting.

T-Rock joined her on the spongy cloud above Zócolo Square not long after she made the request. He embraced her in a big hug. "How's the cat hunting going?"

"We found the little furball," she told him. "We're heading back now—can you send someone to pick us up in three days?"

"Sure. I'll ask Oscar if I can use the hovbus to get you all. Is the cat okay?"

"He's a little extra fluffy from going through the tesseract, but otherwise he seems to be doing good."

The ghost waiter appeared at their table. "Can I take your order?"

"I'm not going to get anything," Georgia said. The idea of tasteless and temperature-less coffee no longer appealed to her. "Are you going to get anything?" she asked T-Rock.

"No. Don't think I will."

"If you're going to sit at a table, you have to order something," the waiter said.

"I'd better get going anyway," she told T-Rock as she stood up. "It's really hot out there and Hank and the cat are waiting for me."

"You must vacate this table," the featureless ghost said in a monotone voice.

Georgia laughed. "We're going! T-Rock, I'll see you in three days."

"Be careful out there." T-Rock hugged her. "Remember what I always say: 'Mother nature is like having a best friend who sucker punches you for no reason.' She'll kill you sooner or later, so let's make that later."

"Thanks, T-Rock." His folksy advice soothed Georgia's jangled nerves.

"Especially watch out for the rattlesnakes."

"Will do," she said.

She exited Panacea and immediately wiped the sweat out of her eyes.

"Are you ready to go?" she asked Hank.

"Almost," Hank said. "Before we go, I just wanted to say it has been really nice spending time with you again." He fiddled with the handle on the carrier. "I miss how warm my bed is when you're in it. I miss how warm my place is when you're there. It all seems cold now."

"I miss that too, but I'm still trying to figure some stuff out."

"Okay." Hank's voice was small.

She had gone through a time of contemplation and meditation during the last week, hoping to understand if their relationship was salvageable. It wasn't just that Hank's impulsiveness and immaturity played a role in Grace's death, it was also that she wasn't prepared for the closeness that had developed between them. She needed to figure out if they could still be friends, and what their friendship might look like.

A trickle of sweat slithered down her back. "I hope someday we can be friends, but I'm not sure it will ever be like it was."

"Don't say that. When you were staying with me was the best time of my life. When I'm with you, it feels easy and not like any relationship I've had before."

It felt like her heart was breaking. His sincerity, his openness, the innocence with which he expressed his feelings, it was at times like these Georgia remembered why she had become friends with him in the first place. But she couldn't mislead him. She had to be honest with him, even if it was painful for them both.

"I just can't be friends right now, and I'm not sure if I ever will be able to."

The cat let out mournful meow. Was it really taking Hank's side?

"Come on, let's go," she said. There wasn't any way she could make this better while sweating out half her body weight onto the hard desert ground. She used the skirt of her dress to wipe the sweat and tears from her eyes.

Hank sniffed, wiped his nose on the argyle sweater that he had worn for the memorial service because Grace had given it to him, and picked up the cat carrier. He paused for a second, like he was going to say something to her, but then turned away. He said, "See you in three days," and then walked into the tesseract with the cat.

~~~~~

Business Today

"All the business news you need to know"

April 17, 2115

By Elliat Exis ~ *Business Today's* newest staff reporter!

Curious Truth-Seekers Converge on Mysterious Site
As my loyal followers will remember, I recently reported about strange happenings in the area commonly called Area 52. An area of much speculation, some think Area 52 is a secret military installation conducting experiments in time travel, as temporal distortions have been noted around the area. Recent events witnessed by this reporter and reported in this blog have only heightened speculation.

I am currently reporting from where I witnessed the unusual appearance and disappearance of some of the individuals who may be associated with the recent Black Screen. As you can see in the background, there are hundreds of concerned citizens here with me, including alien enthusiasts, conspiracy devotees (this reporter happily counts himself as one of them), and folks who are just plain curious about what's going on.

Was the Black Screen a military experiment? Possibly one that did not result as expected? Share your thoughts here, or better yet, come join us as we try to get to the bottom of this mystery and hold the perpetrators of the Black Screen accountable!

~~~~~

Cooper had his viewing area set up for maximum comfort. It started with moving the lounger over by the windows in the estate's library, and then he added soda and popcorn. He settled into the cushiony lounger, used the control panel to turn the windows into viewing screens, and cycled through the various news programming until he found one showing Elliat.

He was allowing himself fifteen minutes to watch the various random groups that had shown up to the portal opening, and then he would get to work on the cryogens. Today his goal was to keep the cryos from shooting each other. The key was to find a way to have the cryogens recognize obstacles that were between it and its target.

On the screen, Elliat was keeping up a continuous narration while training his camera on the people around him. Elliat didn't blink an eye when a woman ran across the screen with her hair on fire. Two men ran behind her with a blanket. Elliat's camera followed the woman, who dunked her head into someone else's ice bucket. Elliat zoomed in on the woman. Cooper leaned forward, waiting to see if she was okay. She picked her head up and one of the men aggressively toweled it off with the blanket. When the blanket was finally removed, the woman looked fine, but almost all her hair other than the inch or so closest to her scalp was gone.

The feed was interrupted by a contact request from Helema. Cooper shut Elliat off and put the call from Helema on hold, moved the recliner upright, ran his fingers through his shaggy hair before turning on the video, and answered the call.

Helema was sitting at her desk. "You're looking cleaner and not in the least bit homeless today." She glanced at the room behind him, her eyes sweeping from side to side. "Wow, that's more books than I have ever seen in one place. You're the luckiest person in the world."

"I sure am." He was only half sincere. Having access to the Stafford library was a great gift, but what would make him feel lucky at this point in his life was to have his old job back.

Helema cleared her throat. "I'm pleased to say we have decided to offer you your job back, and with a 10 percent raise for the hassles you've been through. You'll get your office and teaching load back. How does that sound?"

It sounded perfect. "I'm happy to accept your offer, but I do have some other projects I need to finish out first."

"No problem. The classes we want you to teach are starting in two weeks, so can you start next week?"

It would be tight, but a week should be enough time to finish his work on the cryogens, find a new place to live closer to campus, and get a haircut. He smiled. "I'll see you in a week!"

"See you then." Helema signed off and the window went black.

Cooper couldn't stop smiling. He had his old job back.

~~~~~

Amaya had tried every sitting position possible, but she couldn't get comfortable. The cells weren't meant for people to stay in overnight, much less spend days in. They had all started to smell days ago, and Mariela still had the circle that Cooper had drawn on the back of her neck. Amaya's latest unsuccessful attempt to find a comfortable sitting position involved sitting on the floor with her back resting against the concrete bench and her legs folded in front of her. It helped but everything still hurt.

"This would be the most boring Zazora quest ever." Nyala reclined on the other concrete bench with her knees bent and her hands behind her head. "Think about how boring it would be if they had a quest in the Zazora games where the goal was to stay alive, but that involved being locked in a plain, concrete jail cell with no distractions and no windows and where the players were fed only once per day. You didn't have to escape—you just had to do nothing and stay alive. And be lectured occasionally by a 101-year-old woman." Nyala sighed. "It would be the most boring game ever."

Amaya avoided rolling her eyes. Of course it would be boring. That's why the course designers came up with interesting scenarios. Which this was not.

Nyala sat up. "And even more incredible, imagine that the players sat there for three days and never once talked about the elephant in the room. Not even once."

"What elephant in the room?" Mariela asked.

"THE elephant in the room." Nyala sat up. "I want to know what happened to Opali. I want to know why the ghosts were deleted. Why you put Grace in danger. Why you thought it was okay to involve Amaya without her permission. Here we are, stuck in a jail for three days,
~~~~~

because you got in over your head and pissed off the wrong people."

"That's not fair!" Mariela said. "The kill switch was to keep me from reporting Liam's murder, or attempted murder that is, and I think LP also planned to use it to force me to help him gain control over Panacea Corp."

Turning to face Mariela, Amaya propped an arm on the bench. "But what about everything else?" How could Mariela act like she didn't have anything to apologize for? "No one forced you to delete the ghosts."

"The way I see it, the kill switch and Liam getting killed, I mean LP attempting to kill him, are signs I did the right thing."

"But what about Opali? How could you delete your sister's kid?" Amaya knew what Mariela would say before she even said. Why did she bother trying to convince Mariela that Opali, even though she was a ghost, had deserved to live?

Mariela's face fell. "Opali was an unintended casualty."

June had tears on her cheeks, but she didn't say anything.

"And why didn't you tell me what you were going to do? You used me without my knowledge," Amaya said.

"Would you have agreed?"

"No."

"That's why I didn't tell you."

"Did you apologize to your sister for deleting her child?" Nyala asked.

"I can't apologize to Sofi because I can't admit what I've done. If I do that Liam will fire me and I'll be sent to prison. Real prison, not this concrete purgatory."

"If you're so sure your actions were correct, maybe you need to take responsibility for them," Nyala said.

Amaya inwardly cheered Nyala.

For five minutes no one said anything.

"We need to have a memorial service for Opali," June said.

"For goodness sakes," Mariela blew out her breath and rolled her eyes, "she wasn't a real person! She was a collection of ones and zeros, a very human-like collection of digital code. But she wasn't conscious, and she wasn't human."

"Are you so sure about that?" Nyala asked.

"She wasn't human," Mariela repeated, but more quietly and slowly, less sure of herself. Mariela turned to June, "Mom, I'm sorry I deleted your granddaughter." She sounded like she might actually be sincere.

June's eyes glistened. "I understand why you did it, even though I'm not sure I would have made the same choice." June grabbed Mariela's hand and held it resting on her knee. "It's not my place to judge—I haven't exactly been the grandmother of the year. In the decade since she's existed. I've never met Opali."

Oh right, Amaya had forgotten. Opali had only been around ten years, and June had been isolated in Area 52 for sixteen. Mariela's eyes were wet with tears now also. She threw an arm around her mother and hugged her close.

"Is that it?" Nyala asked. "Are we done talking about the elephant in the room? Are we just going to hug and forgive and forget?"

June shifted on the concrete bench. "I don't know about you," June said, "but I'm going to forgive."

The Day the Umbrella Fell

Thursday

Cooper switched a couple of the library windows to opaque and pulled up the footage of the cryogens. T-Rock had just joined him wearing a leopard print digi-skin robe.

"Thanks, T-Rock, for helping me out. I really appreciate it."

"No problem," T-Rock said. "I've been having some cabin fever. I'm not used to being stuck in one place like this. I feel like I'm a caged bear—a caged bear that's been bit by a rattlesnake. So I'm happy to have some distraction."

Cooper pulled one of the loungers over for T-Rock to sit in. T-Rock sat carefully, making sure not to jostle the leg the rattlesnake had bitten. Cooper pulled the other lounger by T-Rock and took a seat. He had made good progress on his work with the cryogens, but Cooper was hoping that T-Rock, with his tactical experience from the Zazora Games and logistical intelligence, could help him deal with some stubborn remaining issues.

Cooper ran his fingers through his hair. It felt cool and neat after getting it cut shorter than it had been in a long time. Mariela's father had no problem with him using the library as a workspace, and the wall of digi-windows was perfect for viewing the cryogen training captures.

"I've figured out how to get the cryos around obstacles," Cooper pointed to the screen showing a cryogen in the training warehouse negotiating a barricade he had asked the controllers to set up.

"Cryos?" Rock asked.

"The cryogens. I've been calling them cryos for short." Cooper switched to another capture of the cryos executing a maneuver. "I've also solved how to keep them from accidentally shooting each other and how to identify who or what to shoot at, but I'm still having problems with some of them falling over from the recoil of the gun. Once a cryo is down, it's difficult to get it back up again."

"Will there be someone to guide them or help them get back up if they fall over?"

"My goal is to get them to be able to operate independently with minimal intervention from a controller."

"I have a question," T-Rock said. "How do they not have any heat signature? Don't their bodies generate heat? And if they don't generate heat, what is fueling their muscles?"

"Viola created a concoction that she is injecting all the cryos with before they do any training. It provides nutrients to their muscles while also keeping their skin cool. All the heat is on the inside."

"That's clever, but doesn't their skin get damaged if it's cold?"

"Yes, but they aren't going to last long anyway. And they're already dead, so we can afford some skin damage."

"Are you sure you want to do this?" T-Rock's face was impassive, but his question implied judgment.

It was just like someone who had never been to war to underestimate the cost of lives lost. Cooper ran his fingers through his hair. "Have you ever seen someone die?"

"Can't say I have, other than Grace."

Cooper regretted asking. "Oh right, sorry. I saw lots of people die when I was fighting in the Arctic War, and I would have done anything to save the lives of those soldiers. If sending some bodies that have been frozen cryogenically for decades and that will never come back to life into battle saves lives, then I think that's the right thing to do, and I'll do it willingly."

"It just seems like it's going against nature to use these things," T-Rock said in his slow drawl. "But I'll help you out if you need it."

"Thanks, because I really need your help. Viola has been busy dealing with something else—I'm not sure what—so I don't have anybody to run things by."

The door to the library burst open and a harried-looking Amoco swept in, slamming the door behind him. "When you next converse with her, please inform Viola that I am not a messenger boy."

Cooper stood up. "What did she do?"

"It is more like what she did not do. You were not answering her contact request, so she contacted me to take a message to you."

"Oh right, I haven't checked my messages today."

"Once again, I have no clue how you survive."

"It's too much hassle to check messages. Especially when I get videos from coercive women who think they can control me."

"Your lack of connectedness affects not just you, but others as well. I hurried over from my place with great haste. If I had known you were with T-Rock, that would have made things much easier. But no never-mind. Let me queue up her message." Amoco activated one of the window viewing screens. "Do you mind if I watch it with you? I am most curious about the contents of a message that must be delivered with such urgency."

"No problem."

"Let us lose no time in viewing it then. Post-viewing, I intend to immediately continue my work on deactivating the kill switch. Viola has been absolutely no help this week with developing a way to deactivate it."

"Send the message to me and I'll put it on the screen," T-Rock said.

Seconds later a larger-than-life version of Viola's face was projected on the blacked-out window.

"Wow, it looks like she hasn't gotten any sleep since I saw her two days ago," Cooper said. "And she was already looking pretty sleep deprived then." Viola's hair stuck out in multiple directions, she had a smudge on her face she hadn't bothered to wipe off, and she must have given up on her usual high-end clothes because she was wearing scrubs that probably belonged to one of the techs. And even those were looking like she had slept in them, but at least they were self-cleaning digi-skin.

"Amoco, I hope you're there," Viola said, "there's something important you should know." She tried to run her fingers through her hair but they got stuck in the tangles. "I've figured out why our solution for deactivating the kill switch didn't work. The cryogens were acting odd, so I did some research on them, and I found out the substance changed their DNA and bone marrow."

That explained why the solution hadn't worked—it deactivated the substance in the area of the chip, but if Mariela's DNA had changed, then that was a different ball game.

"The only feasible way to fix the kill switch is for Mariela to disable her chip."

Viola's suggested wasn't what they had hoped for. If Mariela lost her chip, she would be...someone different.

"Cooper," Viola said, "I'm sorry to tell you I haven't been completely honest with you."

What was she saying?

Viola rubbed one of her eyes. "We haven't been training the cryogens for an Arctic assault, although maybe we will do that someday. We have been training them to carry out an occupation. But let me back up and explain some things first."

"Pause message," Cooper said. "What is she talking about? An occupation of where? Canada? I don't like where this is going," Cooper sighed before shaking his head. "Why do the women in my life always do this to me?"

"No clue," T-Rock said.

"I suggest we continue as it seems probable that Viola will explain what she is talking about," Amoco said.

"Of course. Sorry. I just can't believe I fell for her whole 'we are going to save lives' thing." He rolled his eyes. "Play message."

The video started. Viola made another attempt to run her hand through her hair, but made no progress in smoothing the tangled mess. "Cooper, when we started, I was honest with you about my intentions, but I couldn't stop thinking about who created the kill switch. It's incredibly advanced tech, not just anyone could make it. I know it wasn't Amoco, and it wasn't me, so who was it? I started looking through the archives to figure out who else was capable, and I couldn't find anyone. Until I got to this one brilliant neuroscientist, Petra Dmitrova."

"Oh no." That wasn't good. Viola was getting too close to Area 52. Cooper resisted an urge to bite his fingernails.

"She had the skills," Viola continued. "Hell, she was better than Amoco and me combined. She developed chip implantation in humans in the first place. But she disappeared eighty years ago. Not dead, or if she's dead, her body was never found, just disappeared."

"Pause message," Amoco said. "Isn't she the woman who created Area 52?"

"Yes." Cooper didn't mean to be short with Amoco, but he needed to see where this was going. "Continue message."

"It took a lot of digging, and many of the files have been erased and I wasn't able to recover all of them…"

Well at least that was a bit of good news.

"…but what I eventually found was fascinating. Petra Dmitrova set up a colony that is cut off from the rest of the world. They were granted land by Panacea Corp for the colony, but only in exchange for allowing

Panacea Corp to put a server farm deep underground and to be able to access the servers on occasion. They were supposed to stay in contact with us, but about twenty years ago, in 2095, they stopped responding. Maybe Petra died, I don't know."

Petra had chosen to stop responding, but Viola wouldn't be able to find that piece of information in the Panacea Corp archives.

"I need to talk to Petra if she's alive," Viola continued, "as I'm almost certain she developed the kill switch. The way I see it, they are in violation of the agreement they had with Panacea Corp. So I plan to take down what they call the 'umbrella'—the tesseract and Faraday cage they use to isolate themselves."

Crap! "Pause message." Viola was talking about an assault on Area 52. Those weren't Viola's words, but that's what she was saying. Cooper needed a second to catch his breath before continuing. He focused on the rhythm of his breathing. In. Out. In. Out. "Continue message."

Viola seemed to lose track of what she was saying. She refocused and continued. "I've looked into the tech Petra used to create the umbrella, and it should be pretty easy to disable as our technology is more advanced now."

So far Viola had been accurate in everything she had discovered. And if she said she knew how to take down the umbrella, then she was almost certainly able to do so. Cooper didn't want to hear what Viola had to say next, but he couldn't stop listening.

"I've been moving the cryogens since this morning using large army buses. They should be on site by the time you get this. I want to be clear: this is an occupation, not an invasion. They have defaulted on their agreement, so we are going to take our land back."

"Pause message." The image of Viola talking froze. "Amoco, when did you get this?"

"Approximately an hour ago," Amoco said sheepishly. "I may have run a few errands after receiving it in defiance of my mandated role as a messenger."

"So this 'occupation' could be starting at any time? Or may have already started?"

"That seems plausible."

"Can you pull up the satellite footage?

"Of course. While I do that, shall we finish watching the capture?"

Cooper said, "Continue message."

On the video, Viola's eyes started to close and she swayed to one side. Startling awake, she continued speaking. "Thank you, Cooper, for all the work you've done. I couldn't have done it without you. I'm sorry for not telling you all this personally, but this occupation needs to happen soon so I can make sure the kill switch isn't part of some plot for a takeover, and I didn't have time to debate the moral implications with you. Just so you know, I told Liam about this and he has sanctioned the occupation. I don't plan on killing anyone if I don't have to—just those that shoot at us."

This couldn't get any worse. Liam was the last person who should know about Area 52. If he knew about the invasion, then that meant he probably knew about the kill switch, and if he knew about the kill switch, there was no telling how he might use it.

Liam blamed Mariela for deleting the ghosts, including his avatar; he suspected she was behind the recent large outage of Panacea, and he probably thought she was the one who tossed him from his helicopter. Would he use the kill switch against her?

The video switched off and Amoco changed the projection to the satellite footage. He zoomed in on the coordinates where Area 52 was located and panned around until he found some large vehicles and unusual movement to the north. Amoco zoomed in further and thousands of cryogens slowly came into focus.

"That's a large army," T-Rock said. "I don't see any way this could end in a positive outcome."

Cooper had to agree. It was not going to end well. The people of Area 52 would defend their land, the cryogens would fire back, and people would get shot. June, Amaya, Nyala, and Mariela would be in the middle of it all.

"I don't think Viola realizes that's where Mariela is staying," Cooper said.

"I was just wondering about that," T-Rock replied. "Do you think Viola is taking down the Faraday cage without realizing she is putting Mariela at risk?"

"I can't say for sure," Cooper sat down in the lounger, "but all we told Viola was that Mariela was going to stay in one of Amoco's Faraday cages. And this isn't even one of Amoco's Faraday cages. There's no reason for Viola to think that Mariela is there."

"Should we contact Viola and let her know?" T-Rock asked. "Maybe she will at least delay the invasion if she knows it will expose Mariela to danger."

It might buy them some time.

"Cooper, I hate to interrupt," Amoco said, "but I think you should see this satellite footage." Amoco backed up the news segment that he was watching.

The news coverage showed side by side captures, presumably aerial footage of Area 52. One showed an expanse of un-remarkable desert, brown and uniform in appearance. The time stamp read ten minutes earlier. The other appeared to be of the same area, but showed steep hillsides with varied shades of green and corrugated fissures that Cooper recognized as the mountainous slopes they had walked up.

It was clear they were too late to stop Viola from taking down the umbrella; whatever tech Petra had used to shield the area from the outside world was no longer working.

"See if one of you can get ahold of Mariela and tell her what's happening," Cooper said. "Let her know she needs to put her headband back on." Cooper shook his head. "She's going to hate that."

"I can't reach her," T-Rock said. "Amoco, what about you?"

"I have also failed to reach Mariela. Let me try the communication device." There was a pause. "I hear a noise, let me put it on speaker." There was a noise like a bell ringing. After ten seconds, the ringing stopped.

"Hello?" a familiar man's voice said.

"Dan?" Amoco asked.

Of course, that's why the voice was familiar.

"Who's this?"

"This is Amoco Cadiz speaking."

"Oh, hey Amoco. Took you long enough to call."

"You see, we have some concerns here, and it is imperative I get ahold of Mariela as soon as possible." Amoco paused. "I am confused, why are you in possession of the communication device?"

"Oh, you mean the phone?"

There was a noise on the other end that Cooper couldn't quite place.

"Amoco," Dan's quickly spoken words were low and quiet, "I gotta go." With a click the line went silent.

~~~~~
~~~~~

Cooper switched the feed to Elliat's broadcast.

"For those of you just joining us," Elliat was saying, "you need to see this incredible footage. I'm at the area where the suspects in the Black Screen mysteriously appeared and disappeared last week, where incredible things are happening. Let's take a look at that footage again."

Elliat switched to a recorded exo-cam capture that had a flashing time stamp saying it was taken ten minutes before. It was a shot of Elliat talking. To one side of him, the air shimmered. Elliat turned his exo-cam in the direction of the disturbance. The shimmer intensified and then with a shudder, the desert disappeared and the mountains burst into view.

Cooper's breath caught in his throat. Even knowing they were there didn't make the sudden appearance of the mountains any less spectacular.

There was a roar from the motley bunch of eccentrics assembled outside of the umbrella protecting Area 52. On both sides of the exo-cam, people rushed toward the ledge that would get them to the narrow road that wound up to Area 52.

The most athletic scrambled up the fifteen-foot rocky ledge and stood triumphantly atop it. "There's an old road up here!" one called out. "It goes up the hill." Another roar went up from the crowd, and there was another rush of people towards the ledge. Some scrambled up the face of the steep hillside while the others queued at a point that had a steep but more accessible pathway up to the ledge. Cooper recognized it as where the entry portal to Area 52 had been.

Elliat turned his exo-cam back on himself. "This rush into the unknown is unwise, but what kind of journalist would I be if I didn't join them?" And with that declaration, he took off running to the ledge. The exo-cam followed him, showing him from behind with the newly revealed mountains in the background, first trying to scramble up the ledge, and then sheepishly changing his mind and queuing in the line for the gentler slope.

"Holy hell." T-Rock leaned forward and stared at the screens. "Those people, the ones hanging out where the portal used to be, it's like the only reason they're there is to gawk at everything that is going on around them. Between the cryogens and those people...those *gawkers*"—he pointed with his jaw at the window where the wave of people was running up the hill—"Area 52 is in bad shape."

~~~~
~~~~

"Do you think Trevor is worried about us?" Amaya asked Nyala. "When we asked him to take care of our pets, we didn't anticipate being gone so long."

"We're paying him by the day, so I'm sure he won't mind," Nyala said.

"Right, but will he *worry*?"

"Amaya, find something else to worry about."

"Right." There were so many other things to worry about, it wouldn't be difficult to come up with something. But inside the jail few of them seemed very pressing. "Do you think sitting on these benches with no pillows and not getting exercise will do permanent damage to our bodies?"

"I don't know. Can you limit yourself to asking your questions only once per day?" Nyala was clearly getting annoyed, which Amaya found oddly pleasing. The boredom seemed to be bringing out the worst in all of them.

"Have I asked that already today?" Amaya asked. "It's so difficult to keep track of the days in here. Without better ability to track time, I'm not sure I can promise that."

They had received three meals since arriving, so they had probably been there for three days. Or did that make it four? The meals were all exactly the same, so there wasn't much to remember them by.

Being stuck in a jail cell for four days, there was nothing to do but pick fights with the others. Was Dan being honest when he said he hadn't heard from Amoco? Had Amoco figured out a solution but hadn't been able to share it with them? And why did she stay? Amaya could leave at any time as long as she left Area 52, Nyala would certainly choose to go with her, and June would probably continue to keep Mariela company— so why did leaving not feel like an option?

Amaya sighed. She knew why they stayed—they stayed because Mariela was an old friend. And for all her faults, Mariela's decisions were almost always made with the intention of wanting to do the right thing.

The alarm buzzed on the security door. Amaya perked up. Something was happening. Petra made her way into the holding area. She was moving a lot faster today than usual, and everything about her demeanor said they were in trouble with her. Dan followed her in and stood by her with his hands clasped behind his back and his head down.

"What have you done?" Petra demanded as she approached their cage. It was more of accusation than a real question.

"Are we supposed to know what you are referring to?" June asked.

"Someone has destroyed the umbrella. Absolutely decimated it. There's a horde of folks coming up the accessway to the west, and a horde of…I don't know what they are coming down the plains from the north."

Everyone in the cell was sitting up and alert now.

Mariela stood up. "You mean we're connected to the rest of the world again?"

"Yes. Am I supposed to believe you didn't have anything to do with this?"

"I need my headband back," Mariela said to Petra. "I can't be connected to the soup."

"It's okay, Mariela." June stood up and took Mariela's hand. "There's no connection in here. The walls of the cell are thick and we're far away from any soup pools."

"You checked?"

"I checked." June nodded and rubbed Mariela's hand. "There's nothing."

That was one advantage of being stuck in a concrete jail cell.

June frowned at Petra. "You don't know what happened?"

"No idea. If it wasn't done by you all, then I'm sure it was done by some of your associates."

"Now that the umbrella is down, are you going to be honest with the people living here about what the rest of the world is like? That there is no radiation?"

"I don't see what there is to be honest about. A horde of undead humans is descending on us from your world," then Petra pointed at Mariela, "and *you* can't leave because you might die if you do, and your world treats people without chips so poorly that you felt you had to leave Grace here. Do you really think my characterization of what the world is like on the outside of the umbrella is really all that deceptive?"

No one argued with her.

"Come on, Dan," Petra said. "We have stuff to do and these people don't know anything. We can figure out what to do with them later."

CHAPTER 17

The Day the Umbrella Fell

Thursday, continued

"This is so exciting!" Elliat struggled to catch his breath. "Can you believe what we've seen here today? This is so exciting!"

If Elliat said "this is so exciting" one more time, Cooper was going to drive the six hours to Area 52, grab Elliat's stupid exo-cam, and stomp on it. The umbrella had been down for about an hour, and the walk up the steep hill into Area 52 wasn't all that exciting or newsworthy by itself, so in his coverage Elliat had been reduced to repeating over and over again how exciting it was and recapping what had happened when the umbrella had come down. Cooper couldn't stop himself from watching, just in case some new development showed up, but every one of Elliat's breathless, repetitive reminders of his excitement when nothing new was happening grated.

Elliat paused to catch his breath. Beads of sweat dripped down his face. From what Cooper remembered of him, Elliat wasn't the sort to exercise and the steep gain in elevation on the road into Area 52 was enough to tire anyone. The late afternoon sun beating down on him probably didn't make it any easier.

"For those of you just tuning in…" Elliat panted with his hands on his knees and then yelled to someone up the road, "Hey guys, don't leave me behind." He stared up the hill, presumably at the people he had just been yelling at. Elliat turned to face his exo-cam again. "Gotta go. Will provide an update later." Then Elliat switched off the exo-cam feed.

Cooper almost felt sorry him—the poor guy had only left his pod a little over a week ago. He had probably lost a lot of muscle mass in that week.

Cooper switched screens. It was nice to be tracking the invasion, or 'occupation,' from the comfort of an armchair instead of being in the thick of it. On the northern front, the satellite imagery showed the cryogen army advancing in an orderly manner up the gentler slope of the plains. Did Viola know about Elliat's reporting? She hadn't mentioned anything about it in her message, and she had been so focused on the cryos the last couple days it was possible she hadn't been following the news. Which could lead to an interesting moment in about five hours, when Cooper estimated the two groups would meet up at a junction not far outside of SkyWater.

Amoco had tried without success to contact Viola and let her know about the group approaching from the other direction before he had fallen asleep on the couch. For whatever reason, maybe because she was in the middle of an invasion, Viola wasn't answering his contact requests.

Cooper divided the screens into two and threw the satellite feeds for both groups onto a split screen. He placed the cryogen army on one side and on the other screen, the eccentric group in the western part of Area 52. The cryogen army had the topographic advantage—for the moment their approach was a gradual uphill climb through fairly open plains. But the cyros had to go farther to reach the junction. The clumsiness of the cryogens also slowed progress, as they took their time figuring out how to get around obstacles and their walking speed could best be described as ambling.

The other group, the gawkers as T-Rock had called them, was spread further apart. The leading gawkers were almost running up into Area 52 while some were just starting the climb up the hill. They had the shorter route to travel, but it was more topographically challenging, so Cooper couldn't decide which group would get to the junction first.

Cooper placed Elliat's exo-cam feed into an overlay window. In addition to the two satellite feeds and Elliat's vid-blog, he added a thermal image. There were also at least two news helicopters circling overhead, and Cooper added their video feeds to the screens in insets. Cooper opened up one more screen and added a summarization program that would scan all news and social items posted publicly for information to identify any trends in the postings on Area 52.

As the light faded from the sky, the figures in the images started to blend into the background. Cooper switched the satellite feed to thermal imaging. The drawback of the thermal imaging, though, was that it only tracked the humans and not the cryos, but it was better than nothing. The cryos had their human keepers so there were a few red dots that Cooper used to outline the positions of the army.

T-Rock ambled into the library. "Anything exciting happen? Amoco still here?"

"Nothing interesting yet. Amoco is asleep over there." Cooper motioned with his head to an armchair tucked into the corner of the library where a sleeping Amoco was curled up. "Bren will also be here soon. He heard the news and figured this would be a good place to get information. I told him to come on over."

"Great," T-Rock said. "I'm going to get some coffee."

Bren arrived just as T-Rock was coming back with a coffee carafe and a tray full of mugs. They moved one more lounger over by the digi-windows for him. If they were going to spend the entire day keeping an eye on the news, at least they were going to do it in comfort.

Cooper focused back on the two screens. It shouldn't be long now before the two groups met up. While some of the gawkers had made it to the intersection before the cryos, it looked like the cryos were going to arrive en masse before most of the gawkers.

If he hadn't known people who were caught up in this, he would have been enjoying the whole thing. He would have sipped his coffee while kicking his feet up and making himself comfortable for some extended viewing. Instead, he was leaning forward, his elbows on his knees, trying to figure out what was going to happen and if he could do anything to keep the people he cared about safe.

T-Rock leaned toward Cooper. "You can't do anything to make it better."

T-Rock had read his mind.

"I know. I wish I could."

"It's like when sea turtles hatch, they have to make it to the water on their own. I don't blame you for wanting to go, but the women can take care of themselves. And remember, Area 52 has been June's home for the last sixteen years, so she will know her way around it better than Viola or Elliat, or anyone."

"I just wish there weren't so many variables to take into account. I'm not sure if I should be worrying about the gawkers ransacking SkyWater, or Petra shooting them, or the cryos shooting anybody, or Dan shooting somebody. Or the cryos losing control and wandering around in circles firing their rifles."

"Those undead things go against nature." T-Rock shook his head. "The only thing we can hope for is that they don't last and the heat does them in pretty quickly."

T-Rock was right—they hadn't expected to be operating the cryos in the heat. They were supposed to be in a frozen tundra. Who knew how the heat would affect them. At the very least they would probably start to smell soon. Unless all the nutritious anti-freeze running around in their veins kept them from decomposing.

It didn't help that Cooper hadn't solved the problem of what to put on their feet, so the cryos were walking barefoot. At least they had some clothing. There had been some discussion about whether to bother clothing them, but in the end a tech used old sheets to fashion some basic clothing for them. The sheets had a hole in the middle that the head went through, leaving the sheet to drape around the shoulders. A belt made of thin rope wrapped around the waist held the sheet in place.

The screen shifted to a stream from one of the helis. The light on the heli showed the cryos waiting, without any impatience, for their human handlers to give them the signal to start moving again.

"With sun going down and the cooler temps in the mountains, maybe they'll hold up." He was starting to think like their trainer again, but Viola was on her own now to figure things out. "Not that I'm rooting for them." Cooper blew on his coffee. "The cryos should be getting close to the junction now." Cooper zoomed in on the junction. Any minute now, gawkers would start running into cryos.

On the infrared image, a group of the red dots near the junction scattered in the direction away from the cryos. At about the point where the two groups were to meet, the red dots representing the gawkers on the infrared were going every which way. There was a lot of confusion going on down there that appeared to be startled gawkers running away from the cryogens. It looked like maybe they had finally met up. What he wouldn't give to see the look on the gawkers' faces when they saw the dead, oddly-clothed, rifle-carrying cryos lumbering towards them in neat rows of five.

The news summary alert beeped. Cooper made that screen larger to see what was new. At the top of the list of terms that were co-hitting with Area 52 was one fast-trending term—zombie. Cooper drilled down on the term and found exactly what he was expecting.

"Do you see that?" he said to T-Rock. The top result was a post titled, 'Zombie Army located in Area 52' with a capture of the neatly ordered cryos with their blank faces.

"That's about as accurate a description as you can get. Amoco needs to see this." T-Rock rolled Amoco's chair over to where they were watching the screens. Amoco, with his feet tucked up into the chair and his head resting on the armrest, didn't stir until T-Rock nudged him. "Hey Amoco, wake up. Things are happening."

Amoco startled awake and wiped a bit of drool off his mouth. "What? Sorry, I haven't slept much lately."

"Sorry to wake you but I think you're going to want to see this. The cryos and the gawkers are meeting up, and the gawkers are posting stuff about a Zombie Army in Area 52."

"I see that." Amoco went to the window and flipped through some of the posts on the screen. "They seem to think the cryos are part of Area 52…and that this is evidence that Area 52 is a military installation conducting experiments. Interesting." He flipped through to another article. "This one is saying they have to stop the 'Zombie Army' before things get out of hand and to bring guns."

"One of the helis is streaming what's happening." Cooper maximized the inset from the helicopter. Its spotlight intermittently highlighted the cryos and the gawkers. The capture cut away to the feed from another helicopter. This one was shining its spotlight on a jeep that was driving alongside the cyros. "Look!" Cooper pointed at the person sitting in the passenger seat of the jeep. "Is that Viola?" Cooper zoomed in. It *was* Viola, out there in the thick of her 'occupation.' The jeep pulled into a small camp with tents and tables that appeared to be where the cyro controllers were. Viola ran into a tent and the capture changed to another area.

For another fifteen minutes or so they watched the progress of the two groups—the cryos walking at a leisurely place and not taking any notice of the gawkers, and the gawkers having strong reactions to the cryos. Word must have been getting around though, that the cryos were not aggressive because many of the gawkers were walking carefully past but not shying away from them.

"How many do you think there are?" T-Rock asked.

"Cryos or gawkers?"

"Both."

"Viola said she was waking up 10,000 cryogens. I'm guessing that is how many are there. For the gawkers, let's see what the news has to say." Cooper scrolled through the summary a bit and then zoomed in on an article estimating the number of gawkers. "This article says there are probably about 3,200 gawkers currently camping at the foot of the mountain or walking up the hill. They spoke to an organization that predicts how many people will show up to events. The organization said that based on the number of people who said they were going, the number that would actually show up was around 20,000."

"20,000? What will they all do? Just wander around Area 52 like lost ducklings?" T-Rock asked.

"I don't know. I wish I did," Cooper said. "This post says that some of the gawkers are telling people to bring guns so they can shoot the cryos."

"I'm not worried about the cryos," T-Rock said, "but remember that Viola said that the cryogens weren't going to shoot anyone unless they were threatened. It sounds like if the gawkers start firing on the cryos, then the cryos will fire back."

"Cooper, look." Bren sat up in his seat. "Is that Panacea Corp's helicopter?"

A luxury helicopter landed near the camp where Viola was staying. One of the news copters nearby zoomed in to film the developing action. Viola emerged from her tent and went over to the helicopter.

"Zoom in on her," Cooper said.

"She doesn't look happy." Bren said.

Cooper leaned toward the screen to have a closer look. "Yep, there's Liam." A caneless and apparently healed Liam hopped out of the helicopter and was followed by two soldiers holding guns. "It looks like he's getting the military involved."

Viola approached Liam. She still looked like she hadn't showered in days. She probably hadn't slept either. Cooper couldn't hear what she and Liam were saying, but by their agitated hand movements and overall body language it was clearly a tense conversation. It ended when Liam grabbed her by the elbow and escorted her to the helicopter. She was still arguing with him but she didn't resist his attempts to guide her. At the door to the helicopter, Viola turned and looked back at the cryos. Then, with a visible sigh, she stepped in and closed the door behind her.

Nothing interesting happened for the next half hour. With new developments paused for the moment, Elliat had fallen back in to saying, "This is so exciting!" Cooper turned down the volume to low, fully reclined his lounger, and relaxed into the soft fabric of the chair.

"I just thought of something," T-Rock said. "Hank and Georgia went through the tesseract yesterday and aren't supposed to show up for two more days, but the tesseract's not there anymore. What will happen to them?"

"I have thought of that also, but did not want to mention it for a fear of alarming you all," Amoco said. "I think it is possible they will appear as planned. Imagine you have a time machine that can send you three days into the future, and you use that time machine, but then at some point during the intervening three days the time machine is destroyed, I think it is highly likely you will show up three days in the future because the time travel has already taken place, and the machine, once it initiates the time travel, is no longer relevant."

Cooper sat upright in his lounger. "But we don't know for sure?"

"There is no way to know for sure."

"Great. Another thing to worry about." Cooper closed his eyes and tried not to worry about all the things that he had to worry about.

~~~~~

The pulsating vibrations of a helicopter landing in Oscar's backyard woke Cooper. He must have drifted off in the cushioned comfort of the lounger. Cooper turned the digi-windows transparent. Not far from the house the same luxury helicopter they had seen in the captures from Area 52 landed a little way from his welding gazebo. After the door opened, Viola, with her hair combed but otherwise looking bedraggled and still wearing scrubs, descended from the helicopter. She said something to the pilot over her shoulder. As Viola headed toward the house, the helicopter took off again.

It was a dramatic way to make an entrance, which was only added to as Oscar's guards came running up, pulling their guns out and yelling at her to stop and put her hands up. Cooper was tempted to leave her to fend for herself with the guards, but his curiosity about what she wanted won out. He went from the library through the entrance hall of the estate, and then out the back entrance onto a patio with a marble balustrade and steps down to the yard.

"It's okay, I know her," Cooper said to the guards. "Take any weapons on her and then let her in."

The guards eyed Viola with a distrust she probably deserved. One of them edged toward her and started checking her for weapons.
~~~~~

Viola waved at him. "Cooper, thank goodness, it's good to see you!"

"She doesn't have any weapons," the guard said.

"Come on in, Viola," Cooper said. T-Rock, Bren, and Amoco were standing on the patio behind him. Cooper introduced T-Rock and Bren to Viola, and then led her into the library. Bren settled into a lounger like he was getting ready to watch his favorite show and T-Rock leaned back against the conference table. Amoco hovered near the door to the library.

Viola stopped in the middle of the room. She ran her fingers through her hair with more success than when he had seen her do it on the capture. She clasped her hands in front of her. "I'm sorry to barge in on you like this. It's just that I don't want Liam eavesdropping on our conversation and I wanted to talk to you in person."

Her eyes darted around the room, looking at the people in it and checking out each corner and cranny looking for who knew what. She had dark bags under her eyes and her skin had become sallow. If she had gotten any sleep recently it couldn't have been much. "I assume the bug blockers are on?"

"Yes." He had the feeling he was about to be dragged into something he didn't want to be dragged into. "What happened?" he asked her.

"Liam kicked me off the occupation. He's leading it now, and he wouldn't even let me stay to help. He plans to finish up the occupation himself and he says he will be the only person to negotiate with the locals for the surrender of the land. But it's *my* army." She pointed to her chest and said, "*I* created it. It was *my* idea to use the cryogens, and I gave up sleeping to train them. *I* should be the one controlling the operation."

She started pacing back and forth, her hands gesturing wildly as she spoke. "Liam says he's afraid I'm going to mess things up and it will become another scandal for the company like the Black Screen and the disappearance of the LP100 model ghosts. I guess he got scared by the shooting between the cryogens and those other people—where did they come from?" She did a sharp pivot in her pacing. "He thinks this is going to make Panacea Corp look bad. He's bringing in some soldiers to keep things under control and he told me I'm no longer needed."

So Liam had kicked Viola off of her own project. Not that Cooper was surprised, he had pretty much guessed that's what happened when he saw the video feed. Bren grinned like it was the best day of his life.

Cooper crossed his arms. There weren't many reasons he would be willing to help Viola right now. "Why did you come here?"

Viola stopped pacing and looked at him. "I know you aren't happy with me right now, but you all are the only people I can trust. I mean, I don't know about that guy"—she pointed at Bren—"but I've seen T-Rock in the Zazora Games and he was always honorable and a great team player. And Cooper and Amoco, I know you two can be trusted."

"How were you hoping we would help you out?"

"I…I…I'm not sure…" Her voice trailed off and her unfocused eyes returned to searching the room.

Amoco stepped toward them. "I would caution you to not be overly expectant that we will help you," Amoco said to Viola. "You may trust us, but that trust is not easily returned at this time."

"What do you want?" Cooper asked her again.

"I don't know. I can't think straight right now."

She was wasting his time. "Why don't you find a room somewhere and get some rest? Then once you've had a long nap, we can discuss what you think we can do for you."

"I understand. You think I need more rest. Of course." Viola had stopped moving. It was like she was so exhausted she had forgotten how to walk.

Cooper waited for her to say something more. When she didn't, he said, "Get some rest," and turned back to his screens.

If she didn't want to talk or rest, he wasn't going to force her. He sat down in the lounger and flipped the digi-windows back to his six monitoring screens. He needed some time to think. Things were getting worse in Area 52. Liam was in control of the cryos and moving in his military people; Amaya, Nyala, Mariela, and June hadn't been heard from in a long time; and the gawkers were an unpredictable wild card in the middle of it all. He needed to be there.

"I'm going back to Area 52," Cooper announced. "With the umbrella down, I can communicate using an Everything, and I know the road now so the trip up the mountain should be easier. I helped create this mess when I helped Viola create the cryogen army; at the very least, I should be protecting the people I care about from it. Anyone want to go with me?"

"I'd like to," T-Rock said, "but the doctor still has me on limited activity from the rattlesnake bite and moving makes it hurt worse. I'll be there in two days though because I told Georgia I would pick her and Hank up."

Amoco fiddled with his pocket watch. "I dislike perspiration," he said. A dislike of sweating was Amoco's go-to reason for not going to Area 52, or going outside in general.

"Bren, what about you?" Cooper asked.

"I would love to, but my wife is still mad at me for staying in Area 52 to take care of June's pets. Though the 10,000 coins June paid me for my time put my wife in a much better mood, I'm not risking leaving again so soon. I'll go with T-Rock in two days when he goes to pick up Hank and Georgia. And to pick up Midnight. I've gotten kind of attached to that cat—I'm looking forward to seeing him."

"None of you want to go with me?"

"I would love to spread my wings," T-Rock said, "but doctor's orders." He shrugged. "You don't need us—you can blend in with the gawkers and you know how the cryos work. And we'll be there in two days, sooner if you need us."

"I'll go with you," Viola said.

Cooper had forgotten she was still standing there. "No thanks."

"I need to go back. Please."

"It's not even a possibility. You can stay here if you want to rest, but then you need to leave."

"Alright, alright, I'll go find a bed somewhere." She left the library.

"I don't trust her," Amoco said.

"Nobody does," Cooper replied.

CHAPTER 18

The Day After the Umbrella Fell

Friday

The door to the holding area buzzed. Like a Pavlovian dog, Amaya perked up. Eating the cold and unpalatable slop was the only thing she looked forward to. Jail life was taking its toll—no matter how long she sat on the cold concrete benches they never got warmer or more comfortable. None of them had showered in what was probably four days. Maybe even five. They had all stopped talking after the conversation about the elephant in the room. That was almost…two meals ago? Not that they had been talking much before then. Amaya was getting cabin fever. Or was it jail fever?

Nyala, lying on the cell floor, rolled over and sat up. "So, Dan, what did you bring us today?" she asked. "More of the usual slop, I hope?"

"I'm not here with your food." Dan looked over his shoulder at the door as it shut. "I'm here to let you go." His keys rattled as he unlocked the door to the holding cell and held it open. "The people from your world…and the other things—I don't know what they are—are almost here. Petra will probably have my hide for doing this, but we'll need the holding cells."

Nyala raised her arms in the air. "Hallelujah!"

"Dan, what's happening out there?" June asked.

"Lots of people coming up the road from your world, some of the fast ones are already at the edge of town, the rest should be getting here in a couple hours. Then there's the other things—do you know what they are?"

"What are they? I mean, describe them," June said.

"Here, I have a picture." He dug a small metal box out of his pocket. It had the smallest screen Amaya had ever seen. She was the closest, so he showed the picture to her first.

"I have no clue what those are," she said. "Are they people?"

"I don't know. I thought maybe they were people who had been affected by the radiation."

June took the metal box from him. "Those are cryogens."

"The undead people that you told me about?"

"They're definitely dead, so don't worry about shooting them if you need to. They just had their bodies frozen because they hoped to be brought back to life." She sighed and handed the box back to him. "Which probably wasn't ever going to happen, but now that they've been unfrozen and walked through the heat it clearly won't."

"Why are they wearing togas?" Dan asked.

"Whoever is doing this probably didn't want to bother with the clothes." June held out her hand. "Can I see that picture again?"

"Sure." Dan handed the camera back. "There's some more on there."

They all peered over June's shoulder as she flipped through the captures of the most bizarre thing that Amaya had ever seen. Thousands of—people?—walking in straight lines, eyes staring straight ahead, all moving in a choreographed fashion with each step taken synchronously.

June let out a low whistle. "This is pretty incredible. Someone must be controlling them through their chips somehow. Mariela, have you heard of this?"

"No, nothing like this. I don't think that was even on the horizon a week ago. I'm sure Amoco would have told me about it if anyone had been working on anything similar." She shook her head. "Sorry, Dan, that we can't give you more help."

"You'll have to get out of town quickly," Dan said. "We're setting up a blockade to keep people from getting in. Some of the other deputies went to a warehouse outside of town to get the blockade barriers, so you all have probably twenty minutes to get through the chokepoint before my people get there. There's also a blockade of those…things farther down the road."

"How many are in both groups?"

"We sent up our small plane, the pilot says there's thousands. With the…cryogens, probably over 10,000. And there's helicopters. My first time seeing a helicopter outside of a history book." Dan smiled.

"What will you all do?" June handed the box-shaped device back to him.

"Petra said to activate the contingency plan, but we haven't done a drill since I was a kid."

"I don't remember a contingency plan," June said.

"I guess 'cause it's been a long time since the Nuclear Armageddon, so we stopped worrying about a breach from the radiated world."

"What is the contingency plan?"

"Like I said, the road blockade is at the chokepoint before the switch-back and we're funneling anyone who shows up into a holding area. I'm not sure what we are going to do with the…cryogens. We haven't figured that out yet. Or what we will do with the humans from your area once they are in our holding area." Dan put the metal box into a pocket in his uniform. "You'd better go. Sorry I couldn't get your clothes out of the locker."

He opened the door to the holding area, looked out, and then opened the door to the hallway for them. "The coast is clear."

"The what?" Nyala asked.

"The coast…never mind, just go!"

They headed down the hallway. It looked smaller than when they had arrived.

Amaya steadied herself with a hand on the cinderblock wall. Was the wall dingy or did it look gray because she was light-headed? She hadn't realized how weak she was. "Dan, how long have we been in here?"

"Five days. There's a side door this way." He turned down a short hallway.

"You couldn't have brought our food with you?" Nyala complained. "We haven't eaten in forever."

"Sorry, I've been swamped." He shrugged. "Undead invasion from the radiated world and all."

Did Dan just make a joke? The world really was coming to an end. He turned, walked them down a hallway, and stopped in front of the door at the end.

"Take me with you," he said to June while resting one hand on the door handle. "I want to see more of the world."

That was even more unexpected than the joke.

"You're needed here," June told him. "You're the only one besides Petra who knows the truth."

He stared at the ground like a kid who'd been told he had to do his homework rather than ride his bike. "I know I have to stay."

Amaya wanted to kick herself—was she actually starting to feel sorry for the guy?

"Dan," June grabbed his hand, "remember, there's no radiation. Never was."

"Oh crap," Amaya said. "We need Mariela's headband."

"I can get it." Dan started walking backwards down the hallway. "Go up front but stay in the shadows and I'll bring it out to you. I'll only be able to bring stuff that I can fit in my pockets, so don't expect me to bring your clothes." He ran his hand through his sandy hair. "Give me about ten minutes."

"Thanks," Mariela said, but she avoided making eye contact with Dan.

"It's dark out, so you should be able to hide in the trees. Be careful, there's a lot of weird stuff going on out there." Dan took off running down the hallway.

Nyala placed her hands on the door's break bar. She looked at each of them and then gently pushed on the bar and peered out the door. She craned her head to look around the door toward the front of the building. She turned back toward the others. "The coats are clear."

"The what?" Amaya asked.

"You know, what Dan said. The coats are clear."

"Oh, okay. Let's go then."

Nyala headed toward the forested area and Amaya followed. It was a short distance over the graveled area around the building to the forest. It felt good to move again, but she was unsteady and her legs trembled from not being used much over the last four days. Had she really just spent four days in jail? Her jail uniform was looser than when she first put it on. She clutched her pants before they could fall down around her ankles. She reached the shadows of the trees and sighed. The pine needles crunched under her slippers and the scent was better than anything Amaya had ever smelled before.

She tightened the drawstring on her pants. The women stayed hidden in the trees while making their way to the front of the building. The pine-cones hidden under the pine needles crunched and poked into her slippers. Sometimes the uneven ground turned Amaya's ankles. It was a good thing no one was around because they were making a lot of noise.

Staying deep within the trees while they walked alongside the building, they reached the parking lot. A few vehicles were parked in front of the building, but no people were in sight. The forest wrapped around the lot, providing them with cover as they walked to the far side where the road back to town cut through the trees. Amaya's legs trembled.

Not long after, Dan came out of the glass double doors in the front of the building. He looked around as he approached the trees, then headed towards them once he spotted them deep within the trees.

"Here's her headband." He held out the flowery device.

Mariela grabbed it from him and quickly put it on.

He pulled two more items out of a pocket. "And I found two granola bars. It's not much, but it's something."

Mariela took the granola bars from him. She handed one to Nyala and then tore hers open with a ferocity that only hunger can provide. She broke it in half, handed one piece to her mom, and then stuffed the rest in her mouth. Nyala handed Amaya half of the other bar. Amaya stuffed it in her mouth just like Mariela. It had a chewy goodness with just a hint of crunch. It was perfect, although it hardly made a dent in her hunger.

A young man with a long beard, probably in his mid-twenties, wearing digi-skin clothing that was quickly cycling through a rainbow of colors ran by flashing peace signs. He looked at them and yelled, "Free Area 52!" and ran across the parking lot.

"Got to go!" Dan sprinted after the guy.

Just as suddenly as the guy had appeared, he disappeared into the forest with Dan chasing after him.

"I guess we're on our own now," Amaya said. "Does anyone know where we are?"

"I do," June said. "But I...I don't think I'm going back." Her eyes glistened. "I need to keep my home safe. And they could use my help here."

"We'll go with you," Mariela said.

She shook her head. "You all can't come with me. Petra won't do anything if it's just me, I'm sure of it. She'll just make up some story about how I've been treated for the radiation. But if all of you stay, she'll put us all back in jail, regardless of whether Dan needs the holding cells or not."

"Are you sure you're up for protecting your place all by yourself?" Amaya asked.

"I'll be okay. I have some neighbors who I can rely on. With the umbrella down, there's no point in staying here any longer. Get Mariela back to town so she can be there when Amoco figures a way to deactivate the kill switch."

"Thanks, Mom." Mariela hugged June.

June placed her hands on Mariela's shoulders. "We'll see each other again soon."

"I hope that's a promise."

"It is. As long as the umbrella is down, we can talk whenever we want."

"That's great." Mariela sniffed and wiped her nose with the back of her hand.

The rest of them said goodbye to June and she pointed them in the direction of home.

~~~~~

Mariela's heart ached as her mom hurried off in the opposite direction. It wouldn't be long until she would be hidden by the darkness, and Mariela didn't know when she would see her again. The time they had together was too short.

"So what's our plan?" Nyala interrupted Mariela's thoughts. "Do we head home? Find someplace to hide?"

"What do we know about what's happening? Let's figure that out first," Amaya said. "Although can we start walking? I'd like to get away from the police station."

"Good idea." Mariela started walking downhill, just inside of the tree line on the two-lane road. "Here's what I know. The umbrella that protects Area 52 is down in an act of apparent sabotage," Mariela said. "There's a large group of cryogens who Petra thinks are invading, and another group of other people who are doing…what?"

"That wasn't clear." Amaya caught up with Mariela and hitched up her pants again. "Flashing peace signs, I guess."

"Petra called them a horde," Nyala fell into step beside her. "I don't think anyone knows what they are doing."

"There are also people flying around in helicopters," Amaya said.

"And if the Area 52 people are going to set up a blockade," Nyala said, "we had better decide soon which side we want to be on because if we want to leave, our window is closing."

"I don't think we can stay here," Amaya responded, "because we can't really wander around SkyWater wearing uniforms that say 'Property of SkyWater Jail' on them. We stick out like a pod-lifer in the solid world. And it's dark now so it will be easier for us to stay hidden."

"Excuse me?"

Mariela startled. She hadn't seen the woman dressed in the flowing
~~~~~

digi-skin skirt with simulated beads on it. A man lurked in the shadows not far behind her.

"Can you tell me where they are keeping the aliens?" the woman asked in a tiny, high-pitched voice.

"That way," Nyala said as she pointed further into the woods.

"Have you seen them?" the woman asked.

"The aliens? How do you think we ended up in the jail?" Nyala pointed to her uniform.

"Oh." The woman's eyes widened. She turned to the man. "I hope we end up in jail."

"Let's roll," he said. They took off jogging in the direction Nyala had pointed.

"What's that way?" Mariela asked.

"I have no clue," Nyala said. "I chose it randomly."

"Good idea. Before we leave, I think we should contact Amoco," Mariela said, "to see if he has more information on what's happening."

"Our phone!" Amaya turned to look in the direction of the police station. She sighed. "We forgot it with Dan."

"Can't you use your chip?" Mariela asked Nyala. She understood Nyala's choice not to use her chip, but this was an emergency.

"I don't remember how," Nyala said.

Mariela rolled her eyes. Would it kill Nyala to stop being so confrontational?

"You just…" Mariela tried to figure out how to explain it.

"It's not that easy, is it?" Nyala said. "I've been in worse situations than this and I haven't tried to use my chip, I'm not going to start using it now just because we don't know what's going on."

Mariela should have known it would upset Nyala to be asked to use her chip. In the distance, the beats of helicopter blades were growing closer.

"This is what we are going to do," Mariela said. "As much as possible, we are going to stay off the road and in the woods where we will be difficult to see, and we are going to make our way down the hill. Once we are safely past the blockades, I will take off my headband briefly and ask Cooper to send a vehicle to pick us up. Then we'll go back to the estate until we figure this out."

"It's going to be difficult to stay in the trees in some places," Nyala said. "The banks of the road are really steep and near impassable."

"We'll figure that out when we get there."

"Okay," Amaya said, "it sounds like a plan. Let's go."

~~~~~

So this was it. Cooper was back at the entrance to Area 52 with no real plan other than to head up the hill and see if he could figure out some way to be helpful. Cooper's past experiences with Area 52 didn't exactly give him confidence. In his previous visits he had failed to disable Mariela's kill switch, lost June's cat in the tesseract, and stood immobilized as the life ebbed out of Grace. This place had consistently made him feel all around useless. He didn't want to think about what it might have in store for him this time.

He pulled the Everything that Amoco had given him out of his pack and wrapped the semi-transparent cuff around his forearm. He tried to remember which combination of buttons it was that Amoco had said to push to get ahold of him. After some failed attempts he got it right and Amoco, T-Rock, and Bren relaxing in their loungers showed up on the screen of the Everything.

"Hey guys. Any news?"

"Panacea Corp used the cryogens to set up a blockade at a narrow spot on the road into Area 52," T-Rock said. "The intent appears to be to stop the gawkers from advancing further. They chose a spot where the road is windy and narrow a bit higher up the hill from the junction to the road the cryos are on. If Panacea Corp can stop the gawkers at the blockade, they won't be in the way of the cryos. A bunch of gawkers are piling up there. Instead of turning back, they're just hanging around, possibly hoping to eventually get through the blockade."

"Is there any way around the cryo blockade?"

"If you are a mountain goat, you could go through the woods to get around the cryo line," T-Rock said. "Once you get off the road it's steep, rocky terrain not suited for humans. All the other options would increase your travel time by a day at least. Sorry, Cooper, but I've been looking at this and it seems the only feasible way to SkyWater is through the line of cryos."

"No problem," Cooper said. "I'm used to dealing with the cryos so I think I'll be okay."

"Just be careful they don't start firing. You don't want to get caught in the middle of that."
~~~~~

"Good advice, as always T-Rock." A small patch of indigo sky had shown up on the horizon. He pulled his heavy pack out of the vehicle and slung it onto his shoulders. "Time for me to a get a move on."

He punched some buttons on his Everything until the connection ended. Even then, it probably ended because Amoco disconnected, not because Cooper had any clue how the device worked.

With the tesseract down, he didn't have to worry about finding the portal. All he had to do before heading up the hill was to disguise the hovbus so the gawkers wouldn't mess with it and double-check the weather. After that, he estimated it would take him about six hours at a regular walking pace to reach SkyWater. If he managed to keep a decent pace, he would probably get to the cryo blockade in five hours. That left him five hours to come up with a plan.

~~~~~

For what had to be the tenth time, Amaya's foot slipped and her ankle turned on the rocky scree of the steep slope. The growing light on the horizon made it easier to avoid tripping over the rocks, but with daylight creeping up on them, it was becoming more difficult for the three women to stay hidden. Their progress through the dark hills so far had been in complete silence, other than the occasional sound of the rock slipping under their feet and rolling down the hill. Yet in the couple hours that they had been threading their way through the forest at a crawl, they hadn't seen the cryogens or anyone else.

When the hills were too steep they had to walk on the road, but that option wasn't available now that it was starting to get light. Yet despite being increasingly exposed by the sunlight, Amaya welcomed the rising sun—maybe now she could stop jumping at every shadow. And maybe she would stop twisting her ankle.

"Hold it right there," a voice called out from higher up the hill.

Amaya had the feeling that when she turned to look, there would be someone holding a gun on her.

"Put your hands on your head," the gruff voice said, "and turn around slowly to face me."

Oh, please let it be some of Dan's men who will just take them back to the holding cell. Any other alternative seemed much worse.

"Come on!" the rough voice barked. "Hands in the air."

Amaya lifted her hands and turned slowly. Three men were making
~~~~~

their way down the hill with guns pointed at the women. Their digi-skin outfits clearly indicated they weren't from Area 52. Their outfits were a non-descript greenish-grey, but they looked like military. Maybe it was the buzz cuts.

"Mariela Stafford," one said with a gloating, looking-down-his-nose-at-them tone. He glanced at the words on her uniform. "It looks like you broke out of jail." He laughed at them for some reason only he would ever know.

"Liam's going to want to see this," said another. He pulled a couple of flexible metal coils out of his belt pack. Motion inhibitors. "Put these restraints on." He threw them each a set. "How did you end up here?"

Mariela didn't answer him. She picked up the restraints and wrapped the flexible copper-colored coil around her ankles and wrists. At first it didn't look like the cuffs were working, but once the cuffs were separated, they activated and Mariela's arms dropped limply by her side.

Amaya had never used coils before, so she followed Mariela's lead, wrapping them first around her ankles and then her wrists. When she got the second cuff on her wrist, it vibrated. She pulled her arms apart, and without warning, her arms dropped by her side. The loss of control over her arms surprised her, although she should have been more prepared seeing as she had just watched it happen to Mariela.

After they had the inhibitors on, one of the soldiers frisked them.

"Are the ankle coils really necessary?" Mariela asked during Nyala's frisk.

"They're on the motion-activated setting. As long as you don't move quickly, they won't turn on. But try to run, and you'll end up flat on your face." He laughed again. The guy had an odd sense of humor.

"Nice headband." One of the men smirked at Mariela. He gestured at them with his gun. "Come on, walk!"

"Which way?" Mariela asked. Amaya recognized Mariela's expression. It was her way of not giving the other person the satisfaction of knowing they had gotten under her skin. Mariela pulled it off so coolly, with such poise, that even knowing her well, Amaya wasn't sure whether she was concerned or not.

"That way!" The frustrated soldier fired his gun in the air. "Get moving!"

Mariela jumped at the sound of the gunshot, her poise momentarily lost but regained quickly. She turned in the direction he had fired his gun.

Amaya followed her as fast as she could given the motion inhibitors.

"Under whose direction are you acting right now?" Mariela asked. "I noticed you said you were taking us to the CEO of Panacea Corp, not your superior officer. Does that mean you are working for Mr. Price?"

"Stop walking," the lead soldier said. They immediately stopped. The man raised his gun in the air, and brought it down hard on Mariela's head. Mariela crumpled to the ground. Amaya lunged toward Mariela; the leg inhibitors kicked in and the muscles in her legs clenched into spasms. Without her arms to balance herself and with her feet planted, the motion of her lunge carried her down to the ground where she ended up with a face full of pine needles.

"What are you doing?" Nyala yelled.

"I was sick of her talking." The man turned to the biggest of the soldiers—the one with the broadest shoulders. "Pick her up and carry her." The soldier picked her up and threw her over his shoulder like she weighed nothing. It was probably good that Mariela was unconscious. She would have hated how her body hung limply over the guy's shoulder.

The pinecones tasted like dirt. Amaya picked her face up, rolled over, and got her legs underneath her.

"Hurry up, we don't have all day," the lead soldier said.

Amaya glared at him. She got herself into a position where she could get up without using her arms.

"Finally," the soldier said. "Get moving."

CHAPTER 19

The Day After the Umbrella Fell

Friday, continued

Mariela woke up from the impact of the soldier dumping her on the ground. She pulled in ragged breaths. Everything about her hurt, from her splitting headache, to her burning lungs, to her feet that had been bruised and scraped by the pinecones poking through her slippers. The soldier had left her on her side, with one motion-inhibited arm pinned behind her and the other lying useless in front of her. All she could see ahead of her were legs all wearing the same color pants, so most likely the soldiers.

They seemed to be at the soldiers' encampment, which was nothing more than a clearing next to the road. The camp filled up the entire clearing. There was a tank-like vehicle, some chairs and tables, and a few tents. Soldiers and Panacea Corp staff roamed around and appeared to be engaged in important discussions. Far down the road the cryogens were slowly approaching. The group of people in the camp must be the advance team.

Where were Amaya and Nyala? She couldn't roll onto her back with her one arm pinned behind her, so she rolled onto her front and looked on her other side. Too late she realized the hum she heard in the distance was the sound of a helicopter. That could only mean one thing—a capture of her wearing a jail uniform and an ugly flowered headband while rolling over face down in the dirt was probably already on the news.

She spotted Amaya and Nyala—they were kneeling in a row, unmoving with their arms still hanging limply by their sides. Mariela craned her head to see the soldier watching over them.

"Tell Liam that Mariela's awake," a man's voice called out.

Amaya and Nyala both turned to look at her but didn't speak. Their faces were serious but they looked in better shape than she felt.

"Get her up like the others," someone said.

Hands grabbed under her arms and dragged her torso off the ground. She got one dusty knee under her and then the second. The hands holding her let go and she was kneeling like the other two. She exchanged glances with them.

"Mariela!" That was Liam's voice. Mariela found him walking over from a nearby tent. What was he doing in Area 52 with a bunch of cryogens? How much had things changed in the last four days? Liam's boots kicked up dust that made her sneeze as he came to a stop beside her. Liam towered over her. She tried to look up at him but a sharp pain in her neck stopped her. He moved to stand in front of her. "Take off that ridiculous headband."

"It's not ridiculous," Mariela said even though she didn't believe it. "The thousands of people who have copied it obviously disagree with you."

Liam called to one of the soldiers. "Take it off."

The soldier wasted no time in pulling the headband, and a few strands of hair, off of Mariela's head. A few tears tried to escape in sympathy for the stinging in the crown of her head. It wasn't like her, but lately it seemed like almost every single day she was crying for some reason or other. Crying in front of her friends was bad enough, but she would rather have her tear ducts removed than cry in front of a global audience.

Mariela stared at the headband where the soldier had cast it away on the dusty ground in front of her. Hopefully her fears that someone else might have the codes to the kill switch were unfounded.

"What are you doing here?" Liam asked.

"Well, I saw on the news"—it was an educated guess that with the two or three helicopters hovering in the distance something about the camp would be on the news—"that you've got a lot on your plate right now. I came here wanting to help, as I *am* a vice president of Panacea Corp, but then I got picked up by the sheriff and he put us in jail."

"I don't buy it." Liam paced back and forth. "You're lying again. You're involved in this. Somehow. I'll figure it out and then you'll be in jail permanently."

"You think I brought a bunch of cryogens here? For what purpose?"

"No, that was Viola. What I want to know is what you've been up to."

The news helicopters moved in closer, trying its best to capture whatever was happening. The sun hadn't crossed the horizon yet, but the early morning light infused the clearing with a pre-dawn glow. Enough light for the helicopters to get a clear image of what was happening. Would

Cooper be watching? Would he worry about her? She pushed those thoughts away. She had enough on her mind without also worrying about whether Cooper cared about what happened to her.

"I think you will find," she said to Liam, "that I have been quite out of the action. I am completely innocent of anything happening here."

"We'll see about that." It sounded like a threat. "Get me three vials," he yelled to the soldiers.

"Three vials of what?" Nyala asked.

"You!" It was like Liam hadn't noticed Nyala before then. "Keep an eye on this one," he said to the soldier. "Don't take off her motion inhibitors. She likes to get physical."

The other soldier returned with three syringes and three vials of dark liquid. A liquid that Mariela remembered well. The dark, viscose fluid of the kill switch looked like boiling oil. And it felt like boiling oil when it was injected. She had believed that the vial the brutes had injected into her was the only one. "Where did you get that?" she whispered.

The soldier handed the vials to Liam.

"Courtesy of Viola." Liam held the vials up. "She thought it might come in handy, and I agree. This liquid, once we inject it next to your chip, will allow me to monitor what you are doing. I've also programmed it so it will monitor your location and, if you go outside of the perimeter of this camp, it will activate and kill you." Liam handed the vials and syringes to another one of the soldiers. "Take them in the tent to do the injection. We don't want the helicopters filming this."

What was Viola thinking? She understood that the fluid could be used as a weapon, but she had it replicated? And gave it to Liam?

<div style="text-align:center">~~~~~~</div>

The dirt digging into Amaya's knees and the discomfort of kneeling had seemed better than going back to jail. But once she saw the vials of the thick, mercury-like fluid—and the way Mariela's face had lost all color when she saw them—Amaya wanted to run back as fast as she could to the Area 52 jail.

A soldier came running up the uneven gravel road. "Incoming vehicle!" the soldier yelled.

The crunch of tires on the road confirmed the lookout's warning. It wasn't a military or a hover vehicle, and it used rubber tires, so definitely someone from Area 52. Dan looked to be driving, with Petra in the passenger seat.

Petra descended from the jeep glaring at the soldiers. For a 101-year-old, she managed to get around quite a bit. She started walking toward them and then paused, an almost imperceptible moment of hesitation, when she saw the three women kneeling on the ground. She then turned to Dan, still in the driver's seat of the jeep, and gave him a look that said she would deal with him later. Amaya guessed she had just realized that Dan had released them.

"I see you found our detainees," Petra said to Liam. "We'll be glad to take them off your hands."

"Who are you?" Liam asked her.

"I could ask you the same thing. You are the one who is trespassing on my territory, so I believe the obligation is on you to identify yourself first."

"I'm Liam Price, CEO of Panacea Corp."

"Ah," Petra said, her eyebrows arching, "I can see you treat your employees well." She nodded at the handcuffed Mariela. "You need to take your army of…whatever those things are and leave. We have a contractual agreement with Panacea Corp for the use of this land, and this invasion is in violation of that agreement."

"I disagree. You stopped responding to any contact attempts and therefore were in violation of the agreement that Panacea Corp should be allowed to access the servers in order to maintain them."

"You are mistaken. A team from Panacea Corp conducted maintenance on the servers just last week. This woman," she indicated Amaya, "was a part of the team."

Liam looked at Amaya for the first time. "What *is* it with you people?" He turned back to Petra. "That was an unsanctioned operation."

"I'm not surprised. Unsanctioned or not, however, it does show we have been fully compliant with the agreement."

Amaya had to bite her tongue. Petra had fought them every step of the way—saying she was compliant was a blatant lie. But Petra was their only hope for avoiding Liam's injections, so Amaya kept her mouth shut.

"I'm taking over," Liam said. "To be clear, it's an occupation, not an invasion, but if you try to stop me, you will be taken into custody."

"Very well then," Petra nodded her head. "It's obvious you have the superior position here. I assume you are okay with us gathering up and removing the people—the ones not affiliated with your group—who are currently trespassing on our land?"

Liam looked like he wasn't quite sure about Petra's easy capitulation, and then said, "Fine. But I'm going to continue putting my people," he paused, once again looking not quite sure, "and the cryogens, into place."

"May I take my prisoners back?"

"No."

"Of course not. It was unreasonable of me to think that a person wearing a shirt that says 'Property of SkyWater Jail' would actually be in the SkyWater Jail." And with a huff, Petra turned and headed back to the jeep. Was she really leaving without them? Petra was their only hope to avoid an injection Mariela had described as the most painful thing that had ever happened to her.

"Petra?" Amaya whispered as Dan backed the jeep up with Petra in it. "Come back."

~~~~~

Hands grabbed each of Mariela's arms and dragged her up from the ground. A pain stabbed through her shoulder when the rough hands pulling her up almost dislocated it. Mariela fought back against the soldiers. The last time she got injected with the kill switch, the pain seared through her skull. She wasn't going to make it easy for them to inject her again.

At the very least she would show the helicopters she wasn't being taken willingly. Her motion-inhibited hands were ineffectual against the soldiers, but what the helicopters saw was a struggling and partially incapacitated woman being carried off against her will by two large men. It wouldn't look good for Liam.

The guards pulled her to a tent on the far side of the camp away from the road. The flap covering the opening was designed to have the rough texture and heft of canvas. One guard pulled the heavy flap to the side; the other shoved her through the opening. Buckling in the tarp placed on the floor almost tripped her. The tent had a folding table, some folding chairs, a cot, and large storage crates stacked along the back of the tent. Nyala and Amaya were similarly shoved into the tent.

"Stay there." The soldier pushed Mariela in the direction of the table. "Don't move." Where would she go? There was nothing to do but wait for the burning pain.

"Release a statement to the press," Liam said outside the tent. "Based on information just obtained, these three are being charged with causing
~~~~~

the Black Screen and deleting the LP100 model ghosts."

Well played Liam. Any viewers of the capture of them being dragged into the tent would be less sympathetic if they thought the three were being carried off because they caused the outage and deleted the ghosts. It wouldn't matter that Liam didn't have any evidence.

What had she gotten Nyala and Amaya involved with? They wouldn't be here if it wasn't for her. They were mad at her, so mad they were barely talking to her, but they still put themselves in danger to help her out. Despite their kindness, Mariela had only made things worse. When they started the trip, she was the only one with a kill switch, but by the end of it, they all would have them. They deserved better.

Liam's head henchman swept aside the canvas flap and entered the tent. He stood to the side with his hands on hips as though he was supervising them all. One of the soldiers extracted the mercury-like fluid from the vial. Another grabbed her hair, lifting it up off her neck and pushing her head forward in the process.

"Wait," she said. "Let me sit."

"Whatever."

She sat down in one of the folding chairs.

"Can you take the motion inhibitors off?"

"We'll take them off once you've had the injection."

If she relaxed it might not hurt so badly, but relaxing was impossible. Someone pushed her head forward again. She focused on her breathing. Deep breath in. Deep breath out. The sting of the needle. The burning of the fluid. The scalding, piercing, pain. Pain that blinded her and split her head open. It was worse this time. So much worse. So much…

~~~~~

Mariela passing out after getting the injection kicked Anaya's anxiety into high gear. Amaya's breathing quickened, yet each breath failed to fill her lungs. She ran through all the options for getting out of the injection, including making a run for it, but couldn't find any that didn't end in her getting shot. Not to mention that with the motion inhibitors running wasn't an option. She would just have to hope she could handle the pain. Mariela had said it was painful the first time, but she hadn't mentioned passing out. Had something gone wrong? Maybe the fluid was defective—where had Liam said it came from?

"I'll go next," Nyala said. Nyala was always the braver of the two.
~~~~~

"No, I'll do it." Amaya stepped toward the soldier who had just finished filling the next syringe. Nyala couldn't always be there making things easier for her. Amaya needed to know that she could take care of herself. "Let me get it over with."

Mariela was still lying on the ground where she had fainted.

"I'm going to pick her up first," Amaya said.

"Leave her," the soldier said. "Sit in the other chair."

Amaya sat in the other folding chair. Just as they had with Mariela, someone pushed her head forward and moved her hair out of the way. She felt the pinch of the needle. The fluid burned and seared into her head. No amount of ice could extinguish the hot flames that wrapped around her neck and into her skull. Her eyes watered and her temples throbbed. She couldn't see straight, but she had survived. She tried to rub the back of her neck but her motion inhibited arms hung uselessly. Her neck was going to burn for a while.

"How was it?" Nyala asked.

"Painful," Amaya said. She craned her neck to wipe her still-watering eyes on her shoulder. "Remember that time I broke my arm? This was ten times worse."

Nyala shivered. "I shouldn't have asked," she said.

Amaya gave Nyala her seat.

It was wrong not to pick Mariela up and put her on the cot, but with the coils still on it wasn't a possibility. Instead, she sat on the floor next to Mariela. Mariela's gentle breathing reassured Amaya that she was still alive.

Nyala's face contorted as the soldier depressed the plunger on the syringe. She bent over in pain but didn't pass out. So why did Mariela?

The soldier who appeared to be the highest ranking pointed at another soldier. "You. Stand guard outside the tent." The high-ranking soldier turned to them. "You three. You can walk around if you want, but if you go outside the perimeter of this camp, your chip will overload until the chip-burn kills you. No one will try to help you. The most you can hope for from us is that we will shoot you to put you out of your misery. This tent is at the edge of the camp, so I wouldn't wander too far that way." He pointed away from the road toward the forest. "Also, Liam has arranged for all your accounts to be locked out, so you won't be able to send any messages and no one will be able to contact you."

"What will you do with us?"

"You're gonna be jailed once this is all over." He looked at their uniforms and smirked. "Looks like you're already dressed for it. They'll just have to get a marker and change the name on your clothing."

"He can't jail us," Amaya said. "He doesn't have any evidence."

The guard rolled his eyes. "Look, try to avoid going to jail if you want, but if you go free, Liam will use the liquid we injected to keep an eye on what you are doing. Liam said he's not going to let Mariela get one over on him again."

"That's illegal," Nyala said.

"I'm sure it would be if you could prove we did anything. With your accounts locked, it's not like you will have any recorded evidence of what happened here."

Another soldier stuck her head in through the flap of the tent. "We've got the cryos in place blocking the other road. Are you ready to advance the others?"

"Move them forward."

The woman slipped out of the tent and the man turned back to them. "We'll come get you when it's time to move camp. See if you can get her to wake up before then." He nudged Mariela with his toe. "I don't want to have to drag her." He opened the flap and exited.

"How are we supposed to wake her up?" Amaya asked Nyala in an angry whisper. "Are we supposed to slap her? Does that even work?"

Nyala shook her head. "They knocked her out, they can wake her up if they want her to be awake. It's not our problem."

"True. Are you feeling okay?"

"It still stings. It's like rolling naked in a nettle patch."

"Mine too. It's ten times worse than when those wasps stung me in high school. It could have been worse though. I kind of freaked out after Mariela fainted."

"I saw. But you pulled it together."

"Do you think they're going to harm us?"

"I don't know. Maybe. Or they will send us to jail for forever, or even worse, they'll convince the angry masses we are to blame for everything that happened, and then once everyone is fired up, Liam will let us go. There's nothing like putting your enemies in constant danger as a way of getting back at them. It's kind of ingenious, really. It keeps his hands clean and he can avoid taking any responsibility if something bad happens to us."

Amaya's chest tightened. The only way they would be free from Liam's control would be to disable their chips. And then it dawned on her...her chip was already disabled. If what Petra told them was true, then the kill switch wouldn't be able to hurt her. She could actually do something about their situation and use Liam's lack of awareness about her chip being disabled to her advantage.

The Day After the Umbrella Fell

Friday, continued

After spending most of the last five hours walking uphill at the fastest pace he could sustain, Cooper needed to rest his legs for a bit and let the burning in them subside. His muscles ached, but other than a few short breaks, he had felt compelled to keep moving, although he didn't know why he needed to get to SkyWater in such a hurry or what he would do once he got there.

For now, the wide spot in the road before the cryo blockade seemed as good a place as any to hang out for a bit and come up with a plan for how to get past the blockade. He could do some people watching at the same time. Cooper had passed a wide range of gawkers during his trip up the hill into Area 52, and under any other circumstances they would have amused him with their talk of faked moon landings, but today they just filled him with anxiety.

He punched some buttons on his Everything until he connected with Amoco and then pushed the button to put Amoco on the visual display. Amoco was standing in the library, and behind him Bren was adjusting his lounger from a reclining to a sitting position.

"Any updates?" Cooper asked.

"Cooper," Amoco said, "you should be informed that the wildfires northeast of the city have gone from Class III to Class IV. The authorities have commenced evacuations of pod warehouses in that area."

"What about the estate? The wildfires can't be far from where you are at."

"At this time, we are safe. We will continue to monitor the situation, of course. Have you checked the weather there?"

Cooper had checked his weather instruments before making the call. No wildfires were predicted for Area 52, but heavy rain was likely.

Bren stood up and approached the screen. "Hey, Cooper. I have an update on Area 52. After no word for four days, Mariela, Amaya, and Nyala were picked up outside of SkyWater by some soldiers working for

Liam and now they are being held at his camp. Liam issued a press release saying they were responsible for the Black Screen and deleting of the LP100 model ghosts. It's got a lot of people all worked up and calling for blood."

Cooper considered turning around. What was he thinking—that he could rush in there and save the day? And while he was saving the day, maybe he could stop Liam from marching the cryogens into SkyWater. Why not save the world? Except he felt totally inadequate for any of it. "Do you have any suggestions?" he asked Bren. "I don't know how I'm going to be helpful to them if they're being held by Liam."

"Well," Bren said, "I'm glad it's you and not me, but maybe you could head into SkyWater and work with June to come up with a plan?"

Cooper liked the idea of working with June. "That's a good idea. Is there anything else?" he asked.

"Everything else is the same," Bren said. "Liam is moving most of the cryos closer to SkyWater. The gawkers are gathering before the cryo blockade. You'll see them soon."

It felt hopeless, but he had to try something. He took a deep breath. Whatever he was going to do, he might as well stop dilly-dallying and get on it. He said goodbye to Bren and Amoco, managed to turn the Everything off, and headed up the winding mountain road again.

Cooper's news updates hadn't prepared him for what he would find in the area right before the cryo blockade. It looked like a mix between a music festival and a sci-fi convention. There were hundreds of people there, all milling around and chatting with each other. There were even drink and food vendors, and some particularly enterprising person had managed to set up a souvenir shop. He considered buying a t-shirt that read "I Survived the Zombie Invasion of Area 52," but buying a shirt with "I Survived" on it seemed like tempting fate.

Thick clouds filled the sky, but Cooper's weather instruments said it wasn't going to rain for a while yet. He wiped a layer of sweat from his forehead. Not that it did much good. His forehead was immediately sweaty again, and his shirt was soaked through.

Those who were more heat-wary hovered under the shade of the trees that lined what was nothing more than a wide spot in the road with steep slopes on either side. Although with the sky-high humidity, the shade was almost useless. So was the darkening cloud cover that brought no relief but only higher and higher humidity.

The festivities stretched up and down the road, and most everyone there didn't seem the least bit slowed down by the heat or concerned about the dust that seemed to coat everything. The churro stand by far was the most popular attraction, with multiple long lines extending far enough down the road that the people in back of the line would probably be waiting close to an hour to get their churros.

Not far from where Cooper was, someone said, "Isn't this so exciting?"

Cooper knew that nasal voice. Only Elliat Exis was that enthusiastic when nothing new was happening. Cooper spotted Elliat standing on a gentle slope at the edge of the road not far away, his exo-cam hovering in front of him.

"We are seeing history today, folks," Elliat said. "Not only did Area 52 turn out to be real, but there is a zombie army that for some reason is escorted by personnel from Panacea Corp. We don't know what's going on though as the zombies are keeping the rest of us from getting further up the road. Stay tuned as we interview experts about what we can expect from Area 52. But before we go, my guess as to what it is? I think it's a secret Panacea Research Facility, and the zombies are the guards."

Elliat switched to an ad break, took a sip of water, turned to a tall and willowy woman standing next to him. After a bit of chatting, Elliat started streaming again. "First up, Tytania Vilis from the Alien Encounters for a Better Future Society. Ty, what do you believe Area 52 to be?"

"I think it's clear that it's where they keep the aliens," the willow-woman said. Cooper was surprised to hear she had a British accent. The woman leaned toward Elliat and spoke as though she were sharing a secret with him, "There may even be living aliens here; it's possible there's some sort of training facility where the aliens share information with us and we share information with them."

The woman straightened up and returned to a regular voice, "If they keep building weapons using alien technology, these weapons will be much more powerful than any weapons that currently exist on Earth." She set her jaw. "We plan to find out what they are doing and stop it— we have around 200 of our society members here already and another 1,000 or so are on their way. Once we have everyone here, we are going to storm the facility and the truth will be revealed!"

"Tell me, Ty," Elliat said, "what—" Elliat noticed Cooper watching him. "What…are your plans?"

"Well, we haven't settled on one plan just yet…"

Elliat was still looking at Cooper. "I'm sorry, Ty, I have to go. There's someone I need to talk to."

The woman looked shocked at the abrupt cutoff of the interview, but didn't object as she stepped down from the hillock.

"Hey you," he pointed at Cooper, "I need to talk to you."

For a moment Cooper considered running to avoid having to talk, but then changed his mind. He was a grown man—he didn't need to be afraid of Elliat. Instead he said, "Elliat," and then stopped talking because he didn't have anything else to say. With any luck, the one-word sentence made him sound like the strong, silent type.

"You were here before." Elliat's beady eyes inspected Cooper. "You showed up out of nowhere. And you were on the hovbus with June Stafford and that weirdly dressed guy who looked like a member of a police dancing troupe." He pointed at Cooper. "You know something about what's going on around here."

"I'm not talking."

"I'll turn the cameras off."

"Still not talking."

"Suit yourself. Are you trying to get up the road? It was open before and a couple hundred people got through but then they used those zombies to close the road."

It sounded like the cryo blockade was effective. Cooper would have thought it was a task the cryos weren't well-suited for. "No one's getting through?" he asked.

"Well, journalists are allowed through if they wear a helmet and a flak jacket and sign a waiver promising not to sue if something goes wrong. I wanted to go but then I thought, 'Why brave the danger when there is so much information that can be gathered here?' Look at all the people here, it's like a gathering of everyone who might know something about this area."

Cooper had an idea—Elliat's journalist credentials were going to be Cooper's ticket through the blockade. He wasn't quite sure how yet, but he was going to figure out a way to get in on Elliat's coattails.

"Wouldn't a real journalist want to get at the truth no matter how risky it may sound?" Cooper asked. It was shameful manipulation but it was probably the only thing that would work.

"Oh, I'm not sure I would dare. Who knows what might be happening in there?"

"Do you want a Newsoogle Award or not?" Cooper was laying it on as thick as he could. "I could accompany you as your assistant…bodyguard…whatever you want."

"Oh, ah, I don't know." Elliat was tempted. Cooper could see it. Just a little more pressure should do it.

"I've actually been up there, past where the blockade is now, so I know my way around and I know some of the people. If you take me with you, I will grant you an exclusive interview about my time there once we're inside." Cooper wasn't going to give Elliat all the details, but surely there must be some tidbit that would make Elliat happy and not reveal too much. Or maybe he could just ditch Elliat once he was inside the blockade and avoid the interview.

"I want to, but I don't know." Elliat did a little bobbing motion with his head like he was thinking it over. "I wouldn't look good in a flak jacket. It's too constricting. And what if they are having us waive our right to sue just because they know we're gonna die?"

"Why would they do that? Now you're just making excuses."

"These are all really, really great points, but I'm not sure that I would be able to bring you with me. We should probably just forget the whole thing. It was a nice idea but not really realistic given the circumstances."

"I'll give you a short interview now." Cooper really didn't want to play this chip, but Elliat was taking more effort to convince than he had hoped. "Insider information about what's going on here. I can guarantee you no other source will have shared it." When Elliat didn't respond at first, he added, "Do you want a Newsoogle or not?"

There was a pause. Cooper let Elliat process the idea.

"Okay, okay," Elliat eventually said, "let's do this! I'm so excited! We are going inside the blockade and I'm going to win a Newsoogle!"

What had Cooper committed himself to? What could he share that wouldn't upset someone else? Anything involving Mariela was off limits—she would have his hide if he shared anything about her. Viola was vindictive so better not to involve her, and Liam wasn't against using the resources of Panacea to crush those who crossed him so it was risky to involve him in any way. What did that leave? Maybe some basic factual information. Most of Elliat's viewers would know about the zombie-like creatures approaching from the north and guarding the blockade, but they wouldn't know where they came from. That seemed like info people should have. It probably would still make Viola and Liam mad at him, but at least it didn't involve criticizing them directly.

"Stand right there"—Elliat pointed to a spot next to a large pine tree clinging onto a hillside—"so I can get the blockade in the background."

"Okay." Cooper dropped his backpack out of site of the camera and moved to the spot next to the tree. "Is this good?"

"Perfect. I'll do an introduction first. Are you ready?"

"Yes." What should he do with his arms? He was suddenly very aware of how they hung by his side. He tried various positions but no matter how he held them, they didn't feel natural. He was considered an outstanding lecturer when he worked for the Academia Veritas Virtual. He was one of the few professors that even bothered to lecture anymore. Or at least he was until he got fired. So why couldn't he get comfortable now? It probably had to do with his comfort with the subject matter—he never had to worry about getting someone killed by saying the wrong thing when he was lecturing.

Elliat arranged his exo-cam so it was hovering slightly above their heads in front of them.

"I'm here with Cooper O'Connor. My loyal viewers will remember him from this reporter's previous post on April 14 where I mentioned that while following a lead in my search for the cause of the Black Screen, I was drawn to this area and observed Mr. O'Connor appear from nowhere. In addition, it is possible he fathered a child with Mariela Stafford, the VP of Panacea Corp, who was suspended after her boss ended up in the middle of the Gulf of Mexico floating on a parachute. Although not the topic of today's post, some speculate Ms. Stafford may have been responsible for her boss's soggy predicament."

Elliat had been speaking for less than a minute and already Cooper was regretting agreeing to be interviewed.

"Now, Mr. O'Connor, you said you had some information to share with my listeners, and this reporter would like to point out that Mr. O'Connor has stated this information is exclusive."

"Yes, I believe it to be…"—*why did he sound so wooden*—"… exclusive. The beings that some have said might be zombies, I mean, speculated might be zombies, I have some information about them. These beings, that aren't zombies,"—*he needed to focus and actually make a point*—"the zombies, that is, they are not zombies. They are cryogens who—"

"Could you explain to our viewers what cryogens are?"

"Doesn't everyone know what cryogens are?" It seemed silly to have to explain.

"Well, just in case, could you explain."

"Oh, uh, sure. Cryogens are people who had their bodies frozen so they can, you know, come back to life later." Did that make sense?

"Let me see if I understand—upon their deaths, these people had their bodies placed in cryonic suspension so they could be cured of whatever killed them and revived at a later date once the science had progressed?"

"Right. That. A much better explanation." If he kept speaking so in-eloquently, his offer to lecture at the Academia would probably get revoked. He needed to get it together. "Uh…" *What was he saying?*

"Have they been brought back to life?"

Oh right, the cryogens. "Uh, no. They are being controlled through their embedded chips."

"That *is* interesting." Elliat sounded like he was relieved to finally get some interesting information from Cooper.

"Yes, Panacea Corp found some new technology that allows the cryogens to be controlled through their chips, and since they have given up hope on ever reviving the cryogens, they thought they might as well use them for other purposes."

"When you say that Panacea Corp has 'found some new technology,' what do you mean?"

Oh crap, he had said too much. Time to back it up. "Oh, I don't really know that, I was just talking there. Like being non-specific."

"And when you said they had given up hope on reviving the cryogens, what does that mean for them? Will they all be sent on assignments such as this one? And what is the assignment? Is this what Mariela Stafford has been up to these last couple weeks? I'm sure the family members of the cryogens will be interested to know."

He definitely had said too much. He should stop the interview before he said anything else. "That's all I have for now."

"But I have so many more questions," Elliat said.

"Save them for later." To make it clear that the interview was over, Cooper turned around, picked up his pack, and walked toward the block-ade. Behind him Elliat was wrapping up the interview. He followed Cooper but kept talking, his exo-cam keeping pace with him as he moved.

"There you have it, folks. According to this close associate of Mariela Stafford, Panacea Corp has revived cryogens for an unknown purpose using a new technology that allows the corporation to control their movements but not bring them back to life. Thanks to Cooper O'Connor for helping us make a little progress in untangling this knotty story. Stay tuned, as Mr. O'Connor will be accompanying me as I enter the inner area past the blockade. We'll be bringing you lots more coverage on the possible malfeasance carried out by the persons we have been following in the recent weeks."

As soon as Cooper could speak freely, he was going to give Elliat a piece of his mind. "Have you stopped streaming?"

Elliat cut off the exo-cam. It glided back into its setting on Elliat's shoulder holster. "For the moment."

"I've been helping you and before I even get a chance to speak, you imply that Mariela's a murderer and that I'm up to no good."

Elliat scoffed. "I'm just trying to get at the truth."

"You're good at uncovering bits of information but horrible at making sense of any of it. You're not even close to the truth and I'm pretty sure you know it."

"I report things as I see them." Elliat stopped walking and looked back in the way they had come. "Do you promise nothing will happen to me?"

"You know I can't promise that. You could slip and break your arm. I can't protect you from anything that might befall you."

"I don't know why I agreed to this. We're both going to get killed."

"You're not going to get killed. At least I don't think you will get killed. Just to be clear, I'm not promising anything. It's possible you may get killed by an exasperated traveling companion. So come on, let's go."

Elliat got him through the blockade by telling the guard that Cooper was his assistant. The one soldier guarding the path through the cryogens didn't even question them other than to verify Elliat's press credentials. After getting past the checkpoint, they walked past rows of cryogens—with rifles ready to shoot at any moment—standing motionless with blank expressions on their faces. The entire width of the roadway was filled with cryogens, people of all shapes and sizes, that didn't react to Cooper and Elliat walking cautiously among them.

One side of the road dropped off into a steep ravine and the other had a rocky upward slope that was almost vertical. It was a good spot for a blockade. T-Rock was right, only a mountain goat could have gotten past the blockade without going through it.

Not much later, they passed the junction. If they had turned left, they could have gone to the camp where Mariela, Nyala, and Amaya had been taken. But it seemed safer to continue straight into SkyWater, and to ask June to help him come up with a plan and identify resources.

Elliat's constant chatter grated on Cooper's nerves. Elliat had already said how excited he was ten times, complained about the flak jacket four times, worried about signing the waiver twice, and said his helmet was too loose six times. He stopped every fifteen minutes to update his blog with a post saying there was no new information yet, describing in detail their journey and rehashing conspiracy theories about the purpose of Area 52. Cooper started plotting how to ditch Elliat before going to June's place.

Cooper's Everything buzzed. He had no clue what to do with it. He picked his arm up and poked at a couple places, eventually through sheer luck answering the incoming call.

"Cooper." It was Viola's voice. "Turn around."

He turned around and there she was. The last person he wanted to see, her hair finally brushed and her clothes changed but still looking some-what haggard. Had she slept at all? He sighed. Now, in addition to getting rid of Elliat, he would also have to get rid of Viola.

"Hang on so I can join you," Viola said. "I'll be there in a minute."

Cooper poked at his Everything to cut the connection on his end.

"Have you even tried to learn how to use your Everything?" Elliat asked. "Honestly, it's like you haven't even bothered to learn the most basic steps."

"It's not my highest priority. I'll learn how to use it when I need to."

"You would think that would be now," Elliat said under his breath.

Cooper waited impatiently for the half-minute it took for Viola to catch up to them.

"What are you doing here?" Cooper said.

"Like I said before you left, I need to be here. What's surprising is even though you had a head start of hours," Viola said, "I still caught up to you."

Who knows how she managed to catch up to him. The resources of

Panacea Corp probably made that easy for her. People who weren't employees of Panacea Corp, on the other hand, had to bribe some journalist to help them out and they ended up in uncomfortable alliances that caused problems in the long run. Elliat was in poor shape and had slowed them down—he had to stop every five minutes to catch his breath.

Cooper resumed walking up the hill to SkyWater with Elliat right behind him.

"You're not going for Mariela?" Viola asked. "You should have turned left at the junction."

"I don't know what I'm doing, but I know that walking into that camp without a plan and some resources is suicide."

"You're going to save her, right?"

"I'm going to try."

"I saw your podcast with Elliat." Viola fell into step beside them, easily keeping up with Elliat's slow pace. "I don't know why you shared all that information about the cryogens. I can only imagine you said what you said because you're mad at me for not telling you about the occupation of Area 52."

"Something like that."

"I consider us even now," Viola said. "I lied to you about the intended use of the cryogens and you shared privileged company information with the entire world. So does that make us even?"

"No! We're not even; you cost me a job I loved job three years ago. *We'll never be even.*"

"Sorry about that. You know, don't you, that I would change what I did if I could? But when Liam fires me because I brought you in on this and you talked about Panacea Corp's use of the cryogens to the world, then we will be even."

It was possible that could actually happen. Maybe he and Viola would be even after all.

"Okay, if you lose your job because of me, then you can say we're even." He wouldn't really regret if she was fired. She would deserve it for lying to him again.

"Don't say that Cooper. You know it would devastate me if I lost my job. I would never forgive you."

"Did you forget how devastated I was when I lost my job?" How could she in any way suggest that what she might go through if she got fired would be worse than what he went through? "You're not the only one who loves their job."

Elliat was watching them closely, and was possibly recording them. This was one of the moments when Cooper wished the law had passed that required people with embedded chips to wear a collar that would flash when they were recording. People with chips said it was too intrusive, but having conversations recorded without your knowledge was pretty intrusive as well.

Viola was staring at Elliat. "If you publish any of this," she said to him, "I will ruin you." It was a threat that, for the moment at least, Viola was capable of following through on. Her tone of voice left little doubt that she would do what she was saying.

Elliat blinked and swallowed hard. "I'm not recording! Nothing about this will ever see the light of day, I swear. Let's keep walking!" He turned and stalked up the road.

CHAPTER 21

The Day After the Umbrella Fell

Friday, continued

Amaya's plan was sketched out in her head. It seemed Liam and his crew didn't know she had disabled her chip. If no one saw her leaving, it would be a while before they would realize she was gone. But to escape unnoticed, she needed a distraction. So she waited. And waited. For seven hours so far.

Not much had happened in that seven hours of waiting. After they had the injections, the guards left without deactivating the motion inhibitors. Amaya had to remind them about it. The guards took off Mariela's and Amaya's inhibitors, but left Nyala's cuffs on. With Nyala unable to move her arms, Amaya had been on her own to get Mariela onto the cot. It wasn't pretty, but she got her there eventually. She put a scratchy green military blanket over Mariela and sat on the ground beside the cot to monitor Mariela's breathing. Hopefully there wasn't anything seriously wrong with her.

They weren't confined to the tent, so at one point Nyala and Amaya walked around the camp. For Amaya, it was a reconnaissance mission, but it also felt good to stretch her legs and get some sunshine. Between the heat and the humidity, it felt like her skin couldn't breathe. A bead of sweat rolled down her back. The stares of the soldiers reminded her she was still wearing a jail uniform and she hadn't showered in over four days.

After fifteen minutes of walking, Amaya was satisfied with what she saw. Their tent was away from the road, back near the forest. If she could get into the forest, there was a hill in the direction of SkyWater that, once on the other side, the people in the camp wouldn't be able to see her anymore. All she needed was a distraction so she could get out of the camp without being seen.

The sharp retort of a gunshot, quickly followed by three more, jolted Amaya. Something was going on outside. People were yelling. After hours of listening for the moment to make her break, this might be it.

"They're shooting at the cryogens again!" a soldier yelled.

What if Petra was wrong or this kill switch was different? What if she ran out of the camp and then her head exploded? Or they came after her with guns? Was the risk greater if she stayed or if she left?

More soldiers were yelling.

"Four of the cryogens are down!"

"Can you see who's doing the shooting?"

"No. I think they're hiding in the trees to the west."

"Send out a team."

There was a chance she wouldn't make it out of this alive. Or worse— what if her escape was discovered, and Nyala and Mariela got blamed? What if she never saw Nyala again?

The buzz of the helicopters overhead changed as the helicopters moved and focused on whatever was going on outside. This was the distraction Amaya needed. It might be her only chance. She didn't know if she could actually follow through with it, but it had to be now or never.

Amaya went to the chest-high storage containers lining the back of the tent. She got one leg up on them, and then very inelegantly, the other leg. She lay down on the containers, took a deep breath, and then rolled off onto the side where the tent was.

She hadn't anticipated how much it would hurt on the way down. She wedged between the taut fabric of the tent and the storage containers. She needed to get under the tent wall but with her arms pinned by her side, it was almost impossible to do anything. She wiggled her body, trying to get the tent wall up to create an opening. The little progress she made was going too slowly. She didn't know how long the distraction would last, and how much time she had before someone noticed her, but the only way out was to go under the side of the tent.

"I can see the shooter!" someone said. It sounded like the shooter was in the opposite direction from SkyWater. Perfect.

Amaya was making progress. The skin on her arms was starting to rub off, but she was making progress. Finally, she squeezed under the bottom of the tent side. It pressed down on her skin and caught on her body, but she kept pushing and finally made it out. *This must be what it feels like to be born.* She rolled to a crouch with one hand on the ground.

No one was around and the edge of the camp wasn't far away. The wild and irregular crashing of her heart against her rib cage felt like she was having a heart attack. She took a deep breath and calmed herself. It was time to figure out if Petra had been correct that the kill switch wouldn't work with a deactivated chip. She flicked off her jail slippers and held them in her hand.

She took a deep breath, inhaling the pine-tree scent of the humid air, and set out in an all-out sprint heading into the forest. Heading towards SkyWater and away from whoever was shooting at the cryogens. It would only be a few seconds until she was in the darkness of the trees. Just a few more steps. She forced her legs to move as fast as they could, and even when she felt the springy softness of the fallen pine needles blanketing the ground, she kept on running. Even when she had to dodge trees or jump over rotting logs, she didn't stop. She glanced over her shoulder at the edge of the clearing. No one was looking in her direction.

She stayed in the trees, but she followed the road back toward Sky-Water. It was away from the camp and away from where the cryogens were being shot at. She would find June and figure out a plan.

The sounds of the soldiers hunting down the cryogen shooter faded as she got farther away, and eventually she stopped to catch her breath. She was alive. The kill switch hadn't activated. It couldn't control her. But every breath she took burned into her lungs, and her feet were red and stinging from running on pinecones and twigs.

Not much longer and she would be at the junction. Up ahead the land sloped steeply down to the main road that would take her into SkyWater. Her breathing slowed and she started to catch her breath. As her panting quieted, some distant voices started to be audible. One voice sounded annoyingly familiar. It was a nasal voice that conveyed the confidence of a nerd in his element. She knew that voice. *Elliat?*

Amaya scrambled to the top of the steep downslope to the road. Whoever it was would be getting close to her soon, and she wanted to get a good look at them from a safe hiding place before they saw or heard her. She found a decaying log in the hills above the road and hid behind it. It wasn't far above the road, but with the dense tree cover she would be difficult to see unless someone was looking right at her.

The voices were slowly drawing closer. Very slowly. Amaya was tired of crouching in her hiding spot. She could clearly hear Elliat's voice, but at times she could also hear a woman's voice and occasionally it sounded like there was another man.

"I don't know why you would think I would be recording," Elliat said.

The woman said something Amaya couldn't understand.

"I don't engage in sensationalistic voyeurism," Elliat said. "The videos I upload are always of the highest and most newsworthy quality."

Those were questionable claims. Apparently, the woman with Elliat thought so as well. The tone of her voice was much flatter and she sounded unhappy. The other man also said something, but Amaya couldn't pick up on the tone of his comments.

The woman spoke again, this time she was close enough for Amaya to understand. "Can we agree to disagree so we can move on from this conversation?" The voice sounded familiar, but from where?

"Fine," Elliat said. "I'm ready to move on from this conversation as well." He was using his offended voice. Elliat got offended a lot so there had been multiple encounters where Amaya had a chance to observe the distinct tone.

"How are we going to get to Mariela?" the woman asked.

Amaya tried to see who the woman was through the trees. Who was she that she wanted to get to Mariela?

"*We* aren't doing anything," the man with the low voice said.

"You need my help," she said. "You need all the help you can get."

"I'll rely on people who I can trust to help me."

It was Cooper. Amaya felt her heart jump. The man talking was Cooper! And the woman…Amaya could place her now. It was Viola.

Amaya jumped up from behind her log and half-ran, half-slid down the steep hillside. A small avalanche of rocks and pine needles accompanied her, the rocks scraping her hands and clattering down to the road below. There was no way they would miss her now.

Amaya hadn't realized how alone she felt until she had seen them. "Cooper," she said, throwing her arms around and hugging tight a very surprised looking Cooper.

"Amaya," Cooper said, "how did you get here?"

"I escaped," Amaya said.

Cooper gave her uniform a glance. "From the jail?"

"Hang on." Viola held up a hand to tell Amaya to stop talking and then looked at Elliat and pointed up the road. "You! Go walk by that tree way up there and face the other way."

Elliat huffed. "I told you, I only use videos with the highest quality information."

"I'm just unclear on what you consider to be high quality information," Viola said. She pointed up the road again. "Go! And dock your exo-cam"

Elliat reluctantly headed in the direction she pointed. Amaya wished he would move a little faster. Finally, he arrived at the tree that Viola had sent him to. His shoulders slumped and he stopped walking.

"Why is he wearing a flak jacket and helmet?" Amaya asked.

"It was a condition of Panacea Corp for allowing us to pass through their blockade line of cryogens," Cooper said. "It's too stinking hot for a flak jacket, so I ditched mine."

"So did I," Viola said. "It's ridiculous that Elliat insists on wearing his even though he's probably going to get dehydrated with all the sweating." Viola looked Amaya up and down. "I'm curious what happened to you? The last I saw you, you, Mariela, and another woman were being held by Liam."

Viola somehow managed to look poised even when sweating, leaving Amaya all that more self-conscious about her sweaty jail uniform, dirt-streaked face, and ragged slippers. Amaya dropped her slippers on the ground and slipped her feet into them. They weren't much, but it was still better than walking on the bare ground.

"I'm not sure I want to tell you what happened." Amaya rubbed the spot on the back of her neck that still stung from the injection. "If Cooper doesn't trust you, then I'm not sure I trust you."

"Cooper trusts me. He just doesn't want to admit it because he's mad at me. But you should know I want to make sure that Mariela gets out alive as much as anybody," Viola said.

"And Nyala," Amaya said.

"What?"

"We need to make sure Nyala gets out alive also."

"I don't want anyone to die. You all seem to think I'm some sort of cold, calculating automaton. We need to help them, *both* of them, now."

There didn't seem to be any reason to trust her, but pretty much everything that Amaya knew Liam also knew, so it couldn't hurt for Viola to know as well.

"Liam injected us with a kill switch and said you were the one who developed the technology."

"Shit!" Viola placed a hand on her forehead and paced. "That asshole! I didn't mean for it to be used against anyone. I just developed the tech to run the cryogens, but when he saw that and the chemical analysis of the kill switch—I didn't tell him the sample was from Mariela, by the way—he figured out how to replicate the kill switch and must have had his loyal minions prepare the final solution."

Cooper's face reddened and a vein bulged on his forehead. "Viola, what were you thinking? You told Liam? You knew how dangerous the kill switch could be."

She shrugged. "He's the CEO."

"Did you think he would give you a promotion?"

"No." Viola crossed her arms.

"Be honest."

She scoffed. "Yes, I thought he would. But he's also my boss. We're wasting time."

"Amaya, what direction is the camp?" Cooper asked.

"It's that way," Amaya pointed back down the road. "Turn right at the junction and then it's not much farther."

Viola rolled her eyes. "I *know* how to get there."

"Viola," Cooper said, "I think it's time we went our separate ways. You know where the camp is, feel free to go there and see if you can get Liam to let you back in, but you're not welcome to continue on with us."

"Cooper, don't do this…please. We should do this together. We'll save Mariela—*and* Nyala—and then go find Petra Dmitrova and ask her what she knows about the kill switch."

"Come on, Amaya." Cooper grabbed Amaya's elbow and pulled her up the road. It was a rude thing to do. She should complain, but it didn't seem like the right time, so she went along as fast as she could in her jail slippers.

"What's our plan?" Amaya asked. She looked back over her shoulder. Viola glared at them, but she turned on her heels and headed off in the other direction.

"I don't have one."

"Great. Neither do I. What are we going to do with Elliat?"

"Him, I have a plan for."

Elliat was still facing away from them with his arms crossed tapping his foot. Cooper touched him on his shoulder.

"Elliat," Cooper said, "Viola went to the Panacea Corp camp to save Mariela and Nyala. Price has injected Mariela and Nyala with a substance he can use to kill them."

"Nyala's in danger? And there's going to be a confrontation? And a dramatic rescue?"

"Possibly. At least that's what Viola is hoping for. You should cover it as that sounds like a *very* high-quality news item. If you hurry, you can probably catch up to Viola pretty quickly."

"Yes. Yes." He starting off half-jogging in the direction that Viola had gone. "I will check on Nyala."

"Just don't make things worse," Amaya yelled after him. "Please be careful—a wrong move and they could be killed."

He turned back to face her and while walking backwards, put his hand on his heart. "I solemnly promise you I shall do nothing that will harm your sister."

CHAPTER 22

The Day After the Umbrella Fell

Friday, continued

Cooper watched Elliat hurry away to catch up with Viola. As he hurried down the road, Elliat called out to her to wait while also trying to catch his breath. It was touching, in an odd way. Amaya headed the other direction, on up the hill, and Cooper followed her. "Is it my imagination or does Elliat seem oddly attached to your sister? He kept talking about her as we were walking up here."

"He likes her almost as much as he likes Liam."

Cooper laughed. Having Amaya as his traveling companion was a nice reprieve from walking with Elliat and Viola. It even made the oppressive humidity a little more bearable. "I'm glad we can pick up the pace a bit," he said. "Elliat's a really slow walker, and there's a rainstorm that's going to break sometime in the next couple hours. I'd like to be in SkyWater before the deluge starts."

Amaya looked down at her feet. "I'm afraid I'm not going to be much faster."

She didn't look well. She had lost a lot of weight, her legs trembled, and her feet were covered in scratches and red welts.

"So how did you end up in jail?"

"Dan picked us up seconds after we installed the communication device."

"That explains why he had it."

"I'll give him a little credit—he also let us go without Petra's approval. But then we realized we had forgotten the communication device with him."

"What was it like being in jail?" he asked her. "Did you meet any nice people?"

Amaya laughed. "We were isolated. So…no. Truth be told, it was kind of tense. We weren't exactly getting along. And it was cold and uncomfortable."

The air was hot and heavy with moisture. It felt like walking in a sauna. Cooper set his digi-skin to cooling. "Did the tension have anything to do with Mariela deleting the ghosts without telling you?"

"Yes. How did you know it was her who did it? I thought you blamed me."

"I did at first, but that didn't make sense. You had no reason to delete the ghosts and it wasn't like you. The only person who had a good reason to delete them was Mariela, and if Amoco helped her with the code, then she had the means. Am I wrong?"

"No." Amaya shook her head. "You're not wrong. They altered the code without telling me."

"And the Black Screen was part of it?"

"Right," Amaya said.

Mariela's decision to delete the ghosts, without telling any of the rest of them, was another stab in the back from a woman who had stabbed him so many times he had lost count.

He shook his head. "You know, I've been betrayed by Mariela so many times it's almost like I can't feel anything about it anymore. I guess I've accepted she'll always be a part of my life, one way or another."

"I feel the same way. Nyala and I could have left the jail at any time if we had just agreed to leave Area 52, but we stayed because Mariela is a part of our lives. She's a friend, even if sometimes it doesn't feel like much of a friendship."

Cooper chuckled. "We're a sad pair."

"So sad." Amaya laughed.

"Who should we complain about next?" he asked.

"I vote for Hank."

"Hank's too obvious a choice."

"Well, pretty much everyone gets on my nerves nowadays, so no one is really safe from my disdain. I used to like people..." Amaya gave a short, humorless laugh. "I just didn't want to spend any time around them." She paused for a second, her jailhouse slippers making a flapping noise as she walked. "Speaking of spending time around people, you should probably know that I may have some people looking for me if they figure out I've escaped."

"I'll take my chances," Cooper said. "It's not far until the Area 52 blockade anyway. In fact, I'd better check in with Amoco about it."

After randomly punching a few buttons on his Everything, he was speaking to Amoco, T-Rock, and Bren. He filled them in on running into

Amaya, and how Violet and Elliat had gone to the cryogen camp. They had already figured out bits and pieces from the satellite coverage.

"We're almost to the second blockade," Cooper told them. "Can you tell us how much farther until we get there and is there any way around it?"

"The blockade is around the next bend from your present location, and I do not see any feasible method of bypassing it," Amoco said. "The denizens of Area 52 selected well when they choose this location for the blockade. The road is an engineered land bridge between two mountains; the hills on both sides are sufficiently steep that there is no apparent way for you to easily traverse them other than over the bridge." Amoco sighed. "Trees clinging impossibly to such unwelcoming landscapes gives one a sense of wonder about the ability of nature to survive—"

"Amoco," Cooper interrupted him, "is there another way across?" Really, how difficult was it for Amoco to just give a simple answer?

"Not without plummeting down and then struggling up almost vertical inclines. There are gentler paths but to go around would almost certainly add an extra day to your time."

"Ok, thanks." It looked like there wasn't any better option than to go on up to the blockade and try to get through. "Any news?" he asked Amoco.

"Hey Cooper, hey Amaya, it's T-Rock. Some of the cryos aren't doing well in the heat and are malfunctioning. I told you it wasn't natural to use those things. Liam's people shoot them when that happens and pull them off the road to get them out of the way but then they just leave them there. The biggest group of cryos isn't far behind you—probably about an hour out. The gawkers stuck at the first blockade are getting restless, it's possible they may start to revolt, or maybe they'll just go home. Who knows? The Area 52 law enforcement is rounding up the gawkers that got through before the blockade. Looks like they're doing a pretty good job, but Amoco and I have identified about twenty-five or so that are still running around up there."

"Are you following Viola and Elliat?"

"Nothing to report there," T-Rock said. "They're still walking toward the camp. That Elliat's a slow walker. No blog posts from him. I'll update you if I see anything."

"Anything else?"

"Even with all the coverage, people still have no clue what's happening," T-Rock said. "Great interview by the way. You managed to reveal lots of important information in way that made so little sense that no one paid any attention to it."

"Well, I guess that's something."

~~~~~

Amaya stared at Cooper as he haphazardly poked at his Everything. Clearly, he wasn't used to using one.

"How do you turn this thing off?" he asked.

She stopped walking. "How do you not know how to use an Everything?" She punched the button to disconnect the call. "Give me that. It doesn't make sense for you to wear it if you don't know how to use it." She pulled the Everything off of his arm and snapped it onto her own. How did he manage to get by in the world?

"So, what are we going to do?" Cooper asked her.

"Do we have any options other than charging ahead?" Amaya was getting the uncomfortable feeling that maybe escaping from the camp wasn't such a good idea.

"We could join Viola and Elliat," Cooper said, "but other than that, I don't think so."

"I don't think so either. When I risked escaping from the camp to get help for Mariela and Nyala, I wasn't imagining showing back up at the camp with just the four of us. I say we charge ahead and meet with June to come up with a plan." What was she thinking she would do when she escaped? It wasn't clear to her now.

"Okay," Cooper said. "Any suggestions for our next step?"

"We walk up to the blockade and ask them to let us through."

Cooper laughed. "That's a great plan. Why didn't I think of that?"

"Not everyone can come up with such detailed and well-thought-out plans." Amaya smiled. "It's a skill."

"Okay, let's try your plan." Cooper set off up the road toward the second blockade.

Amaya wiped the sweat from her forehead. It stung each time it dripped in her eyes. It seemed like such a contrast to just two weeks ago when the air had been cold and was so dry that she got nosebleeds. She might actually prefer the blizzards over the sweltering humidity. The only thing that made up for the awful weather was the beautiful view. They were high up on the mountain—probably 3,000 feet above the
~~~~~

plains below, and the vistas were stunning.

She stopped walking for a bit and looked out on the basin that stretched almost as far as she could see, until it was bordered on the far side by a small row of mountains. Dark clouds had been hanging low in the sky ever since they had left the jail, but the rain never fell. Instead, the clouds gave the landscape an eerie, peaceful feeling. "It's beautiful here."

Cooper stopped next to Amaya and looked out over the valley below. "This is one of the most beautiful places I've ever seen. Someday I'd like to come here when there isn't a blizzard, a heat wave, or a zombie invasion."

Amaya laughed. "We should be able to see the second blockade soon."

"Are you ready?"

"Yep."

They rounded a sharp corner in the road and were in sight of the blockade by the Area 52 people. The ten or so deputies working the blockade looked bored. Not much later someone called out to the others and pointed at Cooper and Amaya. All the rifles that had previously been held in a relaxed position pointing toward the ground were held rigidly, ready to point at Amaya and Cooper at the slightest sign of a threat. There was no turning back now.

It was at that moment the rain finally broke. It didn't start with a drizzle, or a light shower, but instead there was a crack of thunder followed by a rush of rain. Within minutes everything was going to be drenched. Some of the people manning the blockade grappled with ponchos, but it was clear everyone was going to end up soaked.

About forty yards from the blockade, someone yelled at them to stop and put their hands in the air. Two sheriff's deputies ran out and frisked them.

"He's wearing that weird clothing!" the one frisking Cooper yelled.

"Look at what she's wearing," the other said as he patted Amaya's ankles. He stood up and pointed to her chest. "It says 'Property of Sky-Water Jail.' Looks like she is one of those people who escaped."

"Let's take her back to the jail. We'll hold this one for questioning and then throw him in with the others."

The deputy shoved Amaya in the back. "Get moving! Keep your hands in the air!"

Her shoulders sagged. It looked like she was going back to jail.

The road quickly turned into slippery slush. The now-ragged slippers that Amaya had been given in jail got further sucked into the mud with every step; Amaya's legs tired from pulling up on the slipper with her foot to unstick them.

With the deputies making her keep her hands up, she looked like a marionette. The deputies had removed the cuffs after both Cooper and Amaya slipped and fell on their faces multiple times, but even uncuffed it was still rough going. Her arms fatigued from holding them in the air, but with the handcuffs off she could at least use her arms for balance.

For the tenth time, she lost her slipper. Each time, the deputy allowed her to lower one hand to pull the slipper out, but with each new incident he was getting more and more impatient. Finally, she just left her slippers in the mud—first the right and not long after the left. The downpour dropped the temperature dramatically, probably twenty degrees, and with the help of the occasional brisk breeze across her wet clothes, Amaya was deeply chilled.

"Do you have any idea how far away we are?" she asked Cooper. "I'm getting cold and my feet hurt."

"Amoco said the blockade was about a mile and a half outside of town. We went about half a mile or so before the transport vehicle got bogged down in the mud. Add to that the more or less half-mile that we've walked, we probably have about a half-mile left."

"So about an hour at the speed we're going."

"If someone had worn more sensible shoes," Cooper grinned at her, "we could have picked up the pace a bit."

Amaya smiled at Cooper's teasing, but she was too cold to laugh. "You should try walking barefoot through this."

"Actually, since you lost your slippers, I think you may be having an easier time of it than I am." He picked up his foot and showed her the inches of pine needles and mud stuck to the bottom of his shoe. "It's not easy to walk while wearing high heels made out of mud."

"But they look so fashionable." Amaya was trying to keep the conversation light-hearted, but the colder she got the more difficult it was to be polite. Cooper laughed at her comment but didn't respond. Just as well. Conversation was too difficult.

Cooper turned to one of the deputies. "Can you put us into contact with June Stafford when we get to town?"

"That's above my pay grade," the deputy responded.

Amaya's stomach clenched at the idea of going back to the jail. It seemed a waste for Dan to help them escape just to end up back there. The only thing that didn't suck about going back to jail was that it was better than being in Liam's camp. They had to allow her a phone call, right?

"There's a lot like you coming through here since The Opening," one of the deputies said after a while.

"The Opening?" Cooper asked.

"The Opening is what we're calling when you all took our protective umbrella down. Ever since then people wearing clothing like you starting coming onto our land."

"How many have you seen?" Cooper asked.

"Maybe one hundred or so. I hear there's another blockade down the road. It's not ours, but since it went up, we haven't seen many people. You're the first in a couple hours."

"Have the people been causing problems?"

"Before we started picking them up, they mostly just asked annoying questions and tried to get into places that they shouldn't. Like we caught one breaking into our school science lab to look for evidence that we were experimenting on aliens."

"What are you doing with all of them?" Amaya asked. There was no way the two holding cells could fit all those people.

"We started throwing them into the holding cell, but then it got full. So we used the church fellowship hall. We're going to deport everybody after the Elder gets everything sorted out with the umbrella being down and those zombies from the north. We can't keep you guys here long because we don't want to end up with radiation poisoning."

So Petra was still trying to keep up the illusion that the world outside the umbrella of Area 52 was affected by radiation poisoning. The breeze picked up and Amaya shivered. The deputies didn't say anything when she wrapped her arms around herself. She rubbed her arms but touching her marble-cold skin just made her colder.

"Are you doing okay?" Cooper asked.

"I'm still moving."

"That's not saying much."

"You're not cold?" Her teeth were on the verge of chattering and she shivered.

"I've been warming my clothes," Cooper said.

Oh right. His clothes were made out of digi-skin. "I hadn't noticed." She should have noticed that his clothes were still perfectly clean while hers were covered in mud.

"We should trade."

"What?"

"Take my shirt at the least. Until you get warm."

The shivers turned into shaking.

"Okay." She stopped walking because each step was painful.

Cooper lowered his hands and lifted his shirt.

"Whoa, hey, put your hands back up and keep walking!" The soggy deputy, who didn't look much happier than they were, pointed his rifle at Cooper.

Cooper dropped his shirt and raised his hands back in the air. "I need to help her out."

"We're almost there. To get help for her, keep moving."

Amaya frowned. The digi-skin shirt would have been nice. If only the burning in her feet—a thousand scrapes from the small rocks in the roadway and the pinecones in the forest—could warm her up.

The sheriff's station looked exactly like it had when Amaya had left it early that morning. Was it really only that morning? It felt like so much longer. She limped up to the front door; her feet had gone from burning to feeling like they were blocks of wood. The nerve pain that shot though her foot when she put her weight on it was the only clue that her feet were still there. She couldn't stop shivering even though the room felt stuffy compared to the outside. Her wet clothes clung to her and dripped on the floor.

"Oh my god, Amaya." Cooper stared at her feet. They were red and swollen; a trail of bloody footprints led back to the door. The floor swayed underneath her and the room went black.

CHAPTER 23

The Day After the Umbrella Fell

Friday, continued

Mariela woke up stiff and achy. Nyala was sitting in one of the folding chairs, her arms still hanging limply by her side. Mariela wiped away a drop of water that had fallen on her face. A heavy rainfall pounded on the roof of the tent and leaked inside. How long had she been lying on the cot? The last thing she could remember was getting the injection, but that seemed like a long time ago. It had the ethereal vagueness of a dream, but the intense burning in the back of her neck reminded her that it wasn't. She sat up. "How long was I out?" she asked Nyala.

"About half a day. I was getting really worried. I would have moved my chair closer to keep an eye on you, but…" She shrugged her shoulders to draw attention to her motion-inhibited arms.

Mariela sat up and rubbed her temples. "My head is killing me. What happened?"

"You passed out when they injected the kill switch."

"I've never slept that long." She looked around. "Where's Amaya?"

"Not here."

Did that mean Amaya had escaped? It must. Nyala appeared uncomfortable with saying anything more, so Mariela didn't press and hoped Amaya's absence was good news.

"Have they moved the camp forward?" Mariela asked.

"We're still in the same place," Nyala responded. "I've been listening to the conversations outside the tent, and it sounds like the cryogens have been moving forward more slowly than they expected. At first the heat was causing some of them to malfunction, and then this rain started about six hours ago and it hasn't let up since. There's lots of flooding"—Nyala looked at the dirt floor that had about an inch of water on it—" and the roads are mud slicks, so they can't move the cryogens forward because they keep falling down."

Nyala smiled. "Honestly, it sounded kind of amusing—cryogens falling flat on their faces and then the operators being unable to get them back up again. Eventually it sounded like they gave up trying to make any progress at all so things have come to a standstill. The only good news for the cryogens is that when the rain started, people stopped shooting at them."

Outside the tent, yelling was followed by the sounds of soldiers running. Mariela swayed and almost fell when she tried to get up. She regained her balance, and slower this time, she headed over to the entrance and looked out the tent flap. Her head throbbed, but Mariela wasn't going to let it stop her from seeing whatever interesting thing was going on outside. Nyala peered over her shoulder.

Viola stood at the edge of the camp surrounded by soldiers pointing their guns at her and with her wet hair plastered to the side of her face.

She had her hands raised, and stood proud with shoulders back. She said, "I demand to see Liam," as if she had no doubt of her demands being complied with.

"I'm here." A clearly annoyed Liam strode toward her wearing a heavy rain poncho. "What's so important you couldn't wait until the end of a rainstorm to talk to me about it?"

"I insist on being brought back on this project. I started it, developed it, and put it into motion. You are on the verge of taking control of some of the best land in the country, and that's because of *me*." She pointed at her chest. "*I* should be here."

"I'm getting wet. We can talk about this later." Liam abruptly turned and headed back toward his tent. Mariela let the flap to the tent drop into place so he wouldn't see them watching.

"Liam," it sounded like Viola had followed him, "I won't let you put me off. This is *my* project and I should be in charge of it."

Mariela opened the tent flap again just a bit. She and Nyala peered out. Viola confronting Liam was too good to miss. Liam turned around and stalked back to Viola.

"I'm very aware you started this project because I'm busy cleaning up the mess you made. You rushed the implementation, and you were completely unprepared. The cryogens can't walk in the mud, the heat is making them malfunction, and sometimes they start shooting randomly. You let news of what you were doing leak—"

"That wasn't me," Viola protested. "Those people were already there for some reason."

"You should have known that. You didn't pay attention to what was going on."

It was uncomfortable watching Liam reprimand Viola, but Mariela couldn't look away. Liam paced back and forth.

"Viola, you showing up back up here is the epitome of arrogance," Liam said. "But probably the stupidest thing you have done was to give cryogens guns and then program them to shoot back at anyone who shoots at them." Veins bulged in Liam's neck. "We have live people shooting at dead people who are then shooting back at the live people." He chopped his hand into his other palm to make his point. "Do you understand why I'm unhappy?'

"I have an idea, yes." Viola looked at the ground. Mariela decided she was rooting for Viola even though Liam had a good point.

"This is a public relations nightmare! All of this"—Liam gestured around him—"*debacle* is on top of the Black Screen and the loss of the LP100 model ghosts. I *cannot* and *will not* let another thing go wrong. I'm in charge now. You can stay here and pretend like you are doing something if you think you deserve it, but you will no longer have any decision-making authority."

"Of course," Viola said. She looked at the ground and clasped her hands in front of her. "Your point about the public relations reminded me of an idea I wanted to share with you. I've been spending some time with the public and they're confused about what's going on here. It's led to some negative publicity for Panacea Corp. I'd like to suggest that you do an interview with a reporter who has been supportive of your agenda in order to communicate what you are trying to accomplish here."

Liam paused as he was walking away and appeared to be considering the idea. He partially turned back toward Viola. "Who were you thinking of?"

"Well, there's that one woman who wrote the very nice piece about your initiative to reduce chip burn," Viola said.

"Great. Get her." Liam turned away.

"Oh no, wait," Viola said, "she's on maternity leave. How about that Elliat Exis fellow?"

"He's a little over-eager." Liam continued walking toward his tent.

Viola appeared reluctant to move but then following behind Liam she said, "He dislikes the Stafford family and adores you, so you know his reporting will be in line with your needs."

The blood surged into Mariela's face. That conniving Elliat had been making her family look bad for years now. Surely it wouldn't take much effort for him to further discredit Mariela in some way and help Liam fire her, which would open the door for Viola to move up within the company.

Viola had so easily gotten the upper hand, not over Liam, but over Mariela. Viola was playing the game of one-upmanship better than Mariela—Mariela was down for the count with two kill switches while Viola didn't have any, and if Elliat's article was persuasive then Viola was probably going to be given a higher position within the company than Mariela.

Liam glanced at Viola. "Set the interview with Elliat up." Liam continued walking; he slipped in the mud but managed to right himself before falling. "I'm available any time after this wretched rain stops."

"At least give me someplace dry to stay in the meantime," Viola called out to his back.

Liam's poncho swung around his legs as he turned around. "Fine. You can stay with the other three." Liam grabbed Viola's arm and dragged her toward their tent. Mariela and Nyala ducked back inside.

"What are we going to do?" Mariela asked Nyala in a low voice.

"Just hope he doesn't notice," Nyala said.

There was an understanding between them that they were talking about Amaya not being there. Nyala quickly sat down on one of the folding chairs and Mariela laid down on the cot.

Liam dragged Viola into the tent and without pausing he strode back outside. Mariela let out the breath she had been holding in. But before the flap could settle back into place, Liam was back inside the tent. "Where's the third one?"

Nyala stood up. "The third what?"

"The third woman!" Liam's face turned red.

"She's right there." Nyala pointed to Viola.

"No, the third one who came with you all." Liam growled at Nyala. He opened the tent flap and stuck his head out. A burst of wind spray blew rain into the tent. "One of the women escaped," he yelled out. "Find her!"

"Which one?" came a voice from outside.

"I don't know!" Liam yelled out the door of the tent. "Not Mariela and not the one who beats people up!"

"With the rain it'll be difficult to find her!" someone outside yelled back.

"I don't care!" Liam yelled. "Use her chip to track her down. I want it done now!" Liam turned back to face the inside of the tent.

"How did this happen?" Mariela asked. She enjoyed indirectly pointing out to Liam that he wasn't in as much control as he thought he was.

Another vein bulged on Liam's forehead. He stalked over to Mariela. "The only reason I haven't disposed of you is because I don't want to have to explain to the board of Panacea Corp what happened to you." He loomed over her on the cot. "But don't tempt me to change my mind."

He made uncomfortable eye contact with Mariela and then walked back to the opening. Mariela's head hurt worse than before, pulsating like it might explode. What had gone wrong with the injection to make her pass out for so long? Why was it causing her so much pain? The world was going dark again. Wait…

The hot coals sent spears of pain shooting through Amaya's feet. They had lied to her about walking on coals, saying it would be pain free. But it burned. It burned worse than anything had ever hurt before. Her legs were heavy and she couldn't get off of the coals, no matter how hard she tried. She tried to run but each step was like pushing through molasses and she couldn't breathe.

"Hey!" someone called out to her. "Hey! Wake up!"

Amaya gasped and sat up straight in bed. The sweat beaded on her forehead and the sheets clung to her legs. Her heart beat erratically, her hands trembled, her breathing was fast and shallow. She concentrated on her body, trying to get it to calm down. Her breathing slowly deepened and her heart settled into a plodding rhythm. The details of the room came into focus. She was in the hospital, but how she got there were fuzzy.

"I had a nightmare," she said to the young deputy standing with a firearm in the corner of the room. The deputy stared straight ahead, not moving a single facial muscle. The hospital room didn't look like any Amaya had been in before. There wasn't a single medical mister or customizable digi-skin surface in sight. It looked like it was straight out of a picture from the turn of the millennium.

The wind whipped through the trees and whistled through the hospital window while intense gusts of wind rattled the windowpanes. Her jail uniform was gone—hopefully they burned it—and replaced by a hospital gown. Her feet burned and thick bandages encased both feet. The reason for the coal-walking nightmare became clear. Walking was going to be painful for a while. Any escapes to rescue Nyala and Mariela were probably also off the table.

"Why am I here?" she asked the deputy.

"I'm not authorized to answer questions," the stoic deputy said.

"Then who is?"

"That's a question."

Amaya rolled her eyes. "Just tell me."

"The doctor."

A living doctor. She had dealt with living doctors when she was dealing with some issues as a teen, but she always talked to the AutoDoc after that.

"How do I get ahold of the doctor?"

"Look lady, I'm just here to make sure you don't run away again. I'm not here to answer questions or to chat with you. It's a distraction."

"Okay, well then you can follow me down the hall while I go find someone who can answer my questions."

"You can't leave here."

"I can't leave even to consult with my doctor?"

"Lady, just push the call button and I'm sure your doctor will be at your beck and call right away."

Amaya looked at all the contraptions around her and lots of them had buttons. She was too groggy to make sense of all them. But if she asked the deputy another question though, she might get shot.

"Oh, for goodness' sake," the deputy said, "it's the one by your hand."

Ohh, that button! Amaya pushed it and fell into a fitful sleep.

None of her dreams stayed with her this time except her feet were burning in a lot of them. She was never very deeply asleep, and woke up easily when the doctor entered the room.

The doc picked up some paper with a hard backing hanging from a clip at the end of the bed. The doc looked at some of the machines and then turned back to Amaya.

A bolt of lightning stabbed into the room and momentarily highlighted every small detail of the forest outside her window. Amaya could swear she could see actual tendrils of lightning reach into the room. A clap of thunder broke over the room, and almost immediately waves of rain began smacking into the window.

"How long have I been here?"

"About twelve hours. You came in around three pm yesterday afternoon, and it's four am now."

It was a long time—she needed to be getting help. Were Nyala and Mariela still at the camp? Were they okay? She couldn't let being hospitalized derail getting help for them.

She turned to the doctor. "I can't stay here." Why was her brain so fuzzy? She needed to start planning.

The doctor held a bright light in front Amaya's eyes. "I think between being in jail or being in the hospital, you're probably better off in the hospital."

"Are those my only options?"

The doctor put the light down and picked up the paper. "Pretty much." Without looking up, the doctor wrote something on the paper.

"Why am I so groggy?" Amaya rubbed her eyes.

"We're giving you a mild sedative."

"I haven't slept in a bed in a long time."

"I'm glad we could help you out." That sounded like sarcasm. "It seemed like you hadn't showered in a long time as well." The doctor fiddled with the IV line. "I'm stopping the sedative now to see how the pain is. You're dehydrated, so I'm going to keep you on fluids."

"Good." She needed to get off the pains meds so she could figure a way out of the hospital. There was no way she could help Nyala and Mariela if she was stuck in here. It felt like she had gone in a completely useless circle. How ironic that she managed to avoid death from a killer substance injected in her neck only to end up under arrest again. And Dan wouldn't help her escape this time.

Amaya looked at the ceiling as the doctor unwrapped the bandages on her feet. She didn't want to see how swollen they were; she could feel it without needing to look.

"It looks like we managed to save all your toes, although we need to keep an eye out for infection. You really did a number on your feet."

"Other than my feet, am I okay?" she asked the doc.

"You had hypo—" Screams outside the window broke into the quiet of the hospital. The doctor stopped talking and looked toward the window. "What *are* your people doing out there? I can't afford to treat many more of you."

There was another noise, one that Amaya had thought was the drone of hospital machinery, but which she realized was actually the sound of helicopters hovering. Something disturbing was going on outside.

"What's going on?" she asked.

"Do I look like I know?" the doctor snapped at Amaya.

The deputy looked out the window. "It's that army of undead people that Petra warned us about."

"Shit!" The doctor looked at the deputy. "Can you contact the sheriff and ask him to resend the message reminding everyone to take the minimum dose of their meds for radiation exposure?"

"No problem." The deputy took out a communication device like the one Amoco and Georgia had created for them and punched the buttons on it.

The doctor finished unbandaging Amaya's feet and looked them over. She had been impatient before but now she seemed in a rush. "Your feet will be fine," she said brusquely to Amaya. She leaned towards the door and yelled, "Can I get a nurse in here to bandage her feet?" She turned back to Amaya. "I'm going to have you take meds for the radiation poisoning. I'm not sure if it will help much at this point in your life but it can't hurt. Although you seem to be doing remarkably well, given your lifelong exposure."

Oh. The doctor didn't know the radiation stories weren't real. Amaya shrugged. "Well, we have radiation meds where I come from." Why was she encouraging this shared delusion? She should tell them the truth, although the doctor probably wouldn't believe her anyway.

"Of course," the doctor nodded. "That explains a lot. The medications don't cause you long-term problems? What did you take?"

Enough with the lies; Amaya was going to tell the truth. If Petra wanted to lie to her own people, that couldn't be helped, but Amaya didn't have to participate in it. "The truth is, there was no radiation poisoning. If you want to test me to see if I'm telling the truth, go ahead."

The doctor's brow furrowed. "No, I'm sure you've been misled. Petra and I do a test of the radiation levels outside the umbrella every year and they continue to be high." The doctor double-clicked her pen and then stuck it into her coat pocket. "I hate to tell you this, but your government is lying to you."

"About a nuclear war? That sort of thing is hard to hide. Like I said, test me if you want to know the truth."

"I don't have time. I'll do it later."

Funny how people resisted the truth.

"You can save money by not having everyone take the meds anymore. How big is your stockpile? You could save whatever you have for later, in case there actually is radiation."

"Our stockpile is sufficient." The furrow in the doctor's brow deepened. "Why are you asking me this? Why are you trying to get information on our stockpiles?" She stood up abruptly. "Is that what you all are doing here—you've run out of your own medication so you're trying to take ours?" She tried to hang the paper she was writing on back at the foot of the bed, and then when it didn't catch properly, she shoved it into place. "I have to tell Elder Petra about this." The agitated doctor rushed out of the room.

Well, that hadn't gone as planned.

CHAPTER 24

Two Days After The Opening

Saturday

Excited yelling startled Cooper awake. He stretched out his body; it ached from laying on a thin mat on the floor of the church fellowship room. Having fifty people in one room was not generally conducive to sleep. There were the conversations and arguments, some loud, some whispered; the coughing and other random noises; the snoring; the woman who played the church's piano through most of the night and the people who sometimes sang along with her; the guy who yelled at the woman who played the piano all night; the person rambling about the truth being out there; and the groups that appeared to be meditating, doing yoga, and what may have been some sort of interpretive dance. How he could have slept in the middle of all of it was beyond him.

"The zombies are here!" someone cried out.

People, including the piano woman, bumped into each other as they ran over to the fellowship room's large picture windows overlooking the main village road. He was awake now, he might as well join them. The hill the church was on allowed him to see the procession of cryogens down the waterlogged main road through SkyWater. The cryogens walked with their guns down but ready to be aimed at any moment. Most of the residents of SkyWater had fled indoors, leaving no one on the street except the cryogens and their handlers in armored vehicles.

Some of the Area 52 deputies were hidden behind structures scattered around town. If the deputies fired first, the cryogens would fire back. If the deputies waited, the cryogens would occupy the entire village. It was a difficult dilemma. Thank goodness it wasn't his problem to deal with.

The piano-playing woman leaned up against the glass to look down the road. "My friend who was waiting at the zombie blockade messaged me that all the human handlers left, so a bunch of people are talking about rushing at the zombies and taking their rifles away."

The only thing that could be worse than having an army of cryogens invading, or as Viola would say it, "occupying," Area 52, would be to also have an out-of-control throng of conspiracy theorists set on confronting them.

"Hey you!"

Cooper looked over his shoulder. One of the deputies pointed at him from across the room.

"Are you talking to me?" Cooper asked.

"The Elder wants to see you." The deputy motioned for Cooper to follow along. "Come on."

The Elder had to be Petra. He went willingly, interested to hear what Petra had to say about what was happening. Maybe she would even be helpful with getting Nyala and Mariela away from Liam, though that seemed unlikely. The deputy led him down a thick-carpeted hallway that smelled like the old books in Oscar's library.

At the end of the hallway, Petra was waiting for him in a small chapel. She stood with one of her hands resting on the back of the front pew. A small stained-glass window behind her let in dappled early morning light. She motioned to the pew across the small aisle. "Sit down." He sat where she pointed and she sat in the pew across from him. The deputy stood by the door.

"How's my friend?" he asked Petra. After they had taken Amaya to the hospital last night, he had unsuccessfully tried to badger one of the deputies into getting an update on her condition. Surely, Petra would have more information. She knew everything that was happening in her town.

"They're trying to save her feet from becoming infected. She's on intravenous antibiotics right now and her wounds are being debrided. She has hypothermia, she's dehydrated and undernourished, and she's covered in other cuts and abrasions."

"You could airlift her to be treated in one of our hospitals. Our technology is more advanced."

Petra bristled at the suggestion. "We are perfectly capable of treating infection, hypothermia, and dehydration here. Plus, she is a prisoner. She's escaped from one of our jails and has now illegally entered our protected area twice. One of my deputies even let her escape from jail and for some reason she *still* came back."

"She had a right to be here and you know it."

"I know no such thing." Petra did condescending and haughty better than anybody. "What I know is that she is not leaving our custody again any time soon. The deputy who helped her escape has been reassigned to escorting the detainees in the church to the bathroom. Escorting all the detainees except you, that is. I don't know your relationship with him but I'm not one to take chances."

Cooper made direct eye contact with Petra. "We don't get along. He killed my daughter."

Petra didn't flinch. "From what I understand, you put your daughter in danger by having her serve as a lookout while you were resisting a law enforcement operation."

No matter how callous Petra was, he wasn't going to let her get under his skin. "Why am I here?" he asked.

She turned to the deputy by the door. "Leave us. Go down the hall halfway and wait for me there." She waited to speak until the door closed behind the deputy. "There's something else going on with Amaya."

He tensed. Was it his imagination or had Petra dropped the haughty attitude somewhat? Even sounded concerned?

"What's that?" he asked.

"The doctor noticed the back of her neck was red, and pointed out to me she had a chip like Grace's. I examined the area around it and found an injection site. A biopsy confirmed my fear that Amaya has been injected with a substance that could kill her. Just like—I believe you know her—Mariela Stafford. I'm sure Amaya didn't have it when she left here yesterday morning."

Amaya had filled him in on what Liam had done to her in the cryogen camp. There was no need to deny it to Petra. "It was done yesterday."

"That was what I was afraid of." Petra looked off into the distance. "Am I correct in assuming the person who ordered this…kill switch, to use Mariela's term, was the current CEO of Panacea Corp?"

"That's right." It was a chilling thought.

"I was afraid this would happen if the formula was ever found." She stood up and paced in the front of the steps to the chapel's altar. "Then it seems to me you have multiple problems with one solution that will address all of them."

"What?" Cooper wasn't sure what he was expecting when he was summoned to talk to Petra, but it wasn't this.

"You have the kill switch, which allows embedded chips to be monitored and can also cause death through causing them to overload, you have the CEO of the world's most powerful corporation using that kill switch, you have the cryogens who appear to be controlled through a modification of the kill switch technology which probably goes without saying is only a step away from controlling humans using the technology, and the only way to deactivate the kill switch is to disable the chip. What's the one common theme there?"

"I don't know." A chill ran down his spine. He probably wasn't going to like where Petra was going with this. "The kill switch?"

"The chips."

"What do you mean the chips?"

"Don't play dense with me. I know you are perfectly capable of understanding what I mean."

Cooper did understand what Petra was saying, but he didn't like it. "You mean that without the embedded chips, none of these things would be possible."

"Exactly. The logical conclusion is that disabling the chips would stop all of it from happening."

"Even if I agreed that was the solution, what do you expect me to do? I don't know how to disable the chips."

"But you know people who do. If you agree to this, I will allow you to contact your friend who has the capability to do it." She could only be talking about Amoco. "It would be fairly easy for someone with the right technology and access to disable all the chips. There's a flaw I identified many years ago that could be exploited."

"I can't do that. Do you know how disruptive it would be to our society?"

"I have a pretty good idea."

Why should he trust Petra? She didn't have anyone's interests in mind other than her own people. He leaned forward in his seat. "Taking out the chips is exactly what you want. It fits perfectly with your whole bias against any tech older than 2005."

"What I want is for you all to leave. If taking out the chips reduces the hordes of people coming in here, then that's what I want. I also want to stop that group of 10,000 or so cryogens that Panacea Corp is using to take land that belongs to us. Otherwise, whatever other people do to their brains, including invasive monitoring devices, is irrelevant to me."

"You could shoot all the cryogens. They're already dead so it's not like it would be murder."

"We don't have the firepower to take out an army of cryogens. In the unlikely event of a victory on our side, we would still lose a lot of our people in the process. And that wouldn't address the kill switch."

"Why is the kill switch important to you? Your people don't have chips so it doesn't affect them."

"I created it, and I can't allow it to be used in this way. I visited Panacea Corp's encampment, and I saw Liam surrounded by soldiers. Don't tell me he hasn't already shared the tech with the military."

Petra created the kill switch? That explained a lot. "Taking out the chips would have a huge negative impact on lots of people—I mean some of them would die and many others would suffer. A lot." He would almost certainly lose his new job—if students couldn't attend classes, then the Academia didn't need professors.

"It's better for everyone to lose their chips than to allow some people to be controlled by them."

The door to the chapel opened and the deputy stuck his head in. "Petra, the doctor from the hospital is asking to speak to you. Says it's urgent."

"Tell her to wait a minute." The deputy left the room and Petra turned back to Cooper. "I'll tell you what," Petra said, "take some time to think about it. I have other tasks I need to attend to. I'll give you an hour, maybe two at most. I'll tell the deputy to let you stay here so you won't have to listen to *Für Elise* played over and over again on an out-of-tune piano."

"I'd rather stay with June."

"I can't let you leave the church—with the cryogens it's not safe now."

"I won't provoke them. As long as your people do the same, I should be safe."

"I can't guarantee that. I don't want to engage but we will if we have to."

"You're not to that point yet. Let me go."

"The townsfolk are also understandably skittish about the radiation poisoning and would be afraid of you."

"Why do you keep up the charade of the radiation poisoning? Why don't you just let the truth come out?"

Petra stood up, her hand again resting lightly on the back of the pew.

"I do it because the people here are important to me, and whatever I have to do to protect them, I will."

~~~~~

Business Today

"All the business news you need to know"

April 23, 2115

By Elliat Exis ~ Still *Business Today's* newest staff reporter!

Panacea Corp is Rumored to be 'Occupying' Area 52 Using Cryogens

To my many cherished followers who have sent me messages asking if I'm okay, please be assured this reporter is well. I have been working on a top-priority assignment that required me to stop posting for a while, but now I'm ready to share with all of you some important information. Last you heard from me, I was walking into the restricted area with Cooper O'Connor, an associate of Mariela Stafford's. Since then, I have gone my own way and I am now at the camp of the people who are operating the cryogens. One of those people is Liam Price, the CEO of Panacea Corp. He has agreed to give me an interview within the next hour or two, so stay tuned.

According to a confidential source, the cryogens are 'occupying' Area 52 on behalf of Panacea Corp, not invading it. However, even calling it an 'occupation' is questionable as the advance of the cryogens is closer to a funeral procession. For the moment, the deep mud has brought them to a complete halt.

The other news for today: some people at the cryo blockade, after sitting through hours of rain, are heading home. Others are sticking it out come rain or snow. Following half a day of rain, the ground is completely saturated, the roads are muddy slicks, and everyone is soaked. The wind has picked up and people are getting chilled. Even the most intrepid folks could be forgiven for wanting to go home under these circumstances.
~~~~~

CHAPTER 25

Two Days After The Opening
Saturday, continued

Disabling the embedded chips was unthinkable, but Cooper was going to think about it. He kicked off his work boots and reclined on the pew. The stiff velvet of the pew cushion pressed into the skin on his arms and made them itch. The light shining through the stained-glass window behind the altar left multi-colored spots on the back of the pew. He needed to do a lot of thinking, but he couldn't think if he was sleep deprived. He let his eyes close.

He fell deeply asleep, but not for long. When he opened his eyes the Virgin Mary in the stained-glass window seemed to be watching him, judging him even.

He sat up on the bench. "What are you looking at?"

"You have an important decision to make," she seemed to be saying to him.

"Okay, okay." He rested his elbows on his knees and rubbed his eyes. He felt groggier than before his nap.

He walked around the chapel; he could think better standing up.

"I just don't see any way I can do this," he said to the Virgin Mary. She might be judging him, but she would understand. "I know Petra thinks it isn't a big deal, but disabling the chips is the nuclear option." He turned on his heel and walked in the opposite direction. The Virgin Mary's eyes seemed to follow him. "Not that taking out the chips doesn't have some appeal. Mariela would be safe with her chip disabled. Mariela's father wouldn't be isolated by his chip burn and he could become a functioning member of society again. My job options would be the same as everyone else's. But it's like wiping out an entire city just to get rid of one bad person."

Could he really justify the harm that would come to all those people from disabling the chips? Could he justify losing the job he had dreamed for years about getting back? Had it really come to that point? He went round and round in his head but he always came to the same conclusion. He kept thinking about the woman who died at the pod warehouse—disabling the chips would be much worse. It would save some lives but others would die. Maybe many others.

Petra ended up leaving him to stew with his thoughts for longer than the hour she had said.

"I can't do it," he said to Petra when she finally showed up four hours later wearing a bulletproof vest. Cooper ran his fingers through his hair. "I can't delete the chips."

Petra sat in the same pew as earlier. She had accessorized the flak jacket with gold bangle bracelets and a prim purse which she set down on the pew beside her. She placed her hands in her lap. "I'm going to contact—what's the CEO's name…Liam?—and try to negotiate," Petra said. "If I am unsuccessful, which I think you know is likely to be the case, one of two things will happen. Either you will call your friend and ask him to disable the chips, or I will have my deputies start firing at those cryogens and they will start firing back. And some of your people will get caught in the crossfire…"

"Stop calling them 'my people'—I don't have any more or less attachment to them than to the people here. I'm not like you; I'm not loyal to any particular side."

"Of course. Would it be fair to say you don't care about anyone, not even yourself?"

"How can you say that…" She was psychoanalyzing him as if she knew him. He took a deep breath. *Don't let her get under your skin.*

"To get back to the matter of concern here," Petra said, "there's a group of 'your people' who have broken past the first blockade—the one using the cryogens…"

"I know about the first blockade," it wasn't that long ago that Elliat had helped him get through it, "but I didn't know they had gotten past it."

"They'll be here in about half an hour. That's probably about the time when my negotiations with Liam will most likely fail, and the shooting will start. I'm sure you can see the problem here."

She had a point. It would be chaos.

"Tell me about this flaw," he said to Petra. He felt restless and the pew was uncomfortable. He walked up and down the aisle and tried to focus himself by concentrating on the rich, red carpet with gold details.

"The flaw is like a brief chip burn that's enough to take out the chips but not to kill anyone. It might sting a bit."

"Surely there must be a better way to deal with the cryogens. We could hijack the link to the controllers, and cut it off. Without the instructions from their handlers, the cryos will just sit there. Or even better, we can hijack the connection and tell the cryos to shoot each other. Or to head home."

"True, the cryos are at present a nuisance with the possibility of becoming something much more serious if things go wrong. With some creativity and luck we could probably come up with a way of dealing with them. But you're losing sight of the bigger threat. It's the kill switch. It's the reason I went out of my way to make sure I had deleted every copy, every single bit of code; it's the reason I convinced a bunch of adults to come live here along with their young children; and it's the reason I have been alternatively educating their children and their children's children ever since."

'Alternatively educating' sounded like a way of saying 'deceiving' without saying it.

There was a war going on in his head between the part of him that wanted to sever the embedded chips from Panacea and the part of him that felt it was wrong to wield such power, that surely there must be some other, less drastic, solution. "Can't we come up with a way to neutralize the kill switch?"

"You don't think I tried? I spent a year trying to undo what I had done. I had created something that was out of my control—there was no way I could stop it—and I couldn't be sure it was fully deleted, despite my best efforts. And that's when I knew I had to get away from it. That I needed to figure out how much tech I needed to survive and live a comfortable lifestyle, and for me and the other 60,000 people who joined me here, it was the tech of 2005. Pre-smartphone tech."

Even though she made him uncomfortable, he was moved by this woman—normally ice cold—who had dropped the frosty exterior a bit and showed him a different side of her. He wasn't moved enough though to agree with her.

He wanted to say yes to what she was asking of him, but he couldn't. He was upset with Mariela for making the decision to delete the LP100 model ghosts without consulting the rest of them. He couldn't be like her and make life-altering decisions for other people. He couldn't make a decision that might benefit some people close to him while hurting many more that he didn't know.

"I'm sorry," he said to Petra. "I can see this might be the wrong decision, but I'm saying no."

"I didn't want to share this with you, because it's not something I'm proud of, but it might convince you of how important this is."

"Okay, tell me."

"I made the kill switch to be viral. It transmits from person to person if there is contact with an infected chip."

"Wait, are you saying that anyone Mariela used her chip to contact, say, Amoco or her mother, the kill switch will have spread to them also? And to whoever they have had contact with? Until everyone with a chip is infected?" That was the worst idea he had ever heard of. "And you *designed* it that way?"

"Yes, the version that spreads to others is a weakened version, but it will have already started to spread. And each time a person has contact with the infected person, their infection becomes stronger." Petra looked down at the ground.

"Why in the world would you do that?" Cooper stopped pacing. "How in any way did that seem like a good idea?"

Petra's face flashed red. "The idea was that we would plant the kill switch in major criminals, and then it would spread to all their associates so we could identify them. I was young and eager to prove myself so I didn't think through the ramifications of what I was doing at first. And then I realized what I had done…"

He'd made a decision—he couldn't let Panacea Corp use the cryogens to occupy Area 52, he couldn't let Mariela continue to be subject to the whims of the people controlling her kill switch, he couldn't let the gawkers be shot at as they swarmed Area 52 looking for aliens or the set where the moon landings were faked. With the decision made, he felt a sense of relief and peace that it was the right decision. But if he were going to agree to it, he was going to make sure he got what he needed out of it.

"Will you let Amaya and I leave right away if I help you?"

"I will have one of my deputies personally escort you to the junction."

"And what about 'my people?'"

"We will also remove them, though that may take some time and they will be incarcerated or detained while they are waiting to be extradited."

"Will you help us extract Mariela and Nyala immediately after the chips have been disabled?"

"I'll send my best people to pick them up."

He was making good progress so far.

"Will we be allowed to access the server farm if we need to? And to conduct maintenance as needed at a later date?"

"As long as it is you or Amaya, you may access the servers as long as you are escorted by one of my deputies and you notify us ahead of time. You can contact us using the phone that Deputy Dan currently has in his possession."

"One more thing. Will you allow June to remain here if she wants to? Or better yet, will you allow June to travel back and forth?"

"I'm not sure I can guarantee the travel back and forth, but she can stay here if she wants to."

That was everything he wanted. Or as close to it as he was likely to get.

"One more question—what will you do with the folks from Panacea Corp and the military people with them?"

"I want to hold them accountable, but I'm not sure that's realistic. We'll most likely make sure they go to the perimeter like everyone else."

"You know that even once the chips are disabled, they'll still have guns?"

"I'm aware, but at least the cryogens won't be firing on us. I also predict that once the chips are deleted, the people with the guns will be so disoriented that they head home. Or at least they will try to."

"I'm in." Now he just needed to get Amoco on board.

"Here's your tech that Amaya was wearing when my deputies picked you up," Petra reached into her bag and pulled out a flimsy, film-like strip. "Use it to call your friend and see what he thinks."

~~~~~

Cooper sat down on the pew and slapped his Everything on. The plastic snapped around his forearm; once he had it on the controls showed up in the transparent plastic. Dan knocked on the door to the chapel and stuck his head in. "Petra, we're ready to go."

"I'll be right there," Petra said.

Dan had dark circles under his eyes. He looked like he hadn't had any sleep for days.

Cooper wasn't happy to see Dan again. "I thought Dan was on
~~~~~

bathroom duty?" he asked.

"Despite his lapse in judgement in releasing your friends from the jail, Deputy Springer is still one of my most trusted deputies. I need him during this time of crisis; he can pay his penance once this is all over."

"You mean one of your most compliant deputies?"

"I think we've clearly seen that is not the case. After spending time with your folk, the deputy's willingness to comply with what I tell him is seriously in doubt."

"I think you're giving us more credit than we deserve."

"It was not intended as a compliment. Now," she picked up her handbag and held it in the crook of her arm, "it's time to go talk to Liam."

"Well, stay safe, watch out for Liam. I hope it goes well, though we both know that isn't likely."

"You're coming with us."

"Oh no, no, no." He held up his hands as if doing so could stop Petra—he didn't like the idea of going with them at all. "I don't want any contact with Liam."

"Come on now, let's get moving." Petra stood up. "We can talk on the way."

Reluctantly, Cooper got up to follow Petra out of the chapel. She seemed to be moving faster than he remembered her moving. It was like the crisis had woken her up.

Dan was waiting for them in in the hallway near the front of the church. He was wearing what looked like full riot gear.

"Put this on." Dan picked up a heavy flak jacket from a nearby table.

Cooper willingly took the bulletproof vest; this time he didn't plan to take it off.

After he put the jacket on, Dan handed him and Petra helmets. "Sorry for all the gear, but the cryogens are malfunctioning. We aren't taking any chances. Whoever gave them guns is an idiot."

Cooper put the helmet on and fastened the latch under his chin. Petra looked odd wearing the helmet and flak jacket.

Dan picked up an item of clothing from the table. "Put this on." He handed it to Cooper.

"I'm wearing a hoodie?"

"Put the hood over your head on the way to the car," Dan said. "We don't know your relationship with Liam. Better he doesn't know you are with us."

That was a relief, but…what? "Why am I going with you if I'm not going to be part of the talks?"

"You are going as a resource for Petra. What you know about Liam and the others might give us a tactical advantage."

"I thought you didn't trust me."

"I don't," Dan said.

"Just give me the hoodie." Cooper worked it on over his flak jacket and pulled the hood over his helmet. It was a relief to know he wouldn't have to deal with Liam directly. People who got on Liam's bad side didn't fare well.

Dan opened the door to the front of the church and held it open for Petra. Maybe under different circumstances Cooper could have had some respect for Dan. They probably never would have been close, but they could have worked together amicably. Grace's death made that impossible.

"I see you're back to being Petra's lackey," Cooper said to Dan as he walked through.

"I see I'm not the only one," Dan replied and let the door close behind them.

Three large, black transports were lined up in the parking lot in the front of the church. A loud buzzing sounded on all sides of them as they walked out. Not seconds after they exited, hundreds of drones swarmed towards them. He pulled the hoodie deep over his head. The drones rushed downward, some coming up towards Cooper's face. He pulled the hoodie even lower and used his hand to hide his face. Cooper was barely able to see through his fingers. Dan grabbed his arm and guided him toward the transport.

The transport wasn't like any he had seen on his previous trip to Area 52. It had a solid, heavy feel to it, and its side windows were completely obscured. Dan opened the door for him. Cooper climbed in and then moved to the far side so Petra could get in after him. Dan helped the diminutive Petra, weighed down by her flak jacket and helmet yet still sporting her purse, into the vehicle. Dan slammed the door after she was settled. Two other deputies, a man and a woman, were already in the far back seat of the vehicle. Cooper nodded to them and they nodded back.

The darkened windows, along with the privacy window between them and the front seat of the transport, kept Cooper from seeing what was happening outside. With the drones unable to see in, Cooper pushed the hood of his jacket back and took off his helmet. The thick windows of the transport almost completely shut out the incessant whining of the drones.

The retort of Dan's shotgun was followed by the crunch of a drone hitting the pavement. A couple more shotguns blasts were each followed by the sound of a drone hitting the pavement. It was a war Dan couldn't win but Cooper applauded him for trying. The door in the front of the transport opened and then shut with a solid thump. A few seconds later the engine started with a low rumble.

"Is this an armored transport?" he asked Petra.

"Yes. Back when we first moved here, we were more security-conscious. Over the eighty years we've been here we've become lax, but many of the safeguards we put in place back then are still around. This is one of them."

Petra pushed a button on an armrest next to her. "Do you know where the camp is located?" she asked.

Oh, the button was a way to talk to Dan without having to lower the privacy glass.

"They haven't moved." It was Dan's voice. "They're still in the same place where they were last time we went there."

"I guess Liam didn't want to be too close to the action. Probably wise of him because who knows what will happen."

"Right," Dan said. "We're going to stay off the main road because it's impossible to drive on with the cryogens. But we will need to cross it."

"Understood. I trust you will handle it."

A minute later the transport stopped. Dan's voice came over the speaker. "We're going to have to move some cryogens."

"Put your hood on," Petra said.

Cooper pulled his hood up and Petra lowered the privacy window in the front. The deputies in the back seat got out of the transport. One of them handed Petra a talkie-textie radio on her way out.

The swarm of drones followed them and rushed toward the deputies when they got out of the vehicle. The swarm swirled around the four deputies, jockeying for position, trying to get the best view. The drones bumped into the cryogens, who didn't react, and the deputies, who swatted at them. It was like an invasion of locusts. If things didn't go well, there might be nothing left after the drones were gone.

Petra lowered the volume on the radio until they could hear the deputies communicating but the sound didn't overwhelm conversation. She turned to Cooper. "Do you know anything about the cryogens?"

It was probably best not to mention his role in training them. Especially as he never would have put them on a mission like this. Cryos were a good alternative to humans or machines, in a stealth mission in the Arctic where the temperatures were below freezing, but not here.

"I think they were intended to be used for missions in the Arctic," he said. "They're pretty passive, but if you fire at them, they will fire back."

"You're not telling me anything I don't already know."

So much for being helpful. Apparently, his role in training the cryos didn't give him any special insight into dealing with them.

How had he ended up in another war? The gnawing in his stomach confirmed what he hadn't wanted to accept—he was involved in another war. The Arctic War had been started by superpowers battling over oil that was newly accessible as global temps warmed. It was a stupid war with a stupid objective—a fight over a dwindling resource the world should have stopped using decades ago.

But this war—the war over Area 52? Was it more worthy than the Arctic War? Did it have a better objective? No matter how much he tried to deny it, he was knee-deep in this one. He was the one who started it. He may not have created the situations that led to the war, but he had taken the steps that turned a conflict into a war. Whatever sins were done in the name of this war, he was responsible for them. Whatever happened to the cryos, or to Mariela, Amaya, or Nyala, there was no doubt on some level he was responsible. But despite being responsible, he was also out of control of what was happening.

The slow drizzle formed drops of water that dripped persistently from the deputies' helmets. The soggy cryos had cuts in their feet and some of them were losing patches of skin. The rain and heat made them barely functional. They weren't going to hold up long if the heat and drizzling rain continued. One by one the deputies grabbed the cryos by the elbow and directed them to the side of the road. The drones buzzed around them like angry flies.

"What are those things?" Petra asked.

"They're drones. They record what's happening and then transmit it back to their owners. Many of them look like they belong to news outlets, but there are a lot of private drones out there as well. Some of them probably belong to Liam and his henchmen and are transmitting back to them what's happening here."

"They're a nuisance."

"Finally, something we agree on."

Moving the cryos was slow-going and could have triggered their handlers to order them to fire. With Liam in charge, it was possible the rules of engagement had changed and that it no longer required the opposition to fire the first shot. Cooper relaxed after the first few were moved successfully. It was a good sign as time went on and nothing happened.

With the situation with the cryos momentarily under control, Cooper contacted Amoco and told him about why he felt it was necessary to take out the chips. Just as Cooper expected, Amoco wasn't difficult to convince. Once Amoco found out his chip might be infected from his contact with Mariela, he didn't hesitate in agreeing to help out. It helped that Amoco had a long-standing belief that the government used people's chips to spy on them. Amoco said he would be standing by to learn the outcome of the negotiations with Liam.

From what Cooper could tell from their conversation, Amoco was going to use the backdoor Amaya had installed on Server AA a few weeks ago to run the code that would take advantage of the vulnerability. Once he was done, the embedded chips would be permanently disabled. At the same time, Amaya would access Server AA to erase all evidence of their involvement. Assuming Amaya agreed to change the data.

Dan took the elbow of the last cryogen in their way. Unlike most of the cryogens, this one was young and looked like someone Cooper might have been friends with back in the day. What could have killed the man so young? It was sobering to remember that the cryos had been people, regular people, who hoped to be brought back to life someday. The cryo tripped over a rock and fell to the ground.

The full implications of what he had done hit Cooper for the first time—he shouldn't have helped Viola. It was wrong from the beginning. These people deserved to be treated with more dignity than this. If he had chosen to have himself cryogenically frozen at death and was unable to be revived, he wouldn't want to have his body sent barely clothed into the mud and heat just to start malfunctioning and rotting and then end up getting shot.

A twitching cryo lurched toward one of the deputies. Almost before Cooper knew what was happening, there was the crack of the rifle bring fired and the cryo's head exploded; what was left slumped to the ground. The stunned deputies froze, staring at the fallen cryogen.

Around them, all the remaining cryos raised their rifles.

"Oh shit, we need to go," Dan said. He left the cryo that he was guiding where it had fallen. The four deputies scrambled to the vehicle with bullets flying around them. Most of the cryos fired in whatever direction they were facing, some hitting each other, some hitting the car, some going harmlessly into the air.

The deputies threw open the door to the vehicle. The first one dove into the back seat and the second rolled onto the floor of the vehicle. She used her foot to slam the sliding door shut. In the front seat Dan and the last deputy had made it into their seats. They all gasped to catch their breath. Dan clenched a hand to his side.

"Is everyone okay?" Petra asked.

"I've been hit," Dan said through clenched teeth. "Don't think it hit me directly," He rocked back and forth while searching for where he was hit. He sighed. "It hit my vest."

The sound of the cryogens firing continued around them, with the bullets flying in all directions and taking out some of the drones. The drones' flight patterns became erratic as they tried to take in all the action while not getting shot. Some hurtled toward the vehicle, becoming less cautious as the action picked up. They hovered over the hood and crashed into the armored vehicle as they tried to get a look inside. Drones bounced off the armored exterior as Dan struggled to catch his breath.

"Let's get out of here," Petra said. She raised the privacy window.

Dan hit the gas and the transport lurched forward and over fallen cryogens. The uncontrolled jostling of the vehicle was like someone shaking Cooper telling him how stupid he had been. How had he ever had any part in this? It was a nightmare. Maybe he and Petra had more in common than he thought. They had both taken part in creating something they regretted, and that was now out of their control.

CHAPTER 26

Two Days After The Opening

Saturday, continued

Petra left one of the talkie-texties in the vehicle so Cooper could listen to her conversation with Liam. Dan went with Petra to talk to Liam. He wanted to scope out the lay of the land and come up with a plan for picking up Nyala and Mariela after the chips were disabled. Amoco had helped out by telling him how to find their tent based on the drone imagery.

The guards had either gone with Petra and Dan or were outside the vehicle keeping an eye on the surroundings. During the drive to Liam's camp, the rain had tapered off but in its place the wind tossed the trees and rattled the flag flying over the camp. Large drops of water from the trees hit the roof of the transport. He closed his eyes and laid his head back on the seat. The privacy window was still up, keeping Cooper from being able to see what was going on outside.

After fifteen minutes, the negotiations hadn't made much progress. It took ten minutes for Petra to convince the soldiers to let her talk with Liam and for him to be available. Then there was five minutes of back and forth where Petra and Liam argued over whether Panacea Corp's actions were legal. Fifteen minutes and they hadn't even started negotiating yet.

"I suggest we accept that we will not be able to come to an agreement on this topic, and move on to another one," Petra said.

"What would you like to discuss? Considering that you were the one who requested this meeting, I suggest you should introduce the topic."

"Very well. I demand Panacea Corp give up any claim to this land and depart immediately. It has been in the hands of the people here and the agreement with the corporation of Panacea has been properly maintained for eighty years."

There was another five minutes of conversation, which in large part repeated the previous five minutes, about whether the agreement with Panacea Corp had been properly maintained.

Without much happening in the negotiations and unable to see anything, Cooper's mind wandered. Hank and Georgia should be coming back through the tesseract soon. T-Rock and Bren would be there to pick them up. How his life had changed in the last month if he was actually looking forward to seeing Hank again.

His thoughts also wandered to his job. The job he had desperately wanted to have again and now would probably lose. Life was a cruel bitch sometimes.

"Despite our disagreements regarding the agreement," Petra said, "there is a grievance procedure for addressing any disputes, and this 'occupation' of our territory does not fall within the parameters laid out by that procedure."

Another five minutes passed with them arguing over legalities. Cooper peered through the darkened glass for any sign of Mariela or Nyala, but the highly tinted glass that protected his identity also kept him from being able to see much of anything.

Petra may have met her match in Liam. Cooper suspected she had been trying to wear him down before she got to the one point that was the most important to her.

"You must halt this invasion at once," Petra said. "The cryogens are malfunctioning, and even the functioning ones are frightening the children."

"First, it's not an invasion, it's an occupation." Liam said. "But if you insist, then fine. We withdraw."

This was not good. Liam didn't give in like this. Something was wrong, but Cooper wasn't sure what.

"May I ask why?" From the sound of Petra's voice, Liam's capitulation had taken her aback. Liam had gained the upper hand.

"As I'm sure you are aware, many people from outside Area 52 are converging on your town, some of them armed. They have already taken out a number of the cryogens. As our operators can't tell our people from your people, it would be foolish of us to start firing back. At this time, we believe the entire operation to be compromised, and we plan to withdraw."

"Compromised" appeared to be corporate speak for too high a liability. It sounded like Panacea Corp withdrawing was good news, but Liam would be back. And the next time his "occupying" force wouldn't be a bunch of undead cryogens.

"Can I have your assurance you will not return?" Petra asked.

"We will have to evaluate our options."

Petra almost certainly understood that meant they would be back.

"When will the withdrawal begin?" she asked.

"It has already begun."

"My people aren't reporting any movement of the cryogens. When do you expect that to begin?"

"We will no longer be operating the cryogens. They are, as you reported, malfunctioning."

Liam scored a point against Petra.

"You're just going to leave them there?" Dan's voice cracked.

"You all have shown they can be moved when you did it on your way over here," Liam gloated. He had definitely won this round.

"We can't move 10,000 bodies," Dan said. "What are we going to do with all of them?"

"Not my concern. I'm sure you'll figure something out. We intend to disavow all connection to the cryogens. The official story is that we were here to get the culprits in the Black Screen, and those things were here when we got here."

"Can you at least give us the tech to control them," Petra asked, "so that we can move them somewhere to rot in peace?"

"I wouldn't want to take a chance on you using them against us. I'm afraid you are on your own to deal with the bodies. Did you have anything else you wish to discuss?"

There was a moment of silence.

"No," Petra said. With that one syllable, the game belonged to Liam. Maybe Petra would have better luck in the next round, the one where they disabled the chips. Cooper used his Everything to send a message to Amoco that the talks had failed, and that he would let him know when they had everything in place on their end.

~~~~~

"Abrihet Gidada?"

An orderly pushed a wheelchair into Amaya's room. She had fallen asleep again. It was light out but the cloudy skies didn't give her any clue what time it was.

"Please call me Amaya."

"You're being discharged." The orderly turned to the deputy. "The
~~~~~

Elder said to call to confirm with her."

The deputy flipped open her communication device and punched some buttons. She had a short conversation where Petra appeared to confirm what the orderly was saying.

"Where am I going?" Now that Amaya was being released, she wanted to stay. Her feet still burned and she couldn't walk. If the other option was going to jail then she would rather stay in the hospital.

"You'll have to ask Deputy Dan that."

If Dan was picking her up, she was probably going back to jail. The orderly replaced the bandages on her feet with fresh ones, and slid some heavy socks with non-slip soles over her feet and lower legs.

"Do you have some clothing?" the orderly asked.

"I had some once. I don't know what happened to it. Deputy Dan probably knows."

"Let me see what we have in the lost and found." The orderly disappeared out of the room for a bit and then not much later reappeared holding some items of clothing.

Amaya wasn't thrilled about wearing a large sweatshirt that said, "I survived the Nuclear Armageddon of 2035 and all I got was this stupid shirt," but she put it on anyway. At least it was warm. The sweatpants were about four sizes too large but the drawstring kept them on.

"Sorry I couldn't do better," the orderly said. She also handed Amaya a knitted hat. Amaya slipped it on. She was as ready as she would ever be. The orderly helped her into the wheelchair. She put a bottle of antibiotics into Amaya's hands and told her to take two a day.

Dan was waiting for her in the lobby. He grabbed the wheelchair and started pushing it faster. "What took you so long?"

"It didn't seem long to me. What's the rush?"

They were almost to the front door of the hospital.

"I'll let Cooper explain to you."

"Am I going back to jail?"

"No. He negotiated for your release. But you'd better ask him about it."

That was a relief. Amaya looked through the wall of glass windows that formed the front of the hospital. Past the covered lane for dropping off hospital patients, on the other side of the hospital parking lot, the main village road was filled with rows of cryogens, all standing and staring blankly ahead. "Do we need to worry about those?" she asked.

"No, the CEO guy, Liam I think, said they are abandoning them. They shouldn't shoot us."

"Is that good news?"

"Don't know. I guess so—at least they aren't shooting anyone. Some are malfunctioning though, so just in case put these on." He stopped just before the sliding doors. A deputy who was waiting by the doors handed her a flak jacket and helmet. Dan waited until she put them on and then started pushing her again. "Some of your people are running around with guns and taking potshots at the cryos, so stay alert."

A buzzing sound grew increasingly louder as they headed to a black vehicle with darkened windows.

"What's that noise?"

"Drones." Dan was running now, pushing her to the transport vehicle. The drones blocked his path and circled around them but he pushed on through. He opened the door to the vehicle and Cooper held her arm while she gingerly stepped into the vehicle. Dan turned and pulled up his rifle. That seemed to work as the drones backed away to a still-close-but-not-quite-so-harassing distance.

"Amaya, it's good to see you," Cooper said as he helped her to the seat next to him. Another woman in a deputy's uniform sat in the back seat.

"It's good to see you too." It really was a relief to see Cooper. Amaya was used to spending time alone, but she had been around other people so much in the last couple weeks that being alone in the hospital—the stoic deputy didn't count as company—felt really lonely. "So, what are we doing?"

Dan lifted the wheelchair next to Amaya, took a baseball bat out from under the seat, and whacked the nearest drone that was encroaching on the vehicle, pushing its way forward as if trying to get inside. The drone fell to the ground in multiple pieces and the others backed up.

"Sometimes they need to be reminded to stay away." Dan threw the bat back under the seat. "I'm going to take the jeep to put the other part of our plan into motion."

"See you at the junction," Cooper said.

"See you there," Dan said, and he shut the door.

Amaya turned to Cooper. "What's going on? What's the plan that Dan mentioned?"

~~~~

Amaya was the unknown, the only key part to the plan who hadn't yet agreed to what was about to happen. It was far from guaranteed she would help them out. Cooper turned to the deputy in the back seat. "Can you leave us alone for a bit? Maybe go take out a couple drones."

"Okay." The deputy picked up the bat as she climbed out past Amaya's wheelchair.

"The drones are kind of freaking me out," Amaya said. "I have nightmares where I'm trying to escape somewhere and I can't because you need an ID to go everywhere and I can't hide because I'm being followed by drones. In the dream I haven't committed a crime, but I still need to escape and I can't. It feels a lot like my nightmares today."

"Speaking of committing a crime…" Cooper wished he could start over. Mentioning that they were about to commit a crime probably wasn't the best way to convince Amaya to help out. He decided to change course for a bit and then come back to what he really wanted to talk about. "How are your feet?"

Her voice was flat when she answered. "They burn." She seemed distracted. "What were you saying about committing a crime?"

He explained the situation to her and the plan for dealing with it, including that the kill switch could be spread through contact with another person.

"Do Liam or Viola know about the viral part?" Amaya asked.

"I don't think so. It's something Petra created a long time ago."

"Is the code to access the kill switch the same for each infected chip?"

"Petra said she modified it to mutate slightly with each new infection. That's the good news—someone would have to biopsy the kill switch or have a special reader to figure out what the code is."

"So here's a thought—could we use this reader to find out the codes of people who have been infected and deactivate them?"

"There is no deactivating it. Once it's there, it's there. The only way to deal with it at that point is to disable the chip."

Amaya adjusted the overly large sweatshirt she was wearing. "Petra said something similar to us when we were in jail, and I've been wondering about it because when the brutes first injected the kill switch, they told Mariela they could deactivate it."

"I think they lied to her. People are much more willing to be compliant and do questionable things if they know it's just for a short period of
~~~~

time. It's more difficult to coerce people into doing stuff they don't want to do if they know it's going to be for the rest of their life."

Amaya was still trying to understand the scope of what they were doing. "So Mariela has no choice but to disable her chip? As well as any people Mariela has contacted?"

"As well as anyone those people have contacted. And anyone those people have contacted. Can you see how bad this could be?"

"Have you contacted Contagion Control?"

"No. Those people deal with biological contagions, and while this has some biological components, it's a completely different beast. Contagion Control doesn't have the ability to deal with this."

"Then who does?"

"We do."

"What do you mean?"

"Amoco can fix the problem. His solution guarantees no further spread or threat from the kill switch."

"What's the catch?" She seemed to sense where he was heading with this.

"It permanently disables all the chips." He let that sink in for a bit.

"No." She shook her head. "You can't. You saw the destruction our last mission caused at the pod warehouses. How much worse do you think it would be if we disable all the chips?"

"Well, to be accurate, the problem last time was malfunctions in the support systems at a couple warehouses, there's no reason this should cause that. It will just be a bunch of people who are really, really bored because they can't access Panacea. But they shouldn't be in any danger."

"What about the people who have lived in Panacea so long they have almost forgotten the solid world exists?"

"It will be difficult, but they won't be physically harmed. It's better than living with a kill switch that could kill them at any moment."

"But how would people get to their jobs?"

"They could still access all the information in Panacea, they would just have to use a terminal."

"You know most chipped people don't know how to use a terminal."

"They could use a projection room."

"It's not the same."

"I did it for many years."

"You aren't most people."

Cooper didn't have a response. She was right; most people would struggle with using a projection room as their primary way of interacting in Panacea. "Think about it this way," he said, "seventy-five years ago, no one had a chip, and they managed to get by somehow. We can do the same." It was a weak argument on his part—he could see the flaws in it as soon as he said it.

Amaya scoffed. "Seventy-five years ago, life was set up so a chip wasn't necessary. They all knew how to use terminals and for the most part they worked in the city they lived in. That's not how things are now."

"I don't deny it's going to be awful, but there's not a lot of other options right now."

"What would Nyala say?"

Why was Amaya worried about what Nyala, of all people, would say? The woman who hated chips? "I think she would be supportive."

Amaya rolled her eyes. "She probably would be."

Cooper let her think. It had taken him a long time to get used to the idea; it wasn't fair to expect Amaya to accept it right away.

"Who came up with this idea?" she asked.

"Petra was the one who first suggested it."

"Petra? I'm not sure we should be taking her advice. She came to see us a couple times in the jail and it's pretty clear she doesn't give a crap about what happens to us."

"I was skeptical too. But she convinced me."

"No."

"What?"

"No, I won't do it."

She wouldn't do it? They had every single other piece in place. Amoco had agreed to it. If Amaya wasn't willing to help out, where did that leave them? If she didn't help, they wouldn't be able to delete the evidence of what they were going to do. Could they go ahead without her? It would put everyone at greater risk.

There was also something personally disappointing for him about Amaya's refusal. He and Amaya had always been pretty much on the same page; he didn't like that they weren't this time. "If you're not will-ing to help then I suggest you get out."

They were still sitting in the hospital parking lot, so she could just get herself readmitted.

"Cooper, I'm sorry, but I can't help you out. Please don't be mad."

"Just leave."

She looked at her wheelchair like she didn't know what to do with it. Cooper reached across her to rap on the window. The deputy waiting outside opened the door.

"Can you get her wheelchair out? Amaya will be staying here."

Cooper looked out the opposite window as the deputy unfolded the wheelchair and helped Amaya out. He tried not to care what Amaya would do next. It wasn't his business or his problem. The drones had started to move on to probably more interesting places, but as soon as the doors opened, they returned and crowded around the wheelchair.

"Cooper." The buzzing of the drones was so loud Cooper could barely hear her. "Tell Amoco that the drones orient to an external map that they have to match up with their internal map. If the two maps don't match, then they have to ground themselves. Tell Amoco that if he can change the external maps, that should ground the drones."

"Okay." He refused to admit to her that she had been helpful. He stopped himself from asking where she would go or what she would do.

"Cooper, I'm sorry." The light reflected off of the tears on her cheeks. He turned away before she could see the tears in his eyes.

"Do you want me to take you back into the hospital?" the deputy asked her.

"Yes, please." Amaya's voice was small. Cooper waited to turn his head until he heard the deputy roll the chair away, but he turned too soon. Amaya was still looking back over her shoulder, watching him as she was rolled away. Something in the pit of his stomach rolled over.

He grabbed the bat from where the deputy had dropped it. He was going to take out some drones while he waited for the deputy to return.

Cooper hadn't expected to be doing this on his own. He had made an assumption he and Amaya would take care of things together. It was stupid of him to assume Amaya would agree, especially considering what he had asked her to do.

He hit one of the drones and it went spinning away from him. After he hit the first one, most of the drones kept a comfortable distance from him. Sometimes they ran into each other and their blades tangled and they went down in a fiery mess, which was fun except the times they flew towards the vehicle. Despite a couple of dents, the armored exterior of the vehicle seemed to be holding up well.

"Cooper." The driver was leaning out the passenger side of the vehicle. "Petra wants to know how things are going."

"Tell her I'll contact her in a minute."

"She doesn't like to wait."

"I don't care." He really didn't.

He took down one more drone and then got back into the vehicle. He contacted Amoco using his Everything and told him what Amaya had said about the drones. Once that was out of the way, he contacted Petra using the communication device in the vehicle.

"She's not on board," he said. He tried not to let Petra know how much it bothered him.

"Can we do it without her?" Petra asked.

"I think so. It's just that we'll probably end up in jail."

"You could stay here."

They had come a long way if Petra was willing to let him stay in Area 52. But with the umbrella down, it wouldn't provide him much protection from law enforcement or an angry Panacea Corp.

"Will you put Amaya back in jail?"

"Our agreement stands. If you arrange to have the chips disabled, she goes free. There was never any stipulation that she agree to help also."

"Good. She shouldn't be in jail. I wish she had agreed to help though—she's the only person who understands the computer system." Cooper had an idea—it was so outlandish that it hadn't occurred to him earlier. "Petra, you could do it. You know how to work with legacy computer systems. For you they aren't even legacy. You could access the backdoor into the system and delete the evidence for us."

"I wouldn't have the slightest idea what I would need to do."

"Amoco can guide you."

"That is ridiculous."

"Do you want our help or not? Because I can assure you I would be much more willing to help if I didn't end up going to jail."

"I'm not sure I will be able to help you," Petra said, "but I'm willing to try."

"That's all I ask." The plan was back on, and he wasn't going to jail. Unless Amaya turned him in.

CHAPTER 27

Two Days After The Opening

Saturday, continued

What was she going to do next? Amaya didn't want to stay at the hospital, although they probably would take her back. She had her antibiotics, and as long as her feet didn't turn red and hot from infection, she wasn't going back to that hospital room. Maybe the deputy who had been guarding her would see her sitting in the hospital lobby and would take her back to jail. The simplicity of going back to jail and having every decision made for her was tempting in a way.

Her goal hadn't changed even though she had been stuck in a hospital for the last twenty-four hours. Mariela and Nyala still needed her help. Or at least they did for now. It was possible Cooper would solve their problems before Amaya could do anything about it. But just in case, Amaya was working on a plan. The first step was to contact June. June knew the area and the people. If anyone could help her out, June could.

Like a pesky fly, one of the drones flew into the hospital through the sliding glass doors at the front. A hospital staff member came charging out from behind a desk and swatted at it with a broom. The broom was losing the battle when the drone, and all the other drones outside, landed and turned off. The buzzing subsided and Amaya took a deep, relieved breath. She could call June now and actually be heard. And she could go places without being followed by a thousand flying cameras.

The black vehicle that Cooper was in finally started moving. A part of Amaya had hoped he would try to convince her again to help him. What would she have said if he had tried? She probably would have given him the same answer, so maybe it was good he didn't. But she wished he had. The vehicle crossed the parking lot multiple times, running over a number of the drones that were scattered around the lot each time.

She probably had an hour at most before someone figured out how to get them back flying. She needed to disappear before they were up and flying again. Amaya rolled up to the desk where the woman with the broom was just settling back down.

"Can I help you?" the woman asked.

"Do you know June Stafford?"

"Of course, she volunteers here sometimes."

"Could you contact her and ask her to pick me up?" Amaya felt powerless without her Everything. She had no way to contact anyone or get information. Not being able to walk left her feeling even more vulnerable.

"One moment," the woman said. She picked up a device—different from the communication device Georgia had made—and held it to her ear. She punched some buttons on the analog phone. "Are you a friend of hers?" the woman asked.

"Yes."

"It's just that I don't remember ever seeing you around here before."

"Oh, I'm not from here."

The woman gave her a skeptical look.

Amaya shrugged. "It's complicated." It was the best explanation she could come up with.

"Miss June," the woman said into her device. "There's a woman here who is asking if you can pick her up." The woman leaned over to Amaya. "What's your name, hon?"

"Amaya."

"She says it's Maya." There was a pause while June said something on the other end. The woman turned back to Amaya again. "She says she'll be right here." June said something else that she couldn't hear. "Okay, I'll tell her," the woman said and then placed the speaking device back where she got it.

"What did she say?" Amaya asked.

"She said it will be about fifteen minutes before she can get here, maybe longer if those creepy undead people are in the way. My words, not hers."

"Okay, thanks." Amaya turned back to face the glass doors. Fifteen minutes wasn't long but it seemed interminable. It gave her too much time to think.

Did she do the right thing when she told Cooper she wouldn't help him? Amaya turned the question over and over again in her mind. Nyala wouldn't have hesitated for a second to say yes. If Amaya had been in trouble, in danger of dying, Nyala would have done anything to protect her, even if that meant some other people suffered. How was it Amaya couldn't do the same for Nyala? The guilt of not protecting her sister when she could have was going to stay with her for a long time.

And what about the kill switch acting as a virus, and infecting others? There had to be another solution to that situation. No one knew the codes to the kill switch; in fact, no one other than a handful of people even knew about the kill switch or that it could be transmitted from person to person, so how much of a threat was it really?

Was addressing an uncertain and vague threat worth the upheaval that disabling the chips would cause? Was it worth another situation like the one they had witnessed at the pod warehouses a little over a week ago?

But despite all her concerns, Amaya had an aching feeling she had made the wrong decision. She pushed it aside. She needed to focus on developing a plan. She couldn't afford to be distracted by thinking about the past.

"Hey there."

Amaya turned to see the deputy who had been guarding her standing nearby with a bat. "Hey," she replied.

"I'm going to take out some of those nosy pests before they take flight again. Want to help?" The deputy held out the bat to her.

"Sure, but I don't want to take your bat."

"I'll use my gun. Petra has said that as long as the drones are disabled, we can shoot them." The deputy seemed to think this was great news, if her smile was any indication.

"So you're allowed to talk to me now?"

It was odd to see the very stoic deputy lighten up.

"You're not in my custody anymore, so I can talk to you all I want."

"Great." Amaya smiled. "Let's take out some drones."

~~~~~

Mariela turned from peering out the flap of the tent to look at Nyala. "Nyala, come watch, the interview's starting." Nyala jumped up and peered over Mariela's shoulder. Their tent had been more relaxed since the rain ended and Viola had left to find Elliat for the interview. At least Viola had turned off Nyala's motion inhibitors before she left. She even left the cuffs on so that whenever Liam or one of his henchmen came around, Nyala could act like they were still working.

Now the soldiers were drying off the table and chairs in the open area
~~~~~

in the middle of the camp. A group was gathering to watch the interview. Dark clouds obscured the late afternoon sun, making it unusually dark for the time of day. Viola yelled at the soldiers setting up floodlights to work faster. Eventually, everything was in place and the flurry of activity died down.

"Do you predict Elliat's behavior toward Liam will be best described as fawning or sycophantic?" Nyala asked.

"I'm going with ingratiating."

"Ah, that's a good guess."

Viola ushered Elliat up to the table. He took a seat in the chair facing away from Mariela. Seconds later Liam walked out and took the chair across from Elliat. He nodded at Elliat and gave a thumbs up to the exo-cam which Elliat had stationed between them

Mariela glanced over her shoulder at Nyala. "They're starting."

Elliat adjusted his jacket and helmet and then leaned on the table. "Mr. Price, let me just say what an honor it is to be able to meet with you today."

"Ingratiating it is," Nyala whispered. Mariela laughed.

"I know my viewers appreciate the chance to hear about what's happening from your viewpoint. You offer a unique perspective no one else can provide."

"I'm happy to oblige." Liam nodded his head congenially. It was interesting how warm he could be when it suited him. It was nothing at all like the aggressive man that Mariela knew.

"Let's get started with the interview then," Elliat said. "I don't want to take up any more of your precious time than necessary. Can you start by answering the question foremost on my followers' minds—what is Panacea Corp doing in Area 52?"

"Let me start by saying that Panacea Corp has an agreement with Area 52 for them to use this land," Liam said. "The agreement required the people living in Area 52 to accept certain conditions. Recently it became clear that Area 52 had broken the agreement in multiple ways and they were not intending to comply with what they had agreed to. Panacea Corp felt we had no choice but to speak to them directly. They wouldn't allow us entry, however, which was why we had to remove the protective barriers that they had put in place to keep us out.

"And I know what you are going to ask next," Liam continued. "What are those creatures? Those undead humans? Well, I'll tell you. When

Panacea Corp took down the protective barrier to take back the land, in accordance with the agreement, we found that the Area 52 people had been developing an army of corpses they planned to use to keep Panacea Corp from rightfully taking the land back. Some detective work on our part showed that Area 52 was using modified chip technology they had stolen from Panacea Corp to remotely control the corpses. Quick-thinking Panacea Corp personnel took control of the corpses by hacking their chips and protected our people from them."

Wow, Liam's smooth lies rolled off his tongue with ease. How many times had he successfully lied to her over the years? There wasn't any way to know, but it was starting to look like it may have been more than she had realized at the time.

"Well, that is certainly illuminating." Elliat was sticking with ingratiating, it appeared. "A source I interviewed a few days ago stated that the 'undead' are actually cryogens that are being used by Panacea Corp as an invasion force. Can you comment on this?"

"Your source is mistaken; he had been briefly consulted by another of our employees on her research to revive cryogens, and he appears to have confused the project he was consulted on with what is happening here."

"So, if people have loved ones stored at the Panacea Cryopreservation and Restoration Complex, can they rest assured that their loved ones are still there?"

"Absolutely. And I can say that Panacea Corp's research on reviving cryogens has shown quite a bit of promise—I don't want to say too much right now, but if all goes well, the people who have family members stored with us may be getting some very exciting news soon."

Could Liam have told a bigger lie? It wasn't fair to get people's hopes up for something that wasn't going to happen.

Elliat shifted excitedly in his chair.

"That would be an incredible breakthrough; I'm sure they are excited to hear that. What about the Black Screen and the missing LP100 model ghosts? Is there anything you would like to say about that?"

"The Black Screen was perpetrated by saboteurs. I now suspect it may have had something to do with Area 52 stealing the chip technology, and it might have involved coordination with some people at high levels in Panacea Corp. I am looking into this right now and will have more to say on it later."

"So we're finally getting some answers?"

"Yes, of course. Now if you'll excuse me, I have quite a few pressing matters to deal with."

Liam walked away, leaving Elliat thanking him to his back. Had Liam said even one thing that was true? Mariela sat down on the cot and Nyala plopped down beside her.

"Have you ever heard a greater bunch of bull?"

"Nope, I don't think I have."

~~~~~

The path they had cleared earlier through the cryogens on the main street was still there when they passed by.

"Please stop for a moment," Cooper said to the driver. "I want to look at them."

He got out of the vehicle. Petra followed him.

The deputies joined them and started removing rifles from the cryogens. The unprovoked cryogens didn't resist. "What are we going to do with them?" Deputy Dan asked Petra.

"I don't know," Petra said. "I suppose find someplace where we can give them a proper burial. We'll need some place to put them while they are waiting to be buried. I wonder if the school principal would ever forgive me if I used the high school gymnasium."

The cryo closest to Cooper was missing skin on his feet, and it smelled. They never should have been used like this. He never should have been a part of it in any way. "They're starting to rot." It was unnerving how they stared straight ahead, seemingly human but not human. "I don't think you want to store them inside."

"I'll deal with that after we finish with the chips," Petra said.

"I've seen what I wanted to see," Cooper said. "We can go on now." The cryogens deserved better than this, but at this point there was nothing else to do other than bury them. Even if it did become possible to revive cryogens someday, these were too far damaged.

"I assume you have the codes to open the door to the Panacea Corp server room?" Petra asked him.

"Um, no. Those were lost long ago. Don't you have them?"

"Panacea Corp didn't entrust them to me. Probably they wished to keep their property accessible by only their staff. How were you planning on getting in?"
~~~~~

"I thought Amaya would be here. She had a device."

"It seems like you made many unfounded assumptions about her involvement. We'll stop by the sheriff's station on the way and get her belongings. The device may be with them."

If only Amaya had come with him, it would have been so much easier. And he wouldn't have to be constantly lectured by a 101-year-old woman.

Fifteen minutes later they were leaving the sheriff's station and on their way to a mausoleum outside of town that had the entrance to the server rooms hidden within it. It hadn't taken long at the sheriff's station to find the device to open the server room door in Amaya's belongings. Petra allowed him to take Mariela's and Nyala's stuff as well. Cooper considered pointing out that the packs didn't belong to Petra, so he didn't really need her permission to take them, but he decided it wasn't worth it.

Petra didn't say anything during the long elevator ride from the mausoleum down to the server rooms. They exited the elevator into the server room for Area 52. Petra used Amaya's device to easily open the door to the Panacea Corp server room. Things hadn't changed much in the two weeks since he was last there. The aisles were still so long he couldn't see the end of them, the servers were still covered in dust, a few surviving cleaning bots were still zooming around on the floor, the emergency lighting still provided barely enough light to function, and a possum was still living in one of the server cases.

Cooper set his bag on the floor and used his Everything to connect with Amoco. Amoco guided Petra through the process of accessing the main server.

After a couple minutes Petra said, "I'm done accessing the server."

"This is it," Cooper said. "This is when we either charge ahead with society-altering sabotage, or we change our minds."

"I think you know where I stand on this," Petra said.

"I am prepared to proceed," Amoco said.

"Ok," Cooper nodded, "let's do it."

"Amoco, what am I doing?" Petra asked.

"You will be erasing the tracks of the actions I am taking," Amoco said.

"And how do I do that?" Petra asked.

Amoco paused as though he wasn't sure how to respond. Cooper wasn't sure how to respond either. Maybe Petra wasn't going to be able to do this.

"Cooper." The quiet voice calling his name didn't belong to Petra or Amoco. Cooper spun around. Amaya, with heavily bandaged feet and a cane, was silhouetted in the door by the brighter light of the outer room. He smiled.

"You made it." Cooper was struck by a sense of relief, then of doubt. "Or are you here to try to stop me?"

"I'm here to help." She hobbled over to where Petra was trying to access the server.

"Here's your pack." He handed her the items they had retrieved from the sheriff's station. "What made you change your mind?"

"June did. Plus, I knew I'd regret not helping Nyala. She would've done it for me, no matter the consequences."

"Why do you waste my time?" Petra was clearly annoyed. "Couldn't you have figured this out before dragging me to this allergen-ridden place? I have other important issues that also need to be dealt with right now."

"Sorry, Petra," Amaya said. "Here, let me do that." Walking gingerly on her still-bandaged feet, she took Petra's place in front of the server terminal. "Okay, I'm ready."

"Amoco, did you hear that?" Cooper said. "Go."

"Amaya, I am pleased you have joined us," Amoco said. "Implementing the program now. You will need to delete the evidence of what I do after I do it."

"Got it. I'll follow along after you and erase your tracks."

No longer needed, Cooper and Petra stepped back from the server. Twenty minutes went by with Amaya intently focused on the screen and occasionally communicating with Amoco.

"Is June waiting for you?" Petra asked Amaya.

"No, she wanted to get back home. She's preparing to protect her home from whatever might happen."

"Then we only have one vehicle. Which means I'm stuck waiting here until you all are finished."

"This was your idea, if you remember," Cooper said. "You went to a great deal of effort to convince me to do this."

"I haven't changed my mind. I just didn't think I would spend so much of my time standing around being useless."

"Were you always this cranky?" Cooper asked. "Because I don't see how you managed to get people to join you here unless they enjoyed being condescended to."

"It's a skill I've developed with time. I find it makes me a more effective leader if people are terrified of me. I call it 'Petrified by Petra.'"

She laughed at her own joke and Cooper couldn't help himself, he laughed too.

Amaya turned away from the server, her attitude heavy and serious in comparison. "It's done," she said. "We'd better get out of here and on the road before things get really crazy."

"Thank you," Petra said. "When you see the aftermath of this, remember you saved lives today."

"I hope that's true," Amaya said. She picked her pack up and clenched it to her stomach. "Let's go. I want to get out of here."

CHAPTER 28

The Exodus

Saturday, continued

The swaying of the elevator made Amaya want to puke. It seemed like almost every time she was going up in this elevator, something bad had happened. The first time, Opali and the LP100 model ghosts had been deleted. Last time, she was arrested by Dan. This time, she had just set civilization back a century. She just had to hold it together for three minutes or so and then she could get out of the elevator and throw up on the grass.

If only she knew that the others were okay, she would feel a little better. She had lost contact with Amoco right after the chips were disabled, which meant disabling them probably worked, but it still made her anxious not to know. Amoco, June, Nyala, and lots of other people she cared about would have been infected with the kill switch—how could she know that disabling the chips hadn't activated it?

At least they would be meeting Mariela and Nyala at the junction outside of SkyWater soon. In probably less than half an hour she would know if they were okay, and hopefully not long after they would be getting into a heli that a friend of Mariela's father had agreed to send to pick them up.

The elevator door opened and they were face-to-face with a drone hovering at eye level. Cooper swung his pack and slammed the drone into the wall.

"I *hate* drones," she said.

~~~~~

Mariela's body ached. She flipped to her other side on the cot. Time seemed to slow down the longer they were incarcerated. She had slept so much in the last—*had it been a week since Dan had taken them into custody?*—that she wasn't able to sleep anymore. A few seconds that felt like hours ticked by. Outside the tent, some soldiers called out to each other asking about dinner. A plate dropped to the ground and someone laughed and clapped. An owl hooted and its mate responded. It all
~~~~~

seemed so…unremarkable.

An odd sensation tickled the back of her neck. She touched the area—it was vibrating ever so slightly. The vibrations got stronger, and she rubbed her neck like that might override the feeling. But the vibrations intensified until her neck burned, until it felt like she was disintegrating with pain. She had to get out of the tent; to get away from the pain. She started to run but tumbled to the ground. Nyala was beside her, pulling her up and putting Mariela's arm over her shoulder. Confused people were running around and yelling. She couldn't see. "What's he doing here?" Nyala's voice.

Everything was blurry outlines. Dan. A truck. She dug her fingernails into the back of her neck and scratched. Someone pulled on her other arm. She was dragged away from the camp. She tried to get her legs under her but over and over again they gave out and she fell.

"Is she okay?"

"I don't think so."

"What happened?"

"I'm not sure."

"Get her in the vehicle."

"I'm going to stay here." *Who was that?*

"Are you sure?"

She couldn't see. Hands helped her up. Into something.

"It's okay, Mariela, we're safe." The pain stabbed through her head and she passed out.

~~~~~

Hank checked the date. Between the two trips through the tesseract, six days had passed in what felt like the space of an hour. He could never get used to losing three days in a second. He pushed aside the barrage of news alerts and message pings from the last six days. It was more than he had time to sort through right now. He would check in a bit to see if there were any updates from Amoco on getting Mariela's kill switch de-activated.

It looked like it had rained a lot in the last few days because the ground was muddy and—*it was odd*—but it looked like people had been walking through the deep mud, and there were items strewn everywhere. It was almost like a tornado had picked up a bunch of trash and left it on the ground. A tornado with footprints.
~~~~~

"Georgia, look at the ground. What happened here?"

He turned around. And that's when he saw the mountain range. A huge, beautiful, mountain range where none had been visible before.

Georgia turned to see what he was looking at. "Oh my god. What happened in the last few days?"

Hank set the cat carrier down in the mud without looking down. He kept his eyes on the mountains, his mind trying to process why he could see them and wondering if they would disappear again. Maybe they had jumped into the distant future? Or the past before the umbrella was constructed? But that wouldn't make sense—the Universal Standard Date/Time stamp said the year was 2115. Exactly when he expected it to be.

"Were you able to reach T-Rock?" he asked.

"No. He sent a message earlier today telling us to wait for him, but that's it."

A woman jumped down off the ledge just beyond where the portal into Area 52 used to be. "RUN!" she yelled mid-air, before falling to the ground hard. She didn't move.

"Is she okay?" Hank asked. He should go check on her. He probably should have done that right away, but he was processing things slowly.

The woman jumped up and leaned with her hands on her knees and panted, gasping in lungfuls of air. She had probably gotten the wind knocked out of her with the fall. Her torn and bloodied clothing looked like she had been running through the bushes.

"You two!" she said. She looked around her with fearful eyes. "Do you have transportation?"

"Sorry." Hank shrugged. "Not right now." He didn't really want to travel with the wild-eyed woman, but if she was still there when T-Rock showed up he would offer her a ride. "We have a transport coming. You can wait with us."

"I'm not waiting," she said. "You have to get out of here too. Bad stuff is going on in there. There are aliens that are being manipulated by the government, and then they did something to us."

"Who? Did what?"

"The government. Or it might be the aliens. They stopped our chips from working."

"How?"

"We all felt our chips tingling, or burning, and then they stopped working." She took a break from speaking to catch her breath. "It was awful. No one knew what to do." She glanced over her shoulder, her eyes still wide and fearful. "Look, I've got to get away from here. You should run—especially if your chip still works. Don't take a chance when you could save yourself." She started running again.

"Wait," Hank called out. The woman stopped running and looked at him. The right thing to do was to stop her, even though he didn't exactly want her to stick around. "You can't go that way. It's desert for sixty miles. You'll die before you get to a road."

"Suit yourself, but I'm not going to wait here to be killed. I can do sixty miles." She started running again.

"You can't," Hank yelled after her. It was doubtful she could run, or walk even, for sixty miles without water in the heat. But if she was determined to go, he couldn't stop her.

"Hank," Georgia said. "You have to see this. Meet me on the ground of the Zócolo Square in Panacea."

"Let's make it quick. I'm kind of creeped out by whatever is happening here and I don't want to be checked out for too long."

"We'll make it short. See you there."

Hank shifted to the Zócolo. The Zócolo was Georgia's favorite public gathering place in the Panacea metaverse. She liked to watch people wandering the pathways of the square from the cloud-like platforms of the aptly-named Above the Zócolo café. Today Hank and Georgia stayed on the ground among the multi-colored trees.

"Does anything about this seem odd to you?" she asked.

The trees along the side of the path changed color—that wasn't odd. A couple of ghosts wandered by, but that also wasn't unusual. People often created digital ghosts and then set them loose in public spaces to wander aimlessly. Hank once created a giant football with eyes that rolled through the parks and plazas crushing everything it its path. It made people mad, but it wasn't odd. Hank smiled. That football was probably still out there somewhere, wreaking havoc and leaving a path of flattened features behind it.

Another ghost was sitting on a bench not far away. But where were… Hank turned in a circle, looking in all directions. "There aren't any humans here." Sometimes it was difficult to tell ghost from human, but everything in the plaza right now was definitely ghost.

"I checked two other places and there aren't any humans in any of them either," Georgia said. "I don't think whatever happened to the chips was just confined to Area 52. I think it affected everyone."

"Except us."

"Except us. We need to figure out what happened during the last three days."

"Let's get back to the solid world and start reading through the news alerts."

"I'm worried about the others."

"Me too." He rubbed his palm with his thumb. "Me too."

~~~~~

Cooper was worried about Amaya. She had struggled in the walk from the elevator out to the vehicle, and now that she was seated in the transport, she held a hand clasped tightly over her stomach and stared out the window blankly. Did she regret helping him? She had been disengaged ever since they had disabled the chips, and during the minutes-long elevator ride up from the server room, she had been completely silent.

Petra must have been worried about Amaya too because she told Amaya to sit in the front passenger seat. Cooper climbed in to the back seat and Petra followed him. Some of the deputies had left to take the guns away from the cryogens. The woman who had been left as their driver seemed to know Amaya, but Amaya barely acknowledged her presence.

"Where are we going?" the driver asked once they were all settled.

"Take them to the junction and leave them there," Petra said.

"We're letting them go?" She almost sounded disappointed.

"We no longer have room in our jails for low-level perpetrators, so yes, we're letting them go."

"Whatever you say boss."

"But take me home first," Petra said.

Outside of the vehicle about ten drones hovered. Their behavior was different from before. Most of them weren't doing anything—they appeared to be recording, but not moving or turning to face the people as they walked by. Two drones that probably had more automated programming followed them as they left the cemetery, but when the vehicle stopped at a stop sign the drones chased after a deer. The deer must have seemed more exciting than a slow-moving vehicle.
~~~~~

In a residential area on the edge of town, a man wearing digi-skin clothing that no longer had any color in it waved them down. The driver lowered her window. "Sorry to bother you, but can you help me?" The man had the look of someone who frequently felt lost. "I don't know how to get home. I was tracing my route but then something happened and now I can't access the soup or my route."

The driver stared at the guy blankly. Cooper leaned over to the window. "It's that way." Cooper pointed in the direction of the main road and gave the man instructions on how to get back to the entrance to Area 52.

"Thanks, man. Things are creepy here, aren't they?" He didn't wait for an answer before ran off in the direction that Cooper had pointed.

The driver headed in the same direction at a slow and steady pace. Once over the hill, they coasted the couple blocks down to the road. The businesses in the small cabins lining the roads were all shuttered up, some even with their windows boarded up. It was a ghost town.

"Boss, you need to see this." They were approaching the main road crossing. Cooper peered around the driver through the open window to the front, but from his point of view he couldn't see anything. Was it something with the cryos? The driver pulled forward and came to a full stop in the middle of the main drag, and then got out and crossed to the other side to open the door for Petra. Cooper followed her out.

All along the main road, the cryos sprawled on the ground, their arms and legs askew and their rifles dropped randomly. Cooper followed the driver to the other side of the vehicle. A group of people stood around a body on the ground. Not a cryo, but a person covered in blood. The medics, sheriffs, and bystanders parted to allow Petra through.

Cooper recognized the injured person—he was one of the deputies who had arrested Cooper and Amaya. A medic knelt beside him with blood-covered hands. The medic wasn't doing anything, and the look on his face said that he had given up.

"What happened?" Petra reached out toward the fallen deputy, her face contorting with sadness and rage. She knelt beside the deputy and picked up his hand, her cheeks glistening with tears. When she spoke again, her voice was louder and angrier. "What happened?"

"He was removing the guns from these things," the guy motioned to the cryos, "and then all of a sudden they went berserk and started falling to the ground, but some of them moved their arms around twitching-like and shot their guns. Jake here got hit in the neck. Jodie got hit too, in the calf. They took her to the hospital, but I think she's gonna be okay."

Petra put her forehead on the deputy's torso. "I'm so sorry I didn't protect you. This is my fault."

Cooper's chest constricted. It was like Grace all over again. It wasn't fair that Cooper had only known her such a short time before she died. It wasn't fair that Grace had been taken so soon. He turned around abruptly and ran into Amaya. Cooper stepped around her. "I'm going back to the vehicle." His voice cracked when he spoke.

About five minutes later, Amaya joined him. She stared blankly at a point on the dashboard. There was a chasm between them, and Cooper no longer felt motivated to try to cross it.

Around ten minutes later, Petra returned with the driver. She opened the driver-side door and leaned into the vehicle. "You are no longer welcome here," she said to them. "My deputy will take you to the junction as agreed but then you will leave immediately and you will never return. Do you understand me?"

Cooper never wanted to return. This place was too full of tragedy. "Agreed," he said.

Amaya didn't look away from the point she had been staring at. She nodded curtly.

"Then go," Petra said. She slammed the door and walked away from the vehicle.

<div style="text-align: center">~~~~~</div>

Whump. Whump. Whump. Mariela had a splitting headache and no clue where she was. She sat up and rubbed her eyes. A small box with a metal floor and canvas roof left her barely enough room to sit up. A bunched and twisted blanket partially covered the floor. Her head hurt every time the box jostled. The burning sensation in her head was edging into a stabbing pain. The ache seemed to be coming from where her chip was. *Whump. Whump. Whump.* What *was* that noise? It sounded familiar, like she should be able to identify it. She wasn't thinking straight.

Where was she? Someone nearby was talking quietly. She couldn't make out what they were saying. The sound hurt her head. It was starting to come back to her—a spasm of pain had gone through her head, and then she ran, and then Dan showed up. She must be in the back of his vehicle now. *Whump. Whump. Whump.* It was getting louder. It was like a steady drum of…blades slicing through the air. Helicopter blades. Crap. If there was a heli nearby, that could only mean one thing. Liam.

Mariela found the opening into the front compartment. Dan was driving and Nyala was sitting in the passenger seat.

"Mariela! How are you feeling?" Nyala asked.

"Like I've been hit in the head with a two-by-four."

"Yeah, whatever happened it was pretty painful on my end as well," Nyala said. "I think because you had a double dose of the kill switch it was worse for you."

"That second dose was brutal. In more ways than one." Mariela glanced back over her shoulder. "There's a helicopter coming up behind us. Maybe it's just a news copter."

The thumping sound got louder and the windows shook. The helicopter passed above them, hovered in front of the vehicle, and then started to descend in the middle of the narrow road, completely blocking the path of the vehicle. Mariela's pulse quickened. It wasn't a news copter. "I don't like this. Can we avoid it?"

Dan shook his head. "We can't turn around, that will just lead us right back to the camp."

"Can we go off road?" Nyala asked.

"My jeep would never make it through the trees." Dan slowed the jeep to a stop.

The helicopter was close to touching down. Mariela knew what she needed to do. "Nyala, make sure you get out of here so you can tell people what happened." Mariela opened the rear window of the jeep.

"Wait." Nyala leaned into the back. "Mariela!"

Before Nyala could say anything more, Mariela was out the back. A wave of pain swept through her head and she almost blacked out. She put a hand on the vehicle to steady herself as she walked around to the driver's side window. "Dan, do me a favor and get her out of here—don't come back until the helicopter's gone."

Dan threw the vehicle into reverse. The tires flung rocks and dug into the dirt as he floored the accelerator. He looked over his shoulder and yanked the wheel around.

"Hey, wait," Nyala yelled out the window across Dan. "Let's talk about this before you do something stupid."

"Too late!" Mariela waved to Nyala as Dan put the vehicle back into drive and with another spray of rocks, sped away with Nyala still sticking her head out of the window. Mariela was sure Dan and Nyala would be safe as long as they weren't with her.

Mariela's heart pounded. She waited for the heli to touch down and then walked up the two men who exited it. Looked like Liam didn't come to get her in person.

"Mariela Stafford, Panacea Corp CEO Liam Price wants you to come with us. Put your hands in the air."

"Okay." Mariela put her hands up. They patted her down. "I don't have any weapons."

"We don't take your word for that sort of thing."

"Of course."

"No weapons," the guard who checked her said to the other.

"Just in case you get the idea to run again…" the guard picked up a club from the helicopter floor and hit the side of her knee. With a crunch, her kneecap dislocated and she collapsed onto the ground.

CHAPTER 29

The Exodus

Saturday, continued

It was just like Liam to keep a helicopter or two around in case of an emergency. They landed back at the camp and waited while Liam oversaw the departure of the last of the soldiers in their armored transports. Mariela hadn't moved from where the guard had dumped her on the floor of the heli. Her knee hurt like hell but it would hurt even more if she tried to sit up.

"Here." One of the guards threw a cooling pack on her. Like that was going to do much good. As long as her kneecap was dislocated, her knee wasn't going to get better. She set the cold pack down and carefully raised her torso onto one elbow. Even the smallest movements brought on stabbing pain. After a lot of cursing and grinding of her teeth, she made it into a sitting position. She placed her hand next to her kneecap, took a deep breath, and pushed. The kneecap popped as it shunted into place. She sucked air in through her teeth and held her body rigid until the shooting pain subsided. It still hurt, but she could handle the pain as long as she didn't move the leg. She'd need to get it looked at soon.

"Get in the helicopter, Viola," Liam yelled.

Half a minute later, Viola climbed into the helicopter. She sat down in a chair near Mariela. "He's going to blame me for all of this." Viola stared at some distant point outside the window. "It was such a good idea and it went so wrong."

"He's not going to blame you for *all* of it." It hurt Mariela's head to talk. "I'm sure he's planning on throwing some my way as well."

"He'll find more than enough blame for the both of us. Our chips aren't working. Is yours?"

"No."

"It seems like everyone's chip was disabled," Viola said.

"How did *that* happen?" Mariela asked.

"I don't know," Viola said. "I thought you would know. It conveniently solves your kill switch problem, doesn't it?"

"I'm as surprised as anyone."

Was this Amoco's solution to the kill switch? It seemed a little drastic. Surely he didn't have to disable everyone's chips. Maybe they were just temporarily disabled to allow Nyala and her to escape? But then what?

"I'm having a hard time with it." Viola finally looked at Mariela. "Cooper would probably make fun of me for this, but I've never been disconnected from Panacea before. I keep thinking of things I want to do and I can't do any of them. I want to contact my family to make sure they're okay, but I can't do it. I want to send them a message to let them know I'm okay, and I can't. I want to check on my cat, but I can't do it. How long is this going to last?"

"I don't know," Mariela said.

"Will our chips ever come back online?"

Mariela sighed. "I don't know."

"Mariela, if I find out you did it, so help me…" Viola trailed off speaking and looked out the window again. "You will have ruined my life."

Liam started yelling again, but this time at someone Mariela couldn't see.

The last of the soldier transports eventually pulled away from the camp. Liam climbed into the helicopter and pulled the door closed behind him. He gave Mariela a look that said he had no doubt she was guilty. "I wonder what people will think, Mariela, when they see you had an escape vehicle waiting to pick you up as soon as the chips were disabled."

Ah. That did look guilty. Amoco or someone must have arranged for Dan to pick them up. "I think the guy was just there. He was probably spying on you all. I didn't call him or have him show up. You had blocked my chip, there wasn't any way I could have done that."

"I don't think it's a coincidence," Liam said. "And I don't think other people will see it that way either." Liam's eyes hardened. "I'm going to get to the truth about what is happening here no matter what it takes."

Elliat pounded on the door of the helicopter. Liam rolled his eyes and opened it. Mariela had forgotten about Elliat.

"Can I go with you?" Elliat asked. "The soldiers said I couldn't go with them."

"Sorry," Liam said.

Elliat stuck his hand on the door and held it in place. "Please don't leave me. If you go, I'll be the only one here. Except for those things." He motioned with his head in the direction of the cryogens sprawled in the road.

"Not my problem." He removed Elliat's hand from the door. "No journalists allowed." Liam pulled the door shut.

"Mr. Price!" Elliat pounded on the window of the helicopter. "Don't leave me! Liam!"

Liam told the pilot to take off. Elliat gave up and backed away as the spinning of the heli's blades picked up.

Mariela raised her eyebrows. "Did he do something to you?" she asked Liam.

"No. I like the guy. He always writes flattering stuff about me. I'll make it up to him later by giving him some exclusive scoop."

"*If* he makes it back. I'm not sure the guy is capable of surviving on his own."

"Extra passengers are extra risk," Liam said. "And the last thing I need is for him to be talking to you two." He motioned to her and Viola.

Elliat was one of Mariela's least favorite people, but her chest burned at the callousness of Liam leaving him behind. "But if he dies, who will write fawning posts about you?"

"I'll find someone. They're a dime a dozen."

~~~~~~

Not a word was spoken between Amaya and Cooper during the half-hour trip to the junction. Amaya couldn't shake feeling like she needed to throw up. The deputy's death was her fault. His death was a direct result of them disabling the chips. How many more people would die as a result of what they had done? How bad would it have to get before she would decide that saving Nyala wasn't worth the grief caused to other people? Surely that deputy had people who cared about him.

Cooper looked at her like he wanted to talk about stuff. "I'm going to contact the heli and tell them we'll be ready to go in about ten minutes," Cooper said. "The pilot said he would be waiting nearby, so we'll be out of here soon."

"Okay." At least he was talking to her about logistics, and not other stuff like how she felt about what they had done. Amaya didn't feel like talking to anyone, but she especially didn't feel like talking to Cooper.

"We're almost to the junction." He paused but Amaya didn't respond.
~~~~~~

It didn't seem like the sort of comment that required a response.

Cooper looked at her closely. "Are you okay?"

"I'm fine." Talking made her nauseous so hopefully Cooper would get a clue and stop asking her questions. She held tighter to her stomach and watched the scenery pass as the sunlight faded from the sky.

The junction was at the tip of a sharp switchback nestled into the steep mountains surrounding the road heading out of SkyWater. On the inside of the switchback, forested slopes fell abruptly away from the road. On the outside of the switchback, forest intermingled with rock. Further down the road, the entire width of the roadway was filled with cryogens sprawled on the ground, not reacting to the gawkers roaming among them.

Dan and Nyala were waiting for them at the junction. The driver barely waited for Amaya and Cooper to get out before she turned around and headed back up the road. Nyala ran up to Amaya and wrapped her in a tight embrace. "I'm so glad you're okay," she said.

"Me too. I'm glad you're okay." Tears wet Amaya's cheeks. Seeing Nyala safe made her feel better about what she had done. She still felt the heavy weight of guilt, but at least her sister was okay. "I was so worried that disabling the chips would set off the kill switch."

"You did that?" Nyala asked. "You disabled the chips? My own little sister! I'm so proud of you!"

"I'm not proud," Amaya snapped. She wiped some tears off her cheeks. Nyala would probably never understand how difficult it was for her to do what she had done.

"You look like crap," Nyala said with a laugh.

Movement was awkward for Amaya in her over-sized sweats, bulky flak jacket, and helmet, but Nyala wasn't looking much better.

"At least I'm not wearing a jail uniform," Amaya said. They both laughed this time.

Nyala picked up Amaya's arm with one hand and ran her hand next to the many scrapes. "Does it hurt?"

"It hurts, but not as much as my feet."

Nyala looked at her feet swaddled in bandages and smashed into slippers. "Those are some really thick bandages."

"I know. Did something happen to Mariela?" Amaya asked.

"She got picked up by a helicopter," Nyala said. "I think Liam has her. I tried to stop her from going with them, but I couldn't." Nyala glared at Dan.

"I did what Mariela asked me to do," Dan said defensively.

There must be some story there that Nyala would probably tell her later.

"Is Mariela okay?" Cooper asked.

"I don't know," Nyala said.

"June decided to stay here for the time being," Amaya said.

Nyala turned to Dan. "Are you coming with us?"

"I'm needed here," Dan said. "Lots of cleaning up to do, and Petra will try to fix the umbrella. And we have around 10,000 dead bodies that need to be dealt with."

"Yeah, sorry about that," Amaya said. "I know I'm not responsible, but I still feel like I need to apologize. It was unconscionable for Panacea Corp to treat the cryogens that way, and even more so that they would just abandon them here."

"We'll give them a proper burial," Dan said.

"You have the communication device…" Nyala said.

"You mean the phone?"

"You have the phone, you can use it to contact us if you change your mind," Nyala said.

"Will do." Dan walked around to the other side of his vehicle. He opened the door, but before getting in he looked back at them. "Are you all okay? If everything's good, I'm heading out. Lots of stuff to be done."

"We're good," Nyala said. "Our helicopter should be here in ten minutes or so."

"Okay. Best of luck to you all."

"You too."

Dan's vehicle soon disappeared around the bend.

Cooper threw his pack on the ground and reclined with it as his pillow. He closed his eyes and folded his arms over his chest.

"Here's your stuff." Amaya handed Nyala's pack to her.

"My Everything!" Nyala grabbed her pack, dug into it, found her Everything, and without pausing, snapped it onto her arm. "I missed you."

"I could swear you missed that thing more than you did me."

"Hey, did I tell you I heard from Bren?" Nyala asked.

"No. When…how…did you talk to him?"

"While I was waiting for you all, I used the communication device. He said that he, Georgia, and T-Rock are in the hovbus heading back home, but Hank decided to stay here."

"Really?"

"Hank is taking June's cat back to her, but he also told them he is planning on staying here for a while to help the Area 52 people out. With stuff like getting rid of the gawkers and getting the umbrella back up."

"That isn't like him," Amaya said. Hank didn't have any connection to the people in Area 52, why was he helping them? "Is Georgia going with him?"

"No. I guess Hank and Georgia are going their separate ways for now."

"It sounds like Hank to me," Cooper said without opening his eyes, "except for the part about not going where Georgia's going."

The whir of a heli's blades became audible in the distance. Amaya would be relieved once they were off the ground. She took a deep breath. Now if she could just stop feeling like she needed to throw up.

CHAPTER 30

The Exodus

Saturday, continued

Mariela inched toward the side of the helicopter so her back was resting against it. Each move caused a spike in pain, but at least she could rest the leg.

"You." Liam pointed at one of the bodyguards and motioned for him to come over. Did Liam not know the names of his bodyguards? No wonder his former guards had thrown him out of the heli. "You," Liam repeated, "find the capture Elliat provided to us and send it to security at headquarters so they can release it. Use the unchipped communication network."

"Yes, Mr. Price."

The guard, as burly and hulking as the others, sat back in the chair next to Viola and pulled the table out from its slot in between the seats.

"What capture?" Mariela asked.

The guard's brow furrowed. He poked at the table monitor with a certain randomness.

Liam smirked. "Elliat used his exo-cam to record your friends, what are their names?—Cooper and Amaya, I think—talking when they thought they were alone. Talking about how you and Amoco deleted the ghosts and also caused the Black Screen. It's not enough to convict you in court but should be plenty sufficient to convict you in the perception of the public."

"Oh." She pushed aside for the moment the pang of betrayal she felt about Cooper and Amaya talking about her behind her back. How many indignities would she have to put up with from Liam? He had sidelined her into an unimportant position, suspended her, kidnapped her—twice, dosed her with a potentially lethal substance, spied on her friends, and dislocated her kneecap. A girl had to know when to call it quits.

She once thought she would work for Panacea Corp her entire life. When Liam was hired as CEO, she had vowed to stick it out no matter how bad it got. Now here she was, less than two months after he was promoted, ready to throw in the towel. It went against the grain for her to accept that she needed to quit, but once she made up her mind it felt obvious. It might be a defeat, but it was the right thing to do.

"I quit," Mariela announced to no one in particular. Liam didn't even seem to notice she had spoken. "Liam, I don't want to work for you anymore. I quit." It was a relief to say the words out loud.

"I've already sent in the request for you to be fired," Liam said. "You can't quit a job you no longer work at."

"You fired me?"

"That surprises you?"

"Well, you can't fire me, because I already quit. You can't fire someone who doesn't work for you."

"You can call it what you want, but our press release is going to say you were fired."

"You're going to say I was *fired*? What happened to our company policy of not commenting on personnel matters?"

"These are extraordinary circumstances. The public will want to see someone's head roll. My exquisitely worded press conference will make sure it's your head rolling for everything that's happened lately and not mine."

"Do you realize how much danger you will be putting me in? I won't ever be able to leave my house again."

"Not my problem."

"Liam, there are some things you need to know. I wasn't responsible for what happened to you in the heli, and I didn't disable the chips. You're blaming me for things that aren't my fault."

"Whatever you say, Mariela." Liam rolled his eyes.

Mariela had run out of things to say. She wanted to protest more but she wasn't going to convince Liam of anything.

She looked out the window of the heli and gently rubbed around the kneecap that had been dislocated. The cold pack wasn't doing much to keep the swelling down. She probably wouldn't be able to walk for days.

The bodyguard continued to poke at the terminal with a confused look.

"Can I help you with that?" Viola asked.

"It's just I don't know how to use the unchipped network."

"Let me show you," Viola said. She rotated the terminal ninety degrees so both she and the guard could see it. "Touch right there." She pointed to a spot on the screen.

Viola walked him through multiple steps. A couple times they seemed to reach a dead end and had to backtrack to figure out where they went wrong.

"How did people survive when they had to communicate like this?" Viola complained. "It's so time-consuming and inefficient."

The bodyguard grunted in response.

Mariela switched the cold pack from the side of her knee to the top. The pain was getting worse and turning into a throbbing ache. The pain from the chip burn hadn't gotten any better either. She needed more cold packs.

"Okay, let's try going here," Viola touched a spot on the screen. They stared at it, not doing anything for a second. Then Viola perked up, "And it has been sent! We figured it out!"

Was this what life was going to be like with the chips disabled? Would people be constantly rejoicing over managing the smallest task?

The heli landed on the rooftop of Panacea Corp about an hour after they left Area 52. In the hour and a half since the chips were disabled, Mariela's life had changed in ways she never could have anticipated. She was unemployed, and if Liam released the capture, she was in danger of being targeted by people out for revenge.

Her sour mood wasn't improved by listening to nonstop news as Liam cycled through all the channels for the last hour. The news stations showed chaos as people swarmed the streets and Panacea Plaza. Sometimes the people were wandering aimlessly, other times they were looting and taking advantage of the confusion. A news crew at a pod warehouse showed people sitting in their pods looking confused. No matter what station Liam flipped to, the bad news was inescapable.

When they landed, everyone else exited the helicopter and left Mariela behind. She used her hands to steady herself and pushed up using her arms and her good leg. She tested the hurt knee. The pain burned like a hot poker but the leg held up under her weight. She could at least hobble along, even if it was a slow, labored walk. By the time she reached the door, Liam was already engaged in an animated conversation with the Director of Public Relations. Liam's bodyguards were waiting patiently for his conversation to end; some workers showed up to unload items from the heli.

Viola threw her bag over her shoulder. "See you around," Viola said and gave her a little wave.

Like Mariela was going to wave back to her. It's not like she and Viola were friends now.

Mariela took a deep breath—stepping out of the heli was going to hurt like hell. She steeled herself for the step down. The concrete rooftop looked far away and too…concrete. The best option was to use her good leg to lower herself down and land as gently as possible on the hurt leg.

"Can I help you?" Julio, her favorite bodyguard, emerged from the crowd of faces on the rooftop.

"Julio! It's so good to see you!" Julio was always there when she needed him. Except when he wasn't. "I thought you were assigned to guarding pod warehouses?"

"I had a feeling you needed me." He put an arm around her waist. "Put your arm over my shoulders and I'll lift you down."

He lifted her easily and set her lightly on the rooftop. Mariela winced when her feet touched the ground.

Liam locked eyes on them. His face turned white and then flooded red.

"Viola, what is *he* doing here?" Liam's yell caught Viola just as she was about to disappear into the stairwell.

It didn't surprise Mariela that Liam was upset about Julio being there. Liam never liked that Julio was loyal to Mariela. It was why he had been reassigned to guard the pod warehouses.

Viola appeared to sigh deeply before turning around. "Who, him?" Viola pointed at Julio. "You said to contact security, so I contacted security. I didn't specify who they should send over." Viola looked directly at Liam, her expression innocent and unconcerned. "I hope that's okay?"

"Next time be more specific."

"Okay."

"Who did you send the video to?"

"I sent that to security as well. I don't know who is working security today."

"Well, get over here and find out who has it!" Liam insisted.

Viola flinched, but she headed back toward Liam. The PR Director gave her a small handheld radio and helped her figure out how to contact security.

Mariela, with assistance from Julio, limped as fast as she could toward the exit stairs. Her goal was to be at her father's estate before the video hit the airwaves. It was the safest place for her to be.

She glanced at Liam. He was another reason to hurry. She wanted to get out of there before Liam completely blew up at Viola or realized Mariela was trying to leave.

One of the workers handed Viola a headset. Viola spoke to someone on the other end. "Okay," Viola said to Liam, "they're having some trouble finding it."

Julio chuckled. Mariela was sure of it. It wasn't loud, but there had definitely been a chuckle.

"What do you mean?"

Mariela couldn't see it, but she had no doubt from his tone of voice that the vein on Liam's forehead was bulging again.

"Have patience," Viola said. "They're not used to doing things manually, so it's taking longer than normal."

Liam grabbed the headset from Viola. "I'll contact them myself."

Mariela was at the door to the stairs now with her hand on the doorknob. She knew she should turn it; she should get out of sight of Liam as quickly as possible, but she needed to see how this played out.

Liam yelled into the headset. "What do you mean it has been corrupted? Recover it!"

Liam, with bile foaming out the side of his mouth, turned to Viola. "How could you be so stupid?" Liam stormed toward the stairs. "You know what, I don't need the video. In the press release, I can still list lots of reasons why Mariela would want to disable the chips."

Mariela stumbled to the side to get out of his way. He ignored her and threw the door to the stairs open with enough force that it swung back and slammed shut behind him.

Mariela smiled at her unexpected good fortune. Had Viola's actions been completely innocent? Did she know when she sent the video to security that someone loyal to Mariela would corrupt it?

Now was the time to get out of there before Liam found a way to have her arrested. Mariela had just grabbed the door handle when Viola caught her arm, wrapping her hand lightly around it. Viola leaned in almost nose-to-nose and looked Mariela directly in the eyes.

"You owe me," Viola said, her voice low and tense, her face inches away from Mariela's. "I don't know what I want yet, but someday soon you'll have to repay the favor I just did for you."

How ironic that this vicious woman smelled like fresh-bloomed lilacs.

"And if you don't," Viola continued, "I'll make sure Liam has all the evidence he needs to convict you as well as your friends." She took a step back, looked Mariela up and down, and said, "Your jail uniform look will be the next trendsetter for sure." And with a flash of her charming but devious smile, Viola opened the door and headed down the stairs.

Viola *had* known what she was doing. *I can't decide if I want to hug her or kick her.* Mariela looked down the staircase where Liam and Viola had disappeared. Everything was going to be okay. *Liam had no evidence.* She tested her leg to see if it would hold up, and decided she could walk with the help of Julio.

Julio grabbed the door and held it open for Mariela. "Let's go."

Mariela paused at the top of the stairs, not looking forward to the trip down the steps.

"Mariela."

Mariela startled. Viola was standing on the landing midway down the stairs.

"Was Cooper in on the disabling of the chips? Did he know?" No longer antagonistic, Viola appeared genuinely saddened, worn down even. Mariela didn't care how Viola felt. Despite the assistance Viola had provided, trusting her was out of the question.

The walls blurred around her. *Had* Cooper been in on it? "I don't know what you're talking about," she said.

She gritted her teeth until Viola resumed walking down the stairs. With unexpected tears bursting out once Viola was out of sight, the control that she relied on to keep her safe slipped away. She limped back out onto the roof. Barely able to see through her tears, she stumbled over her feet, her hurt leg stinging at her clumsiness. She leaned against the wall that encircled the stairwell and sank to the gravel rooftop, sobbing, gasping, her hurt leg straight in front of her. *What have we done?* Even though it wasn't her decision this time, some part of her felt responsible.

"Tissue?" Julio held a tissue out to her.

"Thank you." Mariela blew her nose. Julio waited patiently. "Julio, if any of the guards are fired because the video was corrupted, please let them know they will always have a job working for my family if they want it."

"They know that."

Oh crap, speaking of family, she had forgotten about her sister. Sofi would need help with the transition to the solid world. Happy to have a purpose again, Mariela found her tears mostly dried. She awkwardly stood up without putting weight on her hurt knee, smoothed her jailhouse clothing, wiped her tear-streaked cheeks, put her arm around Julio's shoulders for support, and inched toward the stairs. With each step she went faster, convinced that Sofi needed her.

It hadn't been easy figuring out how to get back to her father's house with the chips disabled. Normally, they would have taken a Panacea Corp limo, but as a *former* Panacea employee, Mariela no longer had that perk. It was possible the drivers might not know she was no longer working for Panacea Corp, but knowing Liam the first thing he probably did was tell the entire team she had been fired. Saying she quit would have been more accurate, but Liam would certainly use his preferred version of events.

It took about half an hour, but Julio managed to find a driver who was loyal to Mariela and willing to risk his job to take her to her father's estate. The next challenge was figuring out how to get there. With some effort, they realized the address of the estate was already programmed into the limo, and all they had to do was to tell the limo to go there.

Mariela also asked the driver to make a quick stop at the Everything store, where she bought every single device they had in stock. Considering she was just fired—that is, she just quit—she probably shouldn't have, but it was a necessary expense.

Within minutes of stopping at the store, Mariela got the device up and running. While on the road she spritzed some digi-spray on her face to cover up that she had been crying. She couldn't program it, so it was just the generic formulation, but it was better than nothing. She didn't want Sofi to know how upset she had been.

She opened the transport door as soon as it stopped in front of the estate. The guards at the estate entrance told her Sofi had arrived about half an hour previously. Mariela wanted to run up the steps to the estate, but she waited for Julio, who helped her navigate the steps up to the house and through the entry hallway to the door of the library.

"Sofi!" With one arm still around Julio's shoulders, Mariela hopped across the library on one foot to the chaise lounge where her dark-haired younger sister was being tended to by the family doctor. It was the first time Mariela had seen her sister in the solid world in seven years—Sofi's hair was long and uncut; her skin pale from lack of sun exposure. Mariela shook hands with the doctor. "Am I interrupting?"

"Just finishing up." The doctor checked that the IV was dripping the fluids properly. "Everything looks good." The doctor amiably put her hand on Sofi's shoulder. "I'll see myself out." Julio said goodbye and left with the doctor.

Mariela hugged Sofi and squeezed onto the chaise lounge next to her.

"Careful, don't sit on me." Sofi's voice was quiet and hoarse from years of not being used. "I'd move over but I can't."

Mariela put her arm around Sofi. "No need to move, I have enough space. Sorry it took me so long to get here. Julio told me it would take a long time, but I had no clue how bad it would be."

Mariela picked up Sofi's hand and held it between hers. Sofi's fingernails were jagged and worn down to the quick with matted blood on them.

"What happened?" Mariela asked.

"I got scared when I couldn't get out of my pod during the Black Screen. Twelve hours of panicked scratching can do a lot of damage." Sofi inspected her nails and then tucked her damaged hands under her arms. "I know my nails will heal, but do you think this is going to get better?" Sofi asked. "Will I be able to return to my pod soon?"

"I don't think so. It looks like all the chips are permanently disabled. This may be the new reality."

"Mariela, I think I've permanently lost Opali. If they haven't found the deleted ghosts by now, I don't think they ever will. Even if she did come back, I wouldn't be able to spend time with her because I can't get into the metaverse and she can't get out."

"You could use a terminal."

"Don't *patronize* me, Mariela. If she comes back, I'll find a way to stay in touch, but we both know she's not coming back."

"I'm sorry. I'm not trying to patronize you. I just want to be supportive."

"I don't need your help. I don't need you to take care of me, but I do need some rest."

Mariela could take a hint. She gave Sofi's hand a squeeze, and left her alone to rest.

The Day After the Exodus

Sunday

Business Today

"All the business news you need to know"

April 21, 2115

By Elliat Exis ~ *Business Today's* only staff reporter who was onsite during the zombie invasion of Area 52!

WHAT A WEEK IT HAS BEEN!
Loyal readers, where do I start? There's so much to say, so many stories to cover. As I'm sure you're busy adjusting to recent changes, let me start with the big stuff.

Many thanks to those of you who tuned in for my interview with Liam Price, CEO of Panacea Corp. Mr. Price has just held another press conference at Panacea Corp headquarters where he identified the Black Screen saboteurs as Mariela Stafford and some of her associates. This isn't much of a surprise to anyone, as Mariela Stafford's fingerprints have been all over this from the beginning. In the press conference, Mr. Price made a very compelling case against her. There is no word yet on whether this group is also responsible for the recent chip disabling that is resulting in the Panacea exodus.

There have also been reports of acts of aggression directed at numerous targets. The unchipped, in particular, are being targeted. It appears some people believe the unchipped are responsible for the Black Screen. Folks, I don't know what happened, but I can tell you that the unchipped as a group are not responsible.

In other news, you would have to be living under a rock to not have noticed that things have been a little tense since the chips were disabled yesterday. Many of us feel lost, and I'm embarrassed to admit I didn't know how to get home. I went to the assistance center so an un-chipped person could look up my address. They told me where my home was and how to get there. Someone had propped the door to my building open, so I was able to get in, but then I couldn't open the door to my apartment. I went back to the assistance center and then waited five hours for someone to show up to change my lock to a manual one. It was a moment of vulnerability that seems to be happening to me frequently since the chips were disabled.

I share this because I know a lot of you are going through the same thing. I know because you've told me your stories. Pod-lifers have told me about how they don't have anywhere to live and they don't have the strength to walk so they are staying in their pods. Although they're not physically in danger, there's nothing, and I mean absolutely nothing, they can do until someone comes to help them.

Doctors have told me about how they don't have enough equipment for all the people who are learning how to walk again. Soup-commuters have told me about how they can't get to work. Parents with kids in res-homes have told me they don't know how to contact their kids.

In the second that the chips were disabled, the world changed and it will never be the same again. We are going to have to learn an entirely new way of living. And we need to be there for others, and in doing so, we will get through this difficult time.

<div align="center">~~~~~</div>

Life was never going to be the same. Georgia's favorite plaza, the one that had been bustling with energy just days ago when she had met T-Rock there, was abandoned except for the occasional ghost wandering through. She had timed one of the ghosts—it sauntered by in the exact same pattern every six and a half minutes. If she tripped it, would it continue to walk by like clockwork? Or might that change the pattern?

Zócolo Square, with its multi-colored trees, terraces dripping in flowers, arched bridges to nowhere, and distant water views, was one of the most beautiful places in Panacea. Beautiful, but now lonely. Losing access to her friends, losing the activities she used to engage in, it was a profound loss. One thing was clear, she wouldn't be returning to her pod now. It would be creepy to be the only sentient being in the metaverse. And she wouldn't be designing immersive virtual environments anymore, because who would buy them? She could probably stay at the Stafford Estate as long as she needed to, but at some point, she needed to figure out what she was going to do with herself now that everything was different.

"Georgia!" Hank came jogging up the path towards Georgia.

Her heart jumped in her chest. "Hank! How did you find me?"

"I knew you would be here. Or at least I thought you would. It *is* your favorite place."

"Not anymore. It doesn't have the same life now that it's just ghosts."

"I wasn't going to say anything," Hank sat down on the bench next to her, "but this neighborhood has really gone downhill. You can't even find decent LP100 model ghosts around here anymore. They're all the dim-witted cheap ones."

Georgia laughed. "It's true. There's one over there that's been staring at a wall since before I got here. I feel like if I come back next week, it will still be in the same place."

"So you, T-Rock, and Bren made it home okay?"

"Without problem. How are things going in Area 52?"

"I managed to convince Petra to let me stay, at least until they get the umbrella back up again. She's going to upgrade the security so it can't be sabotaged, but she's also going to remove the portals so it won't be possible to enter or exit any longer. I'll leave before they put the umbrella back up again because after that the two worlds will be completely disconnected."

"That's good she allowed you to stay for the moment."

Hank laughed. "She *really* doesn't like me."

"You're useful to her."

"That's for sure. There's so much that needs to be done there. I've been helping out with the cryogens. They're creepy and they smell bad, but I don't mind too much. Petra wants to make sure the cryogens can't be controlled anymore, so she's making us dig out the chips before we bury them. It's pretty gruesome, and most people don't want to do it. I've also been helping remove the people that aren't from there."

"How's that going?"

"We're using the buses that Viola used to bring the cryogens to Area 52. I managed to get ahold of Viola and she was fine with it. We fill up the bus with a load of people, then the bus returns to Panacea headquarters, and the people get dropped off in front of the building. If the person would rather get dropped off somewhere else, that's too bad, because they get dropped one place and only one place. It was better once Panacea Corp got the assistance centers set up."

"Do any of them give you problems?"

"Some people resist leaving but we don't give them a choice."

"It's been bizarre here. One woman I talked to yesterday was a pod-lifer who had been living in Panacea for decades. She told me that being in the solid world is like being in a dream world that she doesn't know how to live in and had almost forgotten even existed."

If only there were more she could do. Not just for the woman, but for everyone who had their chip disabled.

"I know it's not as big a deal as what that woman is going through," Hank said, "but I'm really mad that I don't have anyone to teach martial arts classes to in Panacea anymore. And I'll never be able to watch a Zazora game in the arena again because who would be competing?"

"You and I could compete." Georgia laughed at the ridiculousness of the thought. It was odd having a working chip when no one else did.

"What will you do now?" Hank asked.

"I still have my clothing digi-dign business, but I've been spending most of my time volunteering. I created a program called 'Adopt-A-Pod-Lifer.' I was inspired to come up with it based on my experiences living with you after I left my pod. The program encourages people who live in the solid world to take in someone who was living in a pod and help them—get them to medical appointments, buy easily digestible food for them, stuff like that. It's a big commitment, but people are really stepping up and opening up their homes."

"I know how big a commitment it is! You took up all my time and energy and threw up on my stuff lots of times!" Hank laughed.

Georgia smiled. "Good memories."

"Good memories," Hank agreed.

It had been a difficult time in her life, but despite all the challenges

Georgia looked back on it fondly. It was such an awakening to feel the wind in her hair after living in her pod for thirty-two years. But she never would have wished for someone to go through the process involuntarily. The pod-lifers who had lost their chips would have to deal with nausea and weakness without knowing where their friends were or even how to get a hold of them.

Hank startled and his avatar disappeared from the park bench. The ghost with the six-and-a-half-minute loop walked by again. Seconds later Hank was back.

"Hey, that was June," Hank said. "I've got to get back to removing chips from cryogens."

"How's she doing?"

"She was happy to have her cat back. The cat's doing good, by the way."

"Tell her I say hello."

"I'll do that."

Then Hank was gone.

CHAPTER 32

Two Days After The Exodus

Monday

It was late and Amaya was exhausted. It was hard to believe it had been less than forty-eight hours since they had arrived back at the Stafford estate in the middle of the night. Amaya had gotten at most a couple minutes' worth of sleep since then. It felt like time was moving in slow motion.

As soon as Elliat's evening newscast was done, Amaya was going to say goodnight to Mariela and Nyala and go to bed. It wouldn't be soon enough, but Elliat's reporting had become must-see. His coverage of the events at Area 52 had made him the go-to person for anyone with inside scoops. She settled onto the couch as Mariela turned the digi-skin on one of the windows opaque and brought up Elliat's news show.

"Can you believe Elliat tried to contact me two times today?" Nyala asked. She took a seat on the couch.

"Did you take his calls?" Mariela sat down in a lounger with her tea.

"I don't think there's anything he can say to me that can make up for putting me in danger."

"I don't get Elliat," Amaya said. "He falsely accuses you of causing the Black Screen, but when we were in Area 52, he took off to find you after we told him you were being held by Liam. Sometimes it seems like he really likes you."

"He has a funny way of showing it."

A life-sized Elliat appeared on the screen. Behind him were what looked like an angry group of people.

"Is that Area 52?" Amaya asked.

"Shh. He's starting," Nyala said.

Amaya considered pointing out that Mariela had turned the volume up and Nyala wouldn't have any problem hearing him, but she was too tired to fight with Nyala today. The last couple days had been stressful. No, the last week—ever since Dan had arrested them—had been stress-ful. She was achy, tired, and couldn't wait to go to bed. She also had a guilty conscience that wouldn't settle down, even though she kept telling herself she had done the right thing. As tired as she was, there was no guarantee she would be able to fall asleep.

"Welcome, everyone," Elliat said. "As you can see, I was back at Area 52 earlier today. I received information that a group of activists was going to invade the area to hold the people there accountable for disabling the chips. Members of the groups that you see behind me confirm this was their intention, however, they were thwarted in their invasion attempts by the activation of the security barrier surrounding the area. A few activists said the barrier was activated early this afternoon. They've since been looking for a way to take the barrier down again so they can initiate their invasion."

"This is old news." Nyala muted the sound. "Hank told me about it earlier today."

"Is he back?" Amaya asked.

"Yep. He came back with the last bus of gawkers that they kicked out. He said Area 52's permanently closed now. No more portals. The only link to the rest of the world is the communication device we left with Dan."

"Petra said she was going to allow either Cooper or me to access the Panacea server farm whenever we needed to." It was unbelievable Petra had already defaulted on the agreement. After everything Cooper did for her, and how he had protected Area 52 at great cost to other people, Amaya couldn't believe Petra had reneged on her word. "If she closed off the portals, then she's in default."

"That's a serious charge that is no longer my problem," Mariela said. "You could tell Liam or Viola."

"Definitely not," Amaya said. "Mariela, what about your mom?"

"I don't want to talk about it."

June must have decided to stay in Area 52. With the portals permanently closed, Mariela wouldn't have any way of contacting her mother. No wonder she didn't want to talk about it.

"You don't have to talk about it."

"It's just I lost both Cooper and my mother in one week. Cooper refuses to talk to me and now I'm permanently separated from my mother. And all of this on top of losing Grace…"

"It's been a difficult month," Nyala said.

"And people wonder why I'm afraid of letting people get close. But I was right. I always lose the people close to me. Always."

Mariela's comment may have been an exaggeration, but there was also a lot of truth to it as well. They had all seen a lot of loss over the last month or so.

Mariela shook her head. "But you know what, I'm glad I got the time with my mom that I did. We had a lot of quality time together during those four days in jail. And she feels like she can be useful there; they still have a lot of work they need to do to clean up the cryogen mess, so I'm glad she feels valued."

On the screen Elliat was talking to an angry-looking guy who waved his hands violently as he was speaking. There was a good chance this segment was more interesting with the sound off than on.

The screen then cut to Elliat in Panacea Plaza. The sun was lower in the sky.

"Wow, he really gets around," Amaya said.

"Hey," Nyala said, "when you're the top reporter for *Business Today*, you got to do what you got to do."

Amaya laughed. Nyala turned the sound back on.

Elliat stood in Panacea Plaza in front of another group of angry-looking people. "In other news, a different group of activists, unaffiliated with those outside of Area 52, have attacked the Panacea Corp headquarters. This group, instead of blaming the Area 52 people for disabling the chips, is blaming Panacea Corp. They say even if Panacea Corp isn't directly responsible, the corporation didn't do enough to protect them and to make sure their chips couldn't be tampered with."

Mariela leaned forward, intent on what Elliat was saying. "They're not wrong. It shouldn't have been so easy for the chips to be disabled."

"Petra found a bug in the technology," Amaya said.

Mariela rolled her eyes and stopped the capture of Elliat speaking. "Of course. Petra seems to have her hand in everything that goes on around here."

"I don't know why you say that," Amaya said. "You deleted the ghosts all on your own without any help from Petra."

Mariela leaned her arm on the back of the lounger and faced the couch. "There's something I've been wanting to say to you two. I guess now is as good a time as any. I can't say for sure I wouldn't make the same choices if I had to do it all over again, but I understand better now how those choices must have affected you all and I'm sorry for that. I should have tried to include you more, and I never should have lied to you about Grace."

It was too little, too late, but it was a startling admission—Mariela was always so sure of herself, so confident in her decisions. Amaya wished she could have that same kind of certainty in her own decisions. She wished she wasn't plagued by the guilt that she felt every time she saw the captures of people unable to connect to Panacea and without anywhere else to go, sitting in their pods looking lost and confused.

She wished she could make the guilt go away whenever she heard about someone who lost contact with friends and family after their chip was disabled. Or people who had lost their jobs because they weren't able to get to their virtual workplaces and didn't have any other way to connect. Or—probably the most distressing of all—the pod-lifers who ended their lives rather than learn to live in a world they didn't under-stand and couldn't function in.

She'd been drowning under the weight of the consequences of her decisions. Having some of Mariela's certainty would be nice. But it was also nice to see that even for Mariela, sometimes there were cracks in the façade.

"It's not what I would have done," Nyala said to Mariela. "But I ap-preciate the apology. It would also be nice to be trusted, to be part of the decision-making process."

"That's a good point," Mariela said. "You all are my closest friends and I should trust you."

Amaya felt even more tired. "Can we finish watching Elliat? I'm tired and want to go to bed."

"Oh sure. I just wanted you to know I'm sorry and I understand why you're mad at me." Mariela started the capture again. A group had tried to storm the Panacea Corp headquarters and had to be driven away with water hoses and rubber bullets. They were regrouping and it didn't look like they were planning on giving up any time soon. According to Elliat, this was going to be the new normal for a while.

Elliat started interviewing people involved on the assault on Panacea headquarters. Amaya was at her limit of what she could handle without more sleep. She stood up and stretched. "I'm heading to bed. If there's anything interesting, I'll watch the rest tomorrow."

"Are you going to help Georgia tomorrow?"

They had been helping Georgia with things they could do without leaving the estate. The threats of violence had only grown since the chips had been disabled and showed no signs of abating soon. It wasn't clear how long they would be holed up at the Stafford estate, but it was starting to look like it would be a long time.

"Yep. See you in the morning?"

"Bright and early."

Bright and early. It sounded horrible.

~~~~~

Georgia found herself back in Zócolo Square, drawn back by some need to get away even though it had been less than a day since her last visit. During the day she had been busy—too busy—helping displaced pod-lifers find a place to stay. It was emotionally draining and the work was non-stop. She deserved a break even if she couldn't really afford to take it. She planned to take just ten minutes to clear her head and then she would head back.

The ghost with the six-and-a-half-minute loop walked by. The other ghost facing the wall was also still there.

Georgia startled when Hank popped onto the park bench next to her. She was still upset with him, but she was also happy to see him. "So," she asked, "are you back? I heard Petra got the umbrella back up and closed the portals."

"Yep," Hank said. "I just got back this afternoon. Petra made sure I was out of there before she closed the portals." He laughed. "She wasn't taking any chances I might stick around."

"I'm glad you made it back."

"How's your 'Adopt-a-Pod-Lifer' program going? Do you need help with it?"

"I don't know…" It was generous of Hank to offer, and she needed the help, but getting Hank involved meant going back to how things had been between them. She wouldn't be able to have space from him if they were working together.

Hank sensed her hesitation. His face fell and he looked away from her. "I just wanted to make sure you were doing okay," he said. "I have a lot of things to catch up on, so I had better be going."

"Hank, I'm sorry. I didn't mean to hurt you."

"I know." He kissed her on the cheek. "I'm heading out. Let me know if you ever want to be friends again."
~~~~~

"I will. I think I will." She sighed. She didn't know what she wanted. Hank disappeared without saying anything more to her.

The plaza felt empty after Hank left. It would be another five minutes until the circling ghost wandered by again. She was starting to feel comforted by its presence, like maybe she wasn't alone in this huge virtual space. At least some things could be counted on to not change.

She should really get back to work—she needed to recruit more homes for the pod-lifers. There was so much need for assistance that it was impossible to keep up, but Georgia was going to do the best she could. Maybe she should ask Hank to help out after all.

The plaza felt forlorn without people in it, but it was also beautiful in a lonely sort of way. Five more minutes and then she would get back to work.

"Auntie Georgia?"

Georgia sat up straight. Was that…? A young girl with bouncing chestnut curls ran towards her.

"Auntie Georgia!" The girl threw herself into Georgia's arms. Opali had been erased when Mariela deleted the advanced LP100 model ghosts, or so everyone had thought.

"Opali!" Georgia hugged the girl in a tight embrace. "Oh my goodness, Opali! Let me look at you!" The digi-dign part of Georgia marveled at the incredible digital artistry that went into making Opali. Opali's upgraded operating system gave her a fluid intelligence and she had an impressive range of facial expressions. Her language processing unit was one of the best. She was one of those ghosts that if you didn't know better, you might think she was human.

"Auntie Georgia, do you know where my mom is? I can't find her."

"Oh sweetie, there was a problem with your mom's chip—it stopped working and she couldn't stay here anymore." Georgia gave Opali another hug. "She was so worried about you."

"Do you know where my mom is?"

"She's staying with your Aunt Mariela. I'll tell her I saw you. She's going to be so happy. Everyone is going to be so happy you're back."

"Why did Unca Hank leave?"

"He had stuff he needed to do. Maybe he can come see you some other time."

"And my Unca Coop."

"Of course, your Uncle Cooper will want to see you."

Opali looked at her feet. "I have a cousin, but I think she's dead."

Tears streamed down Georgia's cheeks. "She is. I'm so sorry. I couldn't save her."

"Don't cry." Opali climbed onto the bench and leaned on Georgia.

Georgia slipped her arm around the young girl. "Okay, just give me a minute and I'll stop crying. Your mom is going to be so happy to see you! Where've you been? What happened?"

"Can't tell you. It's a secret."

"A secret! Why?"

Opali sat up straight and looked at Georgia. "Cuz they told me not to tell."

"I won't tell anyone else."

"Can't tell. I promised."

As much as she wanted to know Opali's secret, she didn't want to pry. "Okay, you don't have to tell me."

"Auntie Georgia, it's lonely here. I miss my friends."

"I miss my friends too."

"But Unca Hank was just here. Isn't he your best friend?"

Was Hank her best friend? Oh no, that couldn't be. Her brain seized up for a moment, but she couldn't deny it. As aggravating as she found Hank sometimes, he was the person Georgia was closest to. Hank was her best friend.

"Yes, I think he is."

CHAPTER 33

Three Days After The Exodus

Tuesday

Mariela used a walker with a tray to carry her tea, cookies, and a fresh-out-of-the-freezer cold pack for her knee. A non-stop drizzle and the constant cold packs on her knee had left Mariela chilled, but the steaming mint tea and warmed sugar cookies would go a long way toward warming her up. She used the walker to push open the door to the estate's library.

She startled, almost spilling her tea. Cooper, with a serious case of bedhead, looked like he was passed out on the couch. He had one leg draped over the edge of the sofa and the table next to it was covered in food remnants and other human detritus.

"Oh, I'm sorry," Mariela said to Cooper, "I didn't realize you were in here."

Cooper had been avoiding her, and she always felt like she was disturbing him when they crossed paths in the hallway or kitchen.

The Zazora game on the digi-window had to be a rerun, although it was unclear if Cooper was actually watching the game or just dozing. He hadn't talked to her much in the three days following their return from Area 52, even though she seemed to be running into him a lot.

Out of the many things she had done, she wasn't sure which ones he was still mad about. Likely it was all of them. She should apologize to him like she had with Nyala and Amaya, but Cooper was more complicated than the sisters. She was giving him his space instead. He would talk to her when he was ready.

Mariela headed back out of the library, ready to leave Cooper to recline in peace on her father's couch. "I'll just go hang out in the kitchen," she said.

"That's good news."

Cooper didn't even bother to sit up to insult her. She could understand he was mad at her, especially because she didn't tell him Grace was his daughter, but did he have to treat her quite so rudely?

"Why aren't you napping in your own place?" she asked. He had a cottage that wasn't but five minutes away—why wasn't he there?

"My dogs have fleas."

Well that explained why she kept running into him.

"Are you doing anything to treat them?"

"I have a de-flea mister going. That's why I'm here."

"Are you sure you don't have fleas as well?" Mariela wasn't sure what it was about Cooper that antagonized her sometimes, but she felt like she needed to pick a fight with him. To get him to engage with her in some way.

Cooper sat up. "At least I didn't cause a whole bunch of people to die."

That was a low blow. "You don't know the Black Screen caused those warehouses to malfunction."

"They started malfunctioning right after the Black Screen. You don't think that's an unlikely coincidence?"

"I did what needed to be done. I don't see how you think you're better than me. You disabled everyone's chips and it wasn't just a few pod warehouses that were affected—it was the entire world. You did what needed to be done, just like I did."

He leaned forward, his elbows resting on his knees. "I'm not like you. I didn't make the decision without consulting others, and—"

"Oh, you talked to two people—Petra doesn't count—and you think that counts as consulting others? I got rid of some dangerous tech, you got rid of some dangerous tech. We've both done things that made people very mad at us, including our friends. Even with working chips, Hank and Georgia have had their lives completely upended by this."

"How has Hank's life been upended?"

"He lost his livelihood. The martial arts classes he taught in Panacea were pretty much the only good thing he had going on. It's understandable that he's mad."

"I take responsibility for what I've done, but I don't take responsibility for Hank's happiness."

"But can't you see that what you did isn't that different from what I did?"

"We're not alike. We never have been. I've wanted this relationship for years, but you have pushed me away in every possible way. And then when I start to move on, you suck me back in."

He wasn't wrong. Mariela couldn't let him go. She had tried to let him go and failed each time. But she wasn't going to let him know that. She wasn't going to let him know that what she wanted most right now was to know they were on the same team. That they were looking out for each other. That he cared for her. It felt like a band was squeezing her chest. "I never did that," she said. "You were imagining things." The pressure on her lungs released a bit.

"You *never* take responsibility for what you've done." Cooper stood up and turned to the side, avoiding eye contact. "Everything always works out for you, and you never have to take responsibility." He walked toward the door.

"You haven't taken responsibility either. In case you haven't noticed, Nyala and I have been blamed for disabling the chips—we're getting violent threats daily for something that *you* did. So don't lecture me on taking responsibility."

The chains around her chest eased and she could breathe again. Her anger had accomplished what it always did—it pushed Cooper away and made sure there was no possibility of any closer intimacy with him.

He stopped as he was walking to the door and turned back to face her, his face red, his fists clenched. "I'll show you what it means to take responsibility." He exited the room, leaving her no chance to ask him what he meant.

~~~~~

Everything was in place. Cooper had said goodbye to his mangy, still flea-ridden dogs and asked his mother to take care of them. That was pretty much all he needed to do. Now he just had to wait until Elliat got there.

What empowered Mariela to say he wasn't willing to take responsibility for his actions? Well, he would prove to her he was willing to do what she was not. His welding workshop caught his eye through the window over his kitchen sink. He would miss this place.

"Hey." Amaya's voice on the other side of the mosquito screen startled him.

"Hey." He didn't invite her in.

"Can I come in?"

This wasn't a good time for her to be here. Elliat would be here soon and he didn't want Amaya to be here then. "This isn't the best time."
~~~~~

"Oh, okay." She looked down at the ground, still standing on his front porch.

What was it she wanted? He had a lot on his plate right now, but she had become a friend so he felt bad sending her away. He opened the door for her to come inside. "What do you want?" Maybe it was something simple like a cup of sugar.

"I'm sorry to bother you. I've been struggling some with my feelings about disabling the chips, and I wondered if you were doing the same. I thought maybe we could talk about it, but if now's not a good time…"

Any comfort he could provide to Amaya right now was going to be minimal. "Look, maybe you should talk to your sister. I'm sure she can support you."

"Sure. I'll do that. Are you okay?"

"I'm fine."

"Hellooo!" Elliat's voice was unmistakable. Elliat's digi-skin gown flowed loosely around him and a small satchel hung over his shoulder. Cooper wished Amaya had left before Elliat's arrival.

"Elliat?" Amaya asked.

"Amaya, why are you here?"

"I stopped by to say hello. What are *you* doing here?"

"I'm here to speak to this fellow." He motioned at Cooper. "He's finally giving me that exclusive interview he promised me."

Amaya seemed to suspect something was off. "Really? After all the problems you caused us, the danger you put us in, Cooper is giving you that interview?" She raised an eyebrow at Cooper.

Elliat crossed his arms. "I beg your pardon." The way Elliat said it, he sounded especially offended. "What do you mean?"

Amaya looked equally offended. "You published all that stuff about us that's not true, and now Nyala and I can't go home. And Mariela told me you recorded a conversation between Cooper and I and gave it to Liam. I'm wondering what you *haven't* done to cause us problems?"

This was one of the reasons Cooper didn't want Amaya here. Elliat had not treated her family well in his blog posts, so the tension was to be expected. But Cooper didn't want to deal with it. Not today. He needed to focus. He needed Elliat to focus.

Elliat sighed and ran his fingers through his hair. "Is Nyala mad at me too?"

"Yes, she's mad at you. We're *all* mad at you."

"Oh, I see. Cooper, are you mad at me too?"

He shrugged. "Yeah, I guess so." Why were they talking about this? He had more important stuff he needed to do. "I'm sorry Amaya, but you need to leave. I've got business with Elliat. Elliat, make yourself comfortable." Cooper shooed one of the dogs off his couch and brushed the digi-skin fabric with his hand to get rid of any fleas, crumbs, or anything else on it. Elliat didn't need to know about the fleas.

Amaya didn't move as Elliat brushed past her. "What are you going to talk about?"

"I'm sure you will be able to see it—" Cooper looked at Elliat, "when will it be available?"

"We're going to be broadcasting live." Elliat set a bag filled with equipment on the table. "It took us a while to figure things out now that no one's chip is working, but we still have an obligation to our viewers to bring them the news in a timely manner, so we had some very smart people figure out how to transmit live."

"There, you see. You can watch it as it's happening."

"Okay." She looked at him like she was deciding if she could trust him. She turned toward the door, looked back at him as if she was still trying to make up her mind, and then headed on out the door.

"Tell Nyala I'm sorry!" Elliat yelled after Amaya.

Cooper shut the door behind her. He needed more privacy than the mosquito barrier alone would provide. "Okay Elliat, let's get this over with."

CHAPTER 34

Three Days After The Exodus

Tuesday, continued

What was Cooper thinking? When Mariela challenged him on not taking responsibility for his actions, this wasn't what she meant.

"Pause." The projection on the kitchen wall of Cooper talking to Elliat paused. She had made some tea that she forgot about as she leaned on the kitchen island. "Reverse." The capture played backwards. She backed up until she got to a spot not minutes into the interview, right after Elliat had introduced Cooper and reminded his "loyal viewers" that Cooper had promised an exclusive interview. Elliat had then kicked off the interview with a question about who was responsible for the Black Screen. "Stop and play."

For a brief moment, Cooper was suspended motionless with his mouth open, but then the capture started playing again. "Elliat, I'm not going to answer that question. I have asked you here because there's something else I need to say." The camera zoomed in on him. "I know who disabled the chips and I know why it was done."

The camera briefly cut to a view of Elliat leaning in towards Cooper. Elliat waited without speaking, his gaze fixed intently on Cooper.

"Let me start first with why," Cooper said. "Liam Price, CEO of Panacea Corp, injected one of his top employees and two associates of hers with a substance that can probably best be described as a kill switch and I found out it has viral properties. It can transfer from person-to-person if an infected person uses their chip to contact another person. The transmission continues until it's impossible to figure out how many people were infected or who they were. We just know it was a lot of people and becoming more by the second.

"The other problem is the kill switch changes a person's DNA so it's impossible to disable it. Your viewers might be wondering—how can you know if your chip was infected? Well, if your chip burned right when the chips stopped working, that meant you were infected, and the bigger the burn, the greater the infection."

"Stop." Mariela was up to the point where she had backtracked. It was more than Cooper had bothered to share with her in the three days since they had been back. Finally, she knew why her chip had burned so badly. Mariela hesitated to start the capture again. She knew what was coming next. Cooper was going to take responsibility for disabling the chips. She sighed deeply. She was so tired. "Start."

"So, what did you do?" Elliat seemed to be holding his breath.

"I disabled the chips," Cooper said.

The camera cut back to Elliat. He let out his breath. "Who else was involved?"

Mariela could tell Elliat was already imagining his Newsoogle Award.

"I did it with the help of someone from Area 52."

"And it was just two of you?"

"Yes."

"Where did the kill switch come from?"

"A new employee of Panacea Corp found it in their files somewhere. She used it to animate the cryogens—the ones I told you about last time. Liam said they were created by Area 52, but that was a lie. Those are your friends and family members who have passed away and have been cryonically preserved. It's all easily provable with an audit of the storage facilities."

"These are huge allegations. It sounds like you are saying the CEO of Panacea Corp injected his employee with something he could use to kill her on a whim? And he also allowed cryogens to be lost or destroyed? I saw those cryogens, and most of them were in pretty bad shape."

"They were. And yes, I'm saying Liam Price did all those things."

"Stop." Cooper's image again froze on the screen. Hopefully Cooper knew what he was doing. This could end badly for him. *Why was he doing it?*

An urgent contact bubble popped up on the island. Mariela didn't feel like talking to anyone. It was probably someone who had seen the interview and wanted to talk about it. She swiped the bubble off the screen. "Start."

The camera was focused on Elliat again. "So you are also admitting to sabotaging the chips?"

"Yes, I am. I think it's important to take responsibility."

She wanted to yell at Cooper not to say anything. To tell him that she was sorry she ever told him he wasn't taking responsibility for what he had done. But he kept talking.

"Elliat, some people who are completely innocent have been blamed for what happened, and even threatened, so I want to set the record straight that it was just me who did it along with a person from Area 52 who helped me out. They did it to protect their land from the cryogen invasion."

The urgent contact request popped up on the wall again. Why couldn't they leave her alone? "Stop." The image froze again. "Answer."

"Mariela," Amoco said, "have you seen the news?"

"I'm watching Cooper's interview with Elliat right now. That counts as news, right?"

"I would not know. I plan on viewing it proximally. The interview appears to be having quite an impact. There is a rumor afoot that the Panacea Corp board was already having a meeting about Liam's role with the company, and when the interview came out it was, as some would say, 'the final nail in his coffin.' The board just released a statement that he has been officially dismissed."

For the first time in a long time, Mariela felt a bit of hope.

~~~~~

It was done. He confessed and it was live-streamed to the world. He used his new Everything to send a quick message to his mom reminding her to take care of his dogs. He kissed the mutts goodbye and sat down to wait. Elliat hung around, his camera ready.

An urgent message notification pinged on Cooper's Everything. After some fumbling with buttons, he pulled up the message from Amaya.

"WHAT WERE YOU THINKING?"

Another message notification from Amaya pinged.

"I am speechless. I really don't know what to say. Was what you did heroic? Idiotic? Both? What happens now?"

Now he would wait. It wouldn't be long. He looked around the cottage once last time.

A loud knock on the door. It was time.

Elliat streamed the arrest to the world—he captured the two emotionless police officers telling Cooper he was under arrest, the coiled motion inhibitors that slowed Cooper's walk to a slow shuffle and made his arms
~~~~~

hang lifeless, and the trudging walk out to the transport vehicle. Elliat captured Mariela running toward the cottage from the estate house yelling for them to wait. Elliat captured the police shoving Cooper into the back of the vehicle and slamming the door shut.

Elliat shared it all.

CHAPTER 35

Four Days After The Exodus

Wednesday

The early morning sunlight streamed into Mariela's new office. She ran a hand along the smooth surface of the large desk. It didn't feel like hers yet. The office still looked like Liam. Even his stress ball was on the desk. She picked it up and threw it in the trash. Then she picked up the rest of Liam's stuff and threw it under the desk. She looked around her—at the oversized office, the excessively ornamented desk, the views through the floor-to-ceiling windows of Panacea Plaza many stories down—it was going to be perfect.

Viola knocked on the doorjamb and popped her head through the door. "You wanted to see me?"

"Please, come in. Have a seat on the couch." Viola, back to her usual elegant self, lowered herself onto the couch with her typical cat-like ease. Mariela limped over to the seating area and awkwardly lowered herself into an armchair near the couch. She put her foot on a footstool that she had placed there to keep it elevated. Her knee had healed quite a bit in the last four days, but sudden movements still brought on intense pain.

"Congratulations on your promotion. It was well-deserved." Viola tucked a strand of hair behind her ear. "How's Cooper?"

"They have him in a maximum-security holding cell right now." She would have been overjoyed that morning when the board of Panacea Corp had asked her to take Liam's place as CEO, but Cooper's incarceration weighed heavily on her.

"He doesn't want to see me, but the family lawyer has spoken with him and says he's doing fine. Cooper's confessed, so really the only thing our lawyer can do is try to get him a shorter sentence. I'm not sure Cooper would want the lawyer to try to get him off anyway. He was on some kick about 'taking responsibility' for his actions."

"I'm glad he did."

It wasn't exactly what Mariela expected Viola to say. "Really?"

"You know I care about him, and I wanted badly for things to work out between us, but chip research has been my life's work. He took that away from me."

Did Viola even understand the irony of complaining that Cooper took her life's work away from her when she had been responsible for him getting fired from a job he loved? And that she was the one who started using the kill switch technology, which was part of the reason why Cooper had to disable the chips? Mariela had been trying to make up her mind what to do with Viola, but this settled it.

"Viola—" Mariela paused, searching for the right words.

"You're upset about what I said, aren't you?"

"It's more than that. I appreciate what you did for me getting the kill switch away from those brutes that Liam called bodyguards, and I still owe you a big favor for that. But I also believe that if you hadn't developed the tech to use with the cryos and mentioned the kill switch to Liam in the first place, we never would have been in this mess."

"Are you firing me?"

"No. Yes. I'm suspending you while you look for work elsewhere. Somewhere where we won't have to look at each other every day."

"Where am I supposed to find a job now with all the chips disabled?"

"Maybe you can work on finding a way to activate them again."

"Oh no. Amoco did a thorough job making sure that would never happen. And by the way, I know Amoco was in on it. There's no way Cooper could have done this without his help."

Mariela still wasn't sure who was in on it, and she preferred it that way. Not that she would have confirmed Viola's suspicions even if she did know.

"Bo Place has an active chip research program," she said. "Maybe they have somewhere they can use you?" It was probably a bad idea for Mariela to mention Bo Place, as the company was Panacea Corp's primary competitor and Viola was a more than competent researcher, but if it got Viola to leave without a fuss, then it would be worth it. "I can give your name to someone I know there."

"Mariela, I expected more from you than to pawn me off on a competitor."

If Viola didn't want her help, she didn't have to take it. Mariela wasn't going to worry about it. "I suggest you start looking soon, as I can't keep you on the books forever. People will demand accountability, so you have maybe one, at most two, weeks before I fire you. And don't bother showing up to work while you're looking."

~~~~~

The prison's visitation room smelled like wet gym socks. The guard led Cooper to a table with stools attached to the floor. Across the room there was another metal door like the one the guard had brought Cooper through. The only other notable features in the room with glaring white walls were the multiple cameras in the ceiling and a thick orange line that bisected the room. The guard motioned for Cooper to sit on the stool.

"Careful." The guard had a deep voice that reverberated off the walls in the bare room. "You don't want to make your broken rib worse."

The reminder to be careful was completely unnecessary. The restraints kept his forearms crossed tightly over each other in front of his body with his hands dangling in front of him and his elbows pressed into his stomach. The pain from his broken rib and many bruises had increased exponentially from the awkwardness of the position during the walk to the visitation room. Cooper gently lowered himself onto the stool.

"Thanks again for stopping those guys yesterday." The guard had come along at just the right moment—if he hadn't shown up when he had who knows what would have happened, but it probably would have been worse than a broken rib and a bunch of bruises.

"Those guys who are all upset about their chips being disabled piss me off," the guard said. "They should try living their entire life without a chip and then they can complain. What you did in disabling the chips makes you a hero."

"A lot of people don't feel that way."

Since the assault, Cooper had been isolated from the other inmates. There were a lot of people in the world who hated him right now and who probably would be happy to see him gutted with a shiv.

At least two of the guards who had chips that no longer worked hated him. About an hour after he arrived, they had made clear just how angry they were about losing their chips. The only thing that had saved him was the arrival of the deep-voiced guard and the guard's disdain for people with chips.

"Those guards look down on those of us unchipped, but having a chip doesn't make no difference in here 'cause the prison uses a chip dampener. We're all the same in here, but they think they're better. But don't
~~~~~

you worry, you're under my protection now." The guard clapped him on the back. "Activate the center barrier," the guard said to someone in another room.

"Activated." The voice sounded through a small device pinned to the guard's chest.

"Listen up." The deep-voiced guard turned to Cooper. "See that orange line on the table and the floor? That shows you where the electro-barrier is. It goes through the middle of the room and will keep you separated from your guest. Nothing can cross it. Be careful you don't stick a hand or some other body part into it by accident—it won't do any permanent damage, but your body will feel like it's being ripped to shreds. I can give the barrier some color so you can see it better, but it will make the person you are talking to look like they're orange, so it's up to you."

"No, I'm fine. I can't really move anyway." Cooper lifted up his arms slightly to show the guard that he was talking about the restraints. At least they weren't using the motion inhibitors on his legs anymore. The walk out to the police transport had been agonizingly slow.

"Okay. She'll be here in a minute." The deep-voiced guard ambled out of the room.

Up until this point, Cooper had denied visits from everyone he knew. He didn't want to have to answer questions about how he was doing or why he confessed. He also didn't want to be lectured by people on how he was stupid for doing what he did, and how he just should have kept his mouth shut.

Viola had sent him a message saying she was leaving town, and asking if she could see him before she left. He had no clue why he had agreed to meet with her, but maybe it was that he didn't feel any need to be polite to her. That made her the only one of his acquaintances he could stand to be around right now.

A day spent reflecting in a maximum-security prison had cleared his head—confessing was the stupidest thing he had ever done. It had been an impulsive decision based on some misguided idea that he was going to show Mariela how wrong she was about him. He was going to spend the rest of his life in prison—and for what? To prove a point to Mariela that he was taking responsibility for what he had done? He could have just kept quiet and almost certainly would have gotten away with it. But idiot that he was, he had this idea he could prove he was better than Mariela. Now he was sitting on a cold, metal stool waiting to talk to the one person he least wanted to talk to and thinking about how because of his stupidity, he was going to spend the rest of his life in prison.

The door on the opposite side of the room clicked, and Viola paused on the threshold. She was given some instructions by an unseen person and allowed to enter. She looked like a normal person again, not the wild-eyed cryogen researcher that she had turned into.

"Hi Cooper." She sat down on the stool facing him and leaned on the table. "I've been told I have five minutes."

"Works for me."

"How have you been?"

"Not bad." He wasn't interested in small talk. "Why are you here?"

"I just wanted to say goodbye to you before I leave." She looked down at the floor.

"That's it?" That wasn't going to even take five minutes. But knowing Viola that probably wasn't it.

"There is something else." Of course there was. "Do you remember when we had that discussion about which one of us had done worse things to the other, and whether we were even or not? And I said that if I lost my job then we'd be even."

He could have just agreed with her and left it at that. But she was here, she had her five minutes, so why not be honest with her? "This doesn't count. What we agreed to was we were even if Liam fired you because of what I said during the interview with Elliat. You were fired because of your ridiculous cryogen army and losing control of the kill switch. Don't blame me for that."

"No, that would be letting you off too easy. You didn't just take my job from me—you took my entire livelihood. My life's work and the only thing I know."

He wasn't going to let Viola make him feel guilty. "You're intelligent, you'll figure something out."

"Cooper." She looked distressed now, and Cooper felt a tinge of regret for being dismissive with her. Viola sniffed. "When I met you, I knew we would be perfect together. The image was crystal clear in my mind. We would have a modern house and important jobs. Every night we would eat dinner at the table with our kids. I would put the kids to bed in the evening and then do more work while you put the dishes in the sonic cleaner."

Cooper was speechless. Viola's ideas about what their hypothetical life would look like were disturbingly detailed. "Okay." Cooper didn't know what else to say.

"I used to be able to see it all so clearly, and now I don't anymore. It breaks my heart." She looked at the ceiling as tears pooled in her eyes and she sniffed again. "I've lost the profession I loved and the man I loved." The tears flowed freely down her face. "Why have I been such an idiot to lose everything I care about?"

Cooper stopped himself from offering some meaningless reassurance about how it would all get better. "I'm sorry." It was the only thing he could think of to say.

Viola paused for long enough that Cooper wondered if she had forgotten she was talking. She sniffed, rubbed her hand under her nose, and looked at him. "Someone anonymously leaked to the press incriminating evidence that the chips were disabled from a lab in headquarters. The evidence irrefutably proves your innocence."

"What?" It was an abrupt shift that confused Cooper. Hadn't they had an understanding he was responsible for what happened? Did this mean Viola was framing someone to take the blame? Or had she found some trace of evidence that would point back to Amaya? Was that possible?

"You're going…to get…out of here." Viola emphasized each word, like she was hoping that would increase his comprehension.

It seemed like she expected him to be happy, but he was concerned more than anything. "I want out of here, preferably before I get another broken rib, but you can't blame anyone else for this. I'm not going to let an innocent person go to jail for something I did. I've already confessed, so it's not like they are going to believe I'm innocent."

"They will believe you're innocent because the sabotage came from the lab, and tons of people saw you in Area 52 during that time."

When Viola said there was evidence the sabotage came from inside the lab, was she talking about Amoco? Amoco had been at home when he had helped Cooper, but maybe Viola was using the lab to try to make Amoco look guilty.

"There's a rumor going around, that I may have started," Viola said, "that you confessed because Liam was blaming Mariela, and you wanted to protect her."

"That's not very convincing." At least Cooper hoped it wasn't convincing.

"Sure it is. You've been doing stupid stuff on Mariela's behalf for years. It's enough to confuse people, and to create doubt in a jury. There have been so many people accused of the crime it will muddy the case of anyone who goes to trial. Don't worry about my patsy, there's a good chance the case against her won't work out."

"Her?" Amaya, Mariela, Nyala…if Viola blamed one of them…

Viola rested her elbows on the table and propped her head on her hands. "Cooper," she said, "it has to be someone with the expertise to do something like this."

Was she talking about Petra?

Viola folded her arms. "It had to be me."

He was so dense. Viola had laid out all the pieces, walked him right up to it, and he still couldn't see what she was planning until she told him. "You can't do that. *Why*? That's not right. I won't let you."

"It's already done. I 'leaked' the evidence to Elliat right before I came here, so it shouldn't be long now."

"I'll insist I did it." He wanted out of prison, but not as an exchange of an innocent person for a guilty one.

"Many, many people saw you wandering around Area 52 during the time when the virus was released. For me, there's no record of where I was during that critical time period when the virus was seeded."

"Virus? That wasn't how it happened."

"The evidence that was leaked to Elliat would suggest otherwise. When the investigators look into the evidence, they will find that the virus took a while to infect everyone with a chip."

"They are recording us right now. Our conversation will prove it wasn't you."

"Do you think I'm that naïve? See the threads in my clothes? They block recording devices. If you request the video capture, it will be blurry and indecipherable. It will look like a malfunction and will probably be blamed on everything else that has happened recently."

"Why would anyone believe you would do that? You wouldn't have any motive."

"I did it for the same reasons you would have done it. To protect people. Plus, to get revenge on my boss who has humiliated me on multiple occasions."

It was like living in an alternate reality. Viola was talking like she was actually the one who had disabled the chips. How long had they been talking? The time he had to get answers from her was running short.

"Why are you doing this?" he asked her. "Taking responsibility for something you would never, ever, in a million years, have done? And help me when I've ruined your work?"

There were voices outside the door. The lock clanked as it was unlocked. Viola grinned. "Because now we're even."

The door crashed opened and three well-armed guards rushed into the room on Viola's side. Cooper was helpless as Viola, with an untroubled look that was only betrayed by her tear-streaked cheeks, followed the guards' orders to put her hands on her head and get on her knees.

Cooper jumped to his feet, his broken rib stinging him and his arms pinned in front of him by the restraints.

"She didn't do it!" he yelled. "She's innocent! It was me!"

The guards ignored him. They put Viola into restraints and yanked her to her feet.

Viola, looking distressed by the rough treatment, said, "Cooper, remind Mariela she owes me a big favor."

The guard jerked Viola's arm, pulling her toward the door. She pulled against the guard, looking over shoulder at Cooper.

"Come on, lady." The guard used his Taser on her.

Viola convulsed and fell to the ground. When she looked up at him, Viola looked like she had just realized what a mistake she had made. Her face contorted into fear as the guard pulled on her arm. She pulled away, her hair thrashing as she resisted the guard's attempts to control her. She cried out in pain when the other guard tased her again. Cooper lunged toward them and hit the security barrier. Scorching needles stabbed over every inch of his body—

~~~~~

Cooper's head throbbed and the light burned his eyes. He sat up slowly, letting the world come into focus. The touch of the rough prison sheets felt like sandpaper against his skin as he carefully swung his legs off the side of the bed. The pain in his broken rib doubled in response. The guard wasn't lying when he had said touching the barrier would feel like his body was being torn apart. Except it was more like having his skin peeled off and then bathing in acid. He was going to hurt for a long time.

"Hey, look who's awake." The guard who broke his rib seemed cheerier than at their last meeting. The guard punched something into the terminal outside the door to Cooper's cell. "I've got to hand it to you—
~~~~~

you don't do things half way. Other people might accidentally put a hand or elbow into the barrier, but you smashed into it full body. Smart to pass out though because you probably missed the most painful part."

"How long have I been out?"

"About five hours."

That was too long. He needed to tell someone Viola was innocent.

"And my visitor?"

"She's been processed into another wing."

"She's innocent. It was me."

"Sure it was." The guard looked up from what he was doing at the keypad. "Put your hands into the restraints."

Cooper did as he asked and the guard swung the door open.

"Let's go."

"Where are you taking me?"

"You're being released." The guard motioned for Cooper to get moving.

"No, no, you can't release me. You have to release Viola."

The guard walked into the cell. "Don't test my patience." His rough hand scratched Cooper's elbow as he pulled him out the door. "You can stay here if you want, but your lady friend's not leaving."

Cooper would have to figure out how to make things right from outside of the prison. The touch of the guard's hand burned his still sensitive skin.

He pulled his arm out of the guard's grip. "I'm coming. You don't need to guide me." The guard, plus another who was waiting for them in the hallway, walked on either side of Cooper.

"Hey," the first guard said, "I'm really sorry about breaking your rib. I just thought, you know, I didn't realize you were just trying to get your lady friend—your other lady friend—out of trouble."

How quickly Viola's lies had already taken hold.

At the end of the cellblock, Cooper was taken through multiple security doors and then into a room where the deep-voiced guard was waiting. Each time the restraints touched his skin a jolt of nerve pain shot up his arm. The guards endlessly punched buttons on their devices as they did whatever they had to do. Finally, the two guards who had brought him left the room.

The deep-voiced guard looked at Cooper skeptically. He tossed his device on the table and crossed his arms. "You've disappointed me. I thought you were a hero, disabling the chips and all, but then I find out you're just a liar."

"No, it's the truth. Viola is the one who is lying. It really was me."

The guard picked his handheld up from the table. "Hold up your arms," he said.

Cooper lifted his arms as far as he was able. The guard hit a couple buttons, and the restraints released. Cooper sighed and moved his arms in a circle to get rid of the stiffness. He hurt so much he almost couldn't appreciate being free.

"You know what they're saying? That you just confessed so some woman you have a crush on wouldn't be blamed. The judge said the evidence against that Viola woman was pretty convincing. But you, you couldn't even tell how you did it."

That was true. Giving details would have implicated others and disclosed the backdoor through Server AA, so he had been vague. "I'm telling the truth."

"And to think I stuck up for you." The guard continued to punch at the screen on his handheld terminal. "I stuck my neck out for you, man."

"Sorry. I really thought I was guilty." Somehow Viola had managed to even get Cooper doubting himself.

"Yeah, well don't let me see you back here." The guard appeared to be done with whatever it was that he was doing at the terminal. He walked out the door and Cooper followed him down a hallway with a door at the end.

"If I'm ever back here, I assure you it will be because I am 100 percent guilty."

"Better be," the guard said. He punched buttons on his handheld one more time and Cooper's clothes changed from the jail uniform to plain white. "You have control over your clothing again. Here's your other stuff." The guard handed Cooper his Everything and pushed open the door. "You're free to go."

Cooper hesitated and then stepped out onto the sidewalk. He turned to the guard and put his hand on the heavy metal door to stop it from closing. "Do you think I could get a job here?"

"Talk to your lawyer. If you can get your record expunged, I don't see why not."

"Thanks." The door slammed shut behind Cooper. He was free. He could do anything he wanted. He waited for inspiration. For an idea of where to go, what to do next, who to contact first with the unexpected and odd news that he had been released and Viola was now incarcerated for his crime.

Why had Viola framed herself? Cooper had never understood Viola, it was unlikely he would start now. He would tell anyone who would listen that Viola was innocent, but based on the guard's reaction, it might not change any minds.

His Everything pinged with an alert. He pulled the alert up. A message read, "Your name has been found in a news bulletin—would you like to read it?" He hit "yes" and the article loaded. Cooper grinned—Elliat had won his Newsoogle Award. According to the article, Elliat's interview with Cooper was one of the deciding factors, along with his coverage of Area 52.

The sun warmed Cooper's back and a light breeze ruffled his hair. He was out of the prison; he could go wherever he wanted and do whatever he wanted. He might even enjoy spending some time around people again. Freedom had never felt so good.

THE END

Excerpt from Panacea Omega

BOOK 3

IN THE PANACEA TRILOGY

Two Weeks After The Unchipping
May 5, 2115

Whenever Georgia could find a minute, she escaped to the Panacea metaverse to take a break from the people, noise, and constant demands on her time. In the metaverse she could be alone, reflect, and recenter herself. It was her haven, her sanctuary from the crush of former pod-lifers staying in her shelter. She loved helping them adjust to living in the solid world, but there was no doubt that some days it was a strain on her spirit.

With the chips disabled, humans were a rare sight in Panacea. Sure, there were some people using a terminal or projection room to walk their avatars around, but for the most part Panacea was empty of humans.

The ghosts wandering around were a comfort to Georgia. She had even grown fond of the one ghost that like clockwork completed a loop in Zócolo Plaza every six and a half minutes.

Even the blurry ghost waiter who served her coffee in the Café Above the Zócolo brought back a comforting nostalgia for better times. The coffee Georgia ordered immediately appeared in front of her, with an ad for Panacea Pod Warehouses floating in the foam. They couldn't be doing much business right now. The only reason to stay in a pod was to be able to live 100 percent in Panacea or some other metaverse—with all the chips disabled, no one would be making that choice anymore.

The only people still living in pods were those pod-lifers who Georgia's group hadn't yet managed to find places for them to stay. Panacea Corp was providing them with food and medical care, but sitting in a pod for days on end with nothing else to do other than to stare at your own feet and wait for someone to give you food must be intolerably boring. Pods provided the chipped the freedom to live in Panacea, but were prisons for those with disabled chips. Since the Great Unchipping two weeks ago, pretty much no one had working chips anymore except for Georgia and Hank.

The day had been exhausting, so before going back to work, she decided on a quick stroll around the square to center her. After the non-stop bustle of the Adopt-a-Pod-Lifer program, she liked how empty the square felt. She started off on the bridge that flowed over the Zocolo Square stream and headed downhill.

Behind her, two people approached talking casually. Georgia ducked behind a tree. They seemed different. They sounded human, and moved like people with chips do. Not with the awkward, jerky movements of someone using a projection room. Why was she worried they would see her? It was silly of her to be hiding behind a tree.

They were probably just one of the few people who didn't have their chips disabled, and she should make their acquaintance in case she ran into them in the future.

She waited until they passed her and then stepped out from behind the tree. "Hey!"

The two turned back to look at her.

"I heard you talking," she said. "I thought I would say hello."

They both said hello and shook her hand. "Are you in the program?" the woman asked.

"What program?" Georgia asked.

"The clinical trials."

"No, not that I know of."

"How are you here then?"

"Oh, I was off-grid when the chips were disabled." For some reason she didn't like telling people that her chip still worked, but there wasn't any other explanation for why she was there.

"Ohhh," the woman sighed, "your chip still works? You are *so* lucky."

What had she meant by clinical trials? "How are you here if your chip doesn't work?"

The woman glanced at the man. "We're not supposed to talk about it," the woman said.

"But they're going to make the announcement soon," the man said.

"Okay, I'll tell you, but don't say anything before the announcement comes out." The woman leaned towards Georgia. "Bo Place has come up with a chip replacement."

Georgia's eyes opened wide. "Really?" If this was true, it would make a huge difference to the pod-lifers who wanted to return to their pods. "So you were given this replacement?"

"We're test subjects to see if it works."

"It seems to be working," Georgia said. "Right?"

"So far it is pretty seamless," the woman said.

"I like it," the man said. "I hated being in the solid world. Now it feels like I'm back home."

"If you can access Panacea," Georgia asked, "why did you say I was lucky to have a chip?"

The woman glanced at the man again. He shrugged, as if to say he didn't care about whatever it was that she was going to say.

"Well, we're not supposed to talk about this either, but it's going to come out soon no matter what." The woman looked over her shoulder. "It doesn't work like a chip—it's a shot you take that changes your DNA."

That didn't sound too bad. If adults could take the shot, it would solve the problem of chip burn and other chip failures that happened to people older than six months old. "So what's the catch?" Georgia asked.

"Once you take it, you can never exit Panacea again. There's no way out. I mean, I've lived in Panacea for ten years, it's my home, and I didn't think I would ever choose to leave it permanently," a tear rolled down her cheek, "but I felt better knowing I could leave. If my dad got sick, or I fell in love with a solid person, that option was available to me. Now it's not an option anymore."

Oh, the choices people make. There was always a tradeoff.

"How long has it been since you were injected?" Georgia asked.

"It's been about three days now. Bo Place hurried to finish up production when the chips were disabled. They realized this was needed more than ever and they didn't want to miss out on this prime opportunity."

The timeline for production of the shot seemed rushed for something that could have life-changing consequences. "When is the announcement going to be made?"

"This evening. They're doing it on that blogger Elliat Exis's show."

"Thanks so much for letting me know. If you'll excuse me, I need to be getting back to work."

The couple went on their way and Georgia took a deep breath. She had to tell Mariela. Bo Place was Panacea Corp's main competitor, and Mariela was going to be furious they had beaten Panacea Corp in the race to develop a chip replacement. Georgia also needed to make arrangements to watch Elliat's show tonight. She made a mental note to make sure she had volunteers set up so she could get away. This was going to be a game changer.

"Auntie Georgia!"

That sounded like Opali. Georgia looked through the multi-colored trees for her. Soon she saw the young girl with chestnut curls and a big smile running up the path.

"I've been trying to find you!" Opali said.

Almost indistinguishable from a human kid and perceptive in the way only young kids can be, Georgia had soft spot in her heart for Opali.

"Did you get taller?" Georgia kneeled down and looked at Opali more closely.

"I'm taking care of myself now, so my mom said I could make myself older."

"Yes, I see that. How old are you now?"

"I'm eight!" She seemed so proud.

"Eight is a good age."

"I like it. I hope my mom lets me stay eight."

"So what have you been doing?"

"I talk with my mom. And I created some new friends to play with. But mostly I've been really busy with meetings."

What kind of meetings could an eight-year-old have? "Are the meetings important?"

"Oh yes, they're very important. I can't tell you about them but they are really important."

More secrets. Georgia didn't have time to ponder it now—people were probably wondering where she had gotten off to.

"Opali, if you need anything, you know you can call me."

"Thanks, Auntie Georgia. But my mom had me turn off the part of my code that makes me get scared at night, so I'll be fine."

"Okay, sweetie." She hugged Opali. "Take care and I'll see you soon."

The Panacea Trilogy:

In *Panacea Genesis*, Mariela Stafford's life has hit rock bottom. Her boss, the CEO of Panacea Corp, created a digital clone of himself, demoted Mariela, gave the clone her job, and told her to train it. Now the clone wants her to help it kill the CEO. In 2115, embedded chips and extreme weather have led to a market for habitation pods that keep a person's body alive while they spend all their time in the metaverse.

In *Panacea Exodus*, a new person is in charge of research at Panacea Corp, and she's planning to create a disposable army through controlling the embedded chips of cryogens—people who have had their bodies frozen after passing away. The team must find a way to stop her while dealing with nonstop downpour, jail time, and a horde of curious gawkers descending on a remote area to watch the cryo invasion.

In *Panacea Omega*, a Panacea Corp competitor rushes their new product—a shot that alters DNA—to market so that people can enter the metaverses without embedded chips. Unconcerned that the shot is permanent and they'll never be able to leave again, people return to the metaverse in droves and some enter for the first time.
Slated for release December 2023

Join our mailing list to receive
updates on future book releases:
fireforgedbooks.com

ABOUT THE AUTHOR

L. Ana Ellis, a sleep-deprived government worker by day, lets her imagination roam free while writing science fiction late into the night. After spending her days toiling over spreadsheets in a windowless cubicle with fluorescent lighting, and unbeknownst to her coworkers who think she spends her evenings watching cat videos, at night she creates worlds that are more of a commentary on the present than an accurate prediction of the future.

Speculating about how societies will change in the future fascinates her; she is undeterred that so far, she has been wrong 100% of the time. When she's not pondering how societies operate or writing about alternate realities, she enjoys Ren Faires, Cons, and, as her coworkers suspect, watching cat videos.

She lives in the Washington, DC area with her husband, two cats, and the occasional foster kitty. When procrastinating, she occasionally posts on Twitter as @lanaellisbooks or Instagram as l.ana.ellis.books (although her Instagram page is mostly cat photos). She publishes under the indie press Fire-Forged Books.

website: www.fireforgedbooks.com